Clues to You

Claire Huston

Published by Goldcrest Books International Ltd
www.goldcrestbooks.com
publish@goldcrestbooks.com

ISBN: 978-1-913719-90-6

For Liz
x

Chapter 1

Kate squeezed past another huddle of chattering guests, her gaze fixed on the banner at the top of the noticeboard to the left of the reception desk.

MERRYMAN'S MURDER MYSTERY WEEKEND
May 19th–21st, The Old Grange Hotel
Information for Guests

She halted inches from the display, released the handle of her suitcase and pressed her trembling fingers to her lips to stifle a squeal of excitement. This was it. A proper murder mystery weekend. She was finally here!

Ignoring the clamour of conversation around her, Kate scanned the board and recognised several pages from the information pack she'd received a few weeks ago. The comprehensive brochure was impressive and spoke to how professional a set-up Roger Merryman had created, whatever the more negative rumours about him might—

'Are you here for the murder too?'

The slender man who had interrupted Kate's thoughts was hovering by her right shoulder. He was pale, about a decade younger than her, and seemed to have lost his chin. Sadly his cologne wasn't equally absent: its aggressive muskiness assaulted Kate's nose and throat, making her eyes water.

But it took more than a brain-stunning stench to disable Kate's deep-seated instinct to demonstrate good manners. After all, she was a teacher and endeavoured to lead by example.

'Hello. I'm Kate,' she said.

'Dave,' said Chinless Guy, reaching out a hand.

Kate did her best not to grimace at Dave's limp, rubbery excuse for a handshake as she answered his original question. 'Yes, I'm here for the murder mystery weekend.'

Dave dropped his gaze to Kate's rainbow-patterned suitcase and colourful dress. 'Really? You don't seem the type.'

Kate fought the urge to fidget as she glanced down at her clothes and bag. She had wondered about whether plainer luggage would be more appropriate, something black and sleek. And her dress probably did look odd in the sumptuous entrance hall of a sprawling Victorian manor house, but she'd had to rush straight from work to the hotel.

Icy tendrils of doubt tickling the back of her neck, Kate crossed her arms to conceal the trembling in her hands and stared Dave square in the eye. This weekend she was not regular Miss Brannon. She was Kate, focused sleuth. And focused sleuths did not let strangers make them feel small or out of place.

Unfazed by Kate's silence, Dave continued, 'So, are you into all this mystery game stuff?'

'I like reading classic mysteries,' said Kate. 'And I used to go to mystery parties fairly regularly, but I haven't been to one for almost three years.'

Her lips twitched into a brief nostalgic smile. She had mostly fond memories of the dozen or so murder mystery parties she and her friends had hosted and attended in and around Birmingham before she'd moved to Reading. A friend's birthday had been the beginning and soon the whodunnits became a regular enough event for the attendees to give themselves a comedy name: the Friendly Murder Club. But Merryman's mysteries were in another league.

Her heart skipped as she remembered the moment a year ago when Bella had called to announce she'd managed to book their places: Kate had squealed and nearly dropped her phone while breaking into a dance which was a limb-flailing explosion of pure happiness. And after the devastation of the week before Christmas, the approaching Merryman's weekend had become one of the few strands of silver encircling the increasingly grey cloud of her life.

Kate took a deep breath. The weekend she had been waiting for had finally arrived. And it could be *her* weekend. The start of things getting back on track. A sign that her luck was changing. And with Bella and Ethan on her team, she stood a chance. They had always been so supportive at their amateur parties. Not like other people—well, just one person really—who had gone to great lengths to stop her from winning. Who had always blocked her path to success with his unnecessarily ruthless, sniping, pompous—

'Oh, right,' said Dave, 'so you're a bit of an expert.'

Kate shook her head, dismissing unpleasant thoughts of her past competition. 'Not really. This is the first professional murder mystery I've been to. You know, with actors playing the parts of the victim and the suspects.'

'It's my first murder mystery party full stop.' Dave shrugged. 'None of this is my scene, to be honest. My mates twisted my arm.' He nodded to a boisterous group of men in their early twenties huddled by the reception desk. 'They reckon it'll be a bit of fun, but it seems daft, spending a weekend pretending we're in the 1930s and trying to solve a fake murder. Although I wouldn't knock back the prize money.'

The regular prize for solving a Merryman's mystery was one thousand pounds. But, with no one having solved a case for almost two years, the prize fund had continued to roll over. If someone won this weekend, they would take home fifty thousand pounds. Little wonder non-enthusiasts like Dave were tempted to try their luck.

Dave's gaze roved over the crush of guests in the packed lobby, skimming past the imposing beauty of the grand fluted columns, dark wood panelling and glittering central chandelier. He sniffed, his wide nostrils flaring. 'And this place is so *old*. Though I guess it's not all bad. They have a modern spa somewhere.'

Unsure how to respond to Dave's dismissal of the hotel's wonderful historical details, Kate noticed the rowdy group at reception had received their keys and were scanning the room. She tipped her head in their direction and said, 'I think your friends are looking for you. And I should check in.'

'Right you are,' Dave said. 'I'll see you at the welcome talk. It should be interesting. I've heard a lot about the Merryman bloke who runs these things.' He raised an eyebrow and dropped his voice into a tone dripping with murky insinuation. 'And not much of it good.'

Kate nodded—Dave's comments chimed with many of the rumours she had heard—but she was prevented from asking for details by Dave's friends, who charged into their missing comrade, sweeping him away like a noisy tide and clearing Kate a path to the reception desk.

Kate grabbed the handle of her case and gave it, and herself, a shake. Dave might not have thought she looked the part, but she was determined to have a fun weekend with good friends. And maybe, just maybe, it would be a weekend with a dream ending. Her eyes fluttered closed for a moment and she pictured her team solving the case to rapturous applause and carrying off fifty thousand pounds.

Her insides bubbling at the idea of a rare win, Kate steeled herself as she approached reception. Her tummy might be full of butterflies, and she wasn't wearing a deerstalker or carrying a magnifying glass, but she could do this. Besides, Kate thought—her spirits rising further as she drew up to the desk and placed a steady hand on the countertop— plenty of people made the mistake of underestimating Miss Marple, and look where that got them.

The receptionist gave Kate a smile and, unlike Dave, didn't seem to regard her as an unlikely amateur detective. 'You're here with Merryman's party?' she asked.

'Yes, thank you,' said Kate, returning the smile with gratitude. 'Kate Brannon. The booking was made by Bella Hughes.'

'Of course, Ms Brannon. Here's your key. Your welcome talk is in the library in twenty minutes.'

The receptionist blew out a slow breath and, a wrinkle appearing between her brows, scanned the heaving lobby at Kate's back. Kate recognised that look. She and her colleagues wore it often, mostly on rainy days when the kids couldn't get outside at break times. 'I bet you'll be pleased when we've all arrived,' Kate said.

The receptionist gave a small shrug of resignation. 'It's been non-stop all afternoon,' she said. 'We're short-staffed this weekend.' Her tone fell into one of quiet despair. 'And fully booked.'

'I should let you get on,' said Kate, picking up her key. 'Good luck. And thank you for—'

The rest of Kate's sentence was replaced by a gasp as her gaze snagged on the tall man entering the lobby. His upright posture and stern glare were all too familiar.

No. It couldn't be. Bella said he wouldn't be here.

Her pulse accelerating and mouth dry, Kate ducked behind the nearest group of guests and peered around them to get a better view of the newcomer.

Pausing a few steps over the threshold, he released the handle of his suitcase—sleek, plain black, typical!—and tucked his thumbs into his back pockets. In contrast to the slightly dishevelled appearance of everyone else in the lobby, whose hair and clothes showed signs of hurried journeys, his white shirt and dark grey suit were impeccable and showcased his broad, lean frame.

Kate ducked down further as the man seized his case and made for the reception desk, the crowd parting to make way for his straight-backed stride.

The receptionist glanced up from the desk and her weary smile shifted into a shining grin on seeing her latest guest's lightly tanned fair skin, neatly cropped dark blond hair and the long lashes ringing his green eyes.

Not pure green though, Kate remembered as she stared at the side of his head, her heart hammering against her ribs. If you got close enough, you would see that his irises contained sparkling shards of amber and hazel. But these alluring details were only visible if you could get past the contempt in his gaze.

The receptionist relaxed her smile just enough to say, 'Good afternoon, Mr ...?'

Ravenscroft, thought Kate, a hollowness blooming in her chest as her sunny fantasy of a carefree weekend culminating in a rare triumph crumbled to ash. Max Ravenscroft, her old rival, sleuthing nemesis and destroyer of dreams of detective glory, had deigned to grace them with his presence.

Chapter 2

'Welcome everyone! Welcome to a weekend of delightful company, exquisite food and, of course … murder most foul.'

Roger Merryman grinned and, as he spread his arms, a shaft of spring sunshine streamed through the crimson panes in the library's stained-glass windows. The tinted light caught the tips of his outstretched fingers, making them appear as though they'd been dipped in blood.

Kate shuddered and put a hand to her tummy to calm a new wave of jitters. If she wasn't careful her imagination would run away with her. She couldn't remember having been this on edge for months. And her nerves certainly hadn't been soothed by Max's surprise appearance.

She glanced over her shoulder, relieved there was still no sign of him in the rows of guests hanging on Roger's every word. Perhaps Max was attending a different event at the hotel? Was it too much to hope that their being in the same place at the same time was just a giant coincidence?

Roger clapped his hands. The sharp sound bounced off the library's wood panelling and arched window frames, silencing his audience's nervous laughter and snapping Kate out of her Max-related thoughts. 'As I'm sure you've guessed, I am Roger Merryman. I'm delighted to be your host for this Merryman's Murder Mystery. Please, feel free to hunt me down if you need anything.'

Kate raised an eyebrow. Roger's smile was dazzling white, his suit yellow tartan and his tan rusty orange. Every detail of his appearance screamed for attention. Surely the struggle would be losing him rather than hunting him down?

Roger's gaze slid past Kate, who had snagged a safe seat in the third row of high-backed chairs, and roved over the whole audience before he continued, 'And to those of you who have been before, welcome back and'—he paused, his smile twisting with a hint of something wicked—'better luck this time!'

Kate registered the winces of those who had likely already tried, and failed, to crack one of Merryman's fiendish puzzles. It was possibly little consolation to them that they were in good company: after a couple of early wins two years ago—when Merryman had started running murder mystery events in historic venues across the south of England—not one of the subsequent hundreds of would-be detectives had managed to crack a case. A fact which explained the size of the cash prize currently up for grabs.

'Everything you need to know is in your information packs,' Roger said. 'However, while the crime you are here to investigate will be taking place in 1932, you, my friends, don't have to be anything other than citizens of the twenty-first century. Of course if you have come with a suitcase brimming with period attire, I'd encourage you to wear it. And I'd like to take this opportunity to say that while we always strive for historical accuracy, it is possible that a few liberties may have been taken with timelines and other trifles. Please don't let them bother you.'

Ah, thought Kate as she ran her fingertips across the colourful marker tabs protruding from the edge of the information pack sitting on her lap. Roger's comment suggested that some amateur detectives could be as keen on finding historical inaccuracies as clues.

'Now, I'm sure you'd all *kill*'—Roger winked to acknowledge the guests who indulged his 'joke' with some good-humoured groans—'to get to your rooms and decompress before dinner. Seven p.m. sharp.' He tapped his watch, a chunky gold number which probably cost more than Kate's annual salary. 'But does anyone have any questions they're *dying* to ask?'

'Did the butler do it?'

A burst of tension-relieving laughter scattered the silence, although no one appeared to find the quip as funny as Dave, who was sitting on Kate's left and guffawing until his pasty face turned scarlet.

Roger chuckled politely. 'Yes, very amusing, young man. But to answer your question: no. We don't go in for anything that obvious here. Besides, as it states in your packs'—Roger paused to glare at Dave, who Kate was fairly certain hadn't read past the contents page—'none of the staff are suspects. Only the family and their guests should be under suspicion. And, before anyone asks, there will be no deaths by natural or accidental causes. We only deal in foul play here.' Roger inhaled slowly, his nostrils flaring as he scanned the audience. 'Does anyone have a serious question?'

The atmosphere in the room thickened into a soup of awkwardness as the guests squirmed and tried to avoid Roger's searching gaze. Kate fought the urge to sneeze as Dave shuffled in his seat, sending a tsunami of his musky cologne over her. She turned her face towards her fellow guests. Did none of them have any questions? How was that possible? Yes, it was half past five on a Friday and, from their crumpled office wear and flushed faces, she imagined they might be keen to get up to their rooms and change. But surely they were also aching to know—

'Sorry I'm late! You would not believe the traffic getting out of London. Total madness!'

Kate's frown melted away as the pale blonde woman in a black skirt suit exploded into the room. Bella rarely did anything quietly.

Hoping to balance her friend's exuberance with a subtle gesture, Kate raised her right hand and wiggled her fingers.

'Oh, Kate. Thank the Lord! I should have known you'd be on time. And you saved me a seat.' Bella lurched towards her, threw her bottom onto the chair and her arms around Kate. 'It's so lovely to see you! Is that a new dress?'

Kate returned Bella's squeeze, her grin turning rigid and her cheeks hot under the weight of the bewildered and amused stares coming at them from every corner of the room. 'Yes. And it's nice to see you too. But, um, everyone's …' She let her whisper trail away, tilting her head towards the stunned guests Bella had left in her wake.

Bella twisted in her seat and surveyed the gawking faces

surrounding her. 'Oh, please don't mind me.' She flicked her hair off her shoulder and waved in Roger's direction. 'Carry on!'

Roger's small eyes glistened with a cool light as he inclined his head towards Bella. 'Thank you, my dear. So pleased you could make it. And if there are no further questions, I'm sure I'm not the only one who could *murder* a glass of—'

'Kate has a question!' Bella's hand shot up as Kate's heart plunged to her toes.

'Bella!' Kate snatched her friend's hand out of the air.

'What? You always have questions.'

Bella was right. But Kate's tongue felt as though it had swollen to fill her mouth and her hands were growing clammy. Why was the prospect of speaking in front of an audience of adults so daunting? She never feared she was about to break out in hives when she led junior assembly.

She released Bella's hand. 'Maybe now's not the best time ...'

'Nonsense. We're paying for this weekend. We want to get the most out of it. You have questions, so ask away.' She whipped her attention back to Roger. 'Isn't that right, Mr Merryman?'

'Of course.' Roger cleared his throat, perhaps to take the strained edge out of his voice, and glanced at his watch again before turning his focus to Kate. 'Is there something you'd like to know, Ms—'

'Brannon. Kate Brannon.' Kate swallowed as she considered her options. Making excuses and running out of the room was an attractive thought, but now everyone knew her name the damage was done. Best to get it over with. Stare at Roger, pretend there was no one else in the room and talk as quickly as possible. At least she didn't have to stand up. 'Um, well, I was just wondering …'

'Speak up, young lady! Everyone wants to hear you.'

Roger's bark sent another burst of heat rocketing into Kate's cheeks. She dug her nails into the palms of her hands, cleared her throat and tried again. 'In the information pack, which is excellent'—Roger straightened and Kate was pleased to see a little of the welcoming sparkle return to his eyes—'it says that the actors stay in character the whole weekend. But they must need breaks and so how can we be sure we're seeing them in character or if they're being themselves—'

'Easily answered. The actors never break character. Not for one minute.'

Bella snorted. 'They sleep in character? They go to the loo in character?'

Roger swished his hand back towards his shoulder, dismissing Bella's disbelief as if swatting a pesky fly. 'Our actors will remain in character and the year nineteen hundred and thirty-two unless they are in the privacy of their own rooms which, I must remind you, are off limits to guests. In fact, this is something I would urge you to bear in mind when interacting with the actors. You will get the most out of your time if you try to treat their characters as if they were real people. For example, if you attempt to harangue them into a confession, they will react as any reasonable person would: they'll likely get annoyed or retreat. There will also be some characters who are grieving and you should take that into account …'

As Roger continued, Bella turned to Kate and tilted her

head, letting her long blonde hair form a curtain to hide her face. She put her lips to Kate's ear and, dropping her voice to murmur, said, 'Bet you a tenner we catch one of the actors glued to their phone, checking their Insta, before dinner tomorrow night.'

Barely moving her lips, Kate replied, 'Have a little faith.'

'Twenty. Before lunchtime.'

Kate shook Bella's outstretched hand before tuning back in to Roger.

'… secret. This is one of the reasons it is pointless trying to cajole any of our actors into helping you towards the solution: most of them won't know it.' Roger's moustache twitched as he gave a sharp sniff. 'Besides, a murderer is hardly about to confess, even if offered financial inducements to do so.'

Kate's jaw dropped. Someone had tried to *bribe* the actors into giving them hints? Blimey. The size of the prize pot was clearly driving people to extraordinary lengths. But then some people would do anything to win. Max, for instance. His behaviour at their Friendly Club parties had been almost incomprehensibly competitive—

'Are you OK?'

Bella was watching her, a crease of concern at the bridge of her short button nose.

Kate flashed Bella a smile and nodded. She didn't want to give her friend more reason to worry about her. 'I'm fine.'

'Then cheer up. We're finally here!' Bella glanced up at the ornate gilded plasterwork dividing the painted panels of the ceiling. 'This place is stunning. The real deal. Puts the Friendly Murder Club to shame. And by the end of the weekend we could be fifty thousand quid better off!'

Kate mirrored Bella's smile as she imagined what victory would look like. What if they won? What if they became the first team in years to successfully solve a Merryman's Mystery and walk off with a cool fifty grand in the process?

'Ms Brown? Does that answer your question?'

Kate blinked, her pulse slowing as she retreated from thrilling fantasies and returned her focus to Roger. Who had already forgotten her name. Brown? He had probably been inspired by her dull chestnut hair. Or possibly her eyes, which were an equally uninspiring muddy shade. 'Yes, thank you.'

'Wonderful. Was there anything else?'

Kate bit her lip, remembering her internet research which had unearthed some worrying accusations about Roger Merryman and a slew of wild theories as to why it might be impossible to solve one of his mysteries. It raised an important, perhaps crucial question, which it would be in everyone's interests for her to ask. But maybe—given the controversial nature of the subject, her dread of public speaking and the fact that many of the guests were shuffling to the edges of their seats while glancing hopefully towards the exit—she should speak to Roger later, in private.

She shook her head.

'No?' Roger grinned and rubbed his hands together. 'Marvellous. Thank you, Ms Brown. Well then, I'll see you all at—'

'I have a question.'

The fine hairs at the back of Kate's neck stood on end as the deep, steady voice echoed through her, making her bones vibrate. Slowly, she followed everyone else to turn and stare at Max, who was standing on the library threshold, leaning against the door frame with infuriating nonchalance.

Roger loosed a dramatic sigh, accompanied by a few groans from the audience. 'What would you like to know, Mr—?'

'Max!' Bella raised her hand in an enthusiastic wave. Smothering the urge to rugby-tackle her friend to the ground, Kate once again grabbed Bella's hand out of the air.

Too late. Max's gaze followed Bella's greeting only to skim past her welcoming smile and land squarely on Kate. His eyes widened in recognition and the corner of his mouth twitched.

Kate's breath caught in her throat. He was laughing at her already. Even by Max's standards, that had to be a record.

His gaze still locked on to Kate's, Max answered Roger's question. 'Max Ravenscroft. I have a quick query.' He inclined his head a fraction in Kate's direction and the twitch at the side of his lips curled into the smallest of smiles.

Kate's mouth went dry.

Of course.

She clenched her fists. Of course he was going to ask *her* unspoken question. He was going to get there before her. Again. It was all he ever did. He used his fiendish mind-reading powers to steal all her ideas right out of her head and beat her to the finish line.

Unmoved by Kate's reproving glare, Max pushed off the doorway and slid his hands into his pockets. 'Following on from your response to the excellent question from Ms *Brannon*'—Kate rolled her eyes: how typical of Max to be so pedantic about something like a name!—'I was wondering how we can be sure it's possible for us to win? How do we know that you are playing fair, Mr Merryman?'

Chapter 3

Max's blunt questions landed as Kate had expected. The whispers of a dozen furtive conversations fell silent. Roger's smile fell away, leaving his face a slackened blank, and Kate suspected that underneath the layers of orange paint his skin had paled.

'Ah. Yes.' Roger's grin returned, although his eyes remained cold. 'An excellent question. And I believe this is the perfect moment to introduce you to the most important person here—other than myself'—he paused, but this time his wit was met with silence and he hurried on—'Dorothy Williams, our Games Supervisor. Where are you, Dorothy?'

Roger glanced over his right shoulder as a Black woman, sporting a striking pair of large, red-rimmed glasses, glided into position at his left side. Kate guessed she was in her early sixties, slightly younger than Roger.

The woman's approach was so stealthy that Roger startled when he noticed her. 'Here she is! Dorothy's role is to make sure everyone plays by the rules. If you have any concerns about the running of the game, you can approach either of us. We're a tight-knit team.'

'Thank you, Roger.' Dorothy took a step forwards and produced a large scarlet envelope from behind her back. She held it up as she turned her focus to Max. 'This answers your question, Mr Ravenscroft.'

While the audience's eyes were on the envelope, Kate inspected Dorothy, taking in her neat braids, green silk blouse, black trousers, court shoes and a certain *something* in her aura. It was an intangible air of authority which Kate encountered at work every day. And as Dorothy stared directly at Max as if expecting another challenge, Kate decided she'd happily bet Bella another twenty quid that the woman had been a teacher.

Dorothy lowered the envelope and swept her gaze across the room, waiting for silence before speaking. 'Before you all arrived, I witnessed Mr Merryman putting the solution to this weekend's game into this envelope. I did not read the solution myself. I sealed it and will keep it safe until the game officially concludes on Sunday morning. Then I will open the envelope in private. Subsequently your teams will have the opportunity to present a solution to the mystery here, in the library. If anyone gives the solution which matches the contents of this envelope, they will have won.'

Undeterred, Max asked, 'But you work for Merryman's. How can we be sure you're acting independently?'

As Dorothy levelled a stare at Max so powerful it could have stopped a runaway train, Kate realised she had got it wrong. This woman hadn't been a teacher. She'd been a *head* teacher.

'I have worked for Mr Merryman for six months.' Dorothy sniffed. 'I can provide you with my full credentials if you wish, but I assure you I have held several positions as an independent assessor and advisor. Before that I worked at the highest levels in education—'

Aha! She knew it!

Kate was enjoying the glow of satisfaction from her correct guesswork and listening to Dorothy's impressive résumé, when Bella kicked her foot and whispered, 'So Max is joining us.'

'You said he definitely wasn't coming!'

'Did I?' Bella turned her gaze to the front of the room, avoiding Kate's suspicious glare. 'Yes, well, last-minute changes happen.'

Kate snuck a glance over Bella's shoulder at the subject of their conversation. Though she hadn't seen him in almost three years, Max was as she remembered: tall with a broad frame, toned waist and neat fair hair with a faint russet tone ... although there were also hints of grey at his temples. Those were new.

'Anyway,' Bella said, 'even you can't deny Max is good at this stuff. If you want to win you should be pleased he's on our team. And you know I never understood your problem with him. You should try to get along. I mean, you're single now and you do think he's foxy.'

'Fox-like!' Biting her lip to halt her outburst, Kate glanced up at Dorothy who was still holding the room captive with her career history and didn't seem to have noticed their furtive conversation. Kate swayed a little closer to Bella and dropped her voice to the lowest of whispers. 'I said he was fox-*like*. One time.'

Bella raised one shoulder in a shrug. 'Same difference.'

'It's entirely different. I meant he's crafty, sly, devious—'

'Smart, sharp and sexy.'

Kate rolled her eyes. Now wasn't the time for this argument. Not that there was ever much point arguing with Bella.

Her face beginning to warm, she peeked at Max again. Hmn. Definitely greying at the temples. She tilted her head, considering. It suited him. Dammit.

Unbidden, the words 'silver' and 'fox' started to overwhelm all other rational lines of thought and push the heat in her cheeks up to her hairline. Kate rolled her eyes. This was ridiculous.

She tapped the back of Bella's hand. 'He hates me.'

'Rubbish. Who could hate you?'

'Excuse me, ladies.' Dorothy's stern tone made Bella and Kate startle. 'Did you have any questions?'

Fearing they were on the verge of being given detention for chatting in assembly, Kate rushed to reply. 'No. Sorry, Ms Williams.'

Dorothy nodded and, returning her focus to the audience as a whole, continued, 'And I'm sure you'll all be pleased to hear that Mr Merryman has agreed to a slight amendment to the rules going forward. Usually, each team gets to present one solution to the case. But we've decided to increase that to two.'

Gasps of surprise gave way to a swell of excited chatter, which Roger silenced with a raised hand as he bounded back to Dorothy's side. His deep frown suggested he was far less delighted by the rule change than his guests. 'Yes, yes, it's thrilling news. You now have double the chance of success. Never let it be said that our players don't have a fair shot at the win. Would you like to say anything else, Dorothy?'

'No, that's all,' Dorothy said. 'Good luck, everyone.'

'Indeed,' said Roger, although his sunny tone rang a little false. 'In that case, all that remains is housekeeping. The hotel have advised us that they might experience brief power cuts over the weekend. Some building work is going on nearby which may affect the supply and alarms could be triggered.' Low groans hummed through the room as the audience no doubt imagined the horror of being dragged out of bed by a false fire alarm. Roger pushed on. 'Don't worry, it'll probably come to nothing. Now, if there are no further questions …' Kate followed Roger's stare to the back of the room and to Max. Unperturbed by their host's frosty stare, Max met his gaze and shrugged, his curiosity apparently satisfied. Ha. That wouldn't last.

Roger nodded, his frown relaxing as he clasped his hands together and said, 'Then let the game begin!'

Chapter 4

The room emptied in moments, the guests fleeing in an awkward stampede. A lingering stink of acrid cologne drove Kate and Bella towards the library's open windows where they could enjoy the fresh May breeze.

Bella struck Kate's arm playfully. 'This place is amazing. Look at that fireplace!'

Kate smiled as Bella strode towards the enormous hearth to better admire the elaborate swirls and foliage carved into the stone. She would have been delighted to attend a murder mystery weekend at her local community centre, but the Victorian gothic grandeur of the Old Grange was undeniably a huge plus.

Bella wandered over the bright geometric pattern of the floor rug to the mahogany bookcase to the right of the fireplace. Narrowing her eyes, she trailed her fingers over the spines of the volumes on the nearest shelf, the chunky diamond and twin sapphires in the ring on her left hand glinting in the sunlight. 'Do you reckon these books are real or just empty boxes?'

As Bella made to tug a large wine-coloured book from the shelf, Kate raced to her side. 'I doubt we're supposed to pull them out for inspection, Bels.'

'Yes, Miss Brannon.' Bella rolled her eyes and pushed the book back into place. 'You're such a hard taskmaster. Do you let your kids have any fun?'

'Of course. But I also encourage them not to risk damaging private property.'

'I'm glad you're not my teacher. But'—she swept a hand down to the skirt of Kate's dress to touch the soft navy fabric—'I do love that dress. A new one for your school collection?'

The dress was a recent purchase. When Kate had seen the pattern of bright planets, rockets and the shining trails of shooting stars, she had been unable to resist.

'Bet you can't guess what our science topic this half term has been?'

Bella twisted her features into a picture of faux contemplation. 'By any chance have you been going through the joy of budget reviews and staff performance appraisals?'

Her friend's tone was joking, but a ripple of concern moved Kate to place a comforting hand on Bella's arm. Since moving to London with her fiancé, Ethan, two and a half years ago, Bella's rise through the ranks of the accountancy firm she had reluctantly joined had been meteoric. Her promotion—which made her the company's youngest-ever department head at thirty-three years old—was a fair reflection of her talents and very well paid. But Kate worried the responsibilities of her friend's job were becoming increasingly hard to bear. Bella had been so happy working freelance for small businesses in and around Birmingham. Joining the ranks of one of the firms Bella had described as 'enormous faceless numbers machines' back when they were at university, appeared to be gnawing away at her friend's natural liveliness.

Bella grasped Kate's hand and spun her friend in a twirl, making the skirt of her space-pattern dress flare. They giggled, but Bella's levity was brief. Dropping Kate's hand, she sighed. 'I wish I could wear something like that to work. Look at me'—she pointed at her black skirt suit and cream blouse—'in my finest daily funeral wear.'

Though it flattered her gorgeous curves, it was true that Bella's unofficial uniform did little for her fair complexion. Was she paler than usual? It was hard to tell. Kate hadn't seen her in person since Christmas when they were both home visiting family. Bella had patiently supplied sympathy, hugs and chocolate as Kate rambled and sobbed. But, Kate realised with a pang of guilt, she'd been in such a dark place she hadn't looked for any signs that Bella was being swallowed by her own shadows.

Kate gave her friend an encouraging smile. 'I bet you've got something lovely to wear to dinner tonight.'

'I do!' Bella's grin returned. 'Although I suppose we shouldn't really be waltzing round in sequins if a death is imminent.'

'No one is getting killed tonight. It's just dinner for us to meet the future victim and the suspects. The death will be discovered tomorrow morning.'

'It's a good thing you know what's going on. Work's been crazy lately and I've only managed to have a quick flick through the information pack. And obviously'—Bella sighed—'the eternal house hunt continues.'

'Still nothing good enough for Ethan?'

'No. I'm starting to think he won't be happy until he can design and build his own place. Good luck doing that in London!'

'Should my ears be burning? Is she moaning on about house hunting again?'

Kate spun round to find Ethan approaching. He was wearing a dark suit which matched his fiancée's, the opened neck of his white shirt circled by a loosened navy tie. Even though Bella was wearing four-inch heels, Ethan towered over her and had to stoop as he wrapped a hand around her waist and kissed her. Kate smiled, but the simple display of affection caused a heaviness to swell in her chest. Bella and Ethan had met almost five years ago when she and Paul had set them up on a blind date.

'You took your time getting here.' Bella grasped the front of Ethan's jacket and pulled him closer for another kiss.

'Sorry. I've been explaining to Max'—Ethan gestured to his friend who had trailed him across the room—'something urgent came up at the office.'

A knot formed in Kate's throat as Bella placed her left hand over Ethan's heart. Ethan smiled, laid his hand over hers and kissed the top of her head. They were such a beautiful couple. Ethan with his light brown skin, strong jawline and warm smile, and Bella's fair complexion, button nose and high cheekbones. How could Kate be anything but happy for them? Sure, she wished she shared their luck, but not all love stories could have happy endings.

'It's lovely to see you, Kate.' Ethan stepped forwards to peck her on the cheek. 'Are you OK?'

'Fine, thank you. A little tired. The past couple of weeks have been hectic.'

'Oh yeah, Bella said you had a job interview. Back near your parents' place, right?'

'Yes. The school's about fifteen minutes from Mum and Dad's. I don't know if you know the village. Knowleswood?'

A sharp intake of breath drew Kate's gaze to where Max was hovering, a couple of paces away from the group. He covered his mouth with his hand and let out a feeble cough, but he couldn't fool Kate. He had definitely gasped. What was up with him?

Apparently not having noticed his friend's surprise, Ethan said, 'That sounds familiar. I think that's down the road from Max. Isn't it, mate?'

Max shrugged. 'About ten minutes from mine.'

Ah, thought Kate. That was Max's problem. He found the idea of living within a five-mile radius of her gasp-inducingly horrific.

'Well there you go!' Ethan beamed and slapped his friend on the back. 'If Kate gets the job, you two could revive the Friendly Murder Club.'

Max, who had been studying his shoes, lifted his head. His lips were pressed into a thin line, and when his cool green gaze met Kate's he swiftly returned his attention to the floor. 'Hmn.'

Ignoring his friend's non-committal grunting, or perhaps keen to smooth over his rudeness, Ethan continued his questioning. 'So, how was the interview, Kate? When do you hear back from them? And when would they want you to start?'

Kate blinked to battle a rush of light-headedness she hadn't experienced since the morning of her interview. It had gone really well. She had loved the school. The staff and children seemed happy and the location was perfect. But accepting the job would mean admitting that a part of her life—a part into which she had poured so much of herself—was over. And she wasn't sure she was ready for that. Which was why, when the head teacher had called her the previous afternoon to offer her the job, Kate had asked for the weekend to think about it, promising to give her final answer on Monday morning. 'I think it went OK. They'd want me to start in September.' She gave Ethan a bright smile. 'And I should hear back from them next week.'

'That's great. Great.' Apparently unable to detect her lie, Ethan glanced at Bella before asking, 'How's things with Paul?'

Kate's cheeks ached as she forced her smile to stay in place. She knew Paul was one of Ethan's oldest friends, but did he honestly think she wanted to talk about him? 'Um, fine. I guess. I mean—'

'Ethan.' Max nudged his friend with his shoulder. 'Maybe save the inquisition for the murder suspects?'

Ethan turned his attention to Max, allowing Kate to give her sore cheeks a break. 'Sorry!' Ethan laughed. 'I should have guessed you'd already be focused on the big case. What did I miss at the welcome meeting?'

Bella pointed at Max. 'Nothing much, just Max holding Roger Merryman's feet to the fire about those rumours that the game's rigged. But don't worry, publicly accusing our host of cheating only caused a minor earthquake.'

Ethan's eyebrows shot up. 'Wow, mate. Continuing to make friends everywhere you go?'

Max lifted his gaze to meet Ethan's, but his eyes remained in the shadow of a heavy frown. 'He asked for questions and I used the opportunity to check it's possible to win. And'—he glanced at Bella—'it didn't cause that much of a stir.'

Bella scoffed. 'Merryman handled it smoothly enough, but from the daggers he gave you, I wouldn't be surprised if he's added you to the murder victim list.'

'It was in everyone's interests to hear his answer. I mean'—Max gestured towards Kate—'Kate would have asked the question before me, but she's too polite.'

Kate's lips parted in surprise. How did Max know what she had been thinking? How did he do that? And was 'too polite' his way of calling her a coward?

She snapped her jaw shut. She had to say something. If only to stop her grinding her teeth down to stumps. Damn Max and his demonic mind-reading powers. 'It didn't seem the best time,' she said. 'I had planned to speak to Roger about it later.'

'Yes! You see?' Ethan gave Max a light punch on the arm. 'Kate knows how to go about things with a bit of tact.'

'Maybe. But I've always found direct questioning, as opposed to more delicate, roundabout methods'—Max's gaze flicked to Kate—'to be part of a winning strategy.'

Kate's pulse kicked up a notch as she glared at the side of his smug face. Why did Max need to remind everyone about his almost unbroken record of wins and therefore her losses?

Apparently also unimpressed by Max's argument, Ethan rolled his eyes. 'But this isn't one of our Friendly Club parties. The suspects here are played by professional actors. They aren't going to be tipsy and happy to spill everything in the hope of finishing early and getting home in time to watch *Strictly* on catch-up—'

'Hey!' Bella poked Ethan in the chest. 'Let it go! It was one time.'

Smiling, Ethan continued, 'What I'm saying is, you're unlikely to get stuff out of the suspects if your opening gambit is to fling accusations at them.'

'Actually,' said Bella, 'Roger Merryman said something similar. About taking a cautious approach when questioning the actors. To remember to treat them like real people who might be grieving.'

'There you go.' Vindicated, Ethan's smile stretched into a beam. 'This weekend, I reckon Kate's more diplomatic approach is the one our team should take. And I bet she's already got a plan for us to win this thing. Right, Kate?'

'Um. Well ...' Kate's mouth went dry and her mind blank as Ethan, Bella and Max turned their full attention to her. Oh Lord. Why couldn't she remember any of her strategies? She'd had so many ideas earlier but now they eluded her, leaving her floundering, unsettled by the infernal power of Max's green stare. Unchanged since she had last seen him, it remained intense and unhurried, as if he had all the time in the world to wait for her to mess up.

She swallowed and, focusing on Ethan and Bella, said, 'I do have a few ideas. I've been through the information pack and—'

A noise somewhere between a groan and a roar drowned out the end of Kate's sentence. Kate gasped and clapped her hands to her belly to stifle it. Too late. Ethan and Bella chuckled and Max's lips curled into his trademark smirk. Great. Just when she had begun to hold her own and not look like a complete idiot. That would teach her to skip lunch.

'I'm starving too,' Bella said, giving Kate a sympathetic smile.

'In that case,' said Ethan, turning towards the doors, 'perhaps we should all head up to our rooms and you two can find something to eat.'

'Good idea.' Bella took Ethan's outstretched hand and made for the exit. 'We'll see you guys at dinner.'

Kate hoped her smile would conceal how much she wanted to melt into the floor as Max, smirk still in place, threw her a final glare, turned on his heel and followed the couple out of the room.

She lurched towards her chair and sagged onto it. How was she going to get through a weekend of Max's scrutiny? Especially if Ethan kept bringing up Paul?

Kate closed her eyes and let the peace of the library wrap around her. Counting to ten, she reminded herself that this was her weekend. All she had to do was concentrate on the game. Thoughts of work and ex-boyfriends could wait until Sunday afternoon when hopefully she would have successfully unmasked a killer and figured out what she was going to do about her career.

And in the meantime she could help herself by tracking down some food. Low blood sugar did not help her think clearly or improve her mood. Did Victorian mansions have vending machines? Or maybe if she asked at reception they might—

'Here.'

Kate startled. Max had sneaked up behind her—she had forgotten that a supernatural level of stealth was another of his annoying qualities—and was brandishing a parcel which appeared to be made from white napkins. Warily,

Kate reached up and accepted it. As she unwrapped it, Max said, 'There's a conference going on next door. They had these left over.' He glanced up to catch her eye before returning his gaze to her hands. 'They shouldn't go to waste.'

Kate stared at the small pile of chocolate-chip cookies nestling in the thick cloth in her hands. The scent of sugar made her mouth water and she pressed her lips together lest she start drooling.

'You should eat before the noisy ... creature ... thing lurking in your stomach devours you. Or someone else.' Max rocked back on his heels, his gaze passing over her face before settling on the doorway. 'See you at dinner.'

His long strides carried him from the room in seconds and he had disappeared round the corner before Kate shook off her surprise and realised she hadn't thanked him.

'Huh.' Kate eyed the biscuits with suspicion until another scream of distress from her guts overcame her misgivings. Pondering Max's latest unexpected move, she popped a cookie in her mouth and chewed. What was he playing at?

She sighed as the last morsel of the cookie dissolved on her tongue in a burst of chocolatey sweetness so divine it would have made the hardest of hearts soften towards the person who had provided the treat. But perhaps that was Max's plan. Maybe he was using baked goods and his fathomless green stare to throw her off balance, lull her into a false sense of security, wait until she relaxed and then steal all her ideas.

Gah! Kate sagged forwards and dropped her chin onto her hand. Even though Merryman's latest puzzle was likely to stretch her reasoning skills and intuition to their limits, she had hoped she stood a small chance of cracking the case. But the addition of another mystery—and none other than the diabolical enigma that was Max Ravenscroft—could well make the weekend more than she could handle.

Chapter 5

Kate scurried down the wide staircase, skimming her fingers over the polished mahogany handrail. If she had been wearing her favourite sneakers she could have taken the stairs two at a time. But her three-inch peep-toe heels forced her to hop from one step to the next, and she cursed silently with every painful dainty hop.

It was ten past seven. Thanks to some panicked last-minute preparation—involving skim rereading the character section in the information pack—she was running late and goodness knows what valuable insights into the suspect pool she had already missed.

Slightly out of breath, she cleared the dramatic curve in the stairs halfway to the lobby, glanced up and froze.

The entrance to the dining room was to the right of the stairs. The room's double doors were open. Light and laughter spilled out into the lobby, where it bounced off the wood panelling and gilded frames housing umpteen portraits of bored pale aristocrats. And while the noise and décor were arresting, it was the tall man standing in the shadows to the left of the dining room doorway who caught Kate's eye.

She took another step, wincing as the beaded fringe of her dress rustled against her knees. What was Max doing lurking outside the room? Was he observing the suspects from a distance so he could form his first impressions before speaking to them?

As Kate inched her way to the foot of the stairs, a small movement drew her attention to Max's right hand. Unlike the rest of him, which was so still it could have been carved from marble, his fingers were tapping against his thigh.

Kate frowned. Was it possible that Max Ravenscroft, unflappable ice man extraordinaire, was loitering outside because he was ... *anxious?*

The thought was so distracting, Kate missed her step. She gasped and clung to the handrail to halt her slide. Phew. That could have been worse. Hopefully no one would have noticed—

'Kate?' Max was staring at her, blinking in surprise.

Wonderful. So much for making a dignified, though late, entrance.

'What on earth are you doing?' Max strode towards her, a hand extended to help her down the remaining steps.

Kate ignored Max's outstretched hand as she descended the final few steps to the lobby floor. Only Max could tell someone off for almost breaking an ankle. 'Nearly falling. Thank you for your concern.' She straightened her skirt, pleased her voice sounded steely rather than wobbly.

Kate ran a hand over the warm skin at the back of her neck and watched Max step back and put his hands in his pockets. She itched to ask him why he was hanging around in the gloomy hallway. And she should say thank you for the cookies too. But now she had a clear view of him—in a dapper tuxedo, complete with black bow tie and white pocket square, which showcased his lean, muscular figure—the nervous excitement which had been waltzing around her tummy all afternoon broke into a quickstep. She opened and closed her mouth to speak, but her brain failed to supply her with any useful words.

A boisterous cackle flew out of the dining room. Bella's laughter—it was unmistakeable—landed on Kate like a rousing slap. She glanced towards the source of the sound, then back at Max. 'Thank you for the cookies.'

'You're welcome.'

Kate bit her lip. She should say something else. Something safe which couldn't give Max any opportunity to belittle her. 'You look very smart.'

'Men don't have a huge range of options for formal dinners.' He gestured towards her skirt. 'You have more choice. That dress is … different for you.'

Kate glanced down at the midnight-blue chiffon fringed with gold beaded tassels. It was more 1920s than 30s, but she had wanted to make an effort. And, when she had checked her reflection before running out of her room, she had been quite pleased with the result. Was 'different' Max's backhanded way of saying it looked awful?

'Different how?'

'Your dresses are usually more patterned. Like earlier, with the astronomical design. I suppose because they're for school. They're … child friendly.'

Child friendly? Huh. Was that the charming Ravenscroft

way of saying her clothes were childish and ridiculous? Kate's breathing quickened as the barb sank its sharp teeth into her pride. What was wrong with how she dressed? And why did everyone have an opinion—

'What are you two doing out here?' Bella careered out of the dining room, pulled up in the space between Kate and Max, and ran her gaze over her friend. 'Wow, Kate! You look gorgeous.'

Kate shot Max a pointed stare. *That* was how you gave someone a compliment. 'Thank you. So do you.'

Like her own, Bella's dress could have been classed as 'flapper wear' although, in addition to a fringe on the hem, her green sleeveless number had silver beading covering the bodice in diamond patterns.

'You're missing all the fun,' Bella said. 'And the food is amazing. Obviously. Lucinda's company is catering this weekend.'

Kate gave her friend a thin smile and said a silent goodbye to the hope that the weekend would be a Lucinda-free zone. Over the past year, Bella had mentioned her new stepsister's many marvellous qualities almost every time she and Kate had spoken. And while Kate was happy to accept that Lucinda was nothing short of fabulous, the woman was proving almost as irritatingly unavoidable as Max.

'Let's go, we're missing all the fun,' said Bella. 'You lead the way, Max. You're not going to believe the actors. There's one at our table. She's amazing. So believable.'

Max straightened and strode across the threshold, any misgivings he might have had about entering the room apparently having vanished. But as Kate and Bella followed him into the bright light of the dining room, Kate noticed an intriguing pink flush in the band of skin above the white of his collar.

'Uf! Kate!' Bella bumped into Kate's back. 'Why'd you stop? What are you staring at?'

'Nothing.' Kate lifted her gaze to the blazing glitter of the chandelier and the elaborate ceiling mouldings, studiously avoiding Bella's eye. 'Just trying to take all this in.'

'I know, right? Come on'—Bella grinned and grabbed Kate's hand—'you can gawp at the lush furnishings while you eat. I can't wait to introduce you to Lucille. You'll love her. She feisty, fabulously 1930s and could definitely be our murderer!'

Chapter 6

'And now, at the tender age of thirty-eight, I find myself divorced from husband number three. Never marry a musician, honey. No matter how rich, they're always trouble.'

Kate leant forwards, hoping to hear Lucille Palmer better amid the clamour of the dining room and perhaps absorb some of the woman's charisma. Imagine having been married three times before forty! Kate was thirty-two and without a single proposal to her name. But, she thought, a twinge of regret stirring in her chest, that was partly her fault for having given Paul the benefit of the doubt for so long.

Lucille set down her knife and turned her head towards Kate, sending her gold pendant earrings swinging against her dark brown skin. 'I'm just glad I had the good sense to keep my name. Anyways, Adrian always said that the good readers of *Star Weekly* would be upset if I changed it.'

'Why would they be upset?'

'Because they chose it, darlin'. Another one of Adrian's grand ideas. That the magazine's readers be asked to write in to choose my name. As a contest.'

Kate's jaw dropped. Her name was chosen by strangers as part of a competition? 'But … that's … that's—'

'The business we call show, sweetheart.' Lucille grinned and, as she lifted her hands, the gold threads running along the chiffon sleeves of her dress sparkled. 'You may not like parts of it, but you have to learn which battles to fight if you're gonna to get ahead. And Adrian has been a great promoter.' She touched her champagne glass to her lips and murmured, 'Most of the time,' into the rising bubbles.

Was that a hint of bitterness? A sign of a rift between the starlet and her manager? Kate looked past Lucille, who was sitting to her left, and across the dining room to the top table where Adrian Grieve, their supposed host and owner of the Old Grange, was dining with Roger Merryman and a few other guests. Mr Grieve, a rather corpulent, red-faced man in his late sixties, was a wealthy businessman with successful enterprises in many fields. Including movies and theatre productions.

As Kate watched, Adrian drained his wine glass and—with a single imperious flick of his chubby index finger—ordered a waiter to top it up, before reacting to something Roger had said with a wheezy cackle which quickly descended into a bout of coughing.

'Bet you a tenner that Chuckles over there is the victim.' Bella winked at Kate as she finished the last morsel of her roast chicken.

'Bella!' Kate glared at her friend. The volume of chatter in the room was likely to have covered Bella's words but, as a precaution, Kate lowered her voice to reply. 'We're not supposed to talk about the game like that in front of'—Kate tilted her head to her left and Lucille—'the actors.'

Bella scoffed and grabbed her wine glass. 'Don't be daft, it's fine! She's busy wrapping Max around her little finger. Look!'

Max was sitting on Lucille's left. He was staring into her eyes, his lips parted, hanging on her every word. Kate frowned. She couldn't remember ever having seen Max so entranced. Lucille was a convincing creation, but had Max forgotten she was fictional?

'I get it, though.' Bella nudged Kate, distracting her from Max's fascination with Lucille. 'She's amazing. That American accent is faultless. I hope Merryman is paying her and all the actors properly.'

'I would hope so.' Kate stole another glance at Max and Lucille. She raised her hand to her throat, where a weird scratchiness had appeared.

Kate reached for her water glass while Bella returned to her original theme. 'So, do you think I'm right about shiny Mr Gross over there?'

'His name is Adrian *Grieve*.'

'Uf! Thank God you know who's who and what's going on,' said Bella, taking a sip of her wine. 'And you're really good at this.'

'At what?'

'Talking to'—Bella tipped her head towards Lucille and lowered her voice—'as if she were a real person.'

'Well, it's what the information pack recommends. Anyway, Lucille Palmer might be fictional, but she is being played by a real person. It's not hard to be civil and she is easy to talk to.'

'But it's still weird.' Bella scrunched up her nose. 'I guess maybe the key is to not overthink it and play along. Or keep drinking. Or both.' She picked up her wine glass again. 'Speaking of playing along, are you going to take my bet on whether Mr Grieve over there will soon be found dead in the conservatory having been hit over the head with a lead pipe?'

Kate sighed and took a sip of her water. 'I'm trying to keep an open mind about victims and suspects. Why are you so keen on placing bets this weekend?'

'Anything to liven this up.' Bella gulped down a large mouthful of wine as the wait staff cleared their plates. 'The food is great, the venue is amazing and obviously the company is fabulous—'

'Why thank you, madam.'

'You're most welcome.' The women swapped sly smiles and clinked their glasses together, but as Bella returned her glass to the table her expression was serious. 'But where is the drama, Kate? I thought someone would have keeled over by now or staggered into the room clutching a bloody knife.'

'I hate to disappoint you, but the murder won't be discovered until tomorrow morning.'

'What? You're kidding?' Bella reached for the nearest bottle of white wine and pouted when she discovered it was empty. 'I'm going to need more alcohol.'

'Here you go, honey.' Lucille offered a half-full bottle to Bella, her American accent adding a musical quality to her words.

'Lifesaver. Thank you.'

'No problem. Mr Merryman was keen that we keep

y'all well lubricated.' Lucille straightened in her seat, wiggling her shoulders in a brief shimmy which failed to unsettle the chic finger waves in her bob. 'Have you ladies visited the Comptons before?'

Kate's fingers tightened into a ball as she braced herself for the inevitable mention of—

'Lucinda, my stepsister, lives in the area,' said Bella. 'I've visited her a couple of times.'

'That's nice,' said Lucille. 'I have a couple of friends who spent a while here. They're painters. Is your stepsister an artist?'

'Only with food. Lucinda's a caterer. But her boyfriend's a famous actor.'

'This is my first time here,' Kate said, interjecting before Bella could get into full Lucinda-flow. 'I'd heard a little about it having connections with famous painters, but I don't know much about art.'

'Me either, honey. But I know what I like.' Lucille cast a sideways glance at Max, who was deep in conversation with Ethan. When she returned her gaze to Kate, her smile had a salacious edge to it. 'Would you happen to know how old Mr Ravenscroft is?'

'Um …' Kate floundered. She knew Max was roughly the same age as her, perhaps a little older. 'Thirty-three?'

'Good! I like them at least five years younger than me. And he'—she tilted her head towards Max—'is the sort of man who sets me to imagining a husband number four.'

Kate joined in with Bella's and Lucille's suggestive chuckling, but the irritation in her throat had returned and it made it difficult to enjoy the joke.

'Dessert will surely be along shortly,' said Lucille,

laying her napkin on the table. 'Which is my cue to leave you wonderful people and mingle.' She rose from her chair in a single fluid movement and Ethan and Max half rose from their seats as if pulled upwards by her magnetism. 'Oh, please sit, gentlemen. I look forward to speaking to y'all later.'

Ethan, whose gaze lingered on the rear of Lucille's retreating form, accentuated by her fitted burgundy velvet gown, said, 'She seems nice.'

Bella raised an eyebrow and, the edges of her consonants a little blurry, said, 'Are you talking about her personality or her backside, my love?'

Ethan whipped his gaze away from the top table, where Lucille was sliding into a space next to Adrian Grieve. 'Um, I … I wasn't really—'

'Good evening, everyone.'

The tall, slim young man in a vintage tuxedo pulled out Lucille's recently vacated seat. Projecting a level of confidence to match his height, he directed his gaze to Bella and grinned, revealing two straight rows of small pearly teeth. 'It is my pleasure to join you.'

Kate couldn't tell if his deep tan was authentic but at least the shade of his hands and face matched. And his Italian accent, with its unmistakeable sing-song intonation, was convincing.

'You must be Mr Corsini,' said Kate, pleased she had revised the characters page of the information pack before leaving her room.

Lorenzo Corsini turned his dark stare to Kate, the pomade in his black hair shining under the chandelier's brilliance. 'Please, call me Lorenzo.'

Bella swung her hand in front of Kate, offering it to the newcomer. 'Don't mind if I do. I'm Bella.'

Lorenzo grasped Bella's fingers. 'Of course you are,' he said and planted a kiss on her knuckles.

Bella broke into a fit of boozy giggles. 'You are just what was needed. And look! You come with dessert.'

Waiters deposited a slice of cake in front of each of the guests. The three layers of chocolate sponge, held together with generous layers of chocolate buttercream and covered in chocolate shavings, smelled rich and decadent.

Kate smiled to herself. Someone on the catering team—perhaps the great Lucinda herself—certainly had a wicked sense of humour.

'What's so funny?'

Kate parted her lips to answer her friend, but Bella's question had been directed at Max, who was staring at his cake and wearing a small lopsided smile.

Max glanced up and shrugged. 'Nothing.' He shook his head. 'It's stupid.'

Bella was rarely so easily deterred, especially once she'd had a few drinks. 'Come on! I could do with a laugh. Share with the group.'

'No honestly, it's silly.'

'Now I am also intrigued.' Lorenzo tugged at the cuffs of his dress shirt, the movement making his large silver and mother-of-pearl cufflinks shine. 'Please, tell us.'

The blush which Kate had observed earlier next to Max's collar began to appear in his cheeks and Kate was surprised to find the sight stirred a spark of sympathy. What was the world coming to when she felt sorry for Max Ravenscroft?

But as Ethan joined the others in demanding Max answer Bella's question and Max's grip on his dessert fork became so tight that his fingertips turned white, Kate's instinct to leap to the defence of anyone outnumbered— she wouldn't tolerate bullying behaviour in her classroom or anywhere else—overwhelmed her reluctance to come to Max's aid.

She cleared her throat. 'I'm guessing that Max was simply musing on how appropriate it is to serve a cake which is commonly known as Death by Chocolate.' However, she continued to herself, he didn't want to say that in front of 'Lorenzo' because we're not supposed to discuss the game in front of the actors.

Hoping to bring the subject to a close before they broke any rules, Kate used her fork to scoop up a large piece of the cake. 'I suggest we fall silent for a moment to give this chocolate marvel the respect it deserves,' she said and popped the cake into her mouth.

A smooth slice of heaven, the dessert fulfilled all her expectations. The others seemed to share her opinion, quickly becoming absorbed in demolishing their own slices with gusto. Kate closed her eyes to better savour her second bite and, when she opened her eyes, she found Max staring at her. His smirk had widened into an even smile, there was a hint of sparkle in his eyes and, just before he turned his attention to his dessert, he gave her a small nod of appreciation.

A warm zing of pleasure zipped along Kate's limbs. So he *had* been musing on the name of the cake. Perhaps mind-reading wasn't a skill exclusive to Max after all.

The volume of the entire room dropped for a few

minutes as the dessert cast its spell over the diners. 'Mmm.' Bella swallowed her last piece of cake and reached for her wine glass. 'In the absence of drama, I'll take another slice of that. I must remember to tell Lucinda that this—'

A roar erupted from the top table. Crockery exploded against the floor. Instantly, the little remaining conversation in the room fell silent. Kate whipped round to see Adrian Grieve on his feet, glaring at Lucille Palmer, who had shrunk down into her seat as far as she could.

Adrian's face was a terrifying shade of puce. 'You ungrateful hussy! I made you!' He brandished his napkin as if it were a weapon and continued, 'If you think I'll let you cheat your way out of your contract, you are very much mistaken.' He threw the napkin onto the table and stormed out of the room, leaving Lucille trembling.

But as he reached the threshold, Adrian turned back to deliver a final message. 'Release you from your contract? Over my dead body!'

Kate watched him vanish into the gloom of the lobby, her pulse thrumming and mind racing. Lost in a web of questions and theories, she jumped as Bella's boozy breath tickled her ear. 'I told you. That's one dead man walking.' Bella chuckled. 'I'll take that tenner now if you like.'

Chapter 7

Following the high drama of Adrian Grieve's outburst, after-dinner drinks were a subdued affair.

Whoever had prepared the library had done their best to create a genial atmosphere: soft lighting was provided by table lamps and wall sconces, the furniture had been arranged to encourage guests to cluster in convivial groups, and a generous collection of pillar candles in the hearth diffused faint notes of vanilla and jasmine.

But many guests had decided to forego the chance to further grill the murder mystery cast, probably in favour of an early night. This left parts of the room sparsely populated, although Lucille did her best to fill them with her extraordinary glamour. As if the scene over dessert had never happened, she sparkled between the guests, sprinkling jokes and compliments as she went and dropping into conversations like a human exclamation mark.

In contrast, Kate lurked in the corner nearest the door, wrung out after struggling to engage in conversation with a pair of investment bankers. Apparently City bonuses were not what they had been and they were 'only' going skiing at their preferred luxury resort twice this year. Kate's jaw ached from holding a polite smile in place.

Details of their exorbitant earnings had also led her thoughts back to her own career. She sipped water as bubbles of excitement rolled around her belly. The job at Knowleswood Primary was a great opportunity. If everything went well, she would be head of year after Christmas when the current post holder went on maternity leave. Being nearer home again was another draw. She could spend more time with her parents; Mum would need more help with Dad as time went on. And it would be fantastic not to have to skulk past the school office, desperate to avoid running into the staff inside.

Tallying up the pros and cons, there were a mountain of logical arguments telling her to accept the job. So why was she dithering?

A passing waiter was holding a bottle of mineral water and Kate, keen for a distraction, held out her glass for a top-up before returning to surveying the room. Her gaze repeatedly snagged on her preferred target: Adrian Grieve. The fictional master of the house was leaning his elbow on the mantlepiece and sipping whisky while speaking to Roger Merryman.

Adrian had shed his dinner jacket and calmed his temper, allowing his complexion to fade to a shade of pink far less suggestive of an approaching heart attack. Nevertheless, an unnatural death was likely to befall him before the morning—Bella might be indelicate, but she wasn't wrong—making this Kate's one and only opportunity to speak to him and gain insight into who he thought might wish him harm. And, as she watched Roger Merryman slap Adrian on the back and motion towards the door, she sensed her chance was approaching.

Her pulse picking up, Kate searched her immediate surroundings for somewhere to leave her glass. Where had that waiter—

'Why are you hiding in a corner?'

Kate yelped and almost dropped her glass. 'Bella! Please don't sneak up on me.'

'Oh my God, you're so on edge. You should have a drink. Loosen up.'

Bella's consonants had slackened from blurry to slurry. Kate gave her an indulgent smile. 'I prefer water. You know alcohol hates me. Besides, I have no hope of solving the case if I'm tipsy.'

'You don't already have a lead, do you?'

'No! No one's dead yet. But I do want to check out those newspapers.'

'What newspapers?'

'There's a magazine rack beside the fireplace over there. When I got here the room was fairly empty and I had a quick look. Merryman's have gone to the trouble of mocking up newspapers and magazines from 1932. And if they've put that much effort in, they must be clues, right?'

Bella hiccoughed. 'I think you should take the final minutes of the night off, Katie. This is supposed to be a holiday.'

'Hmn?'

'You're not listening! Who are you staring at now?' Bella swayed into Kate and followed her gaze. 'Mr Merryman and the dead guy?'

'Shh! Theoretical dead guy. Roger's monopolised him all evening. Do you think it's his way of stopping us speaking to Adrian in case he gives anything away? I'd really like to talk to him.'

'Then why don't you?'

'It's like you said earlier, interacting with the actors is still a bit weird. Adrian's supposed to be the host of this party. So do I assume he's invited me and I can swan on over there and chat to him like an old friend? Or am I an invited guest's plus one and he's no idea who I am? Should I get Roger to introduce us or—'

Bella cut across Kate's rambles with a loud sigh. 'You're reading way too much into things. I'll introduce you. Come on.'

'No!' Kate shot a hand out to halt Bella's stride. Roger had made it clear that being too direct might make the characters clam up. What Kate needed was a natural 'in', a subtle way of striking up a conversation, rather than Bella's wrecking-ball approach. 'That's OK, thanks. I'll think of something.'

Bella sighed again. 'You need to relax. Stop worrying too much about who here is 'real' and who isn't. Anyway, if the rumours about Roger Merryman turn out to be true then he's a far bigger phoney than any of the 1930s characters—'

'Shh!'

'Oh, you definitely need to chill. I know! We should go to the spa!'

'Now?'

'Tomorrow, silly. I've booked Ethan and me a couple's massage as a surprise. And that's not the only surprise I've planned for him.' Bella wiggled her eyebrows.

'Bels, I love you, but I don't need to hear about your sex life.'

Bella used the back of her hand to deliver a light blow to Kate's shoulder. 'It's nothing like that. Don't breathe a word'—Bella raised her finger to her lips—'but I've arranged for us to visit a local wedding venue. Compton Hall!'

The name stirred vague recollections from the pictures Kate had viewed when researching the Comptons online. Compton Hall was a huge seventeenth-century red-brick pile, surrounded by acres of parkland and with plenty of features likely to appeal to Bella's architect fiancé. And it was certainly a contrast to Ethan's current venue preference. 'But haven't you decided to get married in a little village in the middle of nowhere?'

'Yep, Haileybrook. It's near the Cotswolds. Ethan has family there or something. But while we're in the Comptons, I thought we should consider another, grander option.'

'Well'—Kate frowned, unsure of how Ethan would react to Bella's surprise—'I guess visiting another place can't hurt.'

'Exactly!'

Bella swayed into Kate again and this time left some of her weight resting against her friend. To Kate's dismay, Bella's eyelids started to droop. 'Um, where is Ethan?'

'Hmn?' Bella lifted her head from Kate's shoulder. 'Oh I dunno. He was in a grump after dinner. Probably gone to bed. Should prob'ly go find him.'

'Would you like me to walk you upstairs?'

'No. No need. I'm fine. You stay here and'—Bella drew

wide circles with her index finger—'do your Miss Marple stuff and things. I'll see you at breakfast.'

Bella teetered her way towards the exit and was crossing the threshold when she grabbed the door frame and swung back to hiss at Kate. 'Roger's out in the corridor. If you want to speak to the dead guy, I'd hurry before someone else beats you to it. Oh!' The guests blocking their view of the fireplace had moved, revealing that Adrian already had company. Company with green eyes, high cheekbones and hints of grey at his temples.

A hard, cold feeling settled in Kate's stomach. Did Max do these things deliberately to annoy her?

'Looks like Max had the same idea as you. Look at him doing his Poirot impression. Just missing the moustache.' Bella glanced at Kate, took in her expression, and giggled. 'You and Max are as bad as each other.'

'What do you mean?'

'This sleuthing business. You both take it far too seriously. It's a game, Kate. No one's dead for real.'

Not yet, thought Kate as she trained her sights on Max. Not *yet*.

Chapter 8

'Of course this section of the building, with its gothic aesthetic—all the stone carvings and pointed arches and so on—was part of the extensive renovations carried out by the previous owner.' Adrian Grieve lifted a pudgy finger in the vague direction of the lobby. 'But if you head towards the gardens at the rear of the house you'll enter the original building, the veritable manor house, which dates back to the second half of the seventeenth century.'

Max nodded. 'Late baroque.'

'Exactly, my boy.' Adrian removed his elbow from the mantelpiece and tilted his head, appraising anew the man in front of him. 'I say, you know your stuff, don't you?'

'I'm an architect.'

'Ah!' Adrian motioned to the windows and the grounds beyond. 'You must take a good look at the place during your stay. It's not often we get visitors who appreciate the grotesques and gargoyles.'

Kate, who had been loitering behind Max, waiting for

an appropriate point to enter the conversation, stepped forwards. 'What's the difference? Between gargoyles and grotesques?'

Adrian inhaled, his ample chest swelling like a bullfrog. 'Well, my dear, gargoyles are decorative waterspouts. They're designed to drain rainwater from the roof. The spout is usually in the mouth of the figure. Grotesques are purely decorative.' He chuckled, a raspy laugh with a wheezy edge. 'Although some of the ones here are ghastly! There's a couple of ugly winged fellows on the tower which used to scare my little Pamela when she was a girl. Nancy used to tease her about it.'

Kate followed his gaze to the other side of the library where two pale, dark-haired, brown-eyed women were engaged in an animated, though hushed conversation. The shorter of the two, wearing a floor-length, backless, bias-cut gown in peach satin, was Pamela Grieve. She pouted as she listened to her sister, accentuating the deep cupid's bow in her upper lip. Nancy Grieve was dressed more demurely than her little sister in a high-neck burgundy chiffon gown with a large bow at the left shoulder. Her hair was twisted into a chignon which swayed as its owner shook her head and glared at her sibling.

Kate narrowed her eyes. What were the sisters talking about? Were they having a disagreement? Or did siblings usually give each other poisonous stares like that? Being an only child, she lacked an insider's insight on the subject. The closest she had to a sister was Bella.

'It must have been a magical place to grow up,' Kate said, switching her gaze from the Grieve daughters to their father.

'Indeed. And all the space, the grounds and whatnot, just marvellous.' Adrian released a long sigh, his gaze becoming misty. 'Those were the best years, back when my dear Cora was still with us. She loved this house. Convinced me to buy it.'

Kate knew she should turn the conversation to Adrian's outburst at dinner. But the distant, wistful expression on his face was impossible to ignore. 'I'm sorry.' Kate extended a hand to touch Adrian's arm, then thought better of it. She was pretty sure touching the actors was strictly forbidden, no matter how convincing their grief might appear. 'You must miss your wife.'

'Every day. They say time heals all wounds. But I still find myself wanting to tell her things.' He paused, his eyes turning glassy. 'Silly things that would have made her laugh. And she feels so close, particularly in certain parts of the house. We used to spend hours together in my study, you know. She would read or do her embroidery by the fire while I got on with business at my desk. And lately, I've even thought—' He dropped his gaze to the floor and cleared his throat. 'Look at me, rambling on. Do either of you have children?'

'No, well, sort of. I'm a primary school teacher.' Kate smiled as she pictured the animated faces of her class. 'So it often feels like I have thirty.'

'Excellent. An admirable profession.' Adrian smiled. 'I had hoped I might have grandchildren by now, but I can't complain. I'm pleased both my girls are settled. Archie Forbes is a good man and Nancy was lucky to find a husband who suits her so well. And Lorenzo will no doubt be a devoted husband to my Pamela.' Adrian turned to

Max. 'And how about you, my boy? Got a whole brood at home?'

'Uh, no.' Max shook his head. 'But I do coach under-tens' football.'

What? Kate's jaw fell as her brain scrambled to process what she'd heard. Max Ravenscroft used his leisure time to help kids?

'Capital.' Adrian put a hand on Max's shoulder. 'I'd like to ask you more about—'

'Mr Ravenscroft! Ms Brown!' Roger Merryman breezed towards them, a rigid grin on his face. 'While I'm delighted you are enjoying each other's company, I think it's time we let Mr Grieve retire.'

Kate glanced about the room, noticing for the first time how empty it was. Nancy Grieve had vanished along with all the other detective guests. Pamela Grieve was in the far corner with her Italian fiancé, her pointed chin tipped upwards to allow her to murmur into Lorenzo's ear. Oh Lord. Were the actors meant to have clocked off a while ago? Had she and Max been forcing them to work overtime?

'Thank you, Roger,' said Adrian. 'It's been wonderful talking to you both'—he smiled at Kate and Max—'but I'm afraid you'll have to excuse me. I'm suddenly rather tired.' He took a deep breath and again Kate heard a rasp and a wheeze so convincing she was tempted to offer to get him a chair. 'I must talk to my daughters and then retire.'

Adrian shuffled towards the door, pausing to murmur something to Pamela before exiting the room. His halting motion was a marked contrast to how he had flounced out of the dining room earlier.

'I admire how keen you are,' said Roger, staring at Kate and Max, his eyes cold and empty of admiration. 'And I know my actors are incredibly convincing and engaging, but please try not to corner them. They are entitled to breaks. Goodnight.'

Kate bit her lip, the skin on her forearms prickling unpleasantly as Roger stalked away. The weekend barely started and she had managed to get herself flagged as a troublemaker. Her! Someone who'd never so much as returned a library book late.

'I didn't get to ask him about Lucille either.'

Lost in pondering her novel renegade status, Kate needed a second to register what Max had said. And, for a moment, her disappointment at not learning the motivation for Adrian's explosion at dinner was soothed. Max the all-knowing super-sleuth hadn't found out what was going on between Adrian and Lucille either. Apparently his direct, no-nonsense questioning methods weren't that brilliant after all.

'Oh, that's a shame.' Kate schooled her features into a pinched expression of regret. 'If Bella's right about him being the victim, there probably won't be another chance to speak to him.'

Max shrugged. 'She may be wrong. And we can still speak to Lucille tomorrow.'

We? Kate eyed Max warily. In theory, Bella, Ethan, Max and she were all on the same side for the weekend. But accepting the idea of being on the same team as Max, rather than being in competition with him, would be ... an adjustment.

'Should we leave?' Max shot a glance at Lorenzo and

Pamela. 'If they were supposed to be off duty at ten thirty, we've already kept them back.'

Kate glanced down at the magazine rack to the left of the fireplace. She had planned to have a skim through its contents when the library was empty. But it was getting late and they should still be there tomorrow. 'You're right,' she said. 'Let's go.'

In the deserted corridor, Kate fell into step beside Max. It was a short walk to the lobby, but the silence between them quickly grew oppressive, the tapping of Kate's black satin heels seeming to grow louder with every step. Kate glanced at Max as they neared the reception area, but his expression was smooth with no sign he felt the stifling squeeze of awkwardness which was settling into Kate's chest. Clearly it was going to fall to her to break the silence, so perhaps this was the perfect opportunity to find out more about possibly the most intriguing thing Max had ever said. 'How long have you been a football coach?'

'I played for the team when I was a kid and, when it became clear I wasn't going to be troubling the big leagues, I started helping out with coaching the younger ones.' Max shrugged. 'And, apart from when I was away at university, I never really stopped.'

'Is that every Saturday?'

'Practice is Tuesday and Thursday evenings and matches are Saturdays during the season. Our kids are in tier two of the local league and they've a shot at promotion this year. Just need to sort out our defence. The kids are fantastic though and we've got some real stars coming up ...'

Kate stared at Max's hands, which cycled through a series of chopping and circling motions, doing more talking than his mouth. It was difficult to keep up with the movements, but as his left hand flew past his face, she noticed his cheeks were flushed.

Well, well. Max Ravenscroft had a passion. And one which didn't involve making others miserable. Wonders would never cease.

They reached the bottom of the stairs and Max drew his football-related ramblings to a close. Kate smiled to herself as she climbed the stairs, imagining Max in football kit, a silver whistle around his neck, surrounded by a group of children, giving them a pep talk. It was such a pleasant picture that she had cleared the first few steps before she realised he wasn't following her.

'Are you not coming up?'

'Actually'—Max rested a hand on the carved end of the handrail and glanced over his shoulder—'I'm going to take a walk outside first. It was warm in there.'

'It was,' said Kate, eyeing the dashes of pink highlighting Max's cheekbones. 'But did you think Adrian looked paler than earlier? And did you hear his breathing?'

'He's an actor, Kate. A good one. I'm sure his health is just fine.'

'Hmn.' He was probably right. She was being daft and maybe projecting too. It was a rare moment lately that she wasn't worrying about her own dad's health. And yet she couldn't shake the dart of unease which was pinching her more insistently than her shoes. The discomfort must have shown because Max swerved his green gaze to study her face, his brows contracting in a frown.

She straightened, meeting his stare. 'What?'

'You're still worried.'

'And you think that's silly.'

'No.' Max shook his head. 'Just unnecessary.' He sighed. 'But I don't believe you can help it. You always worry about everyone except yourself.'

His tone was level and gaze steady. The absence of a smirk or sarcastic eyebrow twitch convinced Kate that, for once, Max wasn't being critical. Instead, she detected a note of sadness at the edge of his voice. Oh Lord, she thought, a heaviness pooling in her stomach. Perhaps there was something worse than Max's hatred. Was this *pity*?

Knocked off-centre by this latest unpleasant possibility, Kate shifted her weight to steady herself and her right shoe scraped the brutal blister which had erupted on her heel sometime after dinner. Miraculously, she managed not to whimper, but her features scrunched into a grimace which didn't go unnoticed.

'You should take off those shoes.' Max gestured towards her feet. 'You've been wincing every time you've put your right foot down.'

'I'm fine.'

Max raised his eyebrows.

'Oh, all right.' Kate stooped to remove the offending footwear. 'I admit it, Poirot. The blessed shoes are *killing* me.'

Kate had expected a Ravenscroft smirk, which was all her attempt at humour deserved, but Max's lips curled into an even smile. It was tight-lipped, but it reached up into his eyes, making the amber shards there sparkle. The sight of this tiny crack in his stony shell sent a thrill speeding through Kate which banished the dull weight in her tummy. Unless, of course, it was a pity smile—

Oh for goodness' sake. Stop staring at him and leave before he goes back to glaring at you!

'I'll let you escape before I hit you with more horrific murder mystery puns.' Kate clutched her shoes to her chest and tipped her head. 'Goodnight.'

She had fled up a few stairs before her progress was interrupted.

'Kate?'

'Yes?'

Turning back, she found Max with one foot on the bottom step. He glanced over his shoulder towards the house's main entrance. 'I don't suppose …'

The fine hairs on Kate's arms stood on end. Was Max about to ask her to go with him on his walk? Why would he want to do that?

She swallowed, her tongue suddenly heavy. 'Yes?'

Max opened his mouth and, as his gaze roved the ceiling, Kate found herself leaning forwards a fraction, as if she were planning to reach out and draw the words from him.

But whatever Max had been going to say was dismissed with a slow blink of his thick lashes and a short huff of air. When he opened his eyes he trained his gaze a few inches above her head and asked, 'You don't think there's any chance someone other than Mr Grieve will be found dead in the morning, do you?'

The tight ball of air Kate had been holding in her chest whooshed out as nervous laughter. 'In good news for Bella and her high-stakes bets, and in bad news for my bank balance, I think that's highly unlikely.'

'I guess we'll find out tomorrow. Goodnight, Kate.'

'Goodnight, Max. Enjoy your walk.'

Enjoy your walk? Her inner voice scoffed at her. *What are you even saying? Quick! Leave before you say something else stupid.*

Kate scurried up the rest of the stairs, hoping that if she moved quickly and channelled enough of her attention into keeping a firm grip on her shoes, she wouldn't give in to the urge to glance over her shoulder. For while the carpet was soft and soothing against her blistered feet, an insistent tingling tickled the area between her shoulder blades and she longed to turn back and confirm her suspicion that the cause was Max's cool green stare.

Chapter 9

The early morning air whispered across Kate's cheeks as she admired the wispy puffs of white cloud stippling the pale blue sky. The limestone façade of the back of the house glowed golden in the sunshine and, as she hurried past the conservatory, Kate hoped the cool spring breeze on her skin and the crunch of the gravel under her blissfully comfy purple sneakers would help her feel more awake.

The fire alarm had screamed shortly after 2 a.m. Thanks to years of regular school evacuation drills, Kate's body reacted before her brain. Half asleep, she jolted upright, blundered out of the enormous four-poster bed and bashed into the antique washstand by the window. Her hip had been throbbing and her foggy mind badgering her to grab the register and shepherd the children out to the playground when the bells stopped ringing. It had taken Kate a few moments to remember where she was and recall Roger's warning about false alarms.

It hadn't been the greatest start to the day, a day Kate

had hoped would bring a change in her luck. But at least taking a walk was paying off: her eyelids no longer felt leaden and her hip had stopped aching.

Kate passed the study window and turned the corner where the harsh cawing of crows signalled her arrival at her destination. Squinting, she raised a hand to shade her eyes as she studied the tower. A storey higher than the rest of the Old Grange, the square feature contained the same slender rectangular windows topped by pointed arches seen in the rest of the building. Although, unlike in other parts of the house, the birds resting on this part of the structure were treated to the company of a set of gargoyles in dragon form. They were straining forwards, their wings half open, as if they were preparing to launch themselves into the air, breathing fire as they flew.

Seeking a better view, Kate took a few steps back and gasped as her heel slipped from the gravel of the path into soft earth. She tutted and, glancing down at the damp soil coating the heel of her canvas shoe, noticed a patch of flattened forget-me-nots in the slender flower bed to her left, under the study window. Someone would have had to be careless to wander off the path, given the narrowness of the small flower border. Kate stooped slightly to better stare at the two symmetrical patches of crushed blossoms which, located as they were directly underneath a window, made her wonder if someone hadn't planted their feet in the flower bed deliberately—

'We'll be finished soon. Tomorrow afternoon.'

The voice came from the direction of the tower. Kate was no expert in accents, but she instantly recognised the dropped consonants and wide vowels of East London.

Intrigued, she inched back towards the corner of the building and peered around it.

The man she knew as Lorenzo Corsini was leaning against the side of the tower. Though he had his back to her, his height and slender frame were unmistakeable, as was the raven sheen of his slicked-back hair. His tan sports coat and contrasting grey trousers were more casual than the tuxedo of the previous evening, but he still cut a smart, striking figure.

Kate caught a glimpse of his profile as he glanced towards the gardens and said, in an accent more Romford than Rome, 'I know, my love. As soon as we're done I'll be straight back to London and we'll sort it out.'

Kate sighed. Bella had won the first of her cynical bets and Kate was down twenty pounds. Not even lunchtime and one of the actors was breaking character, chatting on their phone. And, as if that weren't bad enough, he was using wireless earbuds. Although, on reflection, it was probably inevitable that it would be one of the younger actors who would break ranks: Lorenzo's age was listed as twenty-seven in the information pack, but the smooth-faced actor playing the Italian could easily have been in his early twenties. The arrogance of youth! He wasn't even being sneaky about his phone use. Wouldn't it have made more sense to have gone off to the back of the gardens and whisper? Was next the tower the only spot where he could get good enough reception to make—

The sound of footsteps behind her disturbed Kate's train of thought. As they drew closer, she silently cursed whoever was interrupting her observations and turned to greet them.

Max strode along the path, glaring at her as if she was blocking his way. Kate sighed, the lingering tiredness in her limbs shifting into a deep weariness. Unlike Kate—who had treated herself to a brief lie-in—Max had probably been out in the grounds since dawn, proving his superior detective credentials by combing every inch of the lawns and flower beds for clues.

'Morning,' she said as she took in what she assumed was Max's casual weekend attire. Consisting as it did of tailored charcoal trousers, black brogues and a perfectly pressed, powder-blue shirt, it was basically his work clothes without the jacket and tie. Although, to be fair, he had made a major concession by leaving the top button undone and, as his cuffs were fastened with buttons rather with cufflinks, Kate supposed this could well be Max's idea of loungewear.

'You already knew.'

Max threw the words at Kate like an accusation as he halted a few feet from her.

'Lovely day, isn't it?' Kate channelled as much spirit as she could into a suitably sarcastic greeting, but the words sounded flat rather than cutting. Honestly, where did he get the energy for stomping around first thing in the morning flinging nonsensical comments at people? And did he not think his behaviour might be seen as rude?

Kate lifted her fingers to her temple. She needed breakfast and, ideally, an uninterrupted night's sleep to be able to deal properly with Max's odd, abrupt questions. She should just bid him a civil farewell, turn on her heel—in a smooth, elegant action without a hint of a wobble—and slink off to breakfast. Let him skulk about the grounds to his heart's content.

But her mouth had other plans and, prefacing her words with another resigned sigh, she said, 'I already knew *what*?'

'Hmn?' Max had strolled past her and was staring up at the tower. His gaze drifted down to meet hers and he blinked, as if he were remembering she was there. 'Oh. Yes. I was thinking about the dragons. Last night, when you asked Adrian Grieve the difference between gargoyles and grotesques, you already knew the answer, didn't you?'

Kate knew her poker face was rubbish. So she curled her lips into what she hoped was an enigmatic smile and said, 'Did you know that gargoyle comes from the Old French *gargouille*, meaning throat? It makes it easier to remember that they're the ones that act as waterspouts.'

Max's eyes widened and his eyebrows lifted.

Kate's smile stretched into a grin. There was nothing quite like the rare treat of telling Max Ravenscroft something he didn't know. 'A few years ago, one of the kids in my class visited Notre Dame. And while his holiday highlight was the trip to Disneyland Paris, he did like the gargoyles at the cathedral, drawing them and telling me about them.' A warmth spread through Kate's chest as she remembered how Elliot's eyes had shone while he delivered a breathless string of facts. 'And the grotesques.'

'You already knew the difference,' Max said, 'but you wanted Adrian to relax and talk and you figured he'd be the type of man who … who …'

'Who likes explaining things to people and to women in particular?' She nodded.

'Smart.'

'Thank you.' The words came out automatically in response to his compliment, but they left a strange aftertaste. Kate frowned. She regularly found herself apologising to furniture she bumped into and spent a significant amount of her day encouraging students to remember their manners. So why was trading niceties with Max so unsettling? It was only right she'd thanked him for getting her the cookies the previous day—

Her stomach rumbled. Thinking about the chocolatey biscuits had reminded the creature lurking in her guts that her next mission should be breakfast. Apparently it hadn't a care that she was in the middle of a weird conversation with Max, who had already used its unusually loud complaints as a reason to tease her.

The rumbling escalated to a grumble and Max flicked his gaze towards Kate's midriff. 'It appears the dragons aren't only on the tower walls. Have you not had breakfast yet?'

'Not yet,' said Kate with as much dignity as she could muster when her tummy was determined to embarrass her.

Max pointed at her tummy and said, 'Then I suggest we hurry to the buffet before that dragon of yours gets angry.'

He turned and strode off in the direction of the main entrance and, before she had time to rationalise her actions, Kate found herself scurrying along in pursuit, her irritation with herself growing with every step. How in the world had she ended up rushing along after Max Ravenscroft? And what exactly had he been doing outside? Did he already have a lead or was he trailing her so he could swoop in on any useful clues she uncovered?

She needed to know what he was up to. But how did you ask someone if they were stalking you?

Max was a few steps ahead of her, so Kate raised her

voice to ask, 'Did you not want to be one of the first in to breakfast?'

Max came to an abrupt stop, allowing Kate to draw level with him. 'I went to the dining room and Bella and Ethan weren't there. Neither were you, and I didn't want to eat alone so I came out for a walk. To give you all a chance to come down to breakfast.'

Kate bit her lower lip. Max's explanation was plausible, but the way his stare shied away from hers made her doubt the truth of it.

Max scrubbed a hand across his mouth, said, 'Ethan and Bella are probably down by now. We should go before they send out a search party,' and set off once again at a brisk stride, leaving Kate scrambling to keep up.

As they cleared the tower, Kate scanned the deserted path ahead. Lorenzo had vanished. Drat. He must have slipped away while Max was distracting her. True, Max had only interrupted her eavesdropping on the private conversation of an actor. But what if Lorenzo had been in character and speaking to someone out of sight on the other side of the tower? What if what he'd been saying had been a vital clue and she'd missed it thanks to Max?

Annoyance—with Max for distracting her and herself for letting him—spurred her to quicken her pace. As they entered the porch, her last-minute dash brought her to the front door first. Unwilling to let Max have the final word, she turned to face him. Max Ravenscroft was always confident and calm. She didn't know how he managed to stay so serene, but perhaps his unbreakable composure partly explained his string of victories at their Friendly Club parties. And—though it pained Kate to even entertain the notion—if she wanted to have a chance of solving the case this weekend, maybe she should take a leaf out of his book. This weekend, Kate—focused sleuth—would remain unruffled and poised. Even if she was naturally neither of those things.

Wrapping her fingers around the long door handle, she said, 'Our greatest worries shouldn't be Bella sending out a search party or the threat of angry stomach dragons. What we need to prepare ourselves for is the very real possibility that in our absence Bella will have snaffled all the hash browns.'

She pulled on the handle but the door refused to budge. Kate glared at it. Was it locked? She tried again, this time throwing a small huff of frustration into her effort. It remained closed.

Max stepped forwards and laid his palm against the door, next to where Kate's hand gripped the handle. He was close enough that Kate could smell his cologne, an intriguing mix of citrus and something else, an elusive note which was darker, suggestive, fiery.

Kate froze while her gaze shuttled between the shards of gold in Max's eyes and the door, where Max's hand rested against the oak grain. Kate had always had an inexplicable thing for nice hands. And, she thought, her breath coming a little quicker, Max's were close to being model-worthy with their long agile fingers and neat oval-shaped nails.

Max cleared his throat, drawing Kate's attention to his face. His penetrating stare met her own and her pulse picked up to match the pace of her shallow breathing.

'Allow me.' Max's low voice was barely more than a murmur as he gave the door a gentle push. The handle slipped smoothly out of Kate's hand, taking with it her slender reserves of dignity.

One side of Max's mouth quirked upwards into a characteristic smirk. Great. He clearly thought she was as ludicrous as she felt.

Pull yourself together, Kate! her inner voice chided. *What happened to unruffled and poised? Max isn't going anywhere. If you keep letting him unsettle you to the point you can't operate a simple push-pull door, how do you hope to solve the case?*

Holding the door open, his small mocking smile still in place, Max motioned for her to pass through. 'After you. Ladies … and dragons, first.'

Chapter 10

'There you are!' Bella's heels clicked across the lobby as she intercepted Kate by the dining room entrance. 'I was beginning to think you'd made a start on the hash browns without me.'

'I would never.' Kate threw Bella a quick smile, while giving most of her attention to the dining room, which buzzed with the low hum of conversation and the satisfied sighs of the recently roused enjoying their first hit of caffeine. They all seemed oblivious to the grandeur of their surroundings, though numerous details she hadn't noticed in artificial light the previous evening jumped out at Kate. With the teal velvet window drapes pulled back, the bright colours in the intricate flower patterns on the wallpaper shone out and the gold detailing glittered in the sunlight.

Beyond the diners, in the far left corner, two trolleys were covered in snowy linen cloths and an assortment of cereals, yoghurt and fresh fruit. But Kate's gaze swiftly fixed on the right-hand side of the room, where a gleaming group of stainless-steel warming pans stood on a row of rectangular tables.

'Morning, Bella,' said Max as he strode past Kate's shoulder into the dining room, no doubt making a direct line for the healthy thrill of muesli or porridge.

He was out of earshot—thank goodness!—when Kate's stomach gurgled another protest. Biting her lip, Kate weighed her options. At home breakfast was usually cereal and yoghurt—Paul had never had more than a cup of scalding black coffee and a single slice of toast before leaving the house and had regarded her ability to eat anything sizeable before noon as a lamentable quirk—but he wasn't here and this was a holiday.

'Kate? Kate!' Bella gave Kate's arm a pat with the back of her hand. 'Have you heard anything I said or are you too busy drooling at the thought of bacon?'

'Sorry.' Kate grimaced and did her utmost to ignore the fantastic smell of sausages which was luring her into the dining room. 'What did you say?'

'I said, did you and Max come in together?' Bella raised an eyebrow. 'What were you two getting up to al fresco?'

'Nothing.' The word flew out of Kate's mouth and, as Bella's other eyebrow rose, she realised she'd answered too quickly. Time to back-pedal before her friend got ideas. 'Honestly. I went for a walk outside. It's such a lovely morning I wanted to take a look around, the grounds are beautiful and ... I guess Max had the same idea.'

Bella's blue eyes narrowed into suspicious lines. 'Hmn.'

Kate knew she should stop talking—the guilty often loved to ramble—but something about Bella's persistent gaze loosened her tongue. 'I mean we barely spoke to each other and then my tummy rumbled again and, apart from him making some sarky comments about my noisy innards, that was the end of that.' Kate glanced about the lobby praying for someone to come to her rescue, and her spirits soared when Ethan rounded the curve in the staircase. 'There's Ethan! Oh. Is he all right?'

Ethan's eyelids were heavy and his expression slack. His habitual posture was enviably upright, but now he was slumped and the few strides to Bella's side appeared an effort, as if he were wading through treacle.

'He's fine.' Bella glanced at Ethan. 'Just too much wine last night. And the sodding fire alarm going off in the small hours didn't help.'

'You should have stopped me after a couple of glasses.' Ethan's gaze flicked to Bella then back to the floor. 'And I wouldn't have had so much if you hadn't been drinking too.'

Bella snorted. 'A grown man of thirty-four should own his decisions. Besides, it's not my fault you're a lightweight, darling.'

Kate had never known Bella to suffer a hangover no matter how much she seemed to be looking for one. And today, true to form, she was radiant. While Ethan looked as if he had fallen out of bed and into his creased black T-shirt and faded jeans, Bella was sporting a leopard-print top whose shirred bodice and square neck flattered her curvy figure. Teamed with black capri pants and with one sleeve hanging off her shoulder, the look was quite casual for Bella, although she was wearing a pair of three-inch heels. Kate sometimes wondered if her friend slept in stilettos.

A twinge of sympathy for Ethan's state moved Kate to say, 'They have toast and coffee in there.' She tipped her head towards the dining room. 'And I have painkillers in my room if you'd like them.'

'Thank you, *Kate*.' Ethan stressed her name while glaring at Bella. 'I remember Paul said you were always brilliant to him after he'd had a few too many. He really appreciated it.'

The burning roar of hunger in Kate's stomach turned icy. She had hoped this weekend would be a Paul-free space. He'd always hated her going to the Friendly Murder Club parties. She could still hear his sneering: 'If you want to swan about making a fool of yourself, Kate, go ahead. But count me out.'

'Oh did he?' Bella shot a filthy glare at Ethan. 'Well sadly Paul didn't appreciate Kate enough not to—' Bella froze mid-sentence and, snapping her mouth shut, cast a guilty glance towards Kate before lifting a hand to rub Ethan's shoulder. 'Go in and get yourself some coffee. You'll feel better soon.'

The women watched in silence as Ethan shuffled across to the stacks of cups and Kate was daring to dream she might have heard the last mention of her ex for the foreseeable future when Bella said, 'Sorry about that. But you know Paul's still Ethan's oldest friend. Obviously I wouldn't care if I never saw him again.' Bella scratched the back of her neck. 'But I need to tell you … Ethan's asked the weasel to be his best man. And apparently he's looking forward to it.'

The ice in Kate's belly stole upwards and enveloped her heart. *Oh no. Oh God, no.* 'But … but isn't Ethan asking his brother to do it?'

'He did. But apparently there's some diary issue. His brother says he can't commit to all the wedding prep. So Ethan asked Paul instead.' Bella grabbed Kate's hand. 'Look, if you don't want to be my maid of honour any more, I understand. But the most you'll have to do is stand near Paul for some photos. You won't have to dance with him on the day or do any prep together. I swear.'

Kate glanced down at her hand in Bella's. Her friend gave her fingers a warm squeeze which melted a little of the ice in Kate's chest. The wedding was now likely to be an ordeal but, although the idea made Kate queasy, far harder to bear was the drawn expression of worry on Bella's face.

Kate forced a smile. 'It's not a problem.'

Bella blinked. 'You're sure it's OK?'

No. Not at all. 'Of course. It'll be fine.'

Bella beamed and, letting out a squeal of delight, grabbed Kate into a bear hug. 'I love you! And it'll show Paul too, the great pimpled arse. You'll look bloody gorgeous and we'll find you a supermodel to bring as your date.'

Kate's lips stretched into a genuine smile. The prospect of Paul pining for her while she was radiant and unavailable did have a certain appeal. Although finding a suitable jealousy-inducing date could be a problem.

'Come on,' said Bella, ushering Kate through the door and towards the row of steel warming pans. 'Let's get those hash browns before they're all gone.'

As they crossed the room, Bella nodded in the direction of Ethan, who was taking a chair next to Max at a table near the coffee station. He lowered himself carefully towards the seat, his fingers wrapped around a large mug of steaming coffee.

'I hope that cheers him up,' said Bella as Ethan took a tentative sip of the boiling liquid. 'I'm taking him off to the spa later and then'—she dropped her voice and leant closer to Kate as they arrived at the buffet table—'it'll be time for the surprise wedding-venue trip.'

'Hmn.'

'What?' Bella nudged Kate's arm.

'Oh, it's nothing.' Kate murmured in reply, distracted by the sight of Max polishing off a croissant. She frowned as her stomach grumbled. The lucky git also had a pain au chocolat waiting for him beside a cup of tea. Huh. She would never have pegged him for a pastry sort of person. It seemed too fun, too decadent a choice—

'Hey!' Bella thrust a large plate into Kate's hands. 'What was that "hmn" about?'

'Nothing. I was just wondering how you're going to fit in solving a murder around the spa and wedding trips.'

'Oh, that!' Bella snatched up a pair of serving tongs. 'Don't worry. I've got it all figured out.'

'And, I hate to say it, but I owe you twenty quid.'

'Already?' Bella dropped a rasher of bacon on her plate and moved on to the sausages. 'Who was it?'

'The actor playing Lorenzo . I saw him outside, talking on his phone.'

'Yes! I knew at least one of them would snap. I mean, who can stay in character for an entire weekend? Tell me everything.'

Kate opened her mouth to give more details but her words caught in her throat when a petite woman in an old-fashioned maid's uniform—a long-sleeved black dress complete with white cap and apron with lace trim—sprinted into the room and skidded to a halt in its centre.

Her chest heaving and eyes glistening, the maid made several inarticulate sounds before unleashing a shriek which would have made a banshee reach for earplugs.

Resisting the urge to cover her ears, Kate stared as the woman stopped screeching long enough to shout, 'He's dead! Mr Grieve! They've killed him!'

All eyes in the dining room upon her, the maid sighed dramatically and dropped to the floor in a dead faint.

The silence was interrupted by the sound of chairs scraping back as various diners jumped to their feet. But it was Max who was by the side of the collapsed woman first, kneeling to check she was all right.

Kate's head buzzed with questions. Where had the murder taken place? How soon could they visit the crime scene? And why was the supposedly stricken maid fondling Max?

In the centre of the room, the maid had come round and lifted herself from the floor just enough to lounge in Max's arms, her face unnecessarily close to his. Kate's eyes narrowed as she watched Max muttering to the woman who was staring at him in a doe-eyed way that made Kate uneasy. Why was she stroking his shoulder like that? I mean, surely she should be in shock—

Bella nudged Kate in the ribs and dropped a couple of hash browns onto her plate. 'Come on, we've got to eat this lot sharpish before they announce the order in which the teams get to visit the crime scene.' She snatched a bite out of one of her own hash browns and, muttering through a mouthful of fluffy fried potato, added, 'And I don't know about you, but I never examine a fake corpse on an empty stomach.'

Chapter 11

To Bella's disappointment there was no corpse to examine, fake or otherwise. For while the maid had supposedly found Adrian Grieve dead at his desk in the study, his body had been removed before the guests were allowed to access the crime scene.

Fortunately, Bella was soon distracted by the study's impressive ceiling-to-floor bookcases, which covered the wall to the left of the doorway and had their own set of sliding wooden library steps. The hearty hotel breakfast seemed to have filled Bella with nervous energy and, having done a couple of laps of the room and scanned the shelves, she grabbed one side of the ladder and absent-mindedly rocked it back and forth along its rail. 'I suppose it would have been grim for the actor,' she said, her pout still firmly in place, 'to be stuck over there'—she nodded to the bulky pedestal desk on the other side of the room—'for hours and hours while we poked about.'

'And they might have drifted off and started to snore,'

said Ethan, who was busy staring at the items on the desk. 'Which would definitely go against the whole "staying in character at all times" thing they're going for.'

Bella hummed a dissatisfied note, but her frown lifted and she beamed as she gave the library steps a push and watched them glide away from her. Their movement was halted by Kate, who recognised the impish glee on Bella's face and decided it was time to use her best no-nonsense teacher voice. 'No, Bella.'

'Oh, go on. No one will have to know. I'll jump on and you can give me a shove. We'll take turns!'

Kate's patience with her friend's Tiggerish bounciness was wearing thin. 'We were specifically asked not to use the steps. They're old. You might break them.'

'You're no fun.' Bella flicked her golden hair off her shoulder. 'You really do need to lighten up!'

Kate squeezed her fingers into fists. Why was it that being told to 'relax', 'chill' or 'lighten up' only wound her nerves into tighter explosive packets? Sometimes she swore she could hear the little bombs ticking.

'Hey, guys.' Having completed his inspection of their contents, Ethan slammed the last of the desk drawers shut. 'Could this be something?'

Kate gave Bella a final warning glare and strode across the busy paisley pattern in the floor rug to Ethan's side. She scanned the items on the emerald leather inlay of the desktop: a Bakelite telephone, two silver photo frames, three fountain pens, an open ledger book, a rocker ink blotter and a letter rack containing neat stacks of correspondence. The silver-plated paperknife which had been used to open the letters—a thin steel blade with a wide handle decorated with a foliage relief—was absent from its usual place on the desk because it had been lodged deep in Adrian Grieve's back.

'What do you think that is?' Ethan lifted a squat crystal tumbler from the right side of the desk. It contained a splash of amber liquid and was one of six: the rest of the set and matching decanter sat on a metal drinks trolley behind the study door.

'I don't know,' said Kate. 'Whisky? Or maybe—'

'It's very expensive bourbon,' Max said. 'It says so here on this list.' He tapped one of the pieces of paper tacked to the free-standing whiteboard which had been set up in front of the fireplace. The board was large enough to block access to the hearth and part of the bookcase to the right of the mantle. It was covered in photos, a plan of the ground floor of the building, the preliminary notes of one Dr Chase, the initial police report and an inventory of the room's contents at the time the body was discovered.

Max delivered his correction to Kate's guess without taking his eyes from the board, his gaze as fixed as his posture, which was only a fraction less stiff than that of a conscientious sentry guard.

'Bourbon. Great,' Kate said, a dart of irritation stealing into her voice. *Wonderful*. Max's perfectionist sniping had started already. Perhaps he was going for a new personal best? At least at their monthly parties he used to hold out for a half hour or so before interrupting everything she said, usually to disagree with her ideas.

'So what's the explanation they're giving us?' Bella jumped off the bottom step of the ladder and drifted towards the window.

Kate exhaled, willing the knots in her shoulders to release. This part was thankfully something she could say without fearing Max contradicting her. 'The local constabulary believe that a person or persons unknown entered the study last night ...' Kate joined Bella by the tall, two-panelled window and squinted against the glare. The study was in the south-east corner of the Old Grange and the thick burgundy drapes each side of the window had been tied back, allowing the morning sun to fill the room. 'At some time between midnight and 2 a.m.—which is the estimated time of death—this stranger gained access through the window which the late Mr Grieve had left open, presumably because it was a warm evening. The intruder left a set of footprints in the flower bed.'

She pointed at the steel casement in the left window panel, which had been propped open, and took a deep breath, enjoying the lavender-scented air flowing in from the flower beds outside. On first entering the room, Kate had been struck by a thick swirl of perfume and aftershave, a lingering reminder that all the other teams had accessed the crime scene before them. Their team's number had been drawn last. She was trying not to see this as a bad omen.

Stifling a sigh, she strolled back towards the desk. 'The doctor's notes we've been given state that Adrian Grieve's body showed no signs of struggle or distress which supports the idea that the fatal blow was delivered swiftly enough to kill him instantly. Presumably, Mr Grieve had fallen asleep at his desk and so failed to notice his assailant. This idea is backed up by the fact his eyes were closed when he was found—'

'The killer could have closed his eyes post-mortem,'

Max said, not turning his head from the board. 'And tidied up any minor signs of a struggle.'

'True,' Kate said, spitting the word from between clenched teeth. Did Max enjoy interrupting her? And 'post-mortem'? Really? Why use plain English when you could use a poncey Latin phrase?

Kate swallowed her annoyance. Where had she been? Oh yes. Adrian was probably sleeping when he was stabbed. 'The killer could have done that. But, on balance, I think it is most likely that he was asleep when stabbed.'

'Yes, I agree.' Max levelled his cool stare at Kate. 'But it's important we don't jump to any conclusions, particularly at this early stage in the investigation.'

'I don't think anyone's jumping to anything yet,' said Bella. 'Right, Kate?'

Bella winked at Kate, and Kate gave her friend a smile of silent thanks. 'Right,' Kate said. 'It's too early to rule anything out.'

'Then we're all agreed.' Bella grinned and skipped over to the neat rectangular hole in the wall to the left of the fireplace. 'So, the jury's out on the exact details of Adrian's death. What about the robbery?'

Kate joined her friend by the open safe. 'Whether they emptied the safe before or after killing him is unknown, but they'd have to have been incredibly stealthy thieves to take down the heavy painting—' Kate motioned to the large family portrait of Adrian Grieve, his wife and daughters in a thick gilded frame which rested on the floor against the side of the fireplace—'open the safe, remove the contents and then kill Mr Grieve on the way out of the room.'

'And if you could manage the robbery without disturbing

him, why bother killing him?' said Bella, stretching her hand into the black velvet darkness of the safe.

Kate took a moment to admire her friend's thoroughness before pointing out the obvious. 'It's empty.'

'So they say,' said Bella, patting and prodding every corner. 'But a girl can live in hope of a hidden compartment springing open to reveal bags of uncut gems or, if I were extra lucky, a switch that opens the door to a secret room. Ethan's hoping for the same—look at him!'

Ethan's legs and feet were sticking out from under the desk. His hands were busy, tapping the underside of the tabletop and the inner panels of the drawers.

'Find any hidden compartments, Ethan?' Kate asked.

'Nope. Ouch!' Ethan raised a hand to his head, which he had clipped on the desk as he sat up. Kate winced in sympathy and stooped to help him to his feet. The small mark the blow had left on his brow would probably bruise and was unlikely to improve his existing hangover headache.

'Nothing here either,' said Bella, removing her hand from the safe. 'What are they saying was in there?'

Max tapped his knuckle against one of the pictures on the whiteboard and said, 'Just the jewellery.'

'Pft!' Bella strutted over to stand beside Max and waved her hand across the photographs of the missing items. 'How can you refer to these amazing pieces as "just the jewellery"? Look at the work on this necklace.' She nodded towards a large collar of intricate filagree metalwork studded with an assortment of diamonds. In the centre of the glittering array was a large drop pendant holding a fiery ruby. 'It's like a beautiful cobweb studded with stars.'

Kate smiled at Bella's wistful expression as she joined her at the board. 'You're right, but—and I'm sorry to bring it back to less artistic matters—it is loaded with very expensive stones. The total value of the jewellery in the safe is estimated to be ...' Kate trailed off as she scanned the whiteboard for the paper showing the exact amount. Where was it? She'd seen it a second ago. How hard could it be to—

'Over sixty thousand pounds,' said Max, apparently unable to wait for Kate to correct her ignorance.

Too late, Kate found the missing number. 'Sixty-four thousand to be exact,' said Kate, stabbing her finger at the paper carrying the elusive figures with enough pent-up frustration to make the board wobble.

'That doesn't seem anywhere near enough,' said Ethan as he sank into the padded seat of the swivel desk chair and rubbed his forehead with his fingertips.

'They'll be using the value of the pound in 1932,' said Kate. 'Which today would be roughly ...' Kate scrambled to do the mental calculations before Max—who probably did quadratic equations in his spare time for fun—bested her yet again. And the maths really wasn't that hard—

'Somewhere in excess of four million pounds,' said Max.

Kate bit the inside of her cheek. And had Bella not squeezed her hand and given her another wink, she might have drawn blood. 'Wow!' Bella said. 'That sort of cash is definitely a solid motive for murder.'

Ethan frowned. 'But, even so, the police's theory doesn't add up. Why kill him? Why not just knock the old man over the back of the head, tie him up and scarper with the jewels? And if Adrian did wake up and interrupt them, surely he'd have been stabbed in the front or there would be signs of a struggle at least?'

'You're forgetting the most obvious reason why the police theory doesn't add up, my love,' said Bella. 'Are you sure your head's OK?'

'Yeah, it's fine. What do you mean?'

Without taking his eyes from the board, Max said, 'It doesn't add up because this is a murder mystery party and we've been assured that one of the house guests is guilty. We know this was an inside job.'

'Ah, yes, I knew that. Right.' Ethan coughed, perhaps an attempt to dislodge a knot of mortification in his throat. 'You know, maybe I should ask reception for some ice for my head—'

Ethan was saved further embarrassment by his phone, which shrilled and buzzed from inside his back pocket. Standing up, he glanced at the screen and his frown deepened.

'Aren't you going to get that?' Bella stepped back from the board, her gaze skipping between the phone and her fiancé's face. 'Who is it, anyway?'

'Um …'

Ethan glanced at Kate and the sheepish gleam in his eyes made her stomach drop. Ethan fearing her reaction meant there was only one person it could be.

The frog in Ethan's throat had returned. He coughed again and said, 'It's Paul. Probably calling about best man stuff.'

Kate interlaced her fingers behind her back and fixed her stare on the board, hoping to present an outward picture of untroubled serenity which was completely at odds with her inner anxiety. Next to her, Max inhaled sharply and his posture, which had loosened a little while Bella had been next to him, stiffened.

Intrigued, Kate risked a glance at Max's face. The muscles in his jaw were tense and his eyes had narrowed, giving his gaze an intensity which suggested anger. Why would Paul calling Ethan upset Max? She doubted Paul could have offended him personally because—as far as she knew—Max and Paul had never met. Could Max's reaction be connected to Paul's relationship with Ethan? Had Max hoped to be Ethan's best man and the mention of Paul had dredged up disappointment or resentment?

Kate returned her gaze to Ethan and turned over the idea before dismissing it. Max and Ethan had met at work and had never seemed that close. Max couldn't have expected to be chosen over Paul, an old high school friend of Ethan's. So what was Max's problem?

'I'm going to duck out and take this.' Ignoring Bella's glare, Ethan smiled apologetically at Kate and made for the door.

As Ethan disappeared into the corridor, Bella tapped Kate's shoulder. 'I'm going to go after Ethan. I'm a bit worried about his head.'

His head? Kate raised an eyebrow, suspecting that Bella was more interested in eavesdropping on Ethan's phone call than checking his health.

Bella prodded Max's arm to get his attention and waited until both he and Kate were looking at her to continue. 'I'll only be gone a few minutes.' She extended her index fingers and used them to jab warning shots at her audience. 'Play nicely you two. No more murders till I get back!'

Chapter 12

As the thudding of Bella's heels faded, Max shrugged and turned back to the board, his face once again a smooth mask of concentration.

Kate raised a hand to the bands of muscle at the back of her shoulder and rubbed a stubborn knot. The resulting ache served as a wake-up call: she needed to stop worrying about Paul and get back in the game. Max—his gaze roving the board in slow sweeps—was clearly in some sort of zone and she needed to follow his example if she were to have a hope of solving this case.

Kate raked her fingers through her hair and stared at the photos of Adrian Grieve's body. Her focus narrowed to the handle of the letter opener sticking out of his back. It had been driven deep into his heart. The killer would have had to be strong to do that, surely?

She raised her right hand to the image showing a close-up of the wound. And, as she stared at the photograph, muted alarm bells rang in the back of her mind. There was something wrong with the picture. But what?

Her fingers traced the glittering scroll work on the knife handle, taking in the monogram engraved in curly calligraphic script: an intertwined *A* and *G*. The blade had made a clean puncture through Adrian's white cotton shirt. Narrowing her eyes, she glared at the picture. Still wrong. But why?

Kate closed her eyes and pictured Adrian Grieve's last moments. Asleep, head on desk, breathing heavily. His assailant creeping through the window like a malevolent shadow, gliding across the room, snatching up the letter opener, positioning it over Adrian's heart and ... stab! Keen to get into the safe and away, the shadow left the knife in the corpse, that way they wouldn't have to worry about accidentally getting any blood on—

'Why would Bella say that?'

Max had spoken in such a quiet voice that Kate questioned if she had heard him correctly and was relieved when he continued. 'About not wanting another murder?'

Incredulous, Kate parted her lips, preparing to snap, *'Because you hate me and seem hell-bent on annoying me, of course!'* but then her gaze snagged on the small crinkle between Max's eyes. Did he really not get it?

As she held his gaze, she noticed the flush, which she had observed when going into dinner the previous evening, stealing up his neck once again. It was tingeing the skin dark pink, verging on red—

'Blood.'

Max's frown deepened. 'What?'

'One sec.' Kate held up a hand and returned her attention to the close-ups of Adrian Grieve's back. The area around the paperknife was almost unblemished.

Apart from a tiny red stain at the entrance wound, the white shirt was immaculate. Kate raised a finger to the image and muttered, 'Yet who would have thought the old man to have had so much blood in him?'

Max followed her finger and gaze. His eyes widened and, softly, he said, 'Oh!' just as a louder voice behind them said, 'That's *Macbeth*.'

Kate and Max whirled round to find they had been joined by a smiling, fair-skinned woman with sparkling green eyes and a thick mane of jet-black hair. Her clothing was as dark as her locks—black jeans and a high-necked navy jacket—but, backlit by the sunlight streaming through the windows, she was surrounded by a golden glow. Kate was confident she hadn't met the woman before—she would have remembered someone so striking—and yet, she was strangely familiar.

Staring at their twin expressions of surprise, she laughed. 'Sorry to make you jump. But you were quoting *Macbeth*, right? I'm not a Shakespeare expert but my other half's an actor and he was in a production of *Macbeth* last summer in Stratford. He played Macbeth'—the woman's smile stretched into a proud grin—'and I saw it a few times so I remember that one.'

'Actually, while it is from *Macbeth*'—Max paused and cleared his throat—'I believe Kate was thinking of the use of the line in *Hercule Poirot's Christmas*.'

Yes! Open-mouthed, Kate stared at Max and his unreadable green gaze. How did he reach inside her mind like that? As it was, the particular Poirot story was only fresh in her memory because she'd read it in January. It had been in the December edition of her monthly book subscription box. Which had been a wonderful gift three Christmases ago from Paul. She bit her lip—she still hadn't got around to asking him to cancel it or transfer it into her name. It would involve speaking to him about a kind and thoughtful thing he'd done for her and she wasn't sure she could trust herself not to go soft on him and forget he was a heartless—

'Lucinda!' Bella cannonballed across the room and threw herself onto the dark-haired woman, who returned the hug with equal enthusiasm.

Ah, Kate thought as the two women laughed and embraced. No wonder the interloper had seemed familiar. She'd featured in many of the photos of Bella's dad's wedding she had been shown, Kate making polite noises of interest while Bella enthusiastically pointed out the fabulous Lucinda and her handsome actor boyfriend, Alex Fraser.

Kate's gaze dropped to where Lucinda's hands rested on Bella's back. The left one was bare of a simple twinkling band or a large shiny rock to rival Bella's ring. Bella would be disappointed. In contrast, Kate was rather relieved. It was ungenerous of her, she knew. But occasionally it did feel like she was the last person in the world anyone wanted to marry. After all, she had waited years for Paul to pop the question. Little did she expect that when he finally said he had something important to talk to her about it would be to tell her he'd met someone else.

Bella gave Lucinda an extra squeeze before stepping back to beam into her stepsister's face. 'This is a fantastic surprise! What are you doing here?'

'Seeing how last night's dinner went—'

'Obviously it was delicious,' said Bella.

'Thank you. I'm pleased to say that's been the feedback from Mr Merryman too.' Lucinda smiled, but something about the way she said Roger's name made Kate suspect she wasn't his greatest fan. 'And I wanted to check everything's set for this evening. But really it's all just an excuse to see you.' She gave Bella a playful nudge. 'Where's Ethan?'

'Gone to drink some more water and perhaps have a sneaky lie-down before I take him to the spa. He overindulged last night. You've met Kate and Max?'

'Not properly. Hello, I'm Lucinda.' Lucinda shook Kate's and Max's hands. 'Bella tells me you're really into this detective stuff. From what she's told me about you, Kate, I'm not surprised you have a theory already. And I love that dress!'

The dress was one of Kate's favourites. On a deep green background, a busy pattern of colourful hand-drawn teapots and dainty cups was scattered between delicately outlined inkwells, fountain pens and open notebooks. It might not have been 1930s-style or the typical garb of a serious sleuth, but slipping into it that morning had given her mood a much-needed boost.

Kate ran her hands over the skirt, smoothing its flare from the gathered waistband. 'Thank you. I still haven't found one that's exactly murder mystery themed.'

'No, no, it's perfect.' Lucinda tilted her head, scanning the pattern. 'It makes me think of *Murder, She Wrote*.'

A bubble of happy surprise swelled Kate's chest and she blurted, 'I love that show!' her squeaky outburst almost drowning out Max's own response of, 'Great show.'

Kate glanced at Max and caught his eye for a moment.

Huh. Max Ravenscroft, secret admirer of Jessica Fletcher. Perhaps the man wasn't a complete lost cause after all.

'But sorry, I've taken you off topic.' Lucinda smiled at Kate. 'You were going to tell us about your *Macbeth*-related breakthrough.'

Max and Bella followed Lucinda's eyeline, training their stares on Kate, and suddenly the warm thrill created by Lucinda's compliments shifted into an unpleasant jangling of nerves. Kate's voice carried a tremor of uncertainty as she said, 'Oh … well, sort of. It's probably nothing though.'

'I don't believe that for a second,' Bella said. 'What's up?'

'Kate noticed the lack of blood at the wound site.' Max tapped the photo of Adrian's back. 'Of course it could be explained simply by the victim's position when he died, he may have had very low blood pressure—'

'Or'—Kate bristled. Her theory was a good one and here was Max, doing his best to explain it away before she'd even voiced it!—'it means Adrian was already dead when he was stabbed.'

'Oo!' Bella's and Lucinda's eyes widened.

Bella inspected the photo. 'That's a great catch, Kate.' She nudged Lucinda. 'I told you she was a proper Miss Marple, didn't I?'

Kate shrugged, but Bella's praise sent a rush of heat to her cheeks.

'So, if he was already dead when he was knifed,' Lucinda said, 'does that mean he wasn't murdered? Did he have a heart attack and the killer assumed he was asleep and stabbed him, not knowing it wasn't necessary?'

'A tempting theory,' said Max, 'but sadly impossible in this case.'

'The Merryman rules are clear: the solution must involve foul play,' Kate explained. 'No accidental or natural deaths allowed. So no heart attack or similar.'

'Ah.' Lucinda gave a tut of disappointment. 'In that case, what are you thinking?'

Kate rubbed the back of her neck, lifting her hair away from the flushed skin at her nape. 'Well, according to the preliminary doctor's report there were no other signs of violence, so I'm guessing poison.'

'Poison!' Bella gave a small skip of glee. 'Brilliant! Someone poisons him and then someone else stabs him.'

'Wow,' said Lucinda. 'This is all going a bit *Murder on the Orient Express*.'

Kate grinned at Lucinda's suggestion. While that was an unbeatable classic, the possibility of a poisoning and stabbing had made her think of one of her favourite mystery movies. It had such a brilliant cast. With Kristin Scott Thomas, Helen Mirren and Maggie Smith in a film what more could you—

'Made me think of *Gosford Park*,' said Max.

'Exactly!' said Kate, unable to conceal her amazement as she turned to stare at Max. 'Me too.'

Max shrugged, apparently unimpressed by his spooky telepathic abilities. 'Brilliant film. Terrific cast.'

Bella chuckled. 'Well, if multiple murderers is the solution to all Merryman's mysteries it would explain why no one has cracked one of their cases yet.'

Lucinda frowned and a glint of suspicion entered her eyes. 'When it comes to Roger Merryman, I'm more inclined to believe the rumours that the games are rigged.' She leant towards the others, getting near enough for

Kate to detect hints of cinnamon and vanilla. 'I wouldn't trust that man as far as I can throw him. I always demand full payment for everything up front. Anyway'—Lucinda clapped her hands and beamed—'back to happier things. When was your victim poisoned?'

Kate and Max both opened their mouths and took a breath, but Bella beat them to it. 'Last night at dinner? Oh my God!' Bella gasped and held up her hands. 'What if it was the dessert? Death by Chocolate! Maybe that was a clue after all? The cake killed him.'

'No.' Lucinda's response was emphatic. 'I've made many a dessert and you can trust me when I say: cake doesn't kill you, it only makes you stronger.'

Everyone chuckled and Kate capitalized on the break in conversation to move to the desk and pick up the crystal tumbler. 'I was wondering …' She lifted the glass to her nose and sniffed the amber liquid inside.

'Bitter almonds?' Max said.

'What?' Bella giggled. 'Are you two talking in code now?'

Lucinda shook her head. 'Cyanide can have an almond-like scent.'

Bella grasped Lucinda's arm. 'Lord save me, I'd forgotten you're a Christie nut when you're not in the kitchen.'

'Hey, I can multitask. I'll have you know I sometimes listen to an audiobook while working.'

While Lucinda and Bella continued to trade good-natured barbs, Max wandered over to Kate's side. 'Well?' he asked.

'I can't make out anything unusual.' Kate stared down at the amber liquid. All she could smell was alcohol. And would Merryman's organisers have bothered to put a drop of almond essence or other suspicious scent in the glass even if Adrian was poisoned? 'But I've never had the greatest sense of smell.' She held the glass out to him. 'Do you want to check?'

Determined not to drop the glass and reinforce Max's ideas of her incompetence, Kate kept tight hold of the top of the tumbler until Max's fingers had wrapped around the base. 'Got it?'

Max raised his gaze to meet hers and nodded. As Kate withdrew her hand, her fingers brushed against Max's. The moment of skin-to-skin contact sent a shot of electricity bolting up her arm which left her fingertips tingling. Kate stared at her hand slack-jawed. What was that about?

Max didn't seem to have felt the shock and was busy swirling the liquid around the glass as if preparing for a wine tasting. He raised the glass to his nose and inhaled deeply. 'Nothing I can detect. In any case, while it's a tempting theory, would the game makers have gone to the trouble of putting a little almond extract in this glass on the off chance that someone would think to look for it?'

'I was thinking that too,' said Kate. 'OK, for the moment, let's assume he was poisoned, even if we don't know how. What does that tell us?'

'It's often a woman's choice of murder weapon.'

'But to lodge the paperknife so deeply into his back would have required strength, so perhaps a man was also involved.'

'Could have been a woman with a serious grievance. Rage can be a short-term superpower.'

'Indeed.' Kate knew what that felt like. Once she had

got over the shock and sadness of Paul dumping her, there had been days she had been surprised that her fury hadn't melted the pavement beneath her feet. But even as Kate agreed with Max's insight, she struggled to believe it came from personal experience. What could upset the icy Max Ravenscroft enough to drive him into a rage?

'I guess there's no way of knowing if he was poisoned unless something shows up in the autopsy,' said Max, setting the glass back on the desktop.

'And we can't bank on getting the report before tomorrow lunchtime.'

'True. Then even if we did, there are toxins which could go undetected.' Max tapped the side of the desk. 'But anyway, I think it's safe to rule out your cyanide suggestion.'

A lump caught in Kate's throat as she was transported back to the monthly murder mystery parties where Max seemed to hover at her elbow, his sole purpose to undermine or contradict her. As if she needed someone else to throw doubt on her ideas when her inner monologue was more than capable of doing that unassisted.

She coughed, rallying. 'Oh? And why is that?'

Max, apparently oblivious to the edge to Kate's voice, replied, 'Because cyanide usually causes convulsions. It's not a peaceful way to go.'

Ah. Dammit.

Unwilling to admit defeat—persistence was a trait of all the best detectives—Kate crossed her arms and tried again. 'What about arsenic?'

'Vomiting and abdominal pain.'

'Strychnine?'

'Not a chance. Nausea, vomiting and muscle spasms.'

Kate huffed a short breath in frustration. Max's knowledge of poisons was apparently encyclopaedic and, if she had thought he was interesting enough to be a murderer, would have been worrying. 'Opium?'

'Not impossible. Hmn.' Max tapped a finger to his lip and turned to gaze at the papers on the whiteboard. 'It's a shame that doctor's report didn't mention the state of the victim's eyes.'

'Why?'

'Morphine poisoning would have caused his pupils to contract to black dots before death. It'd be a great clue. Perhaps—'

'OK, Jessica Fletcher fan club.' Bella's raised voice interrupted Max's musings. 'I'm off.'

While chatting, Bella and Lucinda had drifted over to the doorway. 'And I should get back to the kitchen.' Lucinda raised a hand in a farewell wave and put the other on Bella's back. 'It was nice to meet you both. Good luck!'

Kate's stomach lurched as the women neared the threshold. Wait. Was Bella leaving her alone with Max?

Chapter 13

'Hang on!' Kate scurried across the room and grasped Bella's elbow. 'You're going already?'

'Yes. I have to find Ethan and get to the spa. Then we're off out for lunch and on to Compton Hall. We've—'

Lucinda tapped Bella's shoulder. 'Sorry to interrupt, but I have to go. We'll catch up before you leave tomorrow, OK?'

'I'll call you.' Bella grinned at Lucinda as she strolled off down the corridor, but her smile fell as she turned back to Kate. 'You're already halfway to cracking the case. You don't need me here. And I told you yesterday about the spa and venue visit.'

'But I didn't know we'd be last to view the crime scene. It means we're last to interview all the suspects too. I thought you'd be here for at least some of those interviews before you had to leave.'

'But that doesn't matter. We both know subtlety isn't my thing. I'm sure you'll do better getting the info you need out of a group of grieving relatives if I'm not hanging about. And Ethan's no use in his current state.'

'But … but …' Kate floundered. Bella had a point. But even if she and Ethan were unlikely to prove an asset in that afternoon's interviews, she needed them to act as a buffer to Max's interruptions and dismissiveness.

She glanced over her shoulder. Max had taken the glass to the window and was holding it up to the sunlight, tilting the tumbler and inspecting the motion of the liquid. Her insides swirling in a similar way, Kate stepped closer to Bella and dropped her voice to a hiss. 'But me and Max. Alone. How is that going to work?'

'You're both good at this, it'll work great.' Bella took in Kate's expression and patted Kate's arm. 'If you honestly can't bear to be alone with him for a few hours you could split tasks and work individually. Remember, you're not in competition any more.'

'We really don't get on.'

'Kate. Every day, all over the world, millions of people manage to work successfully with people they don't get on with. In my office alone, there are about twenty people I'd happily shove off the building.'

Kate's eyes widened. She had gelled well with almost everyone she'd ever worked with. Except Kirsty, of course. The sneaky cow. And she'd known Bella found her job tiring and stressful, but she had no idea it involved dealing with so many people she couldn't stand.

'And,' Bella continued, 'while you've convinced yourself Max hates you, I'm not a believer. In fact'—she scrunched up her button nose—'have you ever thought that might be more about you than him?'

'What?' Kate trained her stare on Bella, determined not

to blink until her friend gave her a full explanation of her cryptic comment.

Bella ran her tongue over her bottom lip. 'OK. Do you ever think that sometimes … the things you believe other people are thinking about you are actually just your own—'

Her mobile phone chimed and Bella fished it out of her back pocket. 'Crap, it's a reminder about our spa appointment. I have to go.' She tucked her phone away and glanced up at Kate. 'Could you give Max a chance? See how it goes?'

Bella's encouraging, though slightly condescending tone, was reminiscent of how Kate might ask a five-year-old pupil if they could please try putting on their own coat. Kate gave herself a mental shake. She was being unreasonable. Bordering on cowardly.

'All right,' she said. 'I'll do my best. Sorry for keeping you back.'

'You'll be fine,' said Bella. 'And if our team does win this thing, the prize money is all yours. Apart from a generous wedding present for Ethan and me, of course.' Bella grinned. 'Deal?'

'Will Ethan be OK with that? It doesn't seem entirely fair—'

'If you do the work, you win the cash. Ethan will agree and I won't take no for an answer. OK?'

'Fine,' Kate said. 'If you're sure. Besides, at the rate I'm losing bets to you this weekend, you'll end up with half the money anyway.'

'You're so fantastically sensible. It's one of the many things I love about you.' Bella gave Kate's arm a reassuring squeeze and darted off down the corridor. 'See you later.'

'Enjoy the spa,' Kate called after Bella's retreating figure. 'And good luck this afternoon.'

Without looking back or breaking her stride, Bella raised a hand above her head to give a single wave. 'Thanks, babe. You too!'

Kate's heart plummeted to the soles of her feet as she watched Bella's jaunty trot. Thumping her head against the door frame and groaning was an appealing option, but that was too feeble, even for her at her lowest. *Come on, Kate!* She could do this. Max was just one man. An incredibly annoying man, but even so, how hard could it be to get through a few hours in his company?

Kate relaxed her fingers—which she had balled into fists—and gave them a little shake. All she had to do was stick to the case and perhaps spend some time alone before the interviews that afternoon. They had fifteen minutes scheduled with each of the actors. It wasn't much time and it was crucial they made the most of it. She would feel better prepared if she had a chance to clear her mind in peace, let her thoughts percolate and take a final glance at the character details in the information pack.

A pattern of soft thuds crossing the polished oak floorboards behind her warned of Max's approach. He stopped a couple of steps away and clasped his hands behind his back.

'It's nearly lunch—'

'I was wondering if—'

The corner of Max's mouth twitched. 'Sorry,' he said. 'You go first.'

'No, really,' said Kate, while cursing herself for being so polite, 'you go.'

'All right, well, I was wondering … I know Bella and Ethan have gone out and it's nearly lunchtime … but would you mind if we met up after lunch?' Without lifting his chin, Max left off his examination of the parquet long enough for their eyes to meet, although his gaze remained shadowed by his thick lashes. 'Perhaps a few minutes before the first interview?'

Kate blinked rapidly, her surprise tinged with relief and a spot of something else. Was that … disappointment?

Say something, Kate, her inner voice hissed. *You're gawping at him like a stunned fish!*

'Oh. Um, yes!' Kate chuckled nervously. 'Of course.'

'It's just that there are some things in the info pack, on the suspects' backgrounds …' Max coughed. 'I'd like … I'd feel more prepared if I read them again before our interviews. But if you'd rather—'

'No, no. It's fine. Where and when would you like to meet?'

'Five to two? Outside the music room? If that suits you, that is.'

'That's fine. I'll be there.'

'Perfect. Thank you, Kate. I'll see you later. Enjoy your lunch.'

Max strode away, freeing Kate to slump against the door frame unobserved and grimace as the muscles in her neck relaxed with a sharp twang.

Blimey. Irritating Max was difficult to deal with, but at least she knew what to expect. How on earth was she supposed to react if he insisted on transforming into a polite, considerate person who gave her exactly what she needed?

Chapter 14

The library was located on the opposite side of the Old Grange to the study. Out of the direct spring sunlight, the light passing through the stained-glass roses in the highest window panels failed to cast colour on the central floor rug. The dark wood shelves and bindings of thick books in burgundy, emerald and navy contributed to the gloomy atmosphere, and Kate shivered as she ducked through the open doorway.

The furniture was arranged in much the same way as it had been for the previous evening's after-dinner drinks, with elegant wooden chairs clustered in small groups. The most obvious addition to the décor were two wing-backed leather armchairs facing the fireplace.

Responding to an irrational need to create as little noise as possible—perhaps a reflex reaction to years of being shushed by the school librarian?—Kate crept across the rug. Her goal was the magazine rack she had noticed to the left of the fireplace the previous evening.

To ensure all guests had an equal chance to find and inspect clues, the Merryman's information pack contained strict instructions that any materials such as magazines, dropped items of clothing or footprints be left in the place they were discovered. But, as she advanced on the fireplace, doubts spurred Kate to increase her pace. Would she be too late? Would an unscrupulous guest have made off with the newspapers already?

One of the armchairs creaked and groaned. Kate froze a few paces from the fireplace. 'Er, hello?'

More creaking accompanied the appearance of two heads from behind the wings of the chairs. On the left was Dorothy Williams, her sharp eyes peering at Kate through her bright red spectacles. On the right was an older gentleman, who Kate guessed was in his late sixties. He had short grey hair, light brown skin and a neat moustache. All this sat above a thick neck jutting out of a stiff white collar pinched together with a maroon tie.

'Ms Brannon!' Dorothy's eyes twinkled. 'How fortunate.'

'Oh?'

Dorothy and the man rose from their chairs. 'Yes,' said Dorothy. 'This is Dr Leonard Chase, the Grieve family physician. He was about to leave. But you might like to speak to him first?'

Kate's lips parted. There had been no Dr Chase on the list of characters. Was this—her heart skipped at the idea—a secret or bonus feature that not everyone got access to? Had she accidentally stumbled across something which could give her team the edge?

Dorothy raised a finger. 'Just five minutes,' she said.

'The doctor is due back at his practice and then he's away for the rest of the weekend.'

Kate's heart raced. He was leaving. This would be a one-shot deal. Only one chance to ask the right questions. 'OK. Thank you.'

'I'll leave you to it.' Dorothy glided past Kate, giving her a small lopsided smile so enigmatic it would have unsettled the Sphinx.

'It's nice to meet you. Ms Brannon, was it?' asked Dr Chase, motioning to the seat Dorothy had vacated as he sank back onto his own.

'Kate, please.'

Dr Chase gave her a kind smile, the sort Kate imagined would be an essential part of a local doctor's kit. 'What would you like to know?'

Kate arranged the skirt of her dress over her knees and clasped her hands together to hide their trembling.

Calm down, Kate. Remember, the doctor might be convincing, but really he's just an actor who's having to improvise as much as you are.

Kate cleared her throat and decided to start with a safe question. 'How long have you been the Grieve family's doctor?'

The doctor blew out his cheeks, making the ends of his moustache quiver. 'I first visited the family a few months after they moved into the Old Grange. Cora—that's the late Mrs Grieve—was expecting their first child. It wasn't long until I delivered Nancy and I suppose she must be over thirty now. Goodness me, where does the time go?'

'And you've attended the family ever since?'

'Yes. Although, with the tragic exception of Cora's

110

sudden death—God rest her soul—they've only ever had minor ailments. Adrian was extremely upset by Cora's passing. He was devoted to her.'

'That was the impression I got when he spoke about his late wife last night. How did Mrs Grieve die?'

'A brain aneurysm.' The doctor swallowed and his eyes glistened. 'Poor Cora probably had a weakness there since birth. And she was a slender, gentle thing.'

'And nothing was known to have brought on the aneurysm? No falls or knocks to the head?'

'It's funny you ask that.' The doctor frowned. 'I don't wish to speak ill of the dead …'

'Of course,' Kate said, encouraging him to continue.

'There were … rumours that Adrian could be quite rough with Cora. I never saw any evidence of it, but more than one of the villagers witnessed him shouting at her. I believe there was also an incident when he pushed her and she fell to the ground. But Adrian was away on business the day of Cora's death. Although it's perfectly possible she bumped her head or had some other small accident which triggered the rupture.'

Kate narrowed her eyes and wished she could retract all the sympathetic treatment she'd given Adrian Grieve the previous evening. No matter how wistfully he spoke about his wife, the doctor's testimony combined with how he had exploded at Lucille Palmer suggested that he had been a bully. And to think she had worried about his breathing …

Kate leant forwards. 'Doctor, last night I noticed Mr Grieve's breathing was wheezy. And he was coughing too. Were you treating him for anything?'

'No.' The doctor shuffled his feet and the shiny toe of his

right shoe clipped the black rigid-frame medical bag sitting by the chair. His brown trilby, which had been perched on top of the bag, wobbled and fell to the carpet. 'I hadn't spoken to Adrian for a year, well, apart from to say hello if I saw him when out and about. And at church'—he bent down to put his hat back on the bag and muttered—'when he bothered to attend.'

Picking up a hint of resentment in his tone, Kate asked, 'What happened the last time you did speak? A year ago.'

'I'd come here for Adrian's regular check-up.' He bit his lower lip and eyed Kate warily. 'I'm not supposed to talk about my patients to anyone, you understand.'

Kate nodded. The doctor's reluctance to offer up information brought to mind Roger Merryman's warnings about treating the characters as real people and questioning them with sensitivity.

As if he sensed her concerns, the doctor fidgeted in his seat and eyed the exit. Kate gave him what she hoped was an entirely non-threatening, reassuring smile. She would have to tread carefully not to spook her witness. 'I understand completely. But, Mr Grieve is sadly deceased and, given the circumstances of his death, anything you're able to tell me could be helpful.'

Dr Chase stared into the fireplace for a moment, tapping his finger on his chin. 'All right. After all, it can't do much harm now.'

Kate held her breath, barely daring to disturb the silence, until the doctor continued. 'Those symptoms you describe: the wheezing and coughing. They'd already been giving him some trouble. I recommended he consult a specialist. Have some tests done to rule out anything serious.'

'Do you know if he followed your advice?'

'No, I don't. You see, that check-up was the last time I spoke to Adrian. If I called to see him, I was told he was out, although his car was in the driveway. If our paths crossed in the village he would duck and hurry away as if he was afraid to meet me. Me! I'd known him for over thirty years.'

Kate was loath to poke the doctor's wound, but she needed his opinion. 'Do you believe he would have consulted another doctor?'

'I doubt it. Adrian was a stubborn, rather unsympathetic man. I do believe he regarded illness as a weakness or character flaw.' He snorted. 'You know, and I'm aware this may sound perverse, but I think he would have been rather pleased with the shocking manner of his demise.'

'Why do you say that?'

'He would have hated the thought of anything as mundane as old age or a mere disease getting the best of the mighty Adrian Grieve.' He snorted again and glanced down at his watch. 'Oh my goodness, look at the time.'

He scooped up his bag and hat and rose. Kate sprang to her feet, wracking her brain as he adjusted his trilby. What else could she ask? Closing her eyes, she pictured the crime scene. Adrian at his desk. Max at the whiteboard. Max inspecting the bourbon residue. Max, smug toxins expert— That was it!

'Thank you for your time, Dr Chase. I do have one final question.' The doctor threw a longing glance at the door and Kate stepped between him and the exit in case he decided to rush out. 'You did a preliminary examination of Mr Grieve's body, before it was removed?'

'I did.'

'In your report, you said there were no signs on the body to suggest a struggle. No defensive wounds or marks on the arms or hands. But there was no mention of his mouth or eyes. Did you notice anything unusual?'

The doctor threw another glance at his watch. 'I suppose it'll come out from the autopsy anyway.' He pointed to his own dark eyes. 'I noted discolouration. A slight yellowing of the cornea.'

Kate's insides fizzed. She couldn't wait to see Max's face when she told him Adrian Grieve had signs of liver trouble. 'Why didn't you mention it in your report?'

'Adrian was a high-profile person. The rumour mill will go into overdrive about how he died. Those poor girls will be hounded by the press. I expect Nancy will be all right. She was far closer to her late mother than her father. But Pamela was so young when Cora died, she barely remembers her, and she's always been much more attached to her father. Adrian used to call Pamela his little princess. His loss will be a terrible blow to her.'

'I'm not sure I—'

'Scandal, Ms Brannon!' The doctor's voice was a harsh whisper. 'The last time I examined Adrian his eyes were as clear as yours. And while everyone knew Adrian liked a drink, for him to have consumed enough in the past year to cause jaundice … I didn't want to mention it in my report because I was concerned for his reputation. For the family name. This whole affair is shocking enough, but currently Adrian is being viewed as an innocent victim of a terrible crime. God forbid I mention something that could suggest that Adrian had a dependency.'

114

There it was. The good doctor was afraid that Adrian Grieve had become an alcoholic. He was trying to save the Grieve daughters suffering from any second-hand stigma.

'Poor Pamela already has a weak constitution, like her dear mother. She's had such trouble with her nerves and insomnia, I've had to prescribe her sleeping pills the past six months. I pray she'll be able to weather the loss of her father without anyone'—he glared at Kate—'making it harder for her.'

'I wouldn't want ...' Kate flustered, hoping the doctor would cut her off. 'That is ...'

'Dr Chase!' Roger Merryman marched into the room. He bristled in a brown tweed suit and the glare he threw Kate was a stormy mixture of surprise and annoyance. 'I thought you'd already left. We mustn't detain you from your work.'

'I was just going,' said the doctor. 'Good day, Ms Brannon.'

Kate returned the doctor's farewell, her brain buzzing. If the doctor was right about Adrian's alcohol consumption, the important question was: did something drive him to develop the addiction? Was some external pressure pushing him to seek escape in the bottom of a bottle? And did that same pressure lead to his death?

Roger Merryman harrumphed, drawing Kate out of her reverie of questions. '*Again*, Ms Brown, I must remind you that our actors are human beings who need breaks and are not to be constantly harassed.'

Kate stuttered, stunned by the injustice of Roger's accusations. It was *his* Games Supervisor who had given her permission to speak to Dr Chase! Surely Dorothy wouldn't have done that if the actor was off the clock?

Roger lowered his voice and his stare darkened. 'The welfare of my staff is an absolute priority to me. And I'm afraid that if you insist on pestering my actors in their downtime ... Well, I might have to suggest they take their rest when they had been scheduled to attend an interview with one of the teams.' Fixing Kate with a final disapproving glare, he raised a single eyebrow, turned and strode after the doctor.

Kate ran a hand over her face, trying to wipe away the prickling feeling that came with being unfairly chastised. And beneath the surface sensation lay a deeper unease. If she had understood him correctly, Roger had insinuated he'd be happy to deprive Kate's team of their chance to interview some of the suspects. Basically, he had *threatened* her.

Wow. What was Roger's problem? He claimed to be motivated purely by concern for the welfare of his employees, but his behaviour suggested he didn't want his guests to interview potentially helpful witnesses.

A shard of ice shivered down Kate spine. What if Max's initial suspicions weren't merely another example of his contrariness? What if Roger Merryman really was rigging the game against them and all their determined sleuthing was doomed to fail?

Chapter 15

Late!

Kate glanced at the clock on her phone and hissed.

So late!

She scurried down the wood-panelled corridor, her cheeks hot with panic. Max wouldn't be late. He'd have slithered into the music room twenty minutes early with the sole purpose of looking at his watch every minute and tutting at her tardiness.

Kate ducked her head into another room, but the brass plaque on the door said *The Den*. What even was that? Should she worry about it being full of bears?

A groan of frustration escaped her as she looked up and down the corridor. Perhaps she should go back to reception and ask …

The faint notes of a delicate melody danced around the corner in front of her. Oh, thank heavens. *Follow the music, Kate, even you can do that.*

She doubled her pace, trying not to dwell on the fact

that one of the actors had resorted to playing the piano to entertain themselves while waiting for her to show up. How embarrassing!

She threw herself round the corner and slackened her pace. Through the open door ahead on the left, a grand piano came into view. It was singing in response to the touch of a skilful musician and when the booming of her pulse quietened she recognised the ethereal sounds of 'Clair de lune'.

Breathing deeply, she strolled to the entrance, letting her heartbeat slow further. Though embarrassing, at least she had something to show for her lateness. Curled up in one of the library armchairs, Kate had lost track of time while devouring the sandwiches she had grabbed from the lunch buffet and scanning the mocked-up newspapers and magazines. The headlines were dominated by a series of jewel thefts—which Kate filed under 'likely to be relevant'—and a missing persons case—'less likely, but don't rule it out'.

Kate paused in the doorway, unwilling to disturb the performance of such a haunting piece, which always made her picture gentle rain falling on a midnight garden. The pianist was talented, but she supposed many actors were musical and—

Oh.

Max sat on the edge of the piano stool, his expression smooth and untroubled as his fingers caressed the keys. His half-shut eyes and the ghost of a smile suggested the music had transported him somewhere safe and beautiful.

Kate was mesmerised. She had never seen Max so peaceful and relaxed. He'd even rolled up his shirtsleeves to his elbows to reveal strong forearms, the muscles in them flexing as his fingers flew across the keys.

The breeze outside stirred the clouds and a shaft of sunlight fell across the keyboard as the piece floated to its resolution. The beam illuminated Max's large, dextrous hands, casting them in a warm glow. Kate sighed. The man might be insufferable, but he did have great hands.

The echo of the final notes ringing, Max lifted his fingers from the keyboard and, his head hanging forwards and eyes still closed, said, 'Hey, Kate.'

'Hey.' Kate shuffled closer, pleased she was no longer short of breath. She should get her apologies out of the way so they could get on with the serious business of suspect interrogation. But, as she opened her mouth to speak, Max lifted his gaze to meet hers and she was struck dumb by his expression. His eyes were glassy and the welling tears made the gold shards in his irises glitter.

'Um.' Her first attempt at speech having failed, Kate decided it might be better to dwell on the music for a moment longer—to allow Max to come back from wherever it had taken him—before returning to murder. 'You remember the whole of "Clair de lune"?'

One side of Max's mouth twitched. 'I haven't played it for a while but I used to get a lot of practice. It's one of my mum's favourites.'

Oh. Stumped again, Kate searched for an adequate reply. Guys who were nice to their mums were another of her weaknesses. It was one of the ways Paul had won her over. Of course, in an unpleasant twist, his mum had turned out to approve of Kate even less than Paul did.

She advanced another step, resting her hip against the

end of the piano. 'It's one of mine too. Did you play when you were a kid?'

'Mum started taking me to lessons when I was seven. And I kept going until I was a teenager and football took over. I kept playing though. It made Mum happy.'

'I wish I'd learned an instrument. Infant school-level descant recorder does not count. And I was terrible at it.'

Max chuckled and Kate was confident the shine in his eyes was now a sign of amusement. She smiled, despite the persistence of an uncomfortable heat at the back of her neck. Wishing she had taken a moment at lunchtime to grab a hairclip from her room, she scooped her hair up into her hand and glanced about the room. Why was there never a stray newspaper lying about when you needed a makeshift fan?

Waving her free hand ineffectually at the bare skin at her nape, she said, 'Sorry I'm late.'

Max appeared to have got lost once again, his stare focused over Kate's shoulder. He blinked rapidly when she spoke, as if waking from a dream. 'It's fine. The morning interviews ran over so everyone's behind. Lucille Palmer should be here in a few moments though.'

The feet of the piano stool squealed as Max pushed to standing and strode across to the windows. While opening the first casement, he used his free hand to gesture to the area immediately in front of the small fireplace. It was occupied by four padded chairs, each covered in a floor-length blue velvet slipcover. They stood in two pairs on either side of a low circular coffee table. A large bottle of water and six glasses waited on a silver tray on the polished walnut surface. 'I think we're supposed to sit over there.'

'Right.' Kate wandered over to the table. She inhaled sharply as a cooling breeze came through the window, brushing her face and curling around her neck. What a relief! It also made choosing a seat easier: the chairs nearest the window would be in the middle of the wonderful draught and, as a bonus, give her a view of the suspects as they came through the door.

Of the pair of chairs to the right of the fireplace, she opted for the one nearest the hearth. She was smoothing her skirt over her knees when Max sank into the seat next to her. His nearness surprised her and a shock of gooseflesh rose on her arms. The chairs hadn't seemed that close to each other when viewed from across the room, but there were just a few inches between their shoulders. Kate interlaced her fingers, her hands restless. Perhaps she should have fetched the information pack from her room, if only to have something with which to occupy her hands. And fan herself.

Max didn't share her problem. He bent to his left and, lifting the hem of his chair's slipcover, retrieved a dark red A5 notebook and a retractable ballpoint pen from under his seat. Kate turned her head towards the fireplace so he wouldn't see her roll her eyes. Of course Max had come prepared.

The spine of the book crackled as he opened it and leafed through the pages. From the corner of her eye, Kate peeked at his writing and admired the neat cursive script which crossed the pages in confident black strokes and elegant loops. But unfortunately he insisted on turning the pages so quickly she only had the chance to recognise a couple of the suspects' names and—hang on, was that *her* name?

'Was your lunchtime productive?'

Kate must have unconsciously leant towards Max as she was sneaking a look at his notes. His low, quiet voice was so close to her ear that the words tickled. She snapped her guilty gaze to Max's face and straightened in her chair.

'Yes. I went to the library to go through the newspapers and magazines I noticed there.'

Max scribbled a note at the top of a clean page. 'Anything interesting?'

'A string of jewel robberies on high society targets.'

Max's scribbling intensified.

'And,' Kate continued, trying not to watch the movement of the pen, 'remind me to tell you later all about my chat with Dr Chase.'

'You got to meet Dr Chase?' Max's eyebrows shot up. 'The one who wrote the preliminary report on Adrian Grieve's body? But he wasn't on the character list.'

'I know. He was with Dorothy Williams in the library. He must be some sort of bonus character or something. Anyway, short version of our chat: Adrian Grieve's eyes were yellowed. Suggesting—'

'Jaundice. Liver failure.' Max tapped the top of the pen on his upper lip. 'Well that's … interesting.'

Kate smiled. He might not rate her detective skills but, whatever Max had got up to at lunchtime, she doubted he would have stumbled across anything as thrilling as an interview with an unexpected character. Staring at the pensive wrinkle between his brows, she asked, 'How was your lunch?'

'Not nearly as exciting as yours. Only a couple of things to report. Firstly, Roger Merryman was wandering around the dining room handing out vouchers for free spa treatments this afternoon, supposedly as compensation for the 2 a.m. fire alarm. People were keen to take him up on the offer. I suspect few teams will be completing their interviews.'

'I take it you didn't accept one?'

'No. I thanked Roger, but said I'd rather not be distracted from the case.'

'I doubt that made him happy. It might partly explain why he was so grumpy when he ran into me.'

'What? What happened?'

'He turned up when Dr Chase was leaving and had another go at me for holding back the actors. And he think he may have threatened me.'

'He *what?*' Max's eyes widened, his stare turning fiery as a muscle in his jaw began to tic.

'Not personally or anything! But he insinuated that if he thought I was preventing the actors from getting their rest then he could stop us interviewing all the suspects.'

'Hmn.' Max blinked and the hint of violence in his glare vanished as his brows settled into his trademark frown. 'I'm starting to really dislike Mr Merryman.'

'I'm trying to give him the benefit of the doubt, but he's not helping himself. What was the second thing to report?'

Max's frown lifted. 'In better news, they posted a summary of Adrian Grieve's last will and testament on the board in the foyer.'

Kate's heart leapt. Drat. She'd forgotten about checking the noticeboard for updates. 'Who did he leave everything to?'

'The entire estate, including the house, is to be split equally between his daughters.'

'That's disappointing. No secret heir? A surprise donation to the local donkey sanctuary?'

'I'm afraid not. Although there was one interesting item: the jewels in the safe which were the late Mrs Grieve's are to go to Pamela.' Max glanced at his watch. 'Lucille should be here any minute. As you're more diplomatic when asking questions, would you like to start?'

Max reached forwards to pour himself a glass of water and Kate was glad for the break in eye contact. The surprise and pleasure she felt in response to his question—which was dangerously near a compliment—must have been visible on her face. For all her worries about working with Max, their collaboration had begun remarkably smoothly.

Which made it all the more strange that Kate was struck by a perverse desire to needle him. To unsettle his calm surface. She cleared her throat and said, 'I'd be happy to start. Although it'd be helpful for you to jump in if things get tricky.' She paused as Max raised the glass to his lips. 'Seeing how she fancies the pants off you.'

Max spluttered and Kate suspected that the glass being next to his lips had saved the notebook, table and entire surrounding area from being sprayed with water. Kate pressed her lips together to fight her urge to giggle while Max recovered. He threw Kate an annoyed glare. 'I doubt that.'

'No, she definitely does.' Kate said in her cheeriest, sing-song voice, grinning at the red streaks appearing on Max's cheeks. 'You didn't hear her comments last night about how you were ideal fourth husband material.'

Max grunted and took a cautious sip of water, probably to partially obscure his burning face. Kate watched him out of the corner of her eye, enjoying her small, though petty victory.

'Your lunchtime was obviously very busy.' Max directed his glare at her midriff. 'But please tell me you had time to feed that dragon of yours.'

Kate's grin slipped. Oh well. She'd had her fun with Max and should have expected a dig would come in return. 'Don't worry,' she said, 'it won't be disturbing you while you're grilling the suspects.'

'Excellent. I'm beginning to feel responsible for its welfare. In fact, just in case you hadn't eaten …' Max bent to the side of his chair again, lifted the slipcover and, when he straightened, he was holding a small blue plate covered with a white linen napkin.

Blimey. What didn't he have stashed under his chair?

Kate glanced at the plate. 'More stolen cookies?'

Max tutted. 'Not stolen. Liberated. And no. I bumped into Lucinda right after lunch and she gave me this.' He lifted the napkin to reveal a row of four generous slices of fluffy, caramel-coloured sponge. 'Butterscotch cake with toffee icing. Guaranteed all deliciousness, no poison.'

The cake smelled rich and buttery, making Kate's mouth water, but she resisted the urge to grab a piece. If she took a slice now, Lucille was all but guaranteed to sashay in to see her with crumbs at the corner of her mouth and cheeks stuffed like a greedy hamster. And as much as Kate wanted cake, her desire to appear a competent amateur sleuth was greater.

She glanced up at Max. 'Shall we save it for later? After we've finished the interviews?'

'Good idea. Cake for our post interview debrief. I mean,

exchange of ideas. Theories. If you're happy to do that? If you weren't planning to go to the spa or—'

'No, no. That sounds good.'

'Good.' Max released a long, slow breath, covered the cake and placed it on the table. 'Actually, I'd been meaning to ask you—'

'Oh, thank the Lord!' Lucille Palmer filled the doorway with her starry glow as she lifted a delicate hand to her chest and trained her fluttering eyelashes on Max. 'I cannot tell you how glad I am that it's you I'll be speaking with!'

As Lucille glided across the room towards them, her megawatt smile aimed squarely at Max, Kate leant closer to him and whispered, 'Hubby number four.'

Max muttered, 'Shut up,' two words which shouldn't have been capable of making Kate's insides fizz with glee, but most certainly did.

As Lucille slid onto the seat opposite Max, Kate pressed her lips together, composing her features into what she hoped was the serious expression of a professional investigator. Lucille was an important witness and potential murderer. Now was not the time to get caught up in childish diversions.

Luckily for Kate, Lucille was solidly on topic. 'All right, honey,' she said, crossing her ankles and folding her hands in her lap. 'What d'you wanna know?'

Chapter 16

Kate tucked a stray strand of hair behind her ear. This was it. She couldn't muck this up, no matter how weird it was pretending they were in 1932 and the woman sitting opposite them was a key suspect in a fictional murder inquiry. Kate had hoped her surprise meeting with Dr Chase would have better prepared her for this moment, but it still felt odd. Perhaps the only approach was to go for it.

But how to start? Kate tilted her head and considered Lucille, watching the woman cross and uncross her slender ankles. Was her fidgeting a sign she was also a little nervous? Maybe it would be best to begin with manners. She was good at manners. Besides, they put an interviewee at ease. Relaxed people were generally chattier people. 'Would you like some water, Mrs Palmer?'

'Please call me Lucille. And no, I'm fine. Thank you.'

Right. That was manners out of the way. Now what?

Kate scanned Lucille from head to toe. Though sporting

a plain black velvet, high-neck dress, she continued to cast her magnetic glamour. But her expression, when she wasn't attempting to charm Max, was drawn and pensive, a far cry from the stunning perma-smile she had worn the previous evening. Lucille, Kate decided, was putting a brave face on things.

'Thank you for speaking to us. How are you, Lucille? I know you're not immediate family, but I imagine this has been hard for you.'

Lucille's lower lip wobbled. 'You're the first person to ask me that.' She slipped a lace-trimmed handkerchief from inside her cuff and pressed it to the corners of her eyes. 'Truth be told, I'm devasted. And how awful for poor Pam and Nancy. Such a horrible thing to happen. In their family home too. It's unimaginable.'

'I'm sorry. You've known Adrian for such a long time …' Kate trailed off, praying Lucille would fill in the blanks.

Lucille sniffed, then obliged. 'He discovered me in New York City. Eighteen years ago when I was nobody, a small part in a vaudeville show. He signed me, brought me to Europe.' A wistful smile lifted one corner of her mouth. 'He always said he made me a star.'

'And was your relationship with Adrian …' Kate halted. She wanted to word this right. 'On the whole, was it a happy one?'

Lucille chuckled. 'If you wanna know about Adrian's little outburst last night, just ask. Look, it's no secret I've been trying to get out of my contract for years. It's nothing personal. I simply don't need a promoter any more. I can take care of my own affairs. I've raised it with him before,

128

but he never took me seriously. And last night ...' She shook her head, making her diamond earrings sparkle. 'It was my fault. I picked the wrong time to talk to him about it. I wanted to tell him I'd spoken to a lawyer who said it'd be simple to dissolve our agreement. I wanted him to know it wouldn't be any trouble for him. But I didn't explain it very well and as a result, drama! What a show for y'all, huh? But what everyone didn't see was when he came to my room later to apologise.'

Kate and Max leant forwards as one. Kate said, 'Really?' at the same time as Max asked, 'When?'

'Really and truly. And I guess it must have been around eleven thirty. He didn't stay long. Barely five minutes.'

'Time of death is estimated to be between midnight and 2 a.m.,' said Max. 'Which means ...'

'That, apart from the butler, I was probably the last person on this earth who spoke with him? Yes'—Lucille's voice faded to a sad whisper—'the police told me that. At the time I was so happy we were able to part as friends, but now I keep thinking about if that hadn't been the case, I'm not sure I'd be able ...' She hiccoughed a small sob and raised the hanky to her eyes again.

'Lucille, it's wonderful that you and Adrian left things on such good terms,' said Kate, trying to turn the conversation to happier things. 'Do you mind telling us what he said, exactly?'

'As I said, he didn't stay for long.' Lucille blinked back her tears. 'He seemed a little on edge at being in my room. He was always a gentleman towards me and nothing like that ever went on. He never so much as made a pass.' Her mouth twisted into a bitter moue. 'No matter what *some*

129

people may have thought or said, our relationship was platonic.'

The sound of pen scratching on paper told Kate that Max had found those comments as interesting as she did. 'Of course,' she said. 'But I suppose people will talk.'

'Will they ever! There are small-minded people all over. Thank God, Adrian wasn't one of them. And Pam, bless her heart, has always been a peach.'

But not Nancy. Kate made a large mental note to follow that up as Max's scribbling intensified.

Now apparently having warmed to the subject, Lucille continued, 'Adrian said he was sorry for going off at dinner, but he'd been a little under the weather and had one too many "sharpeners" as he called his liquor. All that "over my dead body" stuff was heat-of-the-moment nonsense and he'd been planning to end my contract later this year. That his lawyers were already working on it. When the attorney came by to read the will this morning, I asked him, and it's true. He had received instructions from Adrian to release me from our agreement.'

'So, to be clear, Mrs Palmer.' Max rested his pen in the crease of the notebook and looked Lucille square in the eye. 'You had no good reason to sneak through the window into Adrian's study and stab him with his own paperknife?'

Kate whipped her head towards Max, her jaw slack. There was being to the point, and then there was walloping someone over the head with a question. Was he trying to undo all her good work?

But Lucille threw her head back and roared with laughter. She reached across the table, swiping a hand in the direction of Max's knees. 'Oh darlin', if you're going to ask a girl straight up if she's a murderer, you must use her first name.'

'Very well,' said Max. 'Lucille, did you kill Adrian Grieve?'

'I did not. And let me tell you something else. If I were in the market to kill a man, I wouldn't be sneaking around all quiet and stabbing him in the back. If I ever wanna do that, it will be a full production and all the neighbours will know about it from both of us breaking the furniture and screaming the place down.'

His blunt approach having paid off, Max continued. 'Where were you between midnight and 2 a.m. this morning?'

Lucille's leant forwards, her eyes shining with mischief. 'I was in my bedroom. And if you need to check up on that, you go right ahead and speak to James, the handsome footman who was kind enough to keep me company'—her lips curled into a salacious smile—'all night.'

'Right. OK ... Uh ...' Max stuttered as his neck began to flush.

Lucille giggled at his embarrassment. 'Don't go all coy on me, sugar, you were on a roll. Ask me another one. Go on!'

Max cleared his throat, preparing for another round. 'So you're clearly not a murderer. I don't suppose you're a jewel thief either?'

'I've had three husbands who were all extremely generous. And while I may not be any good at holding on to men, I sure as heck know how to keep a firm grip on the diamonds they give me. I have more than enough jewels. I don't need to be taking anyone else's.' She chuckled again. 'But thank you for asking, sweetheart. God knows, I needed a laugh.'

Kate grinned as Max stammered again and dropped his gaze to his notebook. Real or not, Lucille Palmer was pure goals, if only for the power she had to make Max blush.

Dragging her gaze away from the sweet pink lines blooming along Max's cheeks, Kate turned to Lucille. 'Prior to yesterday, when was the last time you saw Adrian?'

'I bumped into him six months ago in New York. And again in February in Paris. I often collided with Adrian during his world tours.'

'World tours?'

'Every few years he would take himself on a trip across Europe, over to India, perhaps a stop in the Pacific and then on to the States. This year's was a doozy though. He must have stopped off in almost every capital in Europe. And the champagne reception he hosted at the Plaza? Phenomenal. I didn't know so many people could pack into that place.'

'Did you notice anything different about his behaviour lately? Did he seem in good health to you?'

Lucille shrugged. 'It's difficult to say. Perhaps he was a little more tired? He was always such a firecracker. But he wasn't a young man any more and he said he found it harder to keep up. And I suppose ... yeah maybe he was a little down, at times.'

'Why do you think that might have been?'

'Oh, darlin', I don't like listening to rumours and I sure as heck don't like to spread them.' Lucille sighed. 'But there were some whispers that Adrian lost a lot of money in the Crash. Lord help me, I even wondered at times if that was why he didn't want to let me go. If he *couldn't* let me go because I was the goose laying the golden eggs.' She chuckled. 'I dismissed it all as nonsense. How could he throw a party at the Plaza if he was bankrupt? People love to talk you down. Always best ignore them.'

Kate glanced down at Max's pad and was pleased to read *Wall St. Crash caused AG financial problems?* in Max's neat writing.

She returned her attention to Lucille and asked, 'Obviously— given his outburst last night—Mr Grieve had a temper, but would you describe his behaviour generally as bullying or controlling?'

'I would say, rather than being a bully, Adrian knew what he wanted. But he was a rich, powerful man and in my experience they can all be bullies when things aren't going their way. You need to stand up to them. Give as good as you get.'

Lucille's loyalty to her late employer was touching, and she clearly hadn't found his treatment of her controlling, but someone less confident might have. 'Was he ever physically aggressive?'

Lucille's gaze flickered from Kate, to Max and back again. She blinked slowly. 'Not to *me*. And that's all I can tell you about that.'

'OK, thank you,' said Kate. Lucille had drawn a line under the subject. It was probably best to change tack rather than charge on and risk their witness retreating into silence. 'Where are you off to next, after here?'

'Home to Paris, darlin'.'

Max looked up from notebook. '*Avez-vous un domicile à Paris?*'

133

Unfazed, Lucille replied, '*Oui, bien sûr,*' and proceeded to rattle off a complex reply that Kate's rusty high school French had done nothing to equip her to understand.

Apparently Max didn't suffer from the same linguistic difficulties. He nodded along as Lucille spoke—from her animated gestures and tone, Kate could only guess she was expounding a tremendous love for all things Parisian—and when she had finished he responded.

Kate stared at Max, her eyes widening as Max mirrored some of Lucille's effusive hand movements. Her mind reeled, even as a corner of it whispered, *Of course Max is fluent in a foreign language. That's so him!* But apart from this sliver of reason, the rest of her brain was stunned to silence. The hush was filled by the pounding of her heart because—*Oh là là!*—while Max's voice was smooth at the best of times, when speaking French it became warm honey. The sound sent tingles racing down her spine and, despite the cool breeze fanning her back, Kate found she needed to lift her hair away from her rapidly heating nape once again.

'I think that's everything. Kate? Did you have anything else to ask Lucille?'

Kate blinked at Max. 'Hmn? What? Oh, yes ...' She stared at Lucille, hoping inspiration would strike while berating herself for not having brought her own notebook containing a written list of her questions. Then again, how was she supposed to know that Max was about to break out his entrancing French alter ego? 'Um ... Pam and Nancy. They seemed to be having a disagreement last night. I don't suppose you have any idea what that might be about?'

Lucille snorted. 'Money, most like. You know I don't like gossip, but it's public knowledge that Nancy's never been too thrilled with how cosy Pam was with their daddy, still living at home with him an' all. My bet? Nancy's been fretting Adrian was going to leave everything to her unmarried little sister. And now that Pam has that fast Italian fiancé, well … I guess Nancy was getting all het up at the idea of a foreigner being lord of the manor. Not that any of that matters now, with everything being split fifty-fifty.' She sighed and ran a hand over the stiff waves in her hair. 'You two are angels and this has been a true pleasure, but I must leave you.' She rose and, directing her dark gaze at Max, added, 'Hopefully our paths will cross again.'

As she turned and swished to the exit, Max sagged onto the backrest of his chair. But his relief was short-lived.

'Oh, one more thing,' Lucille said, executing a sharp half turn. 'I shouldn't say anything, but you're so darn charming, I can't help myself. Perhaps, when you speak to the others, y'all should go on and ask them about Adrian's life-insurance policy.'

And after a puckish giggle and saucy wink in Max's direction, Lucille completed her pirouette and was gone.

Chapter 17

'What has that ghastly woman been saying? She had the gall to wink at me—actually wink!—as we passed in the corridor just now. I suppose she's been spreading her poison? It's the only thing a common showgirl like her knows how to do!'

Nancy Forbes, née Grieve, blasted into the room like a wrathful hurricane seconds after Lucille's departure. She wielded her cut-glass voice like a weapon, striking her listeners with a barrage of plummy vowels and consonants which stabbed, popped and hissed. A short black cape whirled behind her as she paced. Her hands were enclosed in black gloves which she raised to swat at the air which was insolent enough to dare touch her.

Kate and Max shared a glance, and Kate was comforted by the sight of Max's wide eyes, which spoke of a similar befuddlement to her own.

'Mrs Forbes?' Max rose from his seat, making a valiant attempt to get Nancy's attention.

It failed.

'Who does she think she is? My father may have been blind to her true nature—men are so easily duped by a pretty face and short skirt—but I see her clearly,' Nancy snarled, her long skirts hissing as she spun. It was fortunate her dark chestnut hair was encased in a black net at her nape or she might have taken to rending it to vent her spleen.

'Mrs Forbes?' Max tried again. 'Why don't you take a seat?'

'And you!' Nancy rounded on Max, closing the gap between them in a few strides. The acoustics of the music room amplified her strident tone, making her voice thunderous. 'You're little better than that hussy. Coming in here, interrogating me in my own home as if I owe you answers. I should have you thrown out into the gutter where you belong. I have never—'

'Mrs Forbes!' Kate's pulse had rocketed as Nancy spewed her vitriol over Max and, as she leapt to her feet, it was booming an angry tattoo inside her ears. 'Mrs Forbes, please get a hold of yourself.'

Having shocked Nancy into silence, Kate stepped slightly in front of Max and attempted a more conciliatory tone. 'We're very sorry for your loss, Mrs Forbes. This is, of course, incredibly upsetting for you. However, there is no need to speak in that manner to Mr Ravenscroft who was only trying to be kind. If you are not well enough to conduct a civil conversation then, as you have pointed out so forcibly, this is indeed your house and you are free to leave whenever you choose.' Kate lifted her chin, striking as haughty a pose as she could. 'It'll be a shame for us

137

not to hear your version of events, but I'm sure we'll get a good enough picture from what Mrs Palmer, your sister and Mr Corsini are happy to tell us.'

Nancy blinked, opening and closing her mouth, stuttering a string of aborted syllables and inarticulate gulps.

'I suggest you take a seat'—Kate held a hand towards the seat Lucille had recently vacated—'and a moment to compose yourself.'

Nancy pressed her lips together. Her entire sharp face, from her pencil-thin eyebrows to her pointed nose and chin, seemed to vibrate and twitch as if containing an explosion.

Instinctively, Kate backed up to stand next to Max. The temptation to cower behind him was intense. Something big was coming and, as it turned out, she only had a moment to share a look of concern with Max before Nancy erupted. She howled, the noise striking them like a ten-foot wave, and threw herself onto the chair where she doubled over and sobbed with her whole body.

Kate and Max shared another glance. He tilted his head towards Nancy and gave a tiny shrug.

Holding up her left index finger in what she hoped was a universal gesture for '*I've got this*', Kate reached into her right pocket and withdrew a packet of tissues. She observed the heaving of Nancy's shoulder blades for a second, took a tissue from the packet and shuffled towards her. 'Would you like a tissue?'

Nancy's sobs ebbed into gasps. She glanced up and, despite her cheeks being streaked with two watery lines of mascara, managed to sniff and take the tissue with an impressive degree of imperiousness. 'Thank you,' she said, her voice a faint gasp.

Better, thought Kate. A decided improvement, although the interview was clearly going to be tougher than she'd anticipated. Time to regroup would be useful.

'Mrs Forbes, why don't you take a minute? My ...' Kate glanced at Max. What was the right word? Colleague? No. Too businesslike. Associate? Same problem as colleague. Partner? Goodness, no. Easily taken the wrong way. Friend? Surely Max would baulk at that.

Unable to find the perfect word for whatever there was between her and Max, Kate said, 'Mr Ravenscroft and I will give you some space. Take as long as you need.'

Nancy set about dabbing her eyes with the tissue while Kate crept towards to the windows and beckoned for Max to follow.

Bathed in sunlight, Max's pupils were black dots and the amber flecks in his irises seemed to glitter. 'Blimey, Kate.' His voice was a low whisper and Kate craned forwards to hear him, leaving their faces inches apart. 'That was ...' He rubbed a hand roughly across his mouth and shook his head. 'She's an actor, remember?'

'It's still not OK for her to speak to you like that.' Kate returned his stare. 'I wouldn't stand for that sort of behaviour from one of my pupils, and we shouldn't have to suffer it from her. If you ask me, she got lucky. Bella would have gone off on one about how we're paying guests. Or slapped her and told her to sod off back to RADA.'

Max chuckled. 'All right. And thank you. For what it's worth, I'm impressed. Again. But I suppose I should have expected nothing less from a woman with a dragon in her belly.'

139

Kate fought to prevent her smile from spreading into a grin. She'd impressed Max. More than once.

'How do you want to do this?' he asked.

'You should ask the questions this time. I don't think I've endeared myself to her, but she might feel ashamed enough to be polite to you.'

'Let's hope so. I would tell you to jump in if you have to, but somehow I doubt you'll hold back on her.'

They both turned to observe Nancy. She had stopped crying and wiped off enough of the mascara disaster to no longer resemble a sad panda. The woman certainly had a filthy temper, but was she their murderer?

Kate's nerves—already tickled by Max's praise—jangled in anticipation of round two with Nancy and the prospect of a breakthrough in the case.

And it appeared she wasn't the only one readying themselves for combat. Pulling herself up straight, Nancy discarded the stained tissue onto the coffee table with a contemptuous flick, sniffed, and—in the languid tones of someone who had far better things to do—said, 'I'm ready for you now.'

Chapter 18

'Mrs Forbes, I'd like to start by echoing Kate's sincere condolences.'

Nancy snorted and opened her lips—no doubt to treat them to a delightfully cynical comment—but Kate fired her a warning stare and she closed her mouth, allowing Max to continue. 'When we spoke to your father last night after dinner, he said he was planning to talk to you and your sister before retiring. Did he speak with you?'

'Yes.' Nancy raised a hand to her throat and ran a finger along the string of pearls encircling her neck. They shone with a creamy glow as they caught the sunlight. 'Parkes—the butler—summoned me to Father's study at about ten to eleven. I went there immediately. I was there for about a quarter of an hour. Then I went to bed.'

Kate frowned, trying to remember details from the previous evening. She had left the library with Max right after Adrian, at about twenty to eleven, so Nancy's timings made sense.

Having given Nancy a moment to volunteer the information and received nothing but stony silence, Max said, 'Would you mind telling us what he said to you, during that conversation in his study?'

'If you must know, he mostly wanted to chide me for rebuking Pam. He told me I needed to be kinder to her. Take care of her. As if I haven't been taking care of Pamela ever since Mother died.' On mentioning her mother, Nancy's voice cracked and her reddened eyes filled with tears.

Kate pulled out another tissue and half rose to pass it across the table to Nancy, who took it without so much as a nod of thanks. Unbelievable! Had Max noticed that? Hang on. What was up with Max?

Max was staring at Nancy as tears rolled silently down her cheeks, his own eyes watering in sympathy. Raising his gaze to the ceiling, he pressed his lips together as a muscle ticked in his jaw. Was he all right?

Kate was deliberating whether to touch his hand, when he swallowed and—with a gruff edge to his voice—asked, 'You and your mother were close, Mrs Forbes?'

'We were.' Nancy pressed the tissue to her cheek. 'Pam barely remembers her. She was only four when Mother passed. I was eleven. And I remember *everything*. Father forgot that. I remember all the times he raised his voice, the beastly things he said, the way he made her suffer. His *women*.' Nancy spat the last word, while in her lap her fingers turned a ghastly white as she twisted the tissue into a tight spiral.

Fascinating. Was there a murderous motive in Nancy's powerful resentment of her father? Busy making her own mental notes, Kate was surprised Max's pen was hovering motionless above his pad.

Kate lifted her gaze to his face. His stare was glassy and distant. What was going on with him?

Not wanting to give Nancy time to reflect on her revelations, Kate pressed on. 'Did your father want to talk about anything else other than your sister?'

'Yes, I suppose.' She sniffed. 'Perhaps he realised he had been overzealous with his haranguing because he also told me … that he was proud of me. That he was pleased with how well I could fight my own corner.'

Kate nodded. That was certainly true, if an understatement. 'The jewellery which is missing from the safe …' Kate paused, aware that she was probably about to prod a sore spot. 'Did it belong to your mother?'

Nancy's hand flew back to the pearls at her neck. 'Yes. It was supposed to come to me. That's what she would have wanted. I thought Father would finally give it to me when I married, but he refused. He said I had married a rich man who could buy me all the diamonds I wanted. As if Mother's jewellery could be substituted with any necklace!' She slid her finger back and forth along the pearls so roughly that Kate feared she might break the string. 'He said I was being selfish. I had my memories of Mother and in that I was lucky. That Pam should get the jewellery. And that's what he put in his will.'

'What does your sister think about this?'

'I have no idea. We haven't talked about it. Although I can't imagine she'd have come running to offer me any pieces.'

Kate watched Nancy's fingers close, claw-like, around her necklace. She thought back to the item inventories stuck to the whiteboard in the study, but couldn't recall the full list of what had been in the safe. Ugh! What she wouldn't give for a photographic memory.

There was nothing for it but to take an educated guess. Staring Nancy square in the eye, preparing to catch her reaction, Kate said, 'But your father gave you those pearls, didn't he? And they were your mother's?'

Nancy's fingers sprang away from the necklace as if Kate had sent several hundred volts through it. 'I ... How did you—?' Nancy stuttered. 'Have you been speaking to my sister?'

'Not yet, Mrs Forbes. But I'm sure she hasn't failed to notice you are wearing such a beautiful item. The pearls are stunning. Especially against the black.'

'Yes, well, if you must know, Father gave them to me last night. When I got to the study he was closing the safe having just removed this necklace. He said he knew I had always wanted the whole collection, but that I should content myself with one of Mother's favourites.' Nancy touched the central pearls gently and, for a moment, her prickliness was gone. 'And with the rest of her collection having been stolen, it looks as though I will have no choice in the matter.'

Poor Pamela, thought Kate. The will had made it clear she was meant to get all the jewels, and now their theft meant she would get nothing. And to add salt to the wound, her sister was parading around flaunting the last piece of their mother's collection not stolen.

'Last night in the library, you and your sister were chatting,' said Kate. 'I hope you don't mind my saying so, but the conversation looked a little tense. What were you talking about?'

'That greasy Italian fiancé of hers, of course. I'll never understand how he got Father's approval to marry Pam. Until a couple of months ago, Father had been firmly against the match. I have wondered whether Lorenzo was blackmailing Father. It wouldn't surprise me.'

'But surely your father would approve of Pamela marrying an aristocrat?' said Kate.

'Pah! He claims to be an Italian count, but even if that's true, half that country swans about telling anyone who'll listen they're practically royalty. Nonsense! Besides, I always thought Father had higher aspirations for Pam. He called her his little princess and sometimes I wondered if he dragged her about on all those horrid world tours to find her an actual prince.' Nancy huffed a laugh, her expression softening for a moment before her brow furrowed once more. 'No. All Lorenzo's romantic tales may have worked on Pam and her foolish friends, but I won't be taken in. I know a gold-digger when I see one. You can spot them by their shifty eyes. Too close together. If you're looking for someone capable of killing a man, I'd start there. I mean, foreigners! I always say you can't—'

Kate opened her mouth to interrupt Nancy before she could spill any more of her racist, xenophobic bile, when Max beat her to it. Very quietly, but with an unmistakeable steely warning tone, he said, 'My mother was born and raised in France.'

The icy glare which accompanied his words would have scared most people into holding their tongue, but not Nancy. She raised an eyebrow and replied, 'Well, we all have our cross to bear, don't we?'

Max's green stare turned stormy. He inhaled slowly

through his nose, his chest swelling with indignation and goodness only knows what comeback. Without pausing to think it through, Kate shot out a hand and laid it on his knee.

He startled, his stare leaving Nancy and flying to Kate's hand, then to her face. Their gazes locked.

Don't, Kate urged him silently. *She's looking for an excuse to leave. Don't give it to her. Besides*—Kate raised her eyebrows and tapped his knee twice with her index finger—*she's an actor, remember?*

Max sighed and dropped his gaze. Kate gave his knee a final pat—because apparently she was patting Max now? Max, who was fluent in French because his mum was French. How hadn't she known that before?—and gave Nancy a glare she hoped told the odious woman that she should watch her back for stray letter openers—

The letter opener! It was seemingly an opportunist's murder weapon: it was on the desk next to the victim, just a handy knife. But that monogram on the handle. Kate had assumed it was Adrian's initials: *A* and G. But what if it wasn't a *G*? What if it only looked like one because of the curly script? And the letters were surrounded by a frilly design which could be said to be feminine …

'Excuse me? Have we finished?' Nancy bristled and picked some imaginary lint off her cuff. 'Because if you have nothing else to ask me—'

Kate snapped her mouth closed, then opened it to blurt, 'The paperknife that was used by your father's assailant.'

Nancy blinked. She hadn't been expecting that. Good.

'I noticed the beautiful engraving on the handle and the monogram: an *A* and a *C*, for Adrian and Cora, I presume?'

'Yes. It was one of the many presents Father gave

Mother on their marriage. Along with new stationery carrying her married name, I believe.'

'Do you know if your father usually used that knife to open his letters? If it was typically kept in his office?'

Nancy sprang to her feet, her knees catching the edge of the coffee table, making it vibrate. 'Why on earth do you think I should know anything about it?' She spat her words, her voice once again close to shouting. 'Who have you been speaking to? It's that American hussy, isn't it? She has been spreading more of her poison. I knew she couldn't be—'

'What ho! What the dickens is happening here?'

The speaker was standing on the threshold to the music room. His head came close to brushing the lintel while his slender build filled barely a third of the width of the doorway. His frame was covered in a white shirt, black necktie, and a striking mustard-brown and tan houndstooth suit. Kate's head swam as she tried to focus on the two-tone check pattern which seemed to blur and shudder. Above the dizzying optical illusion the man's face was a smooth pale oval, the pallidness only increased by a pair of milky blue eyes. However, for such a thin person, he had a surprising number of chins.

Facing their scrutiny, he planted his hands on his hips. 'From all the hullaballoo you'd think someone else was being done in! And we've all had quite enough of that, what?'

'Oh, Archie. Where have you been?' Nancy scuttled across to the newcomer and threw herself into his arms, the force of the blow sending his jowls wobbling.

'Good grief, steady on, old girl! I say'—over Nancy's shoulder, the man's eyes goggled at Max and Kate—'who are you and what the deuce have you done to my wife?'

147

Chapter 19

Max rose and, hand outstretched, strode towards the tall man. 'Mr Forbes, I presume?'

'In the flesh,' said Archie Forbes, taking his right hand away from Nancy's back to shake Max's.

'I'm Max Ravenscroft and this is Ms Brannon. We were asking your wife some questions about her father's death and, understandably, she found it rather upsetting.'

'Of course, of course. Perfectly rotten business.'

'I think,' Nancy said, muttering into her husband's collar, 'I'm going to go up to my room and lie down. I have a migraine coming on.'

'One last quick question, Mrs Forbes,' said Kate. 'After you'd spoken to your father, what did you do?'

'I went straight to bed. My maid helped me undress, we said goodnight and I slept soundly till morning. I was dressing when I was brought the news of his passing.' Nancy pressed her fingertips to her brow ridge. 'Now, if that's everything, I must go and lie down.'

'Capital idea, old thing. You pop off, I'll be along in a jiffy.' Archie kissed the top of Nancy's head and watched her leave, a dopey smile of affection giving way to a wistful sigh. 'My wife is a terrific woman, but—and I'm sure you'll find this tricky to believe—she can be a tad highly strung on occasion. Has frightful attacks of nerves. Very rum!'

Kate's lips twitched. She dropped her gaze to the floor, not daring to look at Max. If he betrayed the smallest hint that he found Archie Forbes as amusing as she did, she wouldn't be able to contain the giggles gathering in her throat.

Continuing to be an upbeat contrast to his dour wife, Archie said, 'I suppose you have some questions for me too, what? Not sure I'll be much help with the bally murder. I'm baffled.' He grinned at this open expression of ignorance and pointed at the chairs. 'Sitting over by the fireplace, are we? Topping!' And without waiting for a reply, he lolloped across the room and swung into the chair next to that which had been favoured by his wife.

Kate risked a glance at Max, who raised a single eyebrow and mouthed, *'Topping,'* causing Kate to snort and struggle to turn her laughter into a fit of coughing.

'I say, Ms Brannon,' Archie called from across the room. 'Are you quite all right?'

'She'll be fine,' said Max, making a pantomime of patting Kate on the back as they shuffled across to their chairs. 'Some of these rooms are rather dusty, that's all.'

Kate swallowed the last of her giggles while Max poured her a glass of water. He turned his back to Archie as he handed it to her and mouthed a *'Sorry,'* which Kate suspected—from the smirk in the corner of his mouth— was only half sincere.

'When did you arrive at the Old Grange, Mr Forbes?' Max asked, as he lowered himself onto the seat next to Kate.

'Oh, about half an hour ago, I'd say. I dashed over as soon as I got word. Nancy telephoned in a state, poor thing.'

'Why weren't you here yesterday?'

'Dashed bad luck! All was at the ready to hop in the motor and roll on over here when a spot of constituency business came up. Fortunately Nancy was a total brick about it. Said not to worry, she'd pop over here on her own. I offered to join her late last night, but she'd not hear a bit of it. Told me to put my head down at home.'

Kate swallowed another surge of laughter. She imagined Nancy had jumped at the chance to have a quiet night off from her ebullient husband.

Max continued, his voice reassuringly stern, 'Were you at home alone last night, sir?'

'Rather! Except for the staff. I said goodnight to Higgins, my man—absolute corker, couldn't be without him—at about ten thirty. And he woke me at ten this morning to say Nancy was on the telephone. The news floored me. Terrible shock, took me a while to cotton on to what she was telling me, don't you know? Wasn't at my brightest at the time. Hadn't had my morning tea. Bucks you up, good and proper. Fabulous stuff!'

As Max noted down Archie's alibi, Kate raided her memory of the character profiles in the information pack for material for further questions. Archie was an easy interview, but it was best to keep the speedy rhythm going. 'You've recently become a MP, I believe, Mr Forbes?'

'Yes, I have.' Archie beamed as he slouched back in his

seat, crossed his legs and stretched his left arm along the top of the vacant seat next to him. 'To be completely up front with you, without my Nancy I'm not sure politics is something I would have wandered into. But it's dashed interesting and one must have something to keep one out of trouble, what?'

Ah, of course. Kate nodded as details from the character profile came back to her. Archie Forbes was the sole heir of an unimaginably wealthy spinster aunt. How nice to be in a position to view becoming a Member of Parliament as something to pass the time.

'You mentioned your wife. How long have you been married?'

'Ten bliss-filled years! Nancy had just turned twenty-one when we met. Love at first sight and all that. She practically threw herself into my arms.'

Nancy was twenty-two when she left home, her little sister only fifteen. If she had resented her overbearing father, it was little surprise she'd leapt at the chance to escape with a daft, kind man who she could mould into anything she wished. And Archie also came with the money to promise Nancy lifelong security and independence from her dad.

'Your wife became rather agitated when I asked her a question about the letter opener which was found in Mr Grieve's back,' said Kate. 'Do you have any idea why that might be, Mr Forbes?'

'Oh gosh, yes. That blessed thing has caused no end of trouble.'

Max and Kate exchanged a glance. Kate leant forwards and, as casually as possible, asked, 'In what way?'

Archie blew out a long breath, causing his lips to vibrate. 'Until a couple of months ago that letter opener sat on my wife's writing desk. She used it every day. Put it to tremendous use on her stacks of correspondence.' Archie shrugged. 'I always assumed her father had given it to her as a memento, what with it having belonged to her mother. My wife is dreadfully attached to her mother's memory, you know. She was fairly pipped at having to return the bally thing.'

'Why did she have to return it?' asked Kate, her pulse picking up at the prospect of an interesting lead.

'Her father asked her to. Or maybe Pam did. I'm not sure. Like I said, Nancy got herself into a bit of a tizz about it. I find'—Archie dropped his voice into a more confidential tone—'that it can be best not to ask too many questions when she's upset.'

'And this was two months ago?' Max asked.

'Thereabouts, yes.' Archie nodded, then frowned. 'Who could have guessed where that knife would end up, eh? Poor Nancy. She must wish she'd thrown the cursed thing into the Thames rather than bring it back here to be used against her father!'

'Indeed.' Max finished jotting down a sentence with a flourish, turned back a page in his book, scanned his notes and asked, 'Did you have any sense that your father-in-law had any money troubles?'

'By Jove! You know it's strange you ask, old boy. Why, just last week I heard murmurs at the club that some of Pater Grieve's investments were on rocky ground. But I never lean too heavily on rumours and anyway, everyone took a hit with the Crash and all that.'

'And would you happen to know if Mr Grieve's life was insured or'—Max paused for a second, a spark entering his eyes—'if the stolen jewels were?'

'I've no idea.' Archie shrugged. 'But I'd bet the house that the jewels were insured to the hilt. My father-in-law was a prudent old cove. The person to ask is Pam. She was a sort of secretary to the old man and would know all about his paperwork. Terrific brain has Pam, like my Nancy. Sharp as a box of tacks. Yes, that's my tip: Pam's your girl.'

'Thank you, Mr Forbes. That's all my questions. Perhaps Ms Brannon has something else to ask. Kate?'

'Hmn?' Kate had been deep in thought about insurance on the jewels. The one thing they knew for certain was that the theft and murder were inside jobs. So any insurance on the jewels could be as important as Adrian's life policy. Why hadn't she thought of that? 'Oh, yes, thank you, Max.' She stared at Archie's open stare and patient smile. 'Mr Forbes, I believe Mr Grieve's will has divided his estate between his daughters, including this house,' Kate said. 'Will you and your wife come to live here?'

Archie spluttered before releasing a braying laugh that was more donkey than man. 'No fear of that, I should say! The old girl hates the place. She's barely laid foot in it since we were married. Bad memories from when she was a girl. And she's always on about the expense of running a place like this. Dashed draughty. Leaking roofs.'

'I'm guessing you'd need a small army of staff too,' said Kate.

'A full battalion at least, I shouldn't wonder. Also, Nancy likes her modern comforts and the thought of having to share a bathroom with anyone ...' Archie's face grew serious, his expression that of one who had seen horrors. 'Let's just say, she wouldn't be bucked by the idea.' He shook his head, dismissing the cloud of gloom. 'No, no. Nancy will be happy for Pam to have the house. Then when she marries that Italian fellow of hers, she has a nest ready for her own family.'

'Have you met Mr Corsini, Pamela's "Italian fellow"?'

'Once or twice at some charity bashes. And he and Pam were in Stratford for the opening of the Shakespeare Memorial Theatre back in April. He seems a charming bird and quite devoted to Pam.'

'Your wife expressed some ... misgivings about his character. Principally that he might be after money. Have you seen any evidence of that?'

Archie rolled his eyes. 'Pam's a great one for charity. She and this Italian are involved in all sorts of do-gooding schemes. Nancy heard that Corsini had asked my father-in-law for a hefty contribution to a children's home he's setting up in London somewhere. She got rather exercised about it, I don't mind telling you.'

'Did Mr Grieve give Mr Corsini the money?'

'No, he bally well did not! I told you, he was a downright cautious old cove. Not even Pam could persuade him.'

'Hmn.' Kate tapped her lower lip, replaying the interview in her head, checking for any unexplored avenues. 'Where do you go next, Mr Forbes? Back to your constituency?'

'Absolutely. Can't shirk my duties for too long. A lot going on at the moment.'

'Oh, yes. You said you couldn't get here yesterday because you had to deal with a constituency issue. What was it?'

'A rather peculiar affair, actually. Have you heard of Derek Jones? Missing lad, been in all the papers for months.'

Kate sat forwards, her heart skipping. Was being a lunchtime swat about to pay off? 'Yes. I remember some of the story.' She recalled the picture illustrating the magazine feature she'd skimmed. A striking portrait of a young man with intense dark eyes, a cloud of flaming red hair, full beard and bushy moustache. 'He's in his early twenties and the first anniversary of his disappearance was recently. His family lost contact with him while he was travelling around continental Europe and they've mounted an extensive search for him but had no luck.'

'That's about the size of it. Lad was born and raised in London, bit of a Johnnie nobody to tell you the truth. Then when he was seventeen, the Duke of Berkshire popped his clogs and blow me, but it turned out this Derek chap was next in line to the title! Well, he was rolled into the family estate tout suite and they were doing a pretty good job of sitting on the boy until he came of age. My guess is they'd locked him up in some ghastly finishing school for a few years to give him a jolly good polish before showing him off. Then, barely having passed his twenty-first birthday, he nipped off to Europe and vanished. Dashed inconvenient for all involved, don't you know?'

'Do the family fear for his safety?' ask Max.

'That's the thing, you see. Opinion was divided. Half of the blighters thought the lad had gone off to sow his wild oats and would come back in due course. The other half were convinced he was dead in a French ditch or trapped in a dungeon in some Bavarian castle.'

'And you became involved in this matter because …'

'Turns out the boy's been bally kidnapped!'

Kate—who had quickly become lost in the story—gasped, earning her a smirk from Max. The killjoy. Ignoring his amusement at her reaction to Archie's tale, she asked, 'Someone sent the family a ransom note?'

'Yes. It arrived in an unmarked envelope at his aunt's place in Windsor yesterday morning. The scoundrels want twenty thousand pounds for the lad's safe return.'

Max let out a low whistle as he wrote 'one million ransom' on his pad.

Archie continued, 'The family, not being the sort who have had much to do with the long arm of the law—unless it's their annual donation to the benevolent fund—wanted to know if yours truly, as their Parliamentary representative, could act as something of a buffer between them and the police in working out how to proceed. And, of course, I knew old Rusty from the club.'

'Rusty?' Max and Kate asked together.

'George Russell, the last Duke of Berkshire. The one who shuffled off the old mortal coil without leaving an heir. It was news to me he was a duke, though. Amazing how little one knows about one's pals.'

'I see,' said Max, in a tone which suggested he understood nothing whatsoever. 'And what did they decide? The family? About how to proceed?'

'Now, now, old boy, I'd like to tell everything, I honestly would. But I'm afraid that's top secret. However'—he waggled his eyebrows—'if you keep a beady eye on the papers next week, I predict you'll be seeing some pleasant tidings. The return of the prodigal and all that.'

Kate's mind raced, moving only fractionally quicker than Max's pen. This story had to be important. Merryman would never have given an actor this amount of detail about something inconsequential to the case, surely? Perhaps—she thought, her pulse skipping—this was the key to cracking the whole puzzle.

'Well, this has been delightful, but I'd better scoot upstairs and check on the old ball and chain.' Archie rose, chuckling. 'We must rally round when these frightful things happen. So much beastliness about. Could get a chap down if he weren't careful, I say, what?' With a final grin, he cantered towards the exit, interrupting his jaunty gait for a moment to call back, 'See you later, chaps. Tinkety-tonk!'

Chapter 20

Bathed in sunlight, the limestone windowsill was warm and solid beneath Kate's fingertips. Outside birds sang and soared across the sky which was an unbroken blanket of blue. The breeze carried the light perfume of the roses below the window.

Kate pressed her palms to the stone, clinging to details of her surroundings to tether herself to reality. For while interviewing Archie had been productive and relatively straightforward, it had left her with an uncanny feeling, as if she had wandered into a Wodehouse short story.

Strangely, it had made her thankful for Max. In the middle of a weekend of extended role play, a weird fictional situation in which everyone was voluntarily suspending their disbelief, he was unwaveringly present and solid.

She turned to take in his dark blond hair, its reddish tones blazing through where it was caught by the sun. She smiled as she admired his broad shoulders, so firm, unshakeable and—

Max's shoulders began to shake. Uh-oh. Frowning, Kate pushed off the windowsill. Maybe she wasn't the only one beginning to lose her grip.

A low rumbling came from Max as she took her seat next to him. He lifted his head and, between deep breathy chuckles, managed to gasp, 'Tinkety-tonk!'

Kate spluttered. The rolling sound of Max's laughter was infectious and soon she was giggling too. The hysteria was a welcome release after what had been a tense day and was so overwhelming that, for a moment, Kate came close to slipping off her chair. She would have ended up on the floor if Max hadn't wrapped an arm around her shoulders to halt her slide, causing her to whoop with laughter and both of them to enter a further uncontrolled bout of hilarity.

When their laughter eventually subsided, Kate's face, ribs and stomach ached and her cheeks were wet with tears. Even so, she felt oddly relaxed. Slumping against Max's shoulder, she reached into her pocket and retrieved two tissues with trembling fingers.

'Here.' She passed Max a tissue.

'Thanks.' Max wiped his eyes. 'Kate, did we just interview Bertie Wooster?'

'Ha!' Kate nudged Max in the ribs. 'I kept expecting Jeeves to walk in and announce that Aunt Agatha was on the telephone.'

Max shook his head. 'How many books do you think that guy read to prepare his role?'

'I don't know. But I'd say enough.'

'If you can ever read enough Wodehouse.'

Kate smiled at Max. In response, his lips curled up on

one side to form his trademark smirk which, right now, looked more like a shy smile. His hand, still resting on her shoulder, was a warm, comfortable weight. This was ... this was ... Kate blinked. Hang on. Was this fun? Was she having *fun* with Max Ravenscroft?

'Come on,' said Max, lifting his arm from her shoulder and twisting in his seat to face her. 'Hit me with your theories before Pamela or Lorenzo turn up.'

Kate rolled her shoulders, shaking off the whisper of absence where Max's arm had been. That order was more the Max she knew and dreaded: all business. 'I believe we can rule Lucille out.'

'Agreed,' said Max. 'She has an alibi. And her only motive would have been getting out of her contract, and she did a good job of destroying that.'

'And, even if the time of death is wrong or she somehow set up her alibi so she had cover for the time she was sneaking down to the study to murder Adrian—'

'Unlikely.'

'Indeed, and—to channel Poirot for a minute—'

'The psychology of the individual?'

'Yep. Lucille isn't the type to stab anyone in the back or poison them. So unless there's some crazy twist like, I don't know, it turns out she has some underlying pathology which causes her to murder in her sleep—'

'Homicidal sleepwalking?' Max's tone turned incredulous. 'Without disturbing the footman sharing her bed?'

'There are real-life examples of people killing while asleep. Well, examples of sleepwalking being used as a defence, anyway. Although, I'm not sure anyone's managed it with the amount of stealth Lucille would have needed.'

Max shook his head. 'We should rule her right out. Any explanation as to how Lucille managed to murder Adrian would be too outlandish. The rules of the game clearly state that there will be clues which guide contestants to the correct answer. And, while I don't know much about Merryman's Games Supervisor, I do get the impression that Dorothy Williams wouldn't allow surprise murder sleepwalking to pass as fair play.'

'Let's hope you're right.'

Max turned a page of his notebook. 'So Lucille's out. Nancy?'

Kate tipped her head back to stare up at the scroll motif running along the crown moulding which framed the ceiling. 'Nancy resented her dad and carried gallons of bottled-up anger towards him. From what we've seen, she could have got worked up enough to kill him in a rage. The method of killing would have been poetic too: stabbing him with her mother's paperknife—'

'Which we know she had to return, against her will. I bet she was angry about that. After all the animosity about not getting what she considered her fair share of her mother's jewels, having to return the letter opener must have been difficult. She certainly became agitated when you asked about it.'

'Yes.' Kate rose and strolled towards the piano. It was often easier to think if she was in motion. 'Nancy doesn't really have an alibi. She knows this house well and could have crept downstairs without being seen. Let's, for argument's sake, give Nancy the benefit of the doubt and assume she didn't *plan* to kill her father. She could have gone to the study with some benign purpose. Perhaps she'd been mulling over their talk, had something else to say and returned to the study later. They argue. In her fury, she spots the paperknife which her father demanded she return, robbing her of another piece of her mother. The memories of his poor treatment of her mother came flooding back and it was too much to bear.'

'She snapped, grabbed the letter opener'—Max gripped his pen like a knife and drove it down towards his pad— 'stabbed him, and staged the burglary to throw suspicion on an unknown intruder.'

'If he wanted the damn paperknife so much, she would drive it through his heart? Avenging her mother? That sort of thing?'

'We've seen her upset. I think she'd be capable.'

'I do too. And staging the robbery would have the additional upside of getting her the jewels she thinks should be hers. Do you think there's any chance she involved her husband?'

'None.' Max shook his head. 'Archie Forbes is far too daft to keep any secrets. He almost revealed exactly when and how that kidnapped kid's family is going to pay his ransom. Nancy would never be foolish enough to involve him. If she did this, she did it alone.'

'Agreed. The origins of that letter knife—a wedding present to Cora Grieve from her allegedly faithless, bullying husband—must be significant. Unless'—Kate sighed, why was nothing straightforward?—'they're an enormous red herring.'

Max scooped up his notebook and, without glancing up from the pages, said, 'Either way, that was a nice spot. I didn't look hard enough and assumed the letters on the knife handle were Adrian's initials.'

While Kate's heart swelled in response to Max's praise, she clamped her lips together to prevent herself grinning. She didn't want him to think she was gloating. Especially when she doubted she would have put the pieces together herself if she hadn't had the stunning luck to interview Dr Chase. 'Back in the study I thought they were an *A* and *G* too. And that curly script is so hard to read. It's a miracle I figured it out. To be honest, if it hadn't been for my chat with Dr Chase—'

'Kate!' Max rose from his seat and came towards her, stopping a couple of steps away. 'Don't do that.' He blinked, softening his glare to a pleading gaze, and when he spoke again his tone was also gentle. 'Please. Don't do yourself down. It was a brilliant catch. It doesn't matter how you managed to put the pieces together, what matters is that you did.'

The warm sincerity in Max's gaze travelled down to Kate's belly, where her insides fluttered in a strange, not entirely unpleasant way. When he said, *'Please'*—in a quiet, insistent tone which suggested that nothing in the world would make him happier than Kate taking his compliment—her knees had quivered. Actually quivered! She hadn't known knees could really do that.

Tearing her gaze away from Max, Kate began to pace. Each tap of her soles on the wooden floor was an attempt to reorder her thoughts. What had they been talking about before Max had undergone a bizarre transformation into a kind of stern personal cheerleader? Oh yes, the murder weapon.

Her stride firm—not a trace of a wobble in her knees, thank heavens—Kate returned to the case. 'Having ruled out Lucille and Archie, we're left with Nancy, Pamela and Lorenzo as possible suspects.' She paused as she turned back to face Max, waiting for him to contradict her or at least tell her not to jump to conclusions.

It was a jolt to find Max's gaze trained on her, as if he had been hanging on her every word. 'Yes, go on!' he said, lifting his left hand from where it had been resting on the piano lid to make an impatient circular motion with his hand. 'Er, that is … I mean,' he rushed to add, 'please continue.'

A slight tremor passed along the back of Kate's knees. What was going on with her this afternoon?

'OK,' she said. 'The choice of murder weapon suggests our killer is one of Adrian's daughters. Unless Lorenzo turns out to be a long-lost relative.'

'Not impossible.'

'And I don't think we can rule out a combination of our suspects acting together. Or acting to implicate one another. In fact, it's likely.'

'Absolutely.'

Kate planted her hands on her hips and exhaled slowly. Drat. They needed more information. 'We have to speak to Pam and Lorenzo before we can get any further.' She strolled back to where Max was leaning on the piano, mentally listing their positive discoveries to combat her frustration: they had identified the significance of the murder weapon and narrowed the suspect pool to three, with heavy suspicion on the Grieve sisters.

'Yes,' said Max, 'we need more information. Do you want to put together a list for our questions before they— Kate? Are you OK?'

Kate halted and stared at the floor as a realization hit her. She lifted her gaze to meet Max's. 'Yes, I'm fine. I just ... we can win this, can't we?'

'Of course.' Max answered without hesitation. 'What criminal could possibly outsmart the Friendly Murder Club's best?' Max smiled, a wide grin which reached up into his eyes, making them sparkle.

Kate stared, certain she had never seen Max smile properly before. It wasn't something she would have forgotten easily. It was as if his face had been lit up from the inside, bringing all his features into focus. His gorgeous gold-flecked eyes, straight nose, strong square jaw and full, even lips. Her gaze snagged on his lips as his grin slipped into a more relaxed smile. They looked soft and—

'Kate?' Max held up his notebook in the space between them, breaking the spell. 'Shall we make a list?'

'Um, yeah. Sure. Great.'

Max shot her another grin and her core was immediately struck by a hot spear of desire which made her breath hitch and heart pound. *Oh good Lord above.* How had she not seen it till now? 'Fox-like' wasn't the right word to capture Max. It didn't even come close. Bella had it right again. The man gazing at Kate with an eager shine in his alluring eyes could only be described as undeniably, unavoidably and distractingly *foxy*.

Chapter 21

Most detectives would have agreed that it was better to interview suspects in isolation. But Lorenzo Corsini and Pamela Grieve came as an inseparable package. Unwilling to release her hold on her fiancé's arm, Pamela only loosened her grip long enough for them to squeeze through the music room doorway as one. By the time they took the seats opposite Kate and Max, her hold on his forearm was so tight her fingertips were bloodless, a pale contrast to the fiery red tones of the large ruby in the engagement ring on her left hand.

While grief appeared to have landed like a petrol bomb on top of Nancy's smouldering resentments, it seemed to have hit Pam like a cold sucking wave. Her porcelain doll face, with her eyelids drooping over her large brown eyes and the sharp pink V in her upper lip, was an exhausted pale grey. The colour of her complexion wasn't improved by her clothes, a fitted dress covering her from neck to knee in bottle-green velvet. The only sturdy thing about her was her dark hair, which had been styled into stiff finger waves tucking neatly under her ears.

Lorenzo seemed relatively untroubled, although he did throw regular glances of concern at Pamela. Impeccably dressed as always, the Italian had changed out of the tan-and-grey combo Kate had seen him wearing by the tower earlier in the day, and was now in a sombre navy suit.

Having delivered their condolences, Kate glanced at the list of questions on Max's pad and said, 'Miss Grieve, last night when he said goodnight to Mr Ravenscroft and me in the library, your father said he wanted to speak to you and your sister. Nancy told us she met him in his study. Did he speak to you?'

'Yes,' said Pamela, her voice barely more than a whisper. 'I often went to his study before going to bed, especially if he was going to stay up late working. I was in the library with Lorenzo when Nancy told me Daddy wanted to see me.'

'Do you remember what time you said goodnight to him?'

'Shortly after eleven. Nancy said she'd come straight from the study to fetch me.'

Kate nodded, the timings fitted with Nancy and Lucille's testimonies. 'Was your father working last night when you went to the study?'

'I believe so. He had some correspondence he wanted to deal with.'

'The letter opener which was used to assault your father—' Max broke off when his words caused Pamela to wince. 'Sorry. We believe it was in your sister's possession until recently. Is that correct?'

'Yes. Nancy had removed it from the house at the start of this year while we were abroad. When we got home, Daddy quickly noticed it was missing and asked her to return it. That must have been a couple of months ago.'

'According to Mr Forbes, your sister wasn't pleased at having to return the knife.'

'She wasn't. And even less pleased at having been caught stealing. I suspect she thought Daddy wouldn't notice the knife was gone because she didn't believe he missed our mother or treasured his few mementoes of her.' Pamela's dark stare flickered to Kate's face, then returned to her knees. 'But he liked having it on his desk because he said it was like having a piece of Mother near him.'

Using her gentlest tone, Kate said, 'Coming back to last night, Miss Grieve: you said Nancy had come from the study to fetch you. Do you know what your father and she spoke about?'

'He said he'd given her our mother's pearls. She's wearing them today.'

'How do you feel about that?'

Pamela let out a sigh which contained an unfathomable weariness. 'The jewellery is like the letter opener. Nancy believes that everything that once belonged to our mother should be hers. That it's what Mother wanted. But Daddy always says'—she paused and swallowed—'*said*. Sorry. He said that Mother loved us both and would want us both to have something of hers. But I don't think she would have wanted it to cause an argument between us either. So I'm happy that Nancy has the pearls. Especially now the rest of the collection has gone and it seems they'll be the only item either of us ever has. Maybe now she can be content.'

Pamela shuddered. 'I certainly never want to see that letter opener again.'

'This obsession your sister has with material things is absurd.' Lorenzo patted Pamela's hand where it lay on his bicep. The movement drew attention to the chunky gold signet ring on his little finger, which Kate didn't recall him sporting the previous evening. He had also changed his cufflinks from those he had worn at dinner: today's were rectangles of gold inlaid with onyx. 'The spirit is what is important.' He turned his gaze to Max and Kate. 'Pamela and I have been to parties and met many people who knew her mother. They all tell me she was a wonderful woman who was kind, generous and selfless. Pamela is right. She would not want her daughters to fight over some silly stones.'

Silly stones worth several million quid, thought Kate. 'Do you know if the jewels were insured, Miss Grieve?'

'They should be, along with everything else in the house.' Pamela frowned. 'Daddy liked to keep on top of things like that. The policy was updated about a year ago. A man came from London and went over the whole house with a clipboard and tape measure, putting a value on everything. I'm sure the papers could be found, if it's important.'

Next to her, a pen scratched across paper, but Kate didn't need to glance at Max's pad to know he was making a note to ask to see the papers later. 'You say the insurance man came to put a value on everything. Did your father also have life insurance?'

'Yes. What happened to my mother brought home to him how fragile life can be. I haven't seen the policy, but I believe it's for a substantial sum.' She bowed her head, covered her face with her free hand and muttered something which sounded like, 'Not that it matters.'

'*Cara mia*, do you want to rest?' Lorenzo touched Pamela's shoulder.

'No, it's all right. I'd rather get this over with.'

Kate reminded herself that the pale woman sitting opposite her, who looked on the verge of nervous collapse, was an actor. Even so, she reasoned, it couldn't hurt to change the subject for a while. To steer the conversation back to the living.

Kate smiled, hoping she might set a trend. 'How did you two meet?'

Lorenzo turned to look at Pamela. 'We met in Italy, nine months ago. I was visiting friends who have a house at Lake Como and Pamela was in the area with her father as part of his latest world tour. Our paths crossed at a party. We talked and discovered we had much in common.' He flicked his left wrist dramatically. 'Destiny!'

Pamela listened while staring into the space above Kate's head, a dreamy smile lifting the corners of her mouth.

Lorenzo continued, his left hand keeping time with his speech. 'Mr Grieve invited me to attend the reception he was planning to hold at the Hotel de Louvre in Paris in early February. From there I followed Pam back to England. She has been keeping me out of trouble ever since.'

'You certainly have been busy. From a quick look through the newspapers in the library, I see you're mentioned as having attended a number of events. Although, you don't feature in any of the photographs. Is there a reason for that?'

Lorenzo waved dismissively. 'I have been lucky to receive many kind invitations. Although I am not naturally attracted to the glitter of these occasions. And I do not like having my picture taken. I am—how do you say this?—superstitious about it. I avoid it ...'

He continued speaking, but Kate had ceased to follow his every word. She was entranced by the movement of his left hand, the way his gold ring caught the light as he swished his fingers through the air with the elegance and control of an orchestra conductor. And as the words 'attracted to the glitter' came out of his mouth, the rest of Lorenzo's speech was drowned out by a loud click inside Kate's head as two previously disparate pieces of the puzzle slotted together.

Kate's breathing quickened. She had to get back to the library and pray no one had moved the newspapers. They contained the reports she needed to prove her theory. Lists needed to be made. Then cross-checked. But right now she could at least test her hunch.

She tuned back in to the rise and fall of Lorenzo's accent as she waited for him to finish. 'Have either of you been following the newspaper reports on the recent string of burglaries at the houses of society figures?' Kate asked in as nonchalant a tone as she could muster. 'I only ask because I wondered if there was a connection to the theft here. I'm sure the police have already raised it as a possibility.'

Pamela blinked at Kate as if waking from a trance. 'Um, yes. I heard Waldorf and Nancy had some items of jewellery go missing after one of their receptions at St James's Square.'

Lorenzo's features had relaxed into a blank mask of

boredom and his hands were perfectly still. 'Waldorf and Nancy?' He gazed down at Pamela. 'Remind me, who are they?'

'The Astors.'

'Ah!' Lorenzo rolled his eyes. 'The politicians. A beautiful house but so many people and all of them so dull.'

'It surprises me that you found a gathering at the Astors' boring, Mr Corsini,' said Kate. 'I understand you're a philanthropist. Surely the sort of wealthy and influential people the Astors could gather, including members of the Houses of Parliament, would interest you? If only to persuade them to support your charitable causes?'

'You think those people are happy to hand over money to the less fortunate?' Lorenzo scoffed and leant forwards, his eyes flashing. 'And those politicians are the worst. They talk about helping the disadvantaged, but that's all that do. Talk! The laws they make are there only to keep them and their friends rich. It would be easier to get blood from a stone—'

A mewling sound came from Pamela, interrupting Lorenzo's rant. He turned to take in her pinched expression. 'I am sorry, my darling. I get carried away. I have been insensitive.'

'Where were you both between midnight and 2 a.m. this morning?' asked Kate, although from the way Pamela and Lorenzo continued to gaze deeply into each other's eyes, she had a good idea what the answer would be.

'We must rely on your discretion,' said Lorenzo. 'We were together until early this morning when I returned to my room.'

Kate nodded. While unremarkable in the twenty-first century, such behaviour by an unmarried couple, even one engaged to be married, would have been scandalous in 1932.

Max drew a line under his last note and looked up from his pad. 'The late Mr Grieve's will splits the estate equally between you, Miss Grieve, and your sister. We have also been told that it is unlikely your sister will want to live here. Will you keep the house?'

'What I want hardly matters,' said Pamela, her voice a hollow echo. 'The house will have to be sold.'

'What?' Kate cleared her throat. That had come out as a squawk. 'Why?'

Using a dull monotone which made Kate worry she had taken some of the sleeping pills Dr Chase had mentioned, Pamela said, 'After lunch Daddy's solicitor telephoned. It appears he didn't have all the information this morning when he read the will to us. Daddy made some investments in the last decade which went to the bad. And, well, he was … to put it plainly: broke. The solicitor says the sale of his remaining assets, including the house and estate, won't even cover all of the debts and death duties. Although with his life insurance, that may be enough to set everything square.'

'I'm sorry, Miss Grieve.' Max's brow creased with concern. 'Did you know your father was having financial trouble?'

'I knew he had some difficulties. I helped with his correspondence and filing his papers, and I did notice some unpaid bills. And a couple of times, when he'd had a little too much to drink, he would ramble on about being ruined. But he'd had setbacks before, you see. And he could be a little dramatic when …'

Pamela trailed off and her fine pink lips twisted in concentration as she searched for the appropriate words. Kate sympathised: it must be hard to find a kind euphemism for 'completely sozzled'. Particularly if being 'a little dramatic' involved violence.

'Was your father ever—' Kate drew back and reapproached her question, not wanting to scare an already fragile Pamela into silence. 'Did you father ever frighten you, Miss Grieve? When he had his dramatic episodes?'

'Sometimes.' Pamela's whisper was barely audible. 'He got frustrated.'

'And you, Mr Corsini?' Max said to Lorenzo, who had wrapped his left arm around Pamela's shoulders. 'You asked Mr Grieve to donate to a charitable project and he refused. Was that a cordial conversation? Or did he become dramatic?'

'Mr Grieve was a passionate man,' said Lorenzo. 'He told me he could not contribute to our plan for a voluntary hospital. I did not know at the time he was speaking literally: that he *could not* give us the money because he did not have it. I may have pressed the point a little too far and he became upset. But that was months ago. We have found alternative donors. Everything is going ahead as planned.'

'We also understand that Mr Grieve initially refused to give his blessing to your engagement,' said Max. 'Is that the case?'

Lorenzo shrugged. 'He was very protective of Pamela. But he changed his mind when he understood it was what

174

she really wanted. He was reluctant to lose Pamela and to be alone here in this big grand house—'

Another squeak of distress came from Pamela Grieve. Her stare was glassy and unfocused as she said, 'I'm not sure I ever imagined … I find so many things hard to picture. You know, since the war, so many houses have been sold off piece by piece and then knocked quite to the ground. Cassiobury Park stood for over two hundred years but it was demolished a few years ago. And, you know, its staircase is in the Metropolitan Museum of Art?' The memory stirred Pamela's features into the briefest of wry smiles. 'I saw it when we were in New York last November. So strange that part of someone's home could be in a museum. Consigned to history.'

Pamela's final words were carried on another deep sigh which expressed something ineffable. Was that resignation? Exhaustion? Existential despair?

Kate cleared her throat and asked, in her gentlest voice, 'What will you do next, Miss Grieve?'

Pamela drew in a long, slow breath, but Lorenzo jumped in before she could speak. 'She will do whatever she wants. A house is just a box.' He squeezed Pamela's shoulder. 'Pamela, you were a slave to your father and this house for years. You are finally free!'

The only response from Pamela was a small, mysterious smile. Was that a sign of nervousness, grief or perhaps even relief? Was Pamela Grieve, with her distant stare, finally seeing the light at the end of a long tunnel? And would the chance at escaping from the darkness have moved an apparently mousey, frail woman to kill her father and steal her mother's jewels?

Chapter 22

The study at the Old Grange had grown gloomier as the afternoon wore on. Shadows stretched across the craze of teardrops in the paisley floor rug and over the top of Adrian Grieve's desk, which had been cleared of all the items they had examined that morning. In their place was a single blue plate covered with a white linen napkin.

Behind the desk, staring up at the elaborate ceiling rose around the main pendant light, Kate was executing lazy circles in the antique swivel chair while waiting for Max.

After Lorenzo had half carried Pamela out of the music room, she and Max had fallen into a pensive silence. It was comfortable, and Kate's thoughts had drifted inwards, quickly wrapping her in a cocoon of questions which was only broken when Max suggested they take a quick break and meet in the study to share their ideas. Any objections she might have had to Max setting the agenda for their investigation were quickly quashed when he told her that if she took care of the butterscotch cake he would hunt down some much-needed tea.

'Here we are.' Max used his foot to open the door wider and crossed the threshold carrying a black plastic tray. On it balanced two white mugs of steaming tea, spoons, napkins and his notebook.

'How did you get a tray?' Kate asked as Max set the tea down on the desk next to the plate.

'Connections,' Max said. 'I ducked into the kitchen and dropped Lucinda's name to the staff. That got me a loan of the tray.' He glanced about the room, his keen gaze playing a rapid game of spot the difference. 'So they cleared the desk, closed the safe, put the picture back and moved the whiteboard. Did I miss anything?'

The whiteboard had been repositioned to stand on the opposite side of the room in front of the bookshelves. Kate suspected the move was partly to discourage anyone else from playing with the sliding library steps.

'No, that's everything. Although'—Kate leant forwards to take a mug—'something bothers me about this room.'

Max took the other mug and sank onto the straight-backed chair on his side of the desk. 'Oh? What?'

'I don't know. I get this feeling when I'm in here. That something's off. Like the ceiling is too low or ...' Kate trailed off as she met Max's stare. He must think her paranoid. 'Never mind. I'm probably being daft. Ignore me.'

'I wouldn't ignore your instincts. It could turn out to be important later.' Max took a cautious sip of tea. 'I'll make a note.'

Watching Max put his tea back on the tray and pick up his notebook, Kate was flooded with a warm glow which reached right down to her toes, making them curl against the soles of her canvas sneakers. She stretched her legs out and leant back in her chair, gazing at the speckling of grey at Max's temples. Perhaps during the almost three years since she'd last competed against Max he'd matured and mellowed. Or maybe this supportive, non-dismissive version of him was like a rare nervous animal: timid in group situations and only observable one-to-one.

'Kate? Did I miss something funny?'

Max had looked up from his notebook, his expression halfway between concerned and bemused. Oh no, thought Kate, the smile which had stolen onto her lips slipping away. She'd been staring at Max through the steam haze of her tea with a dopey smile plastered all over her face. And just when she was making headway in giving him a good impression!

'No, no,' she said. 'Just thinking about the case.' She raised her mug to take a drink, hoping to hide her treacherous mouth for a moment, a move which backfired when the tea scorched her tongue. 'What did you make of Pamela and Lorenzo?'

'Pamela seems to have replaced one overbearing man with another.'

Kate pushed her scalded tongue into her cheek. 'You think they did it together? He convinced her to help?'

'Yes. Nancy was upset about her father's death, but Pamela seemed completely wiped out by it. If she was involved in his murder, perhaps it had just been a theoretical thing to her in the run-up to it but then today the reality struck her hard. It would perhaps explain why she looked so stunned and exhausted. If you'd been building up to something so momentous for months, inevitably afterwards you'd be left feeling adrift, perhaps devastated.'

'Hmn.'

'You're not convinced?'

'I'm not unconvinced,' said Kate, 'and I do see them as our best suspects. But Pamela's behaviour is odd. I mean, imagine you'd planned to kill your father for your independence, but also—crucially—your inheritance. You go through with it, only to find there was nothing to inherit. You'd be shocked, frustrated and maybe angry, wouldn't you? And I didn't see any of that in her. At one point she seemed so droopy I wondered if she was medicated. Which led me to think: could there be a connection between her use of prescription medication and her father's death? The doctor told me he's been prescribing Pamela sleeping pills for months.'

Max jerked forwards, his tea sloshing dangerously close to the rim of the mug. 'Veronal! Barbiturate poisoning. Not morphine. Of course!'

'Agatha Christie bumped off a few characters using barbiturates, right?'

'Yes. In *Lord Edgware Dies* for one.'

That rang a bell. Wasn't that another one of the books that had come in her monthly subscription? She'd been receiving a classic mystery story every month for the past two and a half years, since Paul gave her the subscription as a surprise birthday and Christmas gift. While remembering all of the almost thirty titles she had got through the post was beyond Kate, she suspected *Lord Edgeware Dies* was one she had read last year.

'I think that's the story I remember,' she said. 'If Pamela had a handy supply of pills she could have crushed them and dissolved them in her father's food or drink. Although it would have made him sleep before it killed him. It's a bit of a risky one because it's difficult to know exactly how much it would take to kill him.'

'Yes. A point Christie makes in *Lord Edgware Dies* when the doctor calls Veronal "uncertain stuff".'

'Right.' Wow. Max either had an excellent memory or had read the book recently. Did he have the same book subscription box as her? 'Anyway, I'd be surprised if Pamela or Lorenzo had that kind of perfect dosage knowledge. The killer would have needed to hang around to make sure he was dead. Or ...' Kate fell silent, imagining Pamela and Lorenzo in the darkened study, listening to Adrian's breathing slow, waiting impatiently for it to stop. 'If they didn't have time to hang about checking his pulse, or wanted to make it look like the actions of a crazed burglar, they could stab him in the heart.'

Max nodded. 'It's neat and quiet. And, perhaps, the end for Adrian Grieve chosen by someone who wanted him out of the way, but didn't want him to suffer. A daughter who, though constrained by her dad, loved him and didn't harbour fiery resentment towards him. Unlike her older sister.'

'Hmn.'

'There it is again.'

'What?' Kate looked up from her tea.

Max's head was tilted, his lips curled in a lopsided smile. 'That's your unconvinced noise.'

'Ugh!' Kate let her head fall forwards over her mug.

'And that's either frustration or "oh no, I've been busted".'

Kate lifted her head and returned Max's smile. 'A bit of

both. That is, what you say makes perfect sense. It fits. But there are still so many loose threads.'

'Such as?'

'OK.' Kate put her mug on the tray to free her hands. 'Lorenzo's an animated person.' She waved her hands about, imitating a few of his more extravagant gestures. 'But did you see how still he went when I asked about the parties and the robberies?' She shook her head. 'His character is weirdly contradictory. On the one hand, he's a flamboyant bling-lover but then he claims to be camera shy?'

'It's not necessarily that odd,' said Max. 'He may like to show off, but maybe he knows he photographs terribly?'

'That's possible. But I want to go back to those newspapers and dig into the high society thefts. I bet Lorenzo just happened to be at all those parties.'

'Why would a wealthy Italian aristocrat be stealing jewels from the rich and famous?'

'Maybe he's not as rich as he's letting on?' said Kate. 'Or he wants the money for his charitable projects and stealing it is easier than getting socialites to hand it over. Also, as he seems to despise these people, he would hate having to beg them for their help and probably loves the thrill of getting one over on them.'

'Lorenzo Corsini, Italy's answer to Robin Hood?'

'I don't know, but there has to be a connection. And what's happening with this missing kid—what's his name?'

'Derek Jones.'

'Right. And then Adrian's yellow eyes. And—ugh!'

'There it is again. Definitely frustration this time.'

Kate laughed. 'It's complete information overload. And we've no actual evidence to prove anything. We can accuse anyone we like, but we should be able to back it up. I mean, just one example: this is an inside job, right? So where are the stolen jewels? Did the police search everyone's rooms? Something else we don't know.' She dropped her head into her hands.

The scratching of pen on paper told her Max was making another note. 'I'll follow that up when I'm chasing the insurance details and autopsy report. In the meantime, I think we've earned a break.' Kate looked up as Max whipped the napkin from the plate, scattering the mouth-wateringly sweet scent of toffee. 'And we should eat this cake because we have expert testimony that it can only make you stronger.'

Max rose, scooped up a slice of the sponge onto a napkin and passed it to Kate. 'Thank you,' she said and waited until Max had his own slice before taking a bite.

'Mmm.' Kate closed her eyes to better savour the fluffy buttery flavours as the cake melted on her tongue. 'Bella will be cross she missed this.'

Bella! Her and Ethan's trip to Compton Hall should be almost over. How would Ethan have reacted to the surprise? He'd been set on the idea of a Cotswolds wedding and Kate wasn't convinced he'd be delighted with Bella suggesting an alternative venue, even if it was a grand stately home.

The bitter taste of worry overwhelmed the rich flavour of her last mouthful of butterscotch cake. Bella's wedding. It had been a bright spot on the horizon. But now that Paul was going to be best man—

'Kate?' Max wiped his fingers on his napkin and set it on the tray. 'Speaking of Bella, I'm still thinking about that thing she said before.'

'What thing?' Kate hoped her expression was suitably clueless. She knew exactly what thing: when Bella had told them not to kill each other in her absence.

'I ... it's just ...' Max looked up, striking Kate with a stare so direct that she felt it in the centre of her chest, where her heart thudded in nervous anticipation. 'There's no delicate way to ask this,' he said, 'so I'm just going to come straight out with it. Do you hate me?'

Chapter 23

'No.' Kate's answer was immediate and, she realised as she spoke, the truth. Max might have irritated her at almost every Friendly Mystery Club party, frustrating her investigations and making her feel stupid and inferior in the process, but she had never hated him. Partly because she didn't believe he could help being the way he was. She doubted he could have gone against his competitive, contradictory, second-guessing nature if he'd tried. Also, she wasn't sure you could hate someone unless you knew them properly, and Max had always been something of a remote, fox-like—and yes, *foxy*—mystery. Which was probably why she kept circling back to him. She never could resist a puzzle.

As though her reply had defused a ticking bomb, Max let out a rush of breath and his shoulders fell away from his ears. But Kate couldn't share his relief. Her pulse boomed, the skin at the back of her neck prickled with heat and her fingers ached where she had balled them into tight fists.

'No, I don't hate you.' Kate swallowed, her mouth suddenly dry. She could leave it there, but she was unlikely to ever get a better opportunity to clear the air. 'But—' She paused, waiting for Max to look up. 'I know you hate me.'

Max continued to stare at her as his jaw dropped. 'You ...' He opened and closed his mouth a few times, stuttering. 'You think *I* hate *you?*'

Kate pressed her hand to her chest. Her heart felt heavy, although Max's surprise sent a timid shiver of hope down her spine. 'Maybe hate is a bit strong,' she said. 'But I can see you think I'm a bit daft and not really up to all this.' She glanced down at the pretty teacups on her dress. 'That my clothes are childish and not the sort of thing someone who wants to be taken seriously should wear. And I saw how you suffered through all my attempts at cracking the cases at our Friendly Club parties. Me jumping to conclusions and babbling through my ideas out loud. And I ... I don't make notes!' She flung her hand towards where Max's notebook perched on the corner of the desktop. 'I know you think that's bizarre. And winning is clearly important to you and you've been lumbered with me and I'll hold you back—'

'No.'

'And I'm not plain speaking enough and I'm too soft—'

'Kate. Stop.'

'And I know I must be irritating and frustrating to work with—' Kate couldn't stop. She had bottled up so much for so long that now the cork was out, she couldn't stem the flow. And at some point, her gaze had turned so misty that Max had become a blur.

'Kate!' Max strode around the desk and seized the arm

185

of Kate's chair, spinning it to bring them face to face. He sank to his knees so their eyes were on a level. '*Please*, Kate. Stop. Please stop.'

Blinking back tears, Kate gazed at Max's imploring stare. The thump of her heart against her ribs began to slow and the gentle brush of warm skin over the back of her fingers drew her focus down to her knee, where her hand lay in Max's. He squeezed it.

'I am truly sorry,' he said, 'if I have ever—' He grimaced, cutting himself off, apparently displeased with his words. 'I'm sorry I made you feel like that.'

A tear rolled down Kate's cheek and splashed against her skirt. As she lifted her free hand to wipe away another, Max grabbed a clean napkin from the desktop. 'Here,' he said and, as Kate dabbed at her eyes, he went on, 'I've never hated you for a second, Kate. I've never found you annoying. And, while I know less than nothing about fashion—for God's sake, I wear the same boring thing every day—I think your dresses are brilliant. They're pretty and different and fun. Like you. You like making an effort to find the right one for the right occasion because you're a thoughtful person. You'd have to be a complete killjoy not to find them delightful. And I'm sure your kids at school love them.'

The rubber soles of Kate's sneakers creaked as her toes curled. She had never been good at taking compliments. Even so, she mused as she wiped the corners of her eyes— taking the opportunity to peek at the cute dashes of pink blush on Max's cheeks—she wished she'd be able to remember everything he was saying later, when she didn't feel like she'd competed in a hundred metre final.

Apparently satisfied she was no longer having a nervous episode, Max released her hand, rose and perched on the corner of the desk. 'Bella's comments make sense now. Christ, you must have been dreading being left alone with me.' He sighed, his eyes darkening under a heavy frown. 'Those parties. Did I come across as a competitive jerk?'

Laughter burst out of Kate. As Max recoiled in surprise, she clapped a hand to her mouth but the giggles refused to be suppressed. Besides, the sensation of the tension in her chest finally releasing was so wonderful, she didn't want it to stop.

Max's stunned expression settled into a smirk of amusement. 'I take it that "competitive jerk" is an under-statement?'

Kate managed to nod while patting the napkin to the corners of her eyes, the laughter having brought on new tears.

Max groaned. 'Oh no. I can explain. Will you hear me out?'

Kate nodded again. If nothing else, letting Max talk would give her the chance to pull it together and be able to talk without crying or laughing.

'OK. I don't know if you remember the first two murder mystery parties? We were all unsure of what we were supposed to be doing and felt silly pretending to be other people. I was beyond nervous and so relieved I wasn't the murderer, I didn't take a lot else in. But I do remember you.' Max smiled and his gaze, which had drifted to the window, returned to find Kate's. 'Seeing you questioning people, getting their secrets out of them and putting all the pieces together … It was like having a ringside seat watching Poirot or something. Incredible. And, obviously, you figured out who the murderer was both times.'

Kate remembered those first parties. She'd been nervous too, but excited. Her suggestions to Paul that they might attend a murder mystery event had always been rejected. Apparently they were stupid, and he wouldn't be caught dead dressing up and pretending to be 'Lord So-and-so' or his butler. But Kate, who'd always loved mystery stories—from the moment her mum had introduced her to her own childhood copies of *Nancy Drew* and *The Three Investigators*—had found everything at those parties had made sense. She had felt at home in them and, though she hadn't been drinking, had been pleasantly light-headed throughout, as if she had got high off the experience itself.

Max paused, his smile fading. 'But by the third party, the others must have cottoned on to how good you were. Gillian hijacked what should have been your win. She took all your insights and ideas and presented them as her own. Then practically the same thing happened again at the next meeting'—Max's tone rose in disbelief—'but that time it was Peter. Peter! He couldn't work out how to punch his way out of a paper bag much less solve a locked room mystery. And when it happened the fifth and sixth times, I couldn't ...' He winced. 'It was painful watching them do that to you. And you didn't seem to mind or notice what they were up to even though you deserved to win. So I thought, if I tried to encourage you to be a bit more competitive, maybe you wouldn't be willing to let anyone else—'

'Whoa, whoa. Wait, wait ... wait.' Kate held up a hand, her mind whirling in an attempt to make sense of what she'd just heard. 'You're telling me that all the interruptions, the snarky comments, the constant contradicting. All the times you bested me. That was your own special way of *encouraging me to win?*'

Max open and closed his mouth, his face turning a deep pink of mortification. 'Yeah, well, when you put it like that, it does sound backwards.'

'Backwards, upside down and inside out, Max. Please keep explaining.'

'It made sense at the time. Something happened at those later parties. It was like you stopped wanting to come forward. I know that you had the same solution to those cases as me, and I'm certain that you had it first. I could never understand why you didn't speak up and call everyone together to unmask the killer.'

Oh crap. Kate dropped her face into her hands. Max hadn't made much sense at first, but now he had a point. In the first two games the players had to write their solutions down on cards and hand them to the organiser. But as the parties became more sophisticated, it was decided that the game could end as soon as anyone decided they had the solution and—a bit like shouting 'bingo!'—summoned the rest of the players to hear their theory. It was a nice way of adding more drama to the end of the evening and also a homage to the classic denouement of many a great detective mystery. And, unfortunately, it meant death to Kate's winning streak. Max was right—Kate had solved the mystery before all those who called the players together to listen to their ideas—but she'd hung back, her hands clammy and her heart racing, as others had glided into the spotlight. The thought of everyone staring at her while she spoke, judging her, maybe laughing at her—it had made her nauseous then, and even thinking about it now brought on a wave of queasiness.

'Max.' Kate threw the napkin onto the desk and sat forwards. 'At that third party. Didn't you know it was Gillian's birthday?'

'No. I don't remember it being a birthday party.'

'It wasn't, not really. You see, she was turning thirty and saw that as a catastrophe.' Kate shook her head. Personally, she'd never had a problem with ageing. It was far better than the alternative. 'She didn't want to celebrate and was particularly down that evening. She kept telling me about how her best years were behind her and it was all downhill from there.' Kate rolled her eyes. 'The point is, Gillian didn't hijack my solution to the game.'

'Oh.' Max's eyes widened as understanding dawned.

'And Peter. You're right, he wasn't a natural detective at all. But there'd been a restructuring at his company and he was being made redundant from a job he loved. He was miserable. And it didn't matter to me if I won, so—'

'You gave him a win. You gave them all wins. To cheer them up.' Max chuckled and scrubbed a hand over his mouth. 'That is so you, Kate. I should have figured it out.'

'No, if I'm honest …' Kate lifted her gaze to the ceiling. It would be wrong to give Max the impression that she was a selfless saint. And now they'd embarked on the task of clearing skeletons from closets, they might as well do a thorough job. 'Making them happy wasn't my only reason. I know this is going to sound silly but, I can't do public speaking. I don't know what happens to me. I know it's irrational, but even the thought of standing up in front of a group of people and them all looking at me. My brain goes blank and my mouth all tacky. I can't do it. So when they changed the way we had to announce who we thought the killer was, I started handing my solutions over to people who aren't wimps.'

Kate gripped the arms of the chair, bracing herself for Max's incredulity or disdain.

'But you must speak in front of people at school all the time?' said Max.

'Small people. Mostly. I don't know why, but I don't find them intimidating. Perhaps because I'm twice as tall as most of them and I can always see at least one of them picking their nose. But it's one of the reasons I haven't been too keen to climb the "career ladder" that Paul is always going on about. Head of year, deputy head. You end up speaking at school meetings and functions.'

'Kate, a fear of public speaking—'

'I know what you're going to say.' Kate threw up her hands. She'd heard what was coming many times before. Mostly from Paul. 'It's all in my head. There's nothing to be frightened of and I should get over it.'

'Hmn.' Max pressed his lips together and his eyes narrowed as if she'd just asked him a tricky question. 'I was going to say that it's very common. And there are people with loads of experience who have to do it all the time who still dread it. It makes sense. It's nerve-wracking. Anyone who didn't get at least slightly jittery before standing up to talk to a large group of silent, staring people would have to be a natural show-off at best and a narcissistic megalomaniac at worst, surely?'

Kate nodded, unable to think of anything to say. It was

the first time she'd spoken to anyone about her dread of public speaking and not been made to feel unhinged.

'Have you ever considered talking to someone about it?' asked Max.

'Isn't that what we're doing?'

'Yes, and I'm honoured.' He inclined his head in a playful bow. 'But I've been going to counselling for a while and it's helped me sort out loads of stuff. Some of which I didn't even know was an issue.' He bit his lower lip. 'Actually, while we're doing honesty ...'

Kate steeled herself again. What was she supposed to say if Max told her that having to put up with her at those parties sent him to therapy?

'Those parties. I wasn't in a good place. A lot of things at that time, well, they seemed unbearably unfair. I think that's partly why I got so wound up when I thought other people were stealing your ideas. And I was preoccupied and clearly wasn't thinking about how my behaviour must have appeared to you. Sorry. I struggle in group social situations most of the time, but back then I had some extra personal stuff going on, which I won't bore you with. Although'—he smiled, his gaze drifting upwards—'I also believe that's why I enjoyed those parties so much. They were a chance to be someone else for the evening. And watching you working through the puzzles ...' His gaze snapped back to Kate, sharp and keen once more. 'It's like watching a skilled musician play. You're brilliant at this stuff, Kate. And, I imagine I have a way to go to convince you of this, but I think we make a good team.'

The gold flecks in Max's eyes sparkled and his lips curled into a timid smile. As she held his gaze, a pleasant buzz swept through Kate. It was a light-headed feeling, similar to that she experienced on the first day of a new school year. The excitement of beginnings. Possibilities.

Max slowly reached out his right hand to take hers. Her fingers curled around his, settling comfortably against his palm.

A trickle of electricity ran up Kate's arm as she shifted her gaze from their joined hands to Max's face. 'Is this a truce?'

'I'll take that.' Max gave her hand a brief squeeze before releasing it. 'Although I was going to suggest we agree to become'—he paused to adopt the deep dramatic tone of a movie trailer voice-over—'partners in fighting crime.'

Kate laughed. 'You and me? A crime-fighting duo? Like—'

'Hey! Sherlock and Watson!'

Bella's voice made Kate jump up from the chair. Max leapt off the desk and whirled round to face the doorway as Bella cannonballed over the threshold, her expression grim and skin flushed.

'Bella?' What—' Kate's gaze travelled to the fingers of Bella's right hand which were clamped tightly around the heels of her stilettos. Lord alive. If she had removed her shoes to deliver her message more quickly, this must be a true emergency.

'Don't panic. No one's hurt.' Bella rested her hands on her thighs and drew in a deep breath. 'Kate, I have to warn you.'

'OK.' Her pulse accelerating, Kate rounded the desk to stand in front of her friend. 'What's going on?'

'I'm going to kill Ethan.' Bella groaned. 'I made him

bring me back here as soon as I got it out of him. I'm so sorry.'

Kate glanced at Max, but his wide eyes expressed a bewilderment equal to her own and he could only offer her a shrug.

'Bella!' Ethan marched into the study, his steady breathing suggesting that, unlike his fiancée, he hadn't deemed it necessary to sprint through the building to find them.

Unfortunately for Ethan, he had given Bella time to recover. She whirled towards him and jabbed a pointy shoe in the direction of his chest. 'Piss off! I am not speaking to you!'

'Come on, Bels. It's not a big deal. You're getting upset over nothing.'

Bella gasped. 'Don't you *dare* try that crap on me. You know it's not nothing or you wouldn't have been sneaky about it. You would have—'

'Guys! Guys!' Max stepped between the warring couple and, for a second, Kate's concern was trumped by how impressed she was at his bravery. Bella's stilettos were *sharp*. 'What is going on?'

Bella and Ethan left off glaring at each other, their gazes flicking to Max. They both opened their mouths, but the answer to his question came from elsewhere.

'Hello all!'

Kate stared dumbstruck at the man who had strolled into the study, his dark jeans and black T-shirt as casual as his entrance. She blinked at his familiar grey-blue eyes, thin lips and short tawny hair. Although the facial hair—groomed into a neat moustache and short beard—was new. Perhaps she was hallucinating? Please, God, let her be hallucinating. This could not be happening. Why on earth would her ex be here?

Paul grinned and rubbed his hands together. 'Right then. What have I missed?'

Chapter 24

The silence in the study was in marked contrast to the buzz of questions inside Kate's head. The shock of seeing Paul at all—let alone in such an unexpected context—left her frozen, staring at him for any signs he might be a mirage.

Out of the corner of her eye, she could see Bella breaking the death stare she was giving Ethan to dart guilty glances in her direction. Ethan was keeping his eyes fixed on his fiancée, perhaps fearing another outburst. Or a stiletto to the chest.

It was left to Max, once again, to step into the breach.

'Hello, I'm Max. You must be Paul,' he said, extending his hand.

'Nice to meet you, mate.' Paul gave Max's hand a vigorous, maybe overly vigorous, shake. He drew himself straighter and—tipping his chin up—appeared to be trying to look down his nose at Max, which must have been a challenge given Max was slightly taller than him. 'Ethan tells me you're almost as keen on this murder mystery stuff as Kate.' He turned towards Kate and flashed her a grin. 'Hi, Kate.'

Hi? *Hi?* Kate's nails dug into the palm of her hand, making her wince. She hadn't seen Paul in three months and now he deigned to rock up at her mystery weekend with a cheery 'Hi'?

'Hello,' Kate said, the word barely escaping from between her teeth. She turned away from Paul's stare and touched Bella's arm. 'Bella, could I have a quick word?'

'Absolutely.' Bella looped her arm through Kate's and raised her voice to announce to the room, 'We're popping outside for a second.' She levelled a glare at Ethan as they passed him and lowered her voice to growl, 'Amuse yourselves.'

The only light in the corridor other than that coming from the study was provided by a row of brass-coloured wall sconces, throwing weak orange light across the leaf designs on the burgundy wallpaper. The gloom went some way to calming Kate's racing heart. It was as if she and Bella had stepped into the safety of a cave, with the marauding men left outside, still in view but at a safe distance.

Confident they couldn't be overheard, Kate whispered, 'What the bloody hell is happening?'

Bella raked her hands through her hair. 'I know, I know. It's ruddy awful. After that call Ethan got from Paul this morning, he got another couple this afternoon but he was really evasive when I asked him who they were from. I got it out of him eventually. Bloody Paul, calling to say he was joining us here.'

An ache had developed behind Kate's left eye, a warning sign of an incoming stress headache. She closed her eyes. 'Why?'

'Apparently a couple of weeks ago Paul asked Ethan if he wanted to go for a drink this weekend and, obviously, Ethan said he couldn't. And that reminded Paul about us coming to Merryman's. You were both invited originally.'

'That was a year ago! He didn't want to come and was very explicit about it. You know he thinks murder mystery parties are ridiculous. Am I supposed to believe he's had a radical change of heart?'

'He told Ethan it'd be a laugh and a chance for him to spend time with his best mate and talk about best man and wedding stuff.'

Kate snorted. 'Do you believe that?'

'Of course not. But you know Ethan's soft when it comes to Paul and hearing that would have stroked his ego.'

Kate pressed her fingers to the dull pain spreading along her brow ridge and glanced into the study. Ethan was sitting in the swivel chair and, as she watched, he slumped forwards onto the desktop. Presumably he was catching Paul up on the facts of Adrian Grieve's death.

'Kate, I'm with you on this one.' Bella put a reassuring hand on Kate's shoulder. 'If Paul's here, it's to mess with you in some way and that is not happening. Anyway, there's still a chance we can get rid of him.'

'How?'

'We didn't book for him and the hotel is rammed. I'm hoping there's no room at the inn and he'll have no choice but to piss off back to Reading and whatshername.'

'Kirsty. She's called Kirsty.' Kate's temples throbbed as she was struck by a sharp mental image of the woman, with her perfectly curled thick blonde hair and precisely applied chocolate lip gloss. A daily sight, in head-to-toe figure-hugging black, perched behind the school reception glass, stabbing at the computer keyboard with her perfect set of freshly manicured nails. A woman to turn any man's head. Although, knowing Paul as she did, Kate suspected that Kirsty might be part of the reason Paul had suddenly decided to turn up at a weekend gathering he'd said he'd rather die than attend.

'Are you two ever coming back?' called Ethan.

'We'd better go in.' Bella stooped to slide her foot back into one of her shoes. 'But if you want me to'—she swung at the air with her other stiletto, and Kate could imagine her cheerfully repeating the action next to Paul's head—'just say the word.'

'Hopefully that won't be necessary.'

Bella put her choice of weapon back on her foot and wrapped a hand around Kate's arm. As they made their way back into the room she muttered, 'Speaking of annoying men, have you been all right? With Max?'

A warm flutter stirred in Kate's belly. She avoided Bella's gaze as she replied, 'It's been fine.'

'I knew it would be. Solved the case yet?'

'Getting there,' said Kate. 'I'll catch you up on everything later.'

They came to a stop in the middle of the floor rug, Bella's heels sinking into the pile. Ethan rose from the swivel chair. 'Max has been getting us up to speed,' he said, rounding the desk to stand beside Paul. He nodded towards Max, then Kate. 'It sounds like you two have been busy this afternoon.'

Kate opened her mouth to speak, but Paul jumped in. 'It also sounds like a complicated case.' He smiled and slapped Ethan on the back. 'I'm sure you'll be pleased to have an extra team member.'

Staring at Paul's beaming smile of self-congratulation, Kate remembered him moaning about her 'wasting time at stupid parties' whenever she was getting ready to go out to a Friendly Murder Club event and said, 'I'm certainly *surprised* to have an extra team member.'

'How could I miss this? Ethan made it sound great fun. And speaking of which …' Paul waved towards Kate's skirt. 'That outfit! I should have known you'd have dug out one of your jolly frocks for the occasion.'

Her eyes blazing with violent intentions, Bella took a step forwards and Kate shot out an arm to hold her back. She appreciated Bella's support, but she wanted to hold her own ground. Paul was not going to put her on the back foot. After all, he was the interloper here.

She gave Paul a tight smile, ignoring the ache which had migrated to the back of her head, and said, 'You didn't bring Kirsty with you?'

Paul's grin finally slipped. 'No. She had some family commitments she couldn't get out of.'

At the corner of Paul's left eye, Kate spotted a telltale twitch. She had sadly come to notice the tic too late when she was living him. But she sure as heck recognised it now. He was lying.

Her lurch towards physical violence stymied, Bella channelled her anger into a tone that was pure venom. 'Ethan? What did reception say when you asked them about available rooms?'

'Oh yeah.' Ethan turned to Paul. 'I'm sorry, mate. They're booked solid. But there's got to be another place nearby. We can—'

Paul cut across his friend with a chuckle. 'Not a problem. We're all friends here.' He glanced around at them all, his eyes shifting nervously, as if expecting someone to contradict him. 'I'm sure you'll find a way to make a little space for me in one of your rooms. I don't take up that much space.' He beamed at his own quip and turned to Kate. 'I seem to remember, back when Bella was sorting out the booking, that there was only a twin room available for you, Kate.'

Kate stammered as her pulse raced, her blood burning its way through her veins. Was he seriously suggesting—

'Are you serious?' Bella said, her voice rising to a squeak. 'Paul. Expecting Kate to have you in her room is unreasonable, inappropriate and, frankly, borderline insane.'

Bella's bark bounced off Paul who shrugged. 'I don't agree. It's a twin room. We could almost use it without seeing each other. And we'll be able to share the space amicably, we did live together for four years.'

Kate bit her tongue to stop herself reminding him whose fault it was they no longer lived together. That wasn't the pressing issue. 'I don't have twin beds in my room,' she said. 'Only one double.'

Displaying a thicker hide than the average rhinoceros, Paul shrugged again. 'Well, I still don't see why that has to be an issue.'

What? Kate was stumped. Apart from repeatedly screaming '*No*' followed by various profanities or letting Bella pummel him with her shoes, Kate's stunned brain failed to come up with any ideas for how to penetrate Paul's astounding lack of sympathetic imagination. Did he really not understand why Kate might not want to share a room *and a bed* with him? Or was he being deliberately obtuse?

Apparently Paul's obliviousness was shared by his best friend. 'Come on, Kate,' said Ethan. 'It's only the one night after all.'

Bella, whose pale complexion had steadily been turning lobster red, drew in a deep breath, apparently preparing to externalise the screaming that was happening inside Kate's head. However, instead of a banshee-like wail, the silence was broken by Max.

'I have twin beds,' he said in a calm, firm tone. 'He can have one of them.'

Kate turned to Max and hoped her expression conveyed relief, rather than what she was picturing: throwing her arms around his neck and clinging to him in a huge hug of gratitude.

Paul gave Max an insincere smile. 'That's good of you, mate. But I wouldn't want to put you out.'

'It's no trouble at all, *mate*. As you said yourself, with a twin room we can use it almost without seeing each other.'

Bella beamed, her smile unrestrainedly smug as she took in Paul's crestfallen expression. 'Fantastic! Thank you, Max.'

'Yes. *Thank you*, Max,' said Kate.

Max acknowledged her thanks with a half smile. 'No problem.'

'Now that's sorted'—Bella seized her fiancé's hand—'I'd like a word with you, Mr Lees.' She had managed to lead him as far as the doorway when she paused and looked over her shoulder. 'Kate?'

'Hmn?'

Bella gave her a wide-eyed stare and mouthed, '*You OK?*'

No, of course I'm not. My ex, who despises murder mysteries, has turned up and is staying. Max Ravenscroft— of all people—has turned out to be a white knight. And you're leaving me alone. Again.

But rather than share her turbulent internal monologue, Kate glanced at Ethan—whose slightly panicked expression stirred far less sympathy in Kate than it had previously— before locking eyes with Bella. 'Sure. I'll see you later. For cocktails?'

'Wouldn't miss it!' Bella called as she and Ethan vanished into the murky corridor.

Without glancing at Paul, Max took a cautious step towards Kate. At some point in all the mess of the past five minutes he'd retrieved his notebook. He tapped it and said, 'I'll ask about the insurance, autopsy and room searches. Will you be OK getting back to the newspapers?'

The case! Max was right, she couldn't let Paul's arrival distract her. 'No problem.'

'Great.' Max flashed her a smile, turned and strolled towards the doorway, stopping next to Paul. 'Shall we go to reception and get you a key to my room, Paul?'

Paul had been observing Max and Kate, his blue eyes narrowed to keen slits. 'That's a terrific idea.' He slapped Max on the back and ambled deeper into the room, closer to Kate. 'I'll wait here with Kate while you do that. We can catch up.'

Without waiting to register Max's response, Paul spun to face Kate, blocking Max from her line of sight. He smirked at Kate and circled his index finger to gesture to their opulent surroundings. 'I bet you're loving all this, aren't you? Playing Watson for the weekend.'

The sound of pointed throat-clearing behind him made Paul whirl away from Kate. Until that moment, Kate hadn't thought it possible for a fake cough to sound menacing, but somehow Max had managed it.

Fixing Paul with a steely stare, Max said, 'Kate is Sherlock Holmes, not Watson. Here'—he held out a plastic card to Paul—'take my key. I'll get another one later. You must want to unpack. I'll show you to the room now.' He placed a hand in the centre of Paul's back and walked him to the door. 'See you later, Kate.'

As the men entered the corridor, Max turned his head to look at Kate for a second. Before he disappeared from view he smiled, a brief and subtle curl of his lips, and she could have sworn he winked.

Chapter 25

The painkillers had yet to take effect. Kate opened her eyes and stared up at the bedroom ceiling, its white plaster finish as smooth and cool as a fresh settling of snow. Under her head the pillow smelled faintly of lavender and, as she ran her fingers over the creamy cotton sheets, they whispered gently.

It was four o'clock. Cocktails were at six thirty. That gave her time. Time to rest, pray the paracetamol took effect, head down to the library, make her lists—and hopefully a breakthrough in the case—before having to come back to her room to get ready for dinner.

She closed her eyes and stretched her arms wide, but even so her fingers failed to reach the edges of the enormous king-sized bed. It felt strange, so different to her narrow bed in the tiny flat she had rushed to move into after Christmas. Paul had given her little choice. Apparently Kirsty was keen to move in with him. As their home—a small terraced house Kate had spent hours decorating, doing her best to make it comfortable, to reduce the longing she had for the tiny flat she had left back in the Midlands—technically belonged solely to Paul, it meant Kate had to go.

Enough! Kate screwed her eyes tighter shut. Dwelling on anything Paul-related was not going to get shot of her headache. She had to shelve it.

In one of his latest screen incarnations, Sherlock Holmes had a memory palace, a place in his imagination that he visited where he could store anything he wanted to remember. Kate's version wasn't nearly as grand and existed to help her temporarily forget things. It resembled a walk-in wardrobe, the type of impressive closet Kate had only ever seen in Hollywood movies. It was a bright space with gilt-framed mirrors around the edges and a round bench seat in its centre. All its shelves held neat cuboid storage boxes of different colours and sizes.

Releasing a slow breath, Kate pictured folding Paul, like one of his many precious T-shirts, into a crisp square and dropping him into a black box. The lid closed with a satisfying click and she glanced about, looking for a space to store it. Drat! She had hoped this part would be easy, but the shelves were already full. The handwritten label on the front of the largest box proclaimed itself to contain *Hedgehogs*. Rather than reflect Kate's concern for the welfare of one of the country's most endangered species— although she would probably have to create another box for that at a later date—the bright yellow box contained all her worries about the children in her current class.

Kate whirled away from the yellow box, her gaze grazing the *Dad* label on the medium-sized sky-blue box to its left. She quickened her pace: she had to get away from this part of the wardrobe or she risked her headache morphing into a migraine.

The back of the closet was darker, but—thank goodness! —there was a recently vacated space large enough for the new Paul box. Its previous occupant—a bright green box with a subtle gold sparkle—lay on its side on the floor, its contents scattered across the pale teal carpet. The jumble of items included a whistle, football boots, teacups, a notebook and the sheet music for 'Clair de lune'. Kate knelt and picked up the two nearest objects: a cuddly toy fox and a large deerstalker hat.

Kate was smiling when she opened her eyes, her headache having receded to a small spot behind her left ear. Max didn't hate her. Max thought she was a good detective—a Sherlock!—and wanted to be her partner in amateur sleuthing.

Sleuthing that she needed to get back to.

Kate pushed off the bed, ran a hand over her hair and dug through the Merryman's welcome pack to retrieve the complimentary pen and A5 writing pad. Right. Now to get down to the library before those newspapers were cleared away or snaffled by a rival team.

Reaching for the door handle, she caught a glimpse of herself in the full-length mirror on the back of the door and her smile stretched into a grin. The jaunty pattern of pens, notebooks, cups and teapots on her dress lifted her spirits further. She twirled, enjoying the swish of the material, the way the skirt flared and gathered around her knees. Whatever Paul might say, she loved her dresses. She thought they were pretty. And—she remembered, giving her reflection a final once-over—Max agreed with her.

She yanked the door open and let out a squeal of surprise.

Facing her was Max, his fist raised to knock. 'Sorry,' he said, taking a step back. 'I didn't mean to scare you.'

'That's OK. Spooky timing, that's all.' Kate's gaze fell on the notebook clasped in his left hand. 'Were you going downstairs?'

'Yes. I saw Dorothy Williams in the lobby and asked her if she could get us the information we need. She said to give her an hour. And, um'—he glanced down the corridor in the direction of his own room—'I left our surprise guest unpacking.' He eyed Kate warily as he dropped his voice to a whisper. 'For someone staying one night, he's packed an incredibly generous number of plain black T-shirts.'

Kate barked a laugh and the tightness round Max's eyes relaxed. 'Sounds about right. Paul does love monochrome.' As long as she had known him, Paul had favoured dark blocks of colour. And when not at work he usually opted for short sleeved T-shirts which showcased the muscles he worked so hard to cultivate through various adrenalin sports and hours at the gym. 'I expect he also has at least one full set of exercise kit with him?'

Max's eyebrows shot up. 'Actually, yes he does. He asked me for my opinion of the equipment in the hotel gym and was surprised when I had to admit I hadn't been there, but at least I could tell him where to find it.'

Kate's smile twisted into a wince. Max was treating it like a joke, but Paul's behaviour was embarrassing. 'I'm so sorry you have to share your room,' she said. 'I really appreciate it. Thank you.'

'You're welcome.'

'I hope Paul's been overwhelming you with his gratitude as well.'

'Not exactly,' said Max. He dropped his gaze to the floor and muttered, 'But it doesn't matter. I didn't do it for him.'

'Oh. Right.' Goosebumps rose along Kate's arms. Flustered, she shuffled out into the corridor and missed the handle on her first attempt to close the door. 'Well, thank you again.'

Max smiled, a warm glow in his eyes. 'Not a problem. It's just for tonight after all.'

Kate returned Max's smile as she succeeded in shutting the door to her room and, out of the corner of her eye, noticed Max's gaze roaming over her dress.

He said my dresses were pretty, her inner voice reminded her, a clear note of glee colouring the comment.

Max's gaze snapped up to meet Kate's. His stare was a little too deliberate, as if he wanted her to know he absolutely hadn't been looking at any part of her body other than her face. 'Uh, I … the library, then?'

'Sounds good,' said Kate and followed Max down the narrow passageway. Hanging back a step gave her a better view of the faint pink blush rising from under his shirt collar. She blinked and her pace slackened as a notion formed: was it possible that it wasn't only her dresses that Max thought were pretty?

The idea brought a touch of heat to her own cheeks even as she dismissed it as nonsense. Immersion in a make-believe scenario was obviously starting to get to her. If she wasn't careful, her imagination would be carrying her off into a labyrinth of unlikely, dead-end fantasies.

But, as she and Max strolled side by side down the wide staircase, her gaze once again strayed to his neck and down to the hollow at the base of his throat—

Ugh! Kate trained her gaze on her feet, crossed her arms and gave the inside of her arm a sobering pinch. Some Sherlock she was proving to be. A good detective kept their mind on the job, stuck to the facts and did not ogle their crime-fighting partner. How difficult could that be?

Chapter 26

Though the late afternoon sun filled the library with light, Kate and Max chose to hunker down in the shadows cast by the pair of tall wingback armchairs facing the fireplace.

Confident they would remain unseen by casual observers passing the entrance to the room, they immersed themselves in the case, ignoring the distant sounds of clinking crockery and chatter coming from the dining room, where several of their fellow guests were enjoying the final finger buns and dainty sandwiches of the afternoon tea service.

Kate was making progress through the newspapers, which had thankfully been where she had left them: in the wooden magazine rack beside the hearth. She had tucked her feet up into the chair next to her and, her notepad balanced on her ankles, was jotting down the dates and locations of the 1932 jewel thefts and the names of notable attendees at any events at those venues around the time of the robberies. Meanwhile, Max was killing the time until he could return to Dorothy Williams by revising his notes.

Reclining in the seat, his feet stretched towards the grate, he scanned his notebook from under a furrowed brow. Occasionally he would absent-mindedly run a hand across his mouth, a gesture which drew Kate's attention to his lips and derailed her attempts at approaching her task with a methodical, focused mindset.

Another newspaper scanned from cover to cover, Kate made an addition to one of her lists and looked up at Max, expecting to find him engrossed in his notes, his brow creased in deep concentration. Instead a flicker of the whites of his eyes suggested she had caught him peeking at her. She smiled, her pulse picking up a notch at this small sign that he found her at least partly as interesting as she found him. It also meant she could talk to him without fearing she was interrupting some fragile thought process.

'What exactly did Dorothy say when you spoke to her?' Kate asked.

'That she'd do her best to get us the information we needed. My impression was that she's keen to help us. I don't think anyone else has asked her for anything. But the rules of the game clearly state that contestants can ask for any additional information pertinent to the case.'

'Do you ...' Kate paused, remembering the significant stare Dorothy had given her when introducing her to Dr Chase. 'Do you think she wants us to win?'

'She wants the game to be fair. If she suspects Roger Merryman has been underhand in tipping the scales in his favour, she would want to right the balance. She strikes me as the sort of person who doesn't look kindly on shenanigans.'

Kate giggled.

Max raised an eyebrow. 'What?'

'I don't know. Ignore me.' She giggled again. 'I'm sorry, it's been a weird day and I've always found *shenanigans* ...'

'Funny?' Max smiled, his gaze softening with amusement as he watched Kate struggle to calm her laughter. 'It's a good one, I'll give you that. Almost as good as tomfoolery.'

'True. But skulduggery beats them all.'

Max huffed a short laugh. 'I don't know. It's a bit ... piratey?'

'It's totally piratey! You should see the kids in my class on Talk Like a Pirate Day—'

'That is *not* a thing.'

'I'll have you know it is. It's brilliant.'

'When is it?'

'Middle of September.'

Max chuckled, his eyes gleaming with mischief. 'In Universe Kate?'

'I have not made this up! Google it!'

'Please tell me you have a pirate dress.'

'Dress? I'll have you know I have a full costume. With a cutlass and—'

The floorboards behind them creaked. Kate and Max widened their eyes at each other and twisted to peer around the wings of their chairs.

The tinted light from the stained-glass windows bathed Paul in an eerie red glow. He came to a halt in the middle of the floor rug and was glaring at them with the disapproving expression Kate had seen him roll out on kids he'd caught with their shirts slightly untucked. His tone of voice was equally cool. 'I see you two are hard at work.'

Max sank back in his chair so Paul couldn't see him. He

213

waited until Kate met his gaze to lightly smack the back of his hand and mouth, *'Naughty.'* Kate snorted but, catching Paul's stern glare, turned her laughter into a cough.

'I'm going to see if Dorothy's back,' Max said, the worn leather of the chair creaking as he stood.

'Oh? Already? Maybe it's a bit early? Or, um, maybe ...' Kate's honest reaction would have been to shout, *'Please don't leave me with Paul!'* but instead she stammered, her desire not to come across as pathetic warring with her need to escape an awkward conversation with her ex.

Max placed a hand on the back of her chair and gazed down at her. He lifted his eyebrows and gave her a steady look which Kate guessed meant, *You'll have to talk to him eventually, Kate. Best get it over with.* Aloud, he said, 'I'll be back soon. OK?'

'OK,' said Kate, narrowing her eyes slightly in a way she hoped Max would read as *'You'd better be.'*

The men exchanged sharp nods of acknowledgement as Max strolled across the rug. Loath to give Paul the upper hand—he'd already sneaked up on them after all— Kate scrambled to her feet and approached him, hoping to dissuade him from taking Max's seat and getting comfortable.

'So, Kate.' Paul ran a hand over the carefully curated piece of topiary passing for his facial hair. His grave tone made Kate feel as though she had been summoned to the headmaster's office for a serious chat about her future. 'I've been wanting to talk to you ever since—'

'Yes, me too.' It was best to get in quickly with Paul, before he took charge of the conversation

'Really?'

'Yes. About the book subscription.'

Paul blinked rapidly, his eyes wandering side to side, searching for her meaning. 'The book? Oh! The monthly thing. The mystery book thing I got you for Christmas—'

'My birthday.'

'That's what I meant. They're so close together and it's been, what? A year—'

'Nealy two and a half years.'

'Right! Since I signed you up. Sorry, I was slow on the uptake there.'

'OK.' Kate stared at Paul as he chuckled nervously. 'I want to take it over. It's daft that you're still having to put it through my letterbox now we don't live together—'

'Your place is on my way home. It's no bother.'

'That's nice of you, but I'd rather sort it out. So if you let me know who I need to contact—'

'No need for that. It's a gift.' He dismissed her concerns with a slack-handed wave. 'Besides, you don't have time for all that, do you? Ethan told me you had an interview at a school near your parents' house. How did it go?'

The mantlepiece clock ticked into the silence between them as Kate made a mental note to remind Bella not to repeat everything she told her to Ethan. For the first time, she was pleased she hadn't yet told her best friend about her dad's diagnosis.

Avoiding Paul's eyes to make lying easier, Kate said, 'I haven't heard back yet. But it went well.'

'Would you take the job, if they offered it to you?'

Examining Paul's open stare and parted lips, the signs he was hanging on her every word, Kate had to ask the obvious question, 'Why do you care?'

A grunt came as the initial reply, accompanied by a pinching of his brow, as if her sharp question had wounded him. 'It sounds like a great opportunity for you. But—'

The inevitable *but*. Kate crossed her arms, bracing for impact.

'Ethan said you could become head of year soon. Could you cope with that? It would likely involve speaking to groups of parents, doing presentations. And we know you struggle there. And your wardrobe would have to be a bit more ... professional. Are you sure you're prepared?'

A hard lump had formed in Kate's throat. Hating the wobble in her voice, she said, 'I'll be fine.'

'I just'—Paul stepped closer to her and she wrapped her arms more tightly around herself, refusing to retreat—'I'd hate to think of you taking a job you didn't really want, uprooting and moving away, because ... well, because of me.'

Of all the things Paul lacked, nerve and self-belief weren't among them. 'I moved down to Reading because of *you*,' she said. 'If I move nearer home, it'll be for *me*.'

Her combined glare and tone must have been murderous enough for even Paul to take the hint. Apparently deciding it would be wise to move on, Paul ambled over to the window. He stared out into the gardens for a moment then turned back to Kate. 'The gym facilities here are excellent. But Bella tells me you haven't even been to the spa,' he said, his gaze wandering around the room, inspecting the period features and rows of books lining the walls. 'Aren't you taking this too seriously? It's supposed to be a fun weekend.'

'It's a murder mystery weekend. I don't think you can

take the mystery too—' Kate stopped herself. *Don't make the mistake of debating him. Get to the point.* She fixed him with her most penetrating teacher glare. 'Why are you here, Paul?'

'Who wouldn't want to be here?' He swung his arms out to take in his opulent surroundings. 'Work's been hectic lately and I thought I could do with getting away. Taking a break from all the little treasures. A few of us were supposed to be going caving in Wales this weekend, but it got cancelled at the last minute when a couple of the guys got sick. And Ethan's been talking about this Merryman's thing almost non-stop, I was at a loose end and I was invited originally—as I'm sure you remember— so I called Ethan and he said it'd be fine if I dropped in. And it'll be great to spend some time with him and Bella and … you.'

The last word was delivered with a tremor. And something else. Was that *desperation?*

'I see.' A dull ache had reappeared behind Kate's left ear. Sometimes having your suspicions confirmed was painful rather than satisfying. 'Kirsty dumped you.'

'She didn't, it wasn't …'

Kate waited as Paul stammered. She would not come to his aid. He had all but thrown her out of her home at Christmas. Let him squirm.

Paul paused and drew in a deep breath. 'Kirsty and I agreed that it wasn't working out between us,' he said, only meeting her gaze as he finished the sentence.

'All right. But, given how you think murder mystery parties are ludicrous, I still don't understand why you would come here—'

'I'm making an effort!' Paul's lips parted as if his own words had shocked him. Lowering his gaze to the floor, he softened his tone. 'You enjoy all this detective stuff and, in the past, I know I wasn't very supportive of you going to those parties in Birmingham. But this is something you like and it's important to you. So I wanted to try it.'

'But why would—'

'I made a terrible mistake, Kate.' Paul grimaced, as if his previous behaviour revolted him. 'I've been a complete idiot. My head was turned and I hurt you and I'm sorry.'

Slack-jawed, Kate stared at the tears glistening in Paul's grey-blue eyes. As she listened to him, her limbs had grown heavy and throat dry, so she put up no resistance when Paul closed the space between them and seized her hand. 'I'll do anything, anything to make it up to you. Please. We were good together, weren't we?'

'I … I don't—'

'Just give me another chance.' Paul gazed into her eyes and squeezed her fingers. 'Promise me you'll think about it?'

Chapter 27

They must have formed a striking tableau. The pair of them in the middle of the library, frozen in the rainbow light from the stained-glass windows. Paul stooping, staring at Kate and clasping her hand as if begging her to spare his life. Kate, open-mouthed, blinking at Paul in incomprehension and disbelief.

Thank goodness they were alone. The moment was awkward enough without anyone else—

The sound of rapid footsteps in the corridor grew louder. *Typical*.

Kate dragged her gaze from Paul's pleading stare and levelled it on the doorway just as Max bounded into the library. His eyes were shining with excitement. 'Kate! You'll never guess—'

His smile vanished and his features appeared to petrify as he took in the scene in front of him.

'Max!' Kate pulled her hand from Paul's grip and scurried towards Max, leaving Paul behind her. The skin at the back of her neck prickled with discomfort and she smiled widely, hoping to disguise her embarrassment. 'How did you get on with Dorothy?'

'Er ...' Max glanced at Paul, who followed Kate across the room and came to a halt next to her. A vein throbbed in Paul's temple and the set of his jaw was rigid. Max's gaze returned to Kate. 'Should I come back later?'

'No, no,' said Paul, beating Kate to it. 'I wanted to read through the information pack before cocktails later. Get up to speed on the case so I can make more of a contribution to the team.' His lips curled, but his eyes remained cold. 'Perhaps we could chat later, Kate?'

Aching to be free of the awkwardness of the situation, Kate nodded. Although she couldn't imagine what else he could want to say to her. What could possibly top, *'I've split from the woman I dumped you for, realised I stuffed up big time and now want you back'*?

'Wonderful!' Paul beamed, the light returning to his eyes. 'Looking forward to it.'

He hummed as he strolled out of the room, the jaunty tune at odds with the harsh cacophony of notes ringing in Kate's ears. Lord alive, how was she going to explain what had happened to Max? And Bella! She would spontaneously combust!

'Kate?' Max spoke gently and held his hand lightly to her elbow. 'Would you like to sit down?'

Her legs unsteady, Kate allowed herself to be led to the armchairs by the fireplace. The leather seat let out a groan of despair as she sank into it, or she might have made the noise, she couldn't be sure.

'Are you OK?' Max pushed the other armchair closer

to hers and perched on the edge of its seat, leaving his knees almost grazing hers.

'Give me a minute.' Dizziness forced Kate to take the precaution—no matter how mortifying—of dropping her forehead to her knees. Looking daft in front of Max was better than vomiting or passing out. 'I'm honestly not pathetic all the time,' she muttered into her skirt.

'You're not being pathetic if you're about to faint,' said Max. 'Besides, I'm guessing these are exceptional circumstances.'

'You can say that again.' A few deep breaths and Kate could once again hear birdsong and the wind in the trees outside. It was probably safe to lift her head. Slowly.

'Don't rush it,' said Max, a deep crease of concern at the bridge of his nose.

'I'll be fine. I'm sorry, that must have been weird for you to come back and find us—'

'You don't have to explain—'

'I can't imagine what it looked like.'

'It—' Max paused, his forehead furrowing to complement the crease between his brows. 'It looked like he was asking you to marry him.'

'What?' Kate cringed and covered her face with her hands. 'No. That's not what was happening.'

Max's expression relaxed. From between her fingers, she watched as he reached out to peel one of her hands away from her eyes. 'Would you like to talk about something else?'

Gratitude flooded her and she hoped the small squeeze she gave Max's fingers conveyed some of it to him. 'Yes, please. What did Dorothy say?'

'If you're sure—'

'I'm fine. Look! Sitting upright without incident.' She rested her head against the right wing of the chair and met Max's worried stare. 'Sherlock Holmes eat your heart out. Just need to take up the violin. Buy a pipe. And if things get any weirder, perhaps some opium.'

Max laughed. 'As Dr Watson to your Holmes, I would advise against the hard drugs. I'm happy to look into a violin for you but, in the meantime, I have good news and bad news. Which do you want first?'

'Always bad news first.'

'No autopsy report yet. The police did a thorough search of all the suspects' rooms and cars for the jewels or any other incriminating evidence and found nothing. They also searched the grounds and found no recently dug holes or sacks stashed in the middle of bushes or up a tree. I asked whether anyone sent any parcels to the post today—'

'Brilliant! I hadn't thought of that.'

'But unfortunately they didn't.'

'Shame,' said Kate. 'OK, well overall that's not so bad. It's more or less what we expected. What's the good news?'

'Adrian Grieve's life-insurance policy was updated ten months ago to double the amount that would be paid upon his demise.'

Kate sat forwards and her knees brushed against Max's. A fizzing sensation shot from the point of contact up to her head, bringing her thoughts into focus. 'That is interesting.'

'It gets better. Three months ago a clerk at the insurance company says he received a phone call from the office of

Adrian Grieve to check that everything was in order with the policy: that the premiums had been paid satisfactorily and the beneficiaries were listed as Adrian Grieve's daughters.'

The triumphant gleam in Max's eyes was greater than his news warranted. He was holding something back. 'So someone in Adrian Grieve's staff called to check a payout would be all but guaranteed on Adrian's death.'

'Yes. *Someone*.' Max raised an eyebrow.

'Oh,' said Kate, the penny dropping. 'The *office* of Adrian Grieve.'

'Indeed. And Archie said—'

'She was a sort of secretary to the old man.'

'Exactly.' Max beamed. 'The phone call was made by Pamela Grieve. I think we can safely list her as our number one suspect.'

Chapter 28

The conservatory was the ideal location for early evening cocktails. Its glass walls and roof provided spectacular views of the well-maintained gardens while allowing the last hours of the day's orange light to contribute to a warm and intimate atmosphere indoors. Palm plants in large terracotta pots and white wicker furniture absorbed harsher sounds while jazz standards played quietly from hidden speakers, the recording including the odd scratch and skip, successfully recreating the sound of a gramophone.

Tucked in the corner opposite the entrance and surrounded by a bower of climbing jasmine, Kate breathed in the light fragrance of the plant's star-shaped white blooms and scanned the crowd. It was the largest group of people she had seen since the welcome meeting the previous afternoon. Dressed in a mixture of period costume and contemporary clothing, they snatched at the cocktails being ferried serenely around the room by polite waiters before rapidly returning for seconds and thirds.

They might have signed up for a murder mystery weekend, but their rival teams seemed to have far greater enthusiasm for alcohol than amateur sleuthing. Their thirst was apparently rivalled only by their need for beauty therapy; Bella reported that the hotel's spa had been packed during her earlier visit. Clearly Roger's lunchtime distribution of treatment vouchers had been a popular offer.

'Here you go!' Bella shuffled between two groups of revellers, her hands raised above her head to protect the long-stemmed cocktail glasses in her grip. She passed one of them to Kate. 'I don't know why you insist on standing all the way over here. The waiters will never come near us.'

'You asked for an update on the case and I don't want to tell you our theories with that lot listening in.' Kate stared down at the orange drink in her hand. 'What's this?'

'This,' said Bella, pointing at her own drink, 'is a Maiden's Prayer, containing gin, Cointreau, orange and lemon juice.' She took a sip. 'Mm, lovely. That,' she said, jabbing a finger at Kate's glass, 'is the same without alcohol, so basically straight-up orange juice.'

'Thank you.'

'You're welcome.' Bella raised her glass to her lips. The black feathers protruding from the side of her headband stirred as she turned her head to survey the room.

'Where's Ethan?'

'I left him getting ready. Honestly, I don't know what takes him so long. He gets to wear a tux again. We have to come up with something different.'

Something different in Bella's case was a knee-length, full-sleeve silver gown. The material was silky and fluid, and gave Bella the appearance of being covered in liquid mercury. With black heels, feathered headband and her long blonde hair, the overall effect was striking.

'You look great,' said Kate.

'As do you. I love this slinky little number. And the gloves are fantastic. Why haven't I seen you in it before?'

Because, Kate thought, tugging at the ends of the black satin gloves which came up to her elbows, she'd never felt entirely comfortable in it. The fabric was stretchy and forgiving and the straps were wide enough that she could wear her best push-up bra. But she had forgotten how low the neckline plunged. Was she showing more cleavage than was decent?

'You don't think it's a bit ...' Kate adjusted the right strap. Was it was too late to run upstairs and find a wrap or cardigan? Or maybe she could unclip her hair? That would cover her shoulders at least.

'What?'

'Booby?'

Bella guffawed, causing the group of guests nearest to them to startle and shoot them accusatory glances. Unaware or indifferent to the daggers stares being fired her way, Bella said, 'You look gorgeous and your boobs are terrific. Stop worrying.'

An echo of Bella's raucous laughter erupted on the other side of the conservatory, where Archie Forbes was holding court. From across the room it was impossible to tell if the guests surrounding him were laughing with him or at him.

'So you've definitely ruled him out?' asked Bella, staring at Archie as he waved his arm in a wide circle, narrowly missing losing his cocktail to a large palm frond.

'Yes. No motive and not suited to this style of deliberate killing. Or any style, I suspect.'

Bella took another gulp of her drink. 'From what you've told me, it sounds like we're in a Columbo situation.'

A beige raincoat came immediately to Kate's mind. *That* would be a handy way to cover her cleavage. 'What do you mean?'

'Lieutenant Columbo!' Bella rolled her eyes. 'Peter Falk?'

'Of course *I* know who he is,' said Kate. 'How do *you* know who he is?'

'My dad loved that show. Anytime there was a repeat on a weekend he'd be watching. It was that or those shows where people sell up and move somewhere sunny. Which probably explains why he retired to Spain. Anyway, Columbo always knew who the murderer was almost from the start. Then he figured out how they did it. That's where you and Max have got to, right?'

'More or less.' Kate took a sip of her drink and winced at its sharpness. 'But unfortunately I doubt we're going to be able to irritate our suspects until they confess.'

'You might have a point there. I can't see the whole "Just one more thing" and "Mrs Columbo would love your autograph" routine working on that one,' said Bella, tipping her head in the direction of Nancy Forbes. The elder Grieve daughter was standing on the edge of a group who were being entertained by Roger Merryman. Roger had eschewed the white tuxedo of the previous evening for more traditional black. Nancy wore another floor-length black gown and an expression somewhere between pinched disdain and abject boredom.

'It wouldn't take much to convince me that she killed her father,' said Bella. 'She's the sort of person who would stab you and then send you the dry-cleaning bill because you dared to get your blood on her dress. Paul should watch his back.' Bella stepped back to give Kate a view of Paul—who looked as debonair and handsome in a tuxedo as Kate remembered, damn him!—sidling up to Nancy and attempting to engage her in conversation.

Bella finished her drink and, in a single sway towards and away from a passing waiter, exchanged her empty glass for a fresh cocktail. Glaring at Paul, who was nodding as he listened to a miraculously bright-eyed, smiling Nancy, she said, 'He is charming. I'll give him that. Although if he thinks that ridiculous excuse for a beard makes him look like Robert Downey Jr, he's kidding himself.' She took a generous sip of her new drink. 'OK, I've had enough to drink to hear it.'

'Hear what?'

'What Paul had to say to you.' Bella rolled her shoulders back. 'Come on, hit me with it.'

'Do you promise not to go off on one?'

'As if I would! Besides, I already know he's here to get you back.'

'How do you—oh.' Kate shook her head, biting her bottom lip until the pain forced her to release it. 'He told Ethan.'

'Sorry. After I worked out that the two of them were scheming to get Paul over here, I made it clear to Ethan he had better tell me everything. If you ask me, his coming here is a ruddy cheek after what he put you through. I'm sure he is sorry and obviously he wants you back—you're amazing—but turning up here is asking for …'

Bella's commentary continued, but Kate was distracted by a new arrival to the party. Max had followed another team into the conservatory and was lingering in the doorway, casting his green gaze about the room. His tuxedo was identical to that of the previous evening and sat equally as perfectly on his tall frame. His hairstyle was unchanged and his expression was a Ravenscroft classic: a furrowed brow and stern glare above unsmiling lips. So why, unlike last night at dinner, did he now look absolutely, knee-tremblingly gorgeous?

Her pulse racing, Kate closed her mouth and tore her gaze away from Max, sending her long pendant earrings swinging. Sipping her drink, she pondered the change in his appearance. Perhaps it was the light in the conservatory? There was that magic hour thing, wasn't there? The time near sunset that film-makers loved because it made everything look at its best. Or maybe—she gave her drink a suspicious stare—Bella had given her a non-virgin cocktail?

'... and, at the very least, he should have asked you first—oh, look!' Bella interrupted her rant to raise her free hand in an unmissably enthusiastic wave. 'There's Max.'

Bella's wave hit its target. Max's roving stare stilled and his lips quirked into a fond half smile in recognition of Bella's performance, which resembled an amateur attempt to land a passenger jet. But then his stare slid to Kate and his expression froze. He blinked, his eyes widening and smile slipping as his lips parted.

Kate held Max's gaze, her breathing quickening as she took in his slack jaw and enlarged pupils. Her lips twitched into a nervous smile and she raised her hand in a small wave. Finally blinking, Max mirrored her greeting, his hand drifting up to his shoulder like the unconscious movement of a sleepwalker, while a familiar pink blush appeared in his cheeks.

Her own face beginning to heat, Kate dropped her hand and gaze. Frowning, she tightened her grip on her glass as her pulse galloped. What had she just seen? Was it possible that Max, who looked more alluring than ever to Kate, might be attracted to her too?

Chapter 29

'Kate? Kate!'

Kate jumped as Bella poked a finger between her ribs. 'Hmn?'

'I *said*, how have things been going with Max?'

'Max?' Kate swung her gaze back to the other side of the room in time to see Lucille Palmer, resplendent as ever in a new black satin frock, swooping in on her potential fourth husband. She flashed her dazzling smile at Max and ran her hand over the lapel of his jacket. An unpleasant squirming stirred in Kate's belly and, frowning, she turned back to Bella. 'He agrees that the only prime suspects are—'

'No! Not the case. You two. Getting along without killing each other.'

'Oh, it's been fine,' Kate said, hiding her face from her friend by taking a long sip of her drink. She really didn't need Bella's scrutiny right now. She still hadn't processed Max's earlier revelation that he didn't hate her.

That he found her tolerable. Even, perhaps, likeable. But accepting evidence that suggested he found her *desirable*—although potentially only when wearing indecently booby clothing—would require some quiet reflection and mental readjustment. And neither of those were easy to achieve during a Bella-led inquisition.

Kate frowned. 'We had a chat and it turns out you were right: he doesn't hate me.'

'You see!' Bella smiled in triumph. 'I knew you'd got the wrong end of the stick. Although, to be fair to you—'

'Carry on, I like where this is going.'

Bella returned Kate's smile. 'Well, Max's natural default facial expression is serious bordering on brooding. So I can see how you might think he was giving you evils. But that's his face. It's not his fault. Plus, from what Ethan's told me, he's one of those people who eventually relaxes in the company of those he knows well, but struggles with strangers. He always dreaded the networking events the firm used to send him and Ethan to. And while we were all having a great time at the Friendly Murder parties, he was going through a lot of heavy personal stuff.'

When he'd attempted to explain his own behaviour, Max had said something similar. Kate's subconscious had been shuffling and sifting his words, lining them up alongside his reactions to a couple of things Nancy Forbes had said. 'Did the personal stuff have anything to do with his mum?'

'You don't know?' Bella's eyebrows soared. 'Wow. No, I suppose you moved away right when things were at their worst.'

'What happened?'

'Max's mum died. She was sick for a long time. Cancer. He took time off work to help care for her.'

A cold hollowness seized the centre of Kate's chest. Its icy tendrils reached up into her mind as she struggled to imagine what Max had been through. She had missed her parents terribly when she first moved to Reading. Even though she hadn't been living at home, she'd enjoyed being able to drop in to see them at a moment's notice, and not being able to do that any more … There had been days it hurt. An actual physical pain below her ribs. And to think that Max had already experienced one of the things she feared most, especially with Dad's diagnosis …

Kate dropped the hand which had been covering her mouth. 'Why didn't you tell me about this at the time?'

'I didn't know until right at the end. Max kept everything to himself. Ethan knew his mum had been diagnosed but he thought she'd been getting better. And we didn't see much of him. After you moved away that summer, there were only a couple more Friendly Murder Club parties before the whole thing fizzled out.' Bella shrugged. 'Then we moved to London a few weeks before Christmas and were busy with our new jobs. It was only when she was admitted to the local hospice in the following March that Ethan realised what had been going on. She died in the April.'

The laughing guests, palm fronds and view of the gardens blurred as Kate's eyes filled with hot tears. She raised her gaze to the ceiling and blinked, hoping they wouldn't fall. 'But we spoke all the time—'

'God, Kate, I don't know! I suppose if you'd ever mentioned Max, in any of our conversations, I would have said something. But all our chats were about work, Paul, Ethan, your new place—'

'I know, I know.' Kate blew out a steadying breath. 'I'm sorry, I'm not having a go at you. I just. Max ...' A clear image came to mind of Max's peaceful expression when he had been sat at the piano, playing 'Clair de lune', which he knew by heart because it had been one of his mum's favourites.

The pressure in her chest raced upwards and suddenly no amount of blinking could stop the tears from falling. Between gulps, she said, 'He really loved his mum.'

'Hey, it's OK.' Bella snatched a paper napkin from a passing tray. 'Here. Shit, I'm sorry I mentioned it. This is supposed to be a fun weekend, not a crying weekend. I'd suggest bailing and going to the spa right now but it's closed. We could go tomorrow morning though?'

With her back to the low-lying sun, shadows filled the hollows under Bella's eyes. As ever, her friend had applied her make-up with great precision, but the sight of the dark circles she had done her best to conceal brought back Kate's earlier worries about Bella's health. Bella had needed a break from work. But instead of a restful weekend she'd got a grumpy hungover fiancé, Paul turning up out of the blue and her best friend blubbing in the middle of a party.

Kate sniffed and dried her eyes before more tears fell. 'The spa sounds great, but I'm supposed to be solving a murder.' She summoned a small smile. 'I seem to remember promising someone a generous wedding present if I win the prize money.'

'I remember and I'm holding you to it.' Bella grinned. 'I certainly don't want to put you off your prize-winning detective work, but couldn't a quick trip to the spa help? You could zone out on the massage table. Let someone else unwind your muscles while your subconscious unravels the mystery?'

'I'll think about it. How was your appointment earlier?'

'Not as relaxing as I'd hoped. The pools were busy and then the lights went off! Just when I'd managed to forget all about being woken in the early hours by the sodding fire alarm, another bloody power cut. You think they'd have sorted it out by now.' Bella held out a hand to stop a waiter, beamed and thanked him as he passed her another cocktail. This one was bubblegum pink and decorated with a paper umbrella. 'But at least it didn't trip the fire alarm and send us all outside in our towels.'

Poor Bella. Her keenness to down a rapid succession of sickly sweet rainbow-bright beverages was becoming more understandable. Surely something had gone her way lately? 'How did your trip to Compton Hall go?' Kate asked. 'Is it as impressive as you hoped?'

'And then some. The gardens are beautiful too. Although I'm glad we had someone to show us around. The place is a maze of corridors. I swear it was bigger on the inside than the outside.'

'What did Ethan think of it as a possible wedding venue?'

Bella sighed and took a long sip of her drink.

Kate's heart sank. 'Oh no, what happened?'

'I didn't get round to mentioning that was the reason for our visit. He spent half the time we were there on his phone. Mostly dealing with bloody Paul asking for directions. Apparently his satnav kept taking him the wrong way. Sounds like it was trying to do us a favour.'

Bella directed her gaze across the conservatory, where Ethan and Paul were sharing a joke. As she watched the men laughing and sharing playful nudges, her glare and the firm set of her lips softened. Her eyes glazed over with sadness and her expression became so forlorn that Kate didn't see she had any other option than to step forwards and wrap her in a hug.

'Oof! Watch my drink!' Bella laughed as she protested into Kate's hair and returned Kate's squeeze before easing out of her embrace.

'Are you OK?' Kate asked.

'Yeah. It's all fine. But whenever I try to speak to Ethan about wedding plans—firming up a date, booking somewhere—something seems to come up or he changes the subject. And there's the whole thing with Paul being best man instead of Ethan's brother ...' Bella chewed her lip. 'I know there's some family issue going on there, but Ethan won't talk about it. I thought this afternoon, away from everything out at Compton Hall, it would be the ideal time to have a proper chat. But then that got interrupted by—'

'Ladies! Should our ears be burning?' As he sidled past the group of guests next to them, Paul had raised his voice to compete with the background chatter. He grinned and held up the two glasses in his hands. 'We decided to bring you drinks'—he paused to glance over his shoulder at Ethan—'and escort you to dinner. A large white wine for Bella. And Kate, I got you sherbet lemonade. I remembered how much you like it.'

Kate glanced at Bella, worried that Paul would soon be wearing what remained of her bright pink concoction. And her concern only grew when Bella, with a sigh of resignation, accepted the wine glass with an uncharacteristically weak, 'Thank you.'

'Let me take that one for you,' said Paul, relieving Bella of the cocktail glass. 'Here you are, Kate.' He leant nearer and lowered his voice. 'You are looking particularly lovely this evening. Truly stunning.'

'Thank you,' said Kate, a treacherous strip of gooseflesh rising on her arms as she met Paul's direct, appreciative gaze.

Eager to break eye contact, she lifted her glass to her lips. The refreshing, sparkling mixture fizzed pleasantly on her tongue. It was every bit as good as the one she had enjoyed during one of her and Paul's last evenings out as a couple in Reading. She was impressed he had remembered, but not surprised. Paul had his flaws, but he could be thoughtful and attentive.

'Kate.' Paul blinked, the doe-eyed look he'd deployed on her earlier returning. 'I was wondering if you've had a chance to think about what I said earlier—'

Clang! The discordant echo of the dinner gong had never sounded so sweet. It was followed by the clatter of dozens of feet as the guests moved to the exit. Lucille Palmer was one of the first out of the door, proclaiming loudly how famished she was. Kate scanned the crowd, expecting to see Max somewhere in Lucille's wake, but her search was fruitless and a heavy knot of disappointment settled in her stomach, overwhelming the first stirrings of her hunger dragon.

Ethan took Bella's hand. 'We'd better keep up.'

Paul held out his arm to Kate. 'Shall we?'

With a stiff smile, Kate looped her hand around Paul's arm. She was surprised by how her fingers curled easily into their usual place on his bicep and, as they strolled to dinner behind Bella and Ethan—as they had on so many double dates—it was as if their break-up and six months of separation had been nothing but a bad dream.

Chapter 30

'I hear you, old chap. Discipline is key, I should say. I landed in my fair share of sticky spots at school and the masters didn't spare the rod, if you follow. I always say it never did me any harm. Probably did me some good, what?'

Archie guffawed and slapped Paul on the back. Paul joined the chuckling as he finished his glass of wine. 'I don't agree with corporal punishment,' he said, 'but running a tight ship is one of the most important aspects of my role as deputy head—'

Kate swallowed a groan. That had to be the tenth time in the past hour that Paul had mentioned his job title. And how intolerable the students at his school were. When he'd reached the ninth mention, she had considered pushing her dessert plate to one side and letting her forehead crash down to the table. But at least it was a break from him recounting tales of his latest action-adventure exploits: caving, rafting, abseiling … she'd lost track.

It was a symptom of a dinner which had been gloomier than that of the previous evening. The change in setting didn't help. A large wedding reception was being celebrated in the dining hall, so the Merryman's group had been relocated to the games room. Kate had imagined an intimate space which could house a billiard table, but it turned out to be large enough for a tennis court. The wood panelling, burgundy wallpaper and dim wall lighting conspired to give the room the atmosphere of a cave. One owned by a bloodthirsty hunter, Kate noted, as her gaze flickered nervously to the antlers above the fireplace. The main course had been a perfectly cooked venison. It was delicious, but she had found it difficult to swallow. Eventually she had begun to ponder the benefits of vegetarianism while doing her best not to look at the stuffed deer's head in the centre of the wall display. Its empty black eyes seemed to follow her with an accusatory stare.

The arrival of a delicious lemon meringue tart and Archie Forbes—who had taken the seat between Paul and Kate which had been occupied during the main course by Lorenzo Corsini—had lifted Kate's mood a little. He had also worked some of his magic on Bella, with his avalanche of Woosterisms coaxing the first smile of the meal from her. It had been a relief to see some of her sparkle return. Her glum expression had persisted such a long time that Kate considered venturing into the kitchen in the hope of finding Lucinda and persuading her to come and see if she couldn't lift her stepsister's spirits.

Ethan didn't appear to have noticed his fiancée's muted mood. He spent dinner in conversation with Max, with the occasional intervention from Paul, who was sitting on Max's right.

'Righty-ho! Must be off.' Archie threw his linen napkin onto the table and bounced to his feet. 'By the way, old bean, thanks awfully for bending Nancy's ear earlier,' he said, seizing Paul's hand. 'She said speaking to you bucked her up no end and she needed cheering. What a ghastly rotter of a day she's had, poor old thing!'

'Don't mention it,' said Paul, returning the enthusiastic handshake. 'It was a pleasure speaking with her.'

Kate snapped her jaw shut as Archie bounded away. Nancy Forbes—snooty ball of resentment, pricklier than a bed of thistles—had been so charmed by Paul that she'd mentioned him to her husband?

'From what Archie said, you must have got on with Nancy very well.'

'Hmn? Oh, yeah.' Paul smiled, apparently unaware that he had managed to thaw a permafrost ice queen. 'To be honest, I completely forgot I was speaking to an actress. She was a little standoffish at first, but I get the impression she just wanted a sympathetic ear. An incredible woman. Works tirelessly in her husband's constituency and has some interesting political views. I told her I admired her energy.' Paul paused to fill his mouth with the last of his lemon tart. He continued as he chewed, 'She credits that to how well she sleeps, although she does take tablets for that.'

'*What?*'

Kate and Max spoke at the same time. Kate had assumed Max was absorbed in conversation with Ethan, but his interjection and raised eyebrows told her that he

241

too understood the significance of Paul's last throwaway comment.

Taken aback by the twin reaction on either side of him, Paul swallowed and set down his fork while eyeing them warily. 'Have I said something wrong?'

Kate exchanged a glance with Max. Were they letting Paul into the team?

Max gave her the tiniest of nods and Kate's pulse kicked in response, the adrenalin surge causing her hands to tremble slightly as she slid into the empty chair next to Paul. Eyeing the competition at the tables around them, she dropped her voice to a whisper. 'We believe that Adrian Grieve was poisoned by an overdose of sleeping draught.'

Paul's eyes widened. 'And Nancy told me—'

'Shh!' Max and Kate hissed in unison and loudly enough to interrupt Ethan and Bella's hushed conversation.

'What are you lot talking about?' asked Ethan.

'The case,' said Max. 'Paul might have found out something important.'

'Let me get this right,' said Paul. 'By mentioning she regularly takes sleeping pills, Nancy has told me she has a stash of the actual murder weapon in her room?'

Bella threw her hands up. 'Is everyone on drugs round here?'

Max frowned. 'Who else, besides the Grieve sisters, is taking drugs?'

'That Archie bloke must be on something,' said Bella. 'Otherwise I don't know how you explain anyone being that unrelentingly upbeat.'

'And that Corsini bloke is slick enough to be a dealer,' said Paul.

'Our current theory is that he's actually a jewel thief. And possibly a murderer,' said Kate.

'But where are the jewels?' asked Max.

Paul scoffed. 'Wouldn't be surprised if Lorenzo is wearing them under his clothes. He clearly loves his bling. Did you see his cufflinks and that huge gold ring?'

It would have been hard not to notice Lorenzo's cufflinks which, once again, were different from the last time Kate had seen him. Tonight's pair were solid gold, glittering with a row of diamond studs.

Chair feet scraped against the wooden floor as other diners rose to leave the room. Those at Kate's table sat in silence, their eyes fixed but seeing nothing, all of their sight focused on internal contemplation.

Eventually, it was Bella who breached the peace. 'Do you think Lorenzo'—she paused as three guests from another table filed past her chair—'could have been in cahoots with Nancy?'

'Unlikely,' said Max, 'given her delightful views on foreigners. She hates them and Lorenzo in particular. She called him a gold-digger.'

'Unless ...' Paul drummed his fingers on the tablecloth. 'Could that be an act?'

Kate and Max exchanged another glance. Holding her gaze, he raised his shoulders a fraction. They were in cautious agreement: Paul's suggestion wasn't impossible. 'She was very passionate about it,' said Kate. 'Perhaps too passionate?'

'Maybe,' said Max. 'But Lorenzo and Pamela are each other's alibis. How does that work if he's in a theft-murder plot with her big sister?'

Max's excellent observation resulted in more pensive silence and table tapping from Paul.

'How about ...' Paul lifted his index finger from the table. 'Lorenzo tells Pam he's going to steal the jewels. She's on board for that. He doesn't say anything about helping Nancy to bump off the old man. Then he turns up at Pamela's bedroom door in the dead of night with some sob story: "Help me, my love. Something went wrong with the robbery and I had no choice but to stab your dear old dad. Please be my alibi or it'll be the noose for me and that'll spoil all our plans to help the poor and sick."'

Kate wasn't sure what was more shocking: that Paul had presented a possible alternative theory, or the atrocious cod Italian accent he had used to deliver his imaginings of Lorenzo speaking to Pamela. Her brain buzzing, she said, 'That could have happened, within what we know.'

'Great! I'm getting the hang of this. And'—he twisted towards Kate and dropped his voice—'I want to apologise again for the things I said in the past about your murder mystery parties.' He sat back in his chair, his gaze skipping across everyone at the table. 'This is terrific. I see why you're so into it. Hey! We should fix a date to come on another one. Get it in our calendars before they fill up.'

Six months ago, hearing Paul show any enthusiasm for attending a murder mystery weekend would have made Kate's soul sing. But now, this sudden change of heart, combined with him throwing Nancy back into the suspect mix, only made her head ache, a dull pulse of pain reappearing in her right temple.

As Ethan and Paul discussed future group outings, she winced and raised her fingers to the side of her head.

'I might go for a walk,' said Max, his voice cutting across those of Ethan and Paul. 'It's warm in here.' He rose and, his gaze locked on Kate's, took a deep breath. 'Kate, would you like—'

'That's a good idea,' said Paul, shifting in his seat to face Kate and put his back to Max. 'We could go for a stroll too, Kate. Take in the gardens at night. What do you say?'

The bottle of red wine Paul had drunk with his dinner had put a crimson flush across his face. Max, on the other hand, had been drinking water, so the pink dashes along his cheekbones—when viewed along with his clenched jaw and fists, and the pointed stare he was drilling into the back of Paul's neck—spoke of frustration and possibly fury.

The pain in Kate's temple scuttled behind her eye. Fresh air would probably have helped her feel better, but she saw no way of venturing outside without leaving either Paul or Max disgruntled. What she needed were painkillers and silence. 'You know,' she said, training her gaze on the flowers in the centre of the table, 'my headache's come back. I'm going to go to bed. See if a good night's sleep helps give me some clarity on the case.'

'That's the best idea I've heard all evening,' said Bella, shrugging off the arm Ethan had draped across her shoulders and pushing to her feet. 'I'm exhausted. Come on, Kate. Let's go.'

Ethan and Paul fired a few stammers of protest, but they bounced ineffectively off Bella's titanium hide. In seconds she had grabbed Kate's hand and, with a prim and definitive, 'Goodnight, all!' was striding for the exit, towing Kate behind her.

'You've gone an odd grey colour,' Bella said. 'Let's get you some pills and peace and quiet.' She wrapped an arm around Kate's waist as they marched down the corridor towards the stairs. 'Bloody men!' She harrumphed and rolled her eyes. 'You know what? If we're booking in another weekend away, let's do that, but just you and me. A proper spa weekend. Zero men. Zero stress. Deal?'

Despite the sparks of pain arching between her temples, Kate smiled, buoyed up by the thought that, with help from a friend, escape was always possible. She squeezed Bella's waist and said, 'Deal.'

Chapter 31

After giving Kate some highly effective anti-migraine pills—'There were a couple of weeks at work when I was living on this stuff'—and a long healing hug, Bella left Kate to get ready for bed.

Face washed, teeth brushed and pyjamas on—soft purple cotton with hedgehog print—Kate lay on the bed and let the medicine go to work. The pain had subsided into a faint ache almost as soon as Bella had extracted Kate from the dining room. Without anyone else putting her under pressure, it was now up to Kate to calm her swirling thoughts.

Where was her phone? Her mum had sent her a message that morning and she should reply before she worried. She grabbed her phone from the nightstand and tapped out a quick update.

> Haven't cracked the case yet, but getting closer. Will call you tomorrow afternoon to let you know how it goes. Bella and Ethan are well. Hope Dad is OK xx

She didn't mention Paul, of course. Christmas hadn't been that long ago, after all. And while Kate had done her best to put a brave face on things while staying at her parents' over the holidays—trotting out platitudes about how some relationships naturally ran their course, it was no one's fault, and perhaps it was all for the best—it was impossible to hide anything from Mum, who could see through her daughter's over-bright smiles to the heartache beneath.

Kate bit her lip as she added a jaunty smiling emoji to the end of the message, hit send, and threw the phone onto the bed. If she told her parents Paul had shown up at the Old Grange, she'd be on the phone for ages, fighting to convince them that she was fine and they didn't need to jump in the car and hurtle down the M40 to rescue her. The last thing either of them needed was more stress, especially Dad.

The phone landed by the pillows with a bounce. Was this the tipping point? Was this when she would start to worry more about her parents than they did about her?

With a pang close to her heart, Kate thought of Max. He must have been full of worry for his mum for so long. It was amazing he could function at work and find any energy to funnel into attempts to goad her into winning at mystery parties.

It was at the bottom of the present case too: parents and children. She felt it in her bones. Yes, Lorenzo was involved, but he was a flashy accessory. This was about the Grieve daughters and their father. Did the younger kill her father, somewhat reluctantly, for money and independence? Or did the older poison him to avenge her mother, stabbing an already dead Adrian with the letter opener— the treasured memento of her mother he had snatched away from her— as a grisly piece of poetic theatre?

Ugh! Sleep wasn't going to come easily at this rate.

Kate slid off the bed, padded across the thick carpet and opened the curtains. Moonlight cascaded through the window, bathing her in a silvery glow as she stared up at the sky peppered with stars twinkling like diamonds.

Diamonds. The jewels. Where were Cora Grieve's jewels? They had to be in the house or grounds but if the police had turned the whole place upside down …

Kate closed her eyes as a vivid memory surfaced. A wet afternoon in October. The earthy smell of wet leaves underfoot and steam rising from rows of colourful kids' coats in the cloakroom.

She had been six weeks into her new job in Reading, teaching her first class of Hedgehogs. A boisterous afternoon was disrupted by the disappearance of Jackson Miller's pencil. Such an event wouldn't usually have been cause for a full class search, but the pencil in question was pink and sparkly with a dinosaur eraser on the top. However, despite Jackson's moving sobs, no one would confess to having taken it. So every drawer, pocket, bag, box and cupboard was turned out to unearth the missing treasure. But to no avail. At the end of the day, having sent a snotty Jackson home with what she hoped wasn't an empty promise of the pencil turning up the next day, Kate collapsed into the chair behind her desk. She opened the top drawer to retrieve her emergency bar of chocolate only to find, perched on top of a jumble of stationery, the pink pencil of dreams. It hadn't occurred to anyone to look in the teacher's desk.

The moral of the story was that kids were endlessly, inventively, brilliantly sneaky. But, more immediately, it made Kate believe that the stolen jewels were hidden in the one place the police hadn't thought to look for them. The very place they had vanished from: the study. And, as long as no one else had beaten her to the epiphany, they would still be there. Waiting for her to find them.

Her pulse racing and headache forgotten, Kate raced to swap her pyjamas for the dress she had been wearing earlier in the day and shoved her bare feet into her sneakers. There was no time for make-up. Hopefully she wouldn't bump into anyone and if she did she'd have to pray that the hotel's evening lighting would be forgiving.

The rubber soles of her shoes whispered over the carpet in the corridor as she shoved her phone and key card into her pockets—dresses with pockets were the way forward—and scurried towards the stairs. Should she call on Bella? She'd searched the safe so enthusiastically that morning. Maybe she'd want to continue the jewel hunt?

'I never wanted to go there in the first place!'

The sound of raised voices came from Bella and Ethan's room. Kate paused outside, her first clenched, waiting for the right moment to knock on the door.

'Are you expecting me to apologise for doing something nice—'

'Not nice for *me!*' Ethan's voice rose to match Bella's. 'Nice for *you!* You're the one with fancy ideas of getting married in a stately home. I thought we'd agreed on Haileybrook and—'

'*We* didn't agree on anything. *You* decided that's where you wanted to—'

'I have family in the area, Bella. And you said it was beautiful and were happy about it. Why do you want to change things now and for a place I'd never heard of until today—'

'Perhaps if you'd taken a proper look at Compton Hall instead of spending the whole time on sneaky phone calls to your best man, you'd have warmed to the place!'

Kate winced as her hand plummeted to her side. Interruptions were unlikely to be welcome. At least Bella had got her chance to 'talk' to Ethan. Albeit at a higher volume than was healthy. But still. It was something.

Kate descended the grand staircase. The booming beats from the wedding reception disco thumped against the closed fire doors on the other side of the lobby. A hushed glow from a few standing lamps and wall lights illuminated the empty crushed velvet sofas, mahogany side tables and deserted reception desk. Had everyone other than the wedding party gone to bed already?

The narrow corridor leading to the study was also quiet, the only eyes following Kate those of the anonymous aristocrats in the gloomy oil paintings lining the walls. Although, as Kate passed the doorway to the games room, a burst of laughter made her startle. Clearly a few of the Merryman's guests were reluctant to turn in for the night. She had to hope they were all in one group, tipsy and had no desire to take a late-night trip back to the crime scene.

The study door was ajar. Strip lighting along a few of the bookshelves gave enough light to see by but failed to chase the deepest shadows from the corners of the room.

Kate strolled silently to the centre of the study and planted her hands on her hips. Where to start looking?

Ethan had searched the desk. The safe could keep no secrets from Bella. So … the books?

The shelves next to the window carried a few chunky volumes. Kate pulled the first free and turned it over. The navy-blue cover left a grimy dust film on her fingertips but contained nothing more than thousands of lines of tiny text. No hidden cavities stuffed with diamonds.

Kate continued her search. The mantle clock ticked into the silence, the only other sounds the swish of pages and the thud of the hardback covers striking the shelf and sliding against it.

A rhythmic series of crunches drew Kate's attention to the window. Were those footsteps? She tilted her head towards the noise, but concentrated listening only returned the boom of her pulse. She shook her head and shivered. Why did this room give her the creeps? If the murder had been real, the brief presence of a corpse would be explanation enough. But as that was all a sham, there was something else, something she couldn't put her finger on, which made Kate's detective radar tingle.

Bella would tell her to stop being ridiculous. To appreciate the fine, luxurious features of the space. Kate smiled to herself. She could imagine Bella processing through the rooms at Compton Hall, marvelling at how enormous they were—

Hang on. Kate's fingers relaxed and she almost dropped the book she was taking from the shelf. What had Bella said about Compton Hall? That it seemed bigger on the inside …

Kate turned to stare at the opposite wall. The safe was concealed behind the family portrait to the left of the fireplace. Obviously there would be a recess for the flue. So surely it wouldn't be unthinkable to have built another cavity—

The lights went out. A distant noise, like a grumble layered with shrieking, told Kate that the hotel had been struck by another power cut and the wedding party were not happy about it.

Blinking, Kate fumbled for her phone and shuffled over to the window. The electricity would be back soon and, in the meantime, moonlight would be better than nothing.

She was raising a hand to pull back the drape when she heard it again. The crunch of footsteps on the gravel path outside. Her hand trembled where it had frozen in mid-air. The footsteps were getting closer.

A frosty tremor slipped down Kate's spine and she backed away. The weak light from her phone screen strobed ghostly shadows against the curtains, making it look as though they were moving. No, they *were* moving. Someone was climbing through the window!

Her heart hammering, Kate reminded herself that Adrian Grieve hadn't really been murdered. It was all pretend. That whoever the person in the process of clearing the windowsill was, they weren't a knife-wielding maniac. Definitely not. Probably not. Oh Lord, how had this happened to her?

Kate's phone slipped from her numb, rubbery fingers and clattered off the wooden floorboards. Muttering curses, she whirled and stooped to recover it. The toe of her sneaker caught on a lurking edge of the rug and she plummeted to the ground.

Palms stinging and knees throbbing, Kate winced and rolled onto her bottom. For a moment, mortification outweighed concerns about the impending arrival of axe murderers, but then one of the heavy curtains shuddered and a shaft of moonlight hit the parquet, followed by a foot.

Casting frantic glances over her shoulder, Kate shuffled backwards. Why was the door suddenly so far away? If she screamed, would anyone hear her?

In front of the window, a tall figure used the drapes to haul itself to standing. Backlit by eerie moonshine, it stalked silently towards the rug.

Kate clawed at the rough wool beneath her, her breathing turning ragged as she dragged herself back to the door and the chance of escape.

But she wasn't fast enough.

The looming figure drew nearer, towering over her.

Kate cringed and drew her bruised knees towards her chest. Shout. Kick like hell. Run. A fairly solid plan from a brain that was a buzzing hornets' nest of panic.

The figure crouched and, as it reached a hand towards her, Kate sucked in a deep breath, preparing to holler for her life.

But her planned distress call shrivelled into a whimper of surprise as the dark figure said, 'Kate? Are you all right?'

Chapter 32

'Are you hurt? Hold on ...'

Clothes rustled. A small bright light burst from Max's phone and he placed it on the floor next to Kate.

'I didn't think anyone would be in here,' he said. 'I'm sorry if I scared you. Again.'

While Kate's pulse had slowed from an all-out gallop, it was yet to reach a calm trot. Keen that Max wouldn't think she was an easily frightened wimp, she put effort into using a steady voice to reply, 'You didn't scare me. I tripped over the corner of the rug like a complete clown.'

The upward beam of a torch made most people look like a zombie. But as Max leant closer the light highlighted his strong jawline and made the piercing green of his eyes dazzling.

'It's pitch black in here, Kate,' he said. 'I'm sure you're not the only one who'll have had an accident. And I imagine having a weirdo climbing through the window and surprising you can't have helped. Here.'

He held out a hand, she seized it and they rose to their feet together. A few swipes and the torch on her phone joined Max's in illuminating the darkness.

Kate blinked at the white cotton stretched tight across Max's broad chest. Was he wearing a T-shirt? She narrowed her eyes to get a better look. Blimey. She couldn't remember having seen Max in a top that didn't have a collar.

'What?' asked Max.

Oh no. Had she said that out loud? 'Uh, I was just wondering ...' No excuse for her gawping came to mind. The truth then. 'Are you wearing your pyjamas?'

'Oh.' Max huffed a brief laugh and ran a hand through his hair. Hair which looked fluffy, ruffled. Bed head, that's what it was. And teamed with the casual T-shirt ... A flutter stirred below Kate's belly as she took in this unbuttoned, unwrapped Max. It was a good look on him. A very good look.

'I was in a hurry,' said Max. 'Don't worry, I took the time to throw trousers on.'

Shame. Kate pressed her lips together into a tight smile and waited for Max to speak again. If she opened her mouth she risked voicing her thoughts.

Max cleared his throat. 'Is your headache better?'

'Yes, thanks. Bella had some surprisingly strong migraine pills.'

'So you got your opium in the end?'

'Ha! Possibly.'

They shared an awkward smile, Kate doing her best not to leer at Max's chest and bare neck.

Max cleared his throat. 'You're here for the jewels?'

'Yes!' How had she forgotten? Thank goodness Max

could be trusted to be all business. Kate lowered her voice to a more confidential tone. 'Sorry. I mean, yes. They have to be in here somewhere.'

But where? Brandishing her phone in front of her, Kate strode to the fireplace and scanned the shelves to its left.

Max followed her and tapped the wall next to the mantelpiece. 'How did you figure it out?'

'Jackson Miller's missing pencil.'

Max left off tapping the wall to glance at her. 'OK, maybe I was wrong about the Sherlock thing. Because that was definitely more of a Miss Marple-style comment.'

Kate turned to Max and, on seeing his amused smile, gave him a playful shove. 'If that was meant to be an insult, it won't work.'

'Not at all. Jane Marple is a quiet genius. One who probably solved a murder once because she knew someone who lost a pencil.'

'Exactly. In my case, it's a long story involving a class of six-year-olds and an as-yet-unsolved case of theft. Remind me to bore you with it later.'

Max's smile widened. 'I look forward to it.'

Kate propped her phone on the bookshelf at waist height to free both hands for book inspections. 'How about you?'

'When I was walking around the Old Grange this morning—gargoyle spotting, if you remember—'

'I do.'

'There was something odd about this corner of the building. I went out again after dinner to take another look but still couldn't figure it out. And then I was brushing my teeth and it hit me.'

'The room is bigger on the outside than the inside.'

'Exactly. I only managed to pace it out roughly, but I'd guess there's a good metre missing off this side of the room. And once I'd discovered that, I was in a hurry to get in here to see if I was right, and rather than walk all the way round to the main entrance—'

'You decided to climb through the window?'

'Yes.' Max winced. 'It was already open and I didn't think anyone would be in here. Sorry.'

'That's OK. I get it.' Kate pointed to the bookcase to the right of the fireplace. 'The hidden recess has to be behind that bookcase, right?'

She crossed the room to stand in front of the shelving and Max followed her. 'Unless the fireplace swings out,' he said, 'I'd say so. And my guess is that one of the books conceals the opening mechanism.'

There was an unusually rushed, breathless quality to Max's voice. Sneaking a glance at him, as he pulled and prodded the books on the highest shelf, Kate noticed the way he bounced slightly on the balls of his feet, the light trembling in his fingers. She'd seen that kind of nervous energy before in her class, mostly in the build-up to Christmas break.

She smiled and tucked her hair behind her ears, her own hands shaking. The excitement was infectious.

'Which book do you think it is?' said Max.

'I've no idea. Is it too much to ask for a title like *The Key to the Secret Chamber*?'

'*Open Sesame*?'

'*Pull Here to Open the Hidden Door*— Wait! I think I've got it.'

Max grabbed his phone and shone it directly on the rigid

crimson spine of the relatively slim, unassuming volume in the lowest right corner of the bookcase. His shoulder brushed against Kate's, and an extra zing of electricity shot down her already tingling spine.

The title was in all capitals, embossed in gold.

'*Great Expectations*?' he asked.

Kate exhaled slowly as her fingers closed on the top of the book. 'Only one way to find out.' She paused, listening to her and Max's breathing sawing through the dusty air. They had both figured this out. They had got here at the same time. 'We should do this together.'

'What? No, Kate, you do it.'

'Max. If this does open an actual, honest-to-God secret door behind a ruddy bookcase in an old country house, I'm embarrassed to say it will be one of the most awesome things that has ever happened to me. And, I'm going to go out on a limb here and guess you feel the same.'

Max laughed. 'Beyond awesome.' He grinned. 'All right, Sherlock.' He laid his fingers over hers and Kate's pulse kicked at the contact. 'On the count of three?'

Chapter 33

A sharp click, a muffled clang and the bookcase slid outwards by an inch.

Their hands still clasped on the copy of *Great Expectations*, Kate and Max looked at each other, their mouths forming perfect O's and their eyes shining.

'Oh my God,' Kate whispered. 'Nancy Drew, eat your heart out.'

'There's a groove here, like a handle,' Max said, prising the hidden door open.

Kate stepped forwards. She glanced into the darkness behind the bookcase. 'Do you want to go first?'

'Ladies first. I insist.'

A quick inspection using the phone spotlight revealed a small rectangular space, about a metre wide and a metre and a half long. The floor was a rough brick and above Kate's head there were rows of wooden shelving.

'I'll pull the door back over,' said Max.

'Good idea.' The last thing they needed was the members

of the other teams who were still in the games room to stagger past the study door and notice the bookcase standing open.

Having covered the entrance, Max turned to the shelves behind him. 'There's a light here.' The phone torches were joined by a bright orange glow from what looked like a miniature camping lantern sitting on the bottom shelf nearest the door. 'Rechargeable LED. Not exactly 1930s accurate.'

'But useful,' said Kate, putting her phone in her pocket. 'I think what we're looking for it up here.' She rose to the tips of her sneakers and stretched to one of the upper shelves. Grunting with the effort, she swiped at the edge of the brown canvas she had spotted from below. It belonged to a large bag which Kate managed to drag over the edge of the shelf, almost failing to catch it as it plummeted to the ground.

'This has to be it,' she said, her skin prickling with anticipation as she tugged at the cords binding the bag's neck.

Max joined her, his shadow falling over her hands as she reached into the bag. 'More bags inside,' she said. 'These ones are velvet though. There are some boxes at the bottom. Hang on.' Kate pulled out a square, hinged box. It was covered in red velvet and its corners were rounded. Straightening up, she resisted the urge to shake it, like a kid on their birthday. She slid a nail into the side opposite the hinges and glanced at Max. 'OK, let's see …'

Even in the dim lantern light, the necklace inside sparkled, the rows of diamonds glimmering on the fine strands of precious metal like fresh dew on a dawn cobweb.

Kate's smile stretched into a wide grin. They'd done it. They'd found the missing jewels!

'As you said,' Max said quietly, 'Nancy Drew eat your heart out.' He glanced down at Kate, his smile as wide as her own. 'Now what?'

Shoving aside the desire to clamp the bag under her arm and sprint up the stairs two at a time to show Bella, Kate bundled the box into the bag and pushed it up onto the shelf. 'We'll put them back where we found them. We don't want to let the thieves know we're on to them. Or give anything away to the other teams if they should find their way in here.'

Satisfied that the bag was secure, Kate spun away from the shelves. Her smile slipped. What was Max doing crouched in the opposite corner? 'Max? Are you all right?'

'There's something down here.' Max stood, his fingers pinched around a small object. He rolled it into the middle of his palm and held it up to the lantern light.

Kate gawped. It was a cufflink. Silver inlaid with mother-of-pearl. She had seen a pair like it before. At dinner on Friday night.

'That's Lorenzo's!'

She took a swift step closer to the vital evidence, but her toes struck something hard causing her to gasp and stumble.

Max shot out an arm to stabilise her and she grabbed it gratefully. But her relief was short-lived. With a hiss and a bang the door to the small room swung shut, trapping them inside.

Chapter 34

'I'll call reception,' said Kate, stamping fruitlessly on the closure switch Max had already tried to activate a dozen times. 'They'll come and open the door. It'll be fine. All good. No problem.'

The dial tone trilled uselessly. Kate huffed in frustration and tried again.

With his back against the wall, Max slid down to sitting. 'They'll be busy dealing with the power cut.'

'I'll keep trying.' Kate tapped her foot as the robotic beeps continued. If all else failed, she could call Bella, but she didn't fancy interrupting her 'conversation' with Ethan. 'Someone will pick up eventually. I'm sure if—'

A groan came from the floor, where Max had drawn his knees up to his chest and dropped his forehead onto them.

Oh dear. Frowning, Kate hung up and crouched next to him. 'Are you all right?'

Max kept his head down. His voice was muffled as he replied, 'It's fine. Just not great with small enclosed spaces.'

'Ah. Fair enough.' She glanced behind her. 'I could try throwing my shoulder against the door? Bust it open?'

'It's mostly solid oak.'

'I could try throwing my shoulder against it while shouting really aggressively? Scare it open?'

A snort of a laugh and Max lifted his head enough for Kate to see his eyes. 'While I'm sure the door would be terrified, you'd likely hurt yourself. So don't. But thanks all the same.'

Kate shivered, the cool dry air in the small room raising goosebumps on her arms. OK, her escape suggestions had been silly. But Max had laughed. Perhaps distraction was the answer? How long could they possibly be stuck here? Half an hour, tops? She could be witty and interesting for that long, couldn't she?

'No door charging then. I'll try reception again in five minutes. Scoot over.' Kate sat down next to Max, forcing him to shuffle aside to make space. He settled again quickly, but his gaze darted around the chamber, the panicked stare of a trapped animal. 'Hey.' Kate grabbed his right hand, folding her fingers around his. 'Come on, this is your big chance to tell me your life story, don't blow it.'

Max straightened, resting the back of his head on the wall. He stared at their joined hands and laughed again. 'It's not that interesting.'

'I don't believe that for a minute. For a start, you're an architect. That's interesting.'

'Is it?' Max glanced sideways at Kate. 'You're the first person to say that to me.'

'Really? That's surprising. It takes a lot of effort and training to qualify, doesn't it? So that suggests a vocation, which is always interesting. Why did you want to do it?'

'I guess, I like puzzles, as you may have guessed.'

'I had an inkling.'

Max smiled. 'And I thought I'd done such a good job hiding it.'

'So how is architecture like a puzzle?'

'Well, the job often involves a lot of creative problem solving. It was always going to be either architecture or engineering for me.'

'Why did architecture win?'

'I think it's my grandad's influence. He was a member of the National Trust and used to take me to visit grand places like this when I was a kid. He found them fascinating and he liked pointing out all the little details, the design choices … I suppose it began there.'

'So not Lego?'

Max laughed, a proper chuckle which added warmth to the small space. 'I did and do like Lego, I must admit. I can't rule out its influence.' He swayed gently, nudging her shoulder with his. 'Why did you become a teacher? You studied history, didn't you?'

'I did and I enjoyed it.' Kate nodded. 'But in my second year a friend convinced me to join the university's literacy support project which sends students into schools to help kids who struggle with reading. And I loved it. Right from the first visit. There's this—' Kate broke off, catching herself before she descended into one of the rambles about her job which used to make Paul's eyes glaze over.

'What?' Max squeezed her hand. 'What were you going to say?'

'Nothing, it doesn't matter. I was boring on about work. Sorry.'

'Don't be sorry, I was enjoying listening to you.'

Kate stared at Max through narrowed eyes, searching for hints he was being polite. But his gaze was steady and sincere as he said, 'It's great when someone loves their job. It doesn't happen often. I mean—and please tell me if I'm wrong—but from listening to Paul talk at dinner this evening, I get the impression he hates teaching. And, to be honest, I don't even think he likes children.'

Kate snorted. 'You're not wrong at all.' Apart from one or two favourites, she'd never heard Paul praise the students. It had always puzzled her: why would someone who didn't care for children enter a profession which involved dealing with them every day? 'He was truly ecstatic when he landed the deputy head job though. But then, when he started it I never sensed much about the role brought him joy.' Except for the bump in status and salary. He had enjoyed those.

'But you do love your job,' said Max. 'Why is that? You won't bore me, I want to know.'

'OK, let's see.' Kate closed her eyes and pictured the eager faces of Hedgehog class. 'There's this moment, when you're explaining something to a pupil. Perhaps it's a new concept or maybe they're struggling to understand it. And you try different ways to get it across and suddenly ... it really is like a light bulb goes on inside their head. You can see it in their eyes when things click for them and it's honestly such a rush. They're thrilled and you share that with them because they know something new thanks to you. You have changed them forever and at primary level—with the little kids—you see those moments almost every day. It's amazing.' She grinned. 'It also helps that they're hilarious and can be very sweet.'

'I bet they love you too.'

'Oh, I don't know.' She shrugged and, her cheeks beginning to warm under Max's direct gaze, decided to change the subject. 'Enough about me. What would you do with Merryman's fifty grand prize money? If you won this weekend?'

Max loosed a shaky breath. 'I'd want to give some money to my local hospice.'

Of course. His mum. Kate bit her lip, longing to say how sorry she was for his loss, but doubting that reminding a man on the verge of an anxiety attack of his grief was the smartest idea. Instead, she gave his hand a light, encouraging shake. 'I'm sure they'd be delighted. Anything for the football team?'

'Some new kit would be a good idea.' He tilted his head to look at Kate. 'What are you going to do with the money? When you win?'

'Thank you for your confidence. *If* I were to win ...' Kate paused to consider and the image of a sky-blue box labelled *Dad* leapt to the front of her mind. A knot of worry tangled in her stomach. 'I suppose I'd give some money to Parkinson's disease research and care. My dad's Parkinson's was recently diagnosed.'

'Oh.' Max ran his thumb back and forth over the back of her hand. 'I'm sorry.'

'He's OK. At the moment. His meds are good. But ...' Kate sighed, imagining a future where her parents would need more support. But, her senses distracted by Max's gentle touch, the knot in her stomach failed to tighten.

'Is that why you applied for the job in Knowleswood?' Max asked. 'To be nearer home? To help your parents?'

'Partly. And also because …' She'd missed a lot about home. Friends she'd had since school, going out in Birmingham and even daft murder mystery parties featuring an annoyingly competitive jerk. Who was currently holding her hand. Life was so weird. 'I suppose, I moved to Reading for Paul. His job was a great promotion.'

'How did you two meet?'

'One of my first teaching jobs.' A wistful smile crept onto her lips. Paul had been so welcoming, thoughtful and handsome. He'd been easy to fall in love with. They'd found a flat together and were nearly four years into their relationship when he suggested moving to Reading. Why would she have said no? She had believed he was her forever person. 'We'd been together almost six years when we split up.'

'Do you mind me asking what happened?'

'He met someone else.' Bloody Kirsty. Of all the people he could have left her for, why did it have to be the office manager at *her* school? Why couldn't he have found someone at his school? At least that way she wouldn't have to see the woman every day. Listen to her waving her freshly painted nail in circles while regaling everyone with details of her latest adrenalin-seeking adventure weekend with Paul. How she took part in such high-risk activities and kept her perfect manicure was a mystery Kate would never crack.

The back of her left hand tingled. Max was running his thumb over it again, no doubt gently alerting her to the fact her grip had tightened while thinking of Kirsty. She relaxed her hold and Max did the same. 'I'll try calling reception again.'

Kate scooped her phone off her knees and was dialling when Max said, 'They've offered you the job already, haven't they? The school in Knowleswood?'

Kate's lips parted in shock at Max's mind-reading skills. Damn. The man was a witch. 'Yes. I have to let them know on Monday.'

'It sounds like a great job.'

'It is.' Kate turned her gaze to the wall in front of her and lifted the phone to her ear. The dial tone droned tunelessly and with each tone Kate asked herself: why hadn't she already accepted the job? She had never settled in Reading the way Paul had, she wouldn't miss it the way she missed Birmingham. It had to be Paul. Every time she thought she had closed the lid on the Paul box, nailed it shut and buried it at the back of her mental closet, a happy memory would nudge it open. A small reminder of something sweet he'd said or done. Like that darn mystery book subscription. She'd assumed he'd forgotten her birthday—what with it being so close to Christmas and him being wrapped up in his new job—but then the first book had turned up. A beautiful hardback edition of *Murder on the Orient Express*. There had been no note with that first delivery. It turned out there had been a mix-up at the book shop, but Paul always handed her each month's book from then on. He used to get home early when the next book was expected so he could intercept it and present it to her with a kiss and sometimes a box of chocolates. It was adorable. And he'd continued to pop them through her letterbox since she'd moved out.

'Ugh!' She dropped the phone back onto her lap. 'No answer. Sorry.'

'I'm OK.'

'I could call Bella?'

'She might be asleep and someone at reception will answer eventually. I can wait. Honestly.'

Max's breathing was steady, his features relaxed. He was probably all right. Even so, Kate silently cursed the hotel staff for failing to cover the phones. 'It doesn't look like we have a choice. I'll try them again in a minute.'

Max drummed his hands against his knees. 'Kate?'

'Yes?'

'Can I say something about your job offer? I'm sure you don't want or need my opinion—'

'Go ahead. It can't hurt.'

'I'm certain you'll be an asset to the school and will be more than able to cope with anything they ask of you. So, if you liked the place and believe you could be happy there, then I'd take any chance you can to be closer to your parents.' His gaze drifted to the darkest corner of the room and turned distant, unfocused. 'None of us know how much time we'll get to spend with the people we love. So we should try to make the most of every second. Mum—' He swallowed. 'My mum used to tell me that. And she was pretty wise, for what it's worth.'

Max shrugged as if his words meant little, but a glossy sheen in his eyes gave away the sadness beneath the wisdom. Kate ached to fold herself around him in a huge comforting hug but, uncertain the gesture would be welcome, settled for stretching her arm tentatively across his shoulders. When he didn't move away from her touch, she said, 'I'm sorry about your mum.'

'Thank you.'

'I didn't know.'

'I didn't tell many people.' He stared at Kate's pinched brow. 'She wouldn't have wanted anyone to be sad. Mum was keen on celebrating life. It took me a while to catch on to it—it all seemed so unfair—but I've come round and can see now she was right. As usual.'

'I still wish Bella had told me at the time.'

'Would you have cared?' Max glanced at Kate, an eyebrow raised. 'You thought, with cause, that I was a total jerk.'

'Of course I would have cared! If nothing else, it would have gone some way to explaining your jerkiness.'

'That's very kind. Thank you.' The small smile of amusement at the corner of Max's mouth slipped. 'It doesn't entirely excuse my behaviour though.'

'Maybe not. But your behaviour made you memorable.'

'And there I was, thinking you'd gone off to Reading and forgotten about me. Or that you wanted to.'

'Impossible. You're annoyingly memorable.'

'Thanks again. I must put that on my CV. Or perhaps, if we don't get out of here soon, it can go on my gravestone.'

Kate mirrored Max's sardonic smile. 'I'll try reception again,' she said, lifting her arm from his shoulder and picking up her phone.

As the dial tone droned into the silence, Max asked, 'What would you do for yourself? With the prize money? There must be something.'

'It'd be nice to pay off the student loans company and never have to worry about dealing with them again.'

'Amen.'

'And then, maybe ...' Should she tell him? Paul had always given her a pitying look whenever she'd brought

271

it up. Oh, what the heck. 'I'd like to take a trip down to Devon. Agatha Christie had this house—'

'Greenway? It's National Trust now.'

'Yes, it is. And—this will probably sound daft—but at Christmas they sometimes put on these Christie-inspired events.'

'Sounds brilliant.' Max's voice contained a tremor of excitement. 'Can anyone buy tickets?'

'I think so. The events must be incredibly popular though and I imagine tickets sell out quickly, but as long as you get them far enough in advance I guess it would be OK.' Kate paused. She was rambling. 'It sounds like a lot of fun. And Devon's a beautiful part of the world.'

'So beautiful. Lovely beaches.'

'Yes.' Kate stared into Max's eyes, green like a shallow sea, and a clear picture came to mind: them together, strolling hand in hand along a windswept winter beach. Kate's nose was freezing, her hair a straggly mess, and yet she was laughing and holding Max close.

'Lovely,' Max murmured, his gaze dipping to her mouth, before returning to collide with her own.

He fancies you, her inner voice whispered. *If that's your theory, you should try to prove it. You're both detectives, after all. It's practically your professional duty.* Kate released a small sigh and her fingers twitched as she imagined running them through Max's seductively tousled hair. *Come on, Kate*, the voice urged. *Stop staring and kiss the man!*

'Kate?'

'Hmn?' Kate fidgeted, reluctantly returning from the bright expanse of her imaginary beach to the hard floor in the dim cramped room.

'Tomorrow,' said Max, 'after your inevitable victory—'

'Pft!'

'Scoff all you like. I have faith.'

With only inches between them, Kate was unable to tear her gaze away from the unusual heat in Max's stare. Tantalisingly intense, it drifted down to her lips, the base of her throat and then back up to meet her own gaze. 'Um, anyway,' Max said, his voice little more than a low rasp, 'tomorrow, when the game's over ... I wanted to ask you—'

Kate swallowed, struggling to stop her own gaze from wandering away from Max's eyes to his full lips and alluring dusting of stubble. *Pay attention!* her inner voice screamed. *The man's trying to say something important. Something he finds difficult.*

'After ...' Max exhaled. 'I was wondering—'

Max's question was cut off by the click of the stubborn door release catch and a faint squeal of hinges as the entrance to the secret room swung open.

Chapter 35

'Hello? Anyone in there?'

Kate and Max scrambled to their feet as the door swung open. Their saviour stepped into the orange glow cast by the lantern and Kate instantly recognised a thick mane of dark hair and another pair of striking green eyes.

'It's you two!' Lucinda said, beaming at them as she lowered her phone torch. 'I should have known. Bella was right, you guys are terrific detectives.'

'Rubbish escapologists though,' said Max. 'We got stuck in here and reception weren't answering our calls.'

'Power cut's still going on,' said Lucinda, standing back to let Max and Kate out into the relatively humid air of the study. 'The wedding party aren't best pleased, but at least we'd served all the food before the lights went out in the kitchen.'

Kate closed the bookcase door. 'How did you find us?'

'I was walking past, on my way out, and I heard voices the other side of the corridor wall. At first I thought I was imagining it—it's been a long day—but then I remembered the little room behind the bookcase and came to check it out.'

'Does everyone know about it?' Max asked.

'I don't think so. I have a friend—Becky—who works behind the scenes at weddings in the area, and if there's a secret passageway, hidden room or concealed door in a venue, she'll know about it.' Lucinda grinned. 'She showed me this one.'

'We have to thank her for that. And you,' Max said. 'If you could not mention to anyone else that we were in there though, we'd appreciate it.'

'No problem,' said Lucinda. 'I take it this means you're hot on the trail of the killer? Ahead of the other teams?'

'We don't know for certain,' said Kate. 'But we're getting there.'

The strip lighting along the study shelves and the wall sconces in the corridor outside came on, signalling the end of the power cut and leaving Lucinda, Max and Kate blinking at each other in the sudden brightness.

'Thank goodness for that,' said Lucinda. 'The father of the bride was about to burst a blood vessel. They should have hired Becky. She'd have had a backup generator on standby just in case. And speaking of backup plans, I was going to speak to Bella, but now I have you two here, I need to tell you a couple of things about the game. Bella told me you had some concerns about Roger Merryman and the fact no one's won in ages?'

Max and Kate exchanged a glance. 'Yes, we did,' said Kate. 'You know something about that?'

'Well—'

'Mr Ravenscroft, Ms Brown and Ms Green!' The matchlike silhouette of Roger Merryman appeared in the doorway. A large black torch was gripped in the bony fingers of his left hand. He beamed, his wide smile revealing dazzlingly white teeth but failing to reach his eyes. 'I've been checking in on all my guests to make sure they were all right and had a torch should they need one. But I couldn't find you two'—he wagged his finger at Max and Kate—'anywhere. I began to wonder if you were hiding!' He chuckled mirthlessly, his small eyes boring into each member of his audience in turn. 'I hope I haven't interrupted an important conversation?'

A flutter of concern stirred in Kate's chest. She didn't like conspiracy theories or giving in to paranoia, but it was becoming clear that Roger Merryman was up to something sinister. And he certainly didn't seem happy that she and Max were speaking to Lucinda. Why should that upset him?

'Max and Kate were asking me about the catering,' Lucinda replied. 'They loved the chocolate cake from yesterday.'

'Yes, I'm a keen baker,' said Kate, leaping to back up Lucinda's story, 'and was asking Lucinda if she'd give me the recipe.'

'Mr Merryman'—Max glanced at Kate and his eyebrow flickered upward—'I think we should leave these ladies to it.' He put his arm around Roger's shoulders and steered him to the door. 'I know it's late, but I'd like to buy you a drink and bore you with a couple of quick questions about how tomorrow will work. Your set-up is incredibly impressive. I can see why your mystery weekends are the most popular in the country.'

276

Roger's scrawny chest inflated inside his dress shirt, pushing his bow tie outwards. 'Of course, of course. But you won't be getting any hints from me, young man! I'm a sealed tomb of secrets.'

While Kate was frozen to the spot by her admiration of Max's smooth extraction of Roger, Lucinda held up a hand, her head tilted to one side, listening to the men's fading voices. She tiptoed to the door and peeked round the frame. 'They've gone. But let's go to the kitchen as a precaution. Roger will never show up there. He considers it part of the servants' quarters and beneath him.'

Lucinda led Kate down the corridor and through a door labelled *Private*. A small thrill buzzed along Kate's nerves. Secret rooms and now a behind-the-scenes tour of the building. What was going on tonight? She should be in bed, not scampering after Bella's supernaturally fantastic stepsister like an obedient sheep.

'Here we are,' said Lucinda, opening yet another fire door.

The kitchen was an ultra-modern contrast to the well-preserved Victorian gothic of the rest of the Old Grange. It was filled with stainless-steel surfaces and huge buzzing fridges, cool panels of fluorescent lights and shiny white tiles.

'OK, where to begin?' Lucinda rested her lower back against one of the island units and unbuttoned her black chef's jacket, revealing a purple cotton top beneath. 'Roger wasn't as snooty a couple of years ago. Success has gone to his head. Have you seen his car?'

Kate shook her head.

'It's some sort of convertible sporty thing. Sorry, I'm no

good with makes, I drive a transit van most of the time. But the point is it has personalised plates.'

'Oh dear.'

'Personalised to read BIG R0G.'

Kate winced. 'Say no more.'

Lucinda folded her jacket over her arm. 'Before we talk about whatever's going on with Merryman's, if you don't mind, I wanted to ask you if you think Bella's OK?'

A wave of exhaustion hit Kate along with Lucinda's unexpected question. Her mind sluggish, she waded through her memories of her recent conversations with Bella. 'Yes and no. I think she's all right, but in the way that Bella would be all right even if the world was ending.'

Lucinda grinned. 'I know what you mean. She'd find the last available supply of wine, pass round glasses and tell everyone to cheer up, it could be worse!'

Kate's smile was brief. 'But then, I worry that her job is draining her and she doesn't enjoy it at all. And her and Ethan were having a row earlier about their wedding plans. I think it's all getting to her.'

'I get the impression she only took that London job because Ethan wanted to move there,' said Lucinda. 'And now, with the big promotion and the money, she doesn't feel like she can walk away from it.'

Drawing parallels to her own situation with Paul, Kate asked, 'Do you think she wants to move back home? Back up to Birmingham?'

'No, it's more she doesn't want to be in London. And back home, well, her family's not there. Her dad's out in Spain with my mum. And her sister—I get the impression she's a bit of a nomad?'

Summer, Bella's little sister, continued to capitalise on every advantage being the younger sibling gave her. With her big sister in a steady relationship and full-time employment, she felt free to job hop her way around the globe.

'She was in Thailand, last I heard.'

'Hmn. Do you have a sister?'

'No. Just Bella. Not that "just" is a word that should ever go before Bella.'

Lucinda grinned, her green eyes sparkling. 'Me too. And that's how she sees you as well, by the way. She never stops talking about you. She'd kill for you.'

Kate fidgeted with her skirt, bubbles of happiness warming her insides. To think, she might be on a par with the marvellous Lucinda! 'She's the same with you. And, to be fair, I reckon Bella could be persuaded to kill fairly easily.'

Lucinda laughed, her cackle bouncing off the steel and tiled surfaces. 'I can't disagree. And, speaking of murder'—she clapped her hands—'back to the business of this weekend. I had a quiet chat with Dorothy Williams tonight after Roger ordered one of my staff to put double the usual amount of alcohol in the cocktails. When he refused, Roger attempted to do it himself, at which point I stepped in.' The sharp tone in which she delivered the last three words convinced Kate that when Lucinda put her foot down, even Roger Merryman took notice.

'What did Dorothy say?'

'Since the start of this year, she's seen Roger behaving in ways which worry her. It turns out that trying to get the guests drunk and so, I'm guessing, less able to focus on solving the mystery, is just his latest trick. This afternoon Dorothy had gone to get something from her car and on the way back to the hotel spotted Roger bundling one of the actors out of the building. Apparently it's normal for there to be at least one surprise character who isn't mentioned in the info pack and all the contestants are supposed to get an opportunity to question them.'

Her pulse quickening, Kate bit her lip to stop herself interrupting. Lucinda had to be talking about Dr Chase.

'Roger left and Dorothy pounced on the guy,' continued Lucinda. 'He said he was preparing to mingle with the guests and drop the hints in his brief, when Roger swooped down and all but threw him out, telling him to go home immediately if he wanted to get paid. Having prepared his role, the actor was understandably annoyed—my Alex would have been furious.'

A dreamy smile curled Lucinda's lips as the topic turned to her boyfriend. And who could blame her? Alex Fraser was very handsome. And he also happened to play a leading role in *Napier*, one of Kate's favourite TV police dramas.

Before they both wandered off topic, Kate said, 'Is that why Dorothy brought him back and introduced him to me?'

'She was hoping he could speak to any of the guests, but she was pleased it was you. She sees you're taking the competition seriously and wants someone to have a fair shot at winning.'

'Why does she believe Roger may be sabotaging the game?'

'She didn't say. My guess? If he had to hand over

fifty grand to someone, it'll be "bye-bye" to the car and tailor-made suits. He's got used to a certain lifestyle, one funded—at least partly—by money he hopes he never has to pay out, and one he doesn't want to give up.' Lucinda shrugged and strolled towards the door. 'We should go. Max has already taken one for the team in leading Roger away and keeping him busy. We should rescue him.'

'Oh God, you're right. Poor Max.' Guilt spurring her steps, Kate scurried to follow Lucinda down the corridor. 'Do you think they'll be in the games room?'

'Or the bar. I'll pass by both, get in Max's eyeline and wave goodbye. He'll get it, right?'

'Definitely. He's good at picking up on signals.'

They entered the lobby. The reception desk was still unmanned and their footsteps echoed off the wooden flooring. Lucinda stopped at the foot of the staircase. 'Tell me to mind my own business if you like—'

Uh-oh. That was never a promising start.

'What's going on with you and Max?'

'Um, I'm … it's not…' The skin on Kate's throat and chest became uncomfortably warm as she floundered for an answer. What *was* going on with her and Max?

Lucinda tilted her head, studying her. 'He obviously likes you. A lot. And you seem a great match. I mean, you two were trapped in a small room together and no one died. That's a good sign.'

Kate laughed nervously, prickles of heat climbing to her cheeks. Perhaps sensing her discomfort, Lucinda changed the subject. 'Give me your number.' She swiped at her phone screen and passed it to Kate. 'I'll send you the chocolate cake recipe. To cover our backs. Make our excuse to Roger look good.'

Impressed with Lucinda's thoroughness, Kate tapped her number into the contacts list and handed the phone back. 'Thank you. If it's not too hard, I might try to make it.'

Lucinda nodded. 'Good luck. With everything. I'd better go and find Max. Oh—' She whirled back to face Kate, her eyes wide with a new thought. 'After holding out against many hints and some persistent nagging, I finally caved and asked Alex if Bella could spend a day on the *Napier* set. You obviously like detective stories. Would you like to go too?'

A stinging in her eyes told Kate she was staring, goggle-eyed, at Lucinda. But her mind had frozen, unable to come up with any response that wouldn't involve grabbing Lucinda in a bear hug, lifting her off the floor and screaming, 'Yes!'

That wouldn't do. Kate liked to aim for dignified, even if she often missed. Blinking, she cleared her throat and said, 'That would be lovely. Thank you.'

'Great. I'll be in touch.'

Kate watched Lucinda exit the lobby. 'Oh my God,' she said, whispering the words to herself as a broad grin spread across her face. 'A day on the set of *Napier*!'

The possibility of one of her dreams coming true put a spring in Kate's step as she turned and bounded up the stairs, wondering with each step if—one day—she might oust Bella from her position as the fabulous Lucinda's number one fan.

Chapter 36

Her mind fizzing with fantasies about behind the scenes at the *Napier* set, Kate's smile didn't slip until she was perched on the edge of her bed, changing back into her pyjamas.

Max! She raked her hands through her hair, kicking herself for having forgotten him. She should have waited for him at the top of the stairs or in the corridor. After all, hanging around outside his door was out of the question: Paul was inside, intruding on Max's well-deserved privacy.

On the bedside table, her phone jangled and buzzed. Kate's pulse thudded: maybe it was a message from Max. Although, he didn't have her number, did he?

A quick glance at the screen resulted in a cold shower of disappointment. It was Bella:

Team meeting tomorrow at breakfast. Hash browns and brainstorm to prep our presentation. Hope your head is better and you're getting some sleep! I'll message your Watson now xx

Kate huffed a laugh. Only Bella could demand your attention while simultaneously ordering you to sleep. Composing her reply, the tapping of her fingers against the phone was loud in the midnight silence.

Head much better. Thanks for the pills. Have lots to tell you! News about

Kate paused, her fingers suspended above the screen. On the other side of her bedroom door, a device had chimed and buzzed. A suspicion forming, Kate glided over to the door and peered through the spy hole. Aha! Out in the corridor, Max was staring down at his phone, no doubt reading his summons to the team breakfast meeting.

Kate rushed to open the door, her fingers slipping on the handle.

Max looked up, the surprise in his eyes warming into a smile. 'Hi.'

'Hi.' Kate returned his smile, unable to think of anything to add, distracted by Max's tousled hair, T-shirt-clad broad chest, and her inner voice singing, *He fancies you! He fancies you!*

Max seemed equally lost for words. 'I ... I was thinking— Oh! Sorry, I'm keeping you from bed.'

His gaze had dipped to her knees before rising and getting stuck somewhere around her shoulder. What was he looking at? Kate glanced down. Oh crap. Purple pyjamas with cartoon hedgehogs.

'It's fine,' she said, shuffling to her right so the door hid more of the fabric while making a frantic mental note to buy some alluring pyjamas. Was that even a thing? Slinky pyjamas had to exist, right?

Pulling at the edge of her top, she risked a shy glance at Max and muttered, 'Hedgehogs.'

'Hedgehogs are excellent,' said Max. 'Who doesn't like hedgehogs?'

'Slugs?'

'Exactly. Case closed.'

Kate giggled and forgot to feel shy. She pointed at Max's phone. 'You've also received Bella's instructions?'

Max nodded. 'I was coming to ask what Lucinda told you, but you can fill us all in at breakfast. That way you only have to explain once.' He returned his phone to his back pocket. 'I'll go and let you rest before your headache comes back. But this'—he dipped into his front pocket and brought out Lorenzo's silver cufflink—'is for you. You should keep it, until we have to produce it as proof of our theory.'

A breath caught in Kate's throat as she extended a hand to receive the cufflink. It was a small gesture, but she was touched that Max was entrusting her with something important. Their fingers brushed against each other as the silver stud passed from his hand to hers and a spark of electricity jumped between them.

Slowly, Max lifted his gaze from their hands to Kate's face. The temperature of the air in the deserted corridor seemed to rocket as she stared into his gorgeous green-gold eyes.

'Well'—Max exhaled shakily—'goodnight.'

He moved a fraction closer and Kate's pulse kicked. Was he going for a hug? A goodnight kiss on her cheek? Should she go in for the hug first?

Kate never found out what Max's intentions had been. He swayed to his left. Inhaling, Kate swayed to her right, and was rewarded with the tantalising citrus-spicy scent of his cologne before their lips collided.

Max pulled back, his eyebrows having soared so high they were in danger of hitting his hairline. 'I'm so sorry,' he said. 'I wasn't, not that I wouldn't want to, obviously, I mean, you're amazing—'

Kate smiled as Max babbled and the pink dashes on his cheeks darkened to scarlet. She hadn't been mistaken. Max *did* fancy her. Even when she was under unflattering corridor lighting and wearing pyjamas festooned with cartoon hedgehogs.

Her heart thudding against her ribs, Kate stepped forwards so her bare toes were almost touching Max's shoes. She laid a hand against his chest, rose to the balls of her feet, and kissed him into silence.

Max froze for a moment, then lifted his right hand to cradle Kate's cheek. His fingertips slid into her hair and brushed the tender skin below her ear.

Kate toes curled into the soft carpet as a wave of heat swept through her, turning her legs to jelly. It was the first time she'd experienced a kiss that was this bone-meltingly fantastic and as Max's other hand settled at her waist she was tempted to throw her arms around his neck, drag him into her room and slam the door behind him.

Her skin tingled and a small moan escaped her as Max's hand moved from her waist to the small of her back. He applied a gentle pressure to the base of her spine, encouraging her to lean into him. Kate responded eagerly to the hint, pressing herself to the hard planes of Max's chest. Her mind and body aglow, Kate's knees trembled and her thigh vibrated—

Wait. *What?* What was *that?*

Puzzled, and slightly dazed, Kate pulled away from

Max as the vibration was accompanied by a tinny jingle, followed by more buzzing and chiming from Max's back pocket.

They chuckled nervously as they retrieved their phones. A quick glance at the screen revealed another message from Bella:

Don't forget—breakfast is being served early and in the games room tomorrow. Get some sleep. I'll remind Max xx

'Bella?' Kate asked.

'Yeah.' Max returned his phone to his pocket. 'We should probably get some rest.' He shrugged, his lips curling into a lazy smile of drowsy happiness.

Kate met Max's warm gaze, but a chill trickled down her spine. Was that it? Nothing more than a stolen midnight moment before tomorrow returning to all business?

'But, in case it needs saying'—Max took Kate's hand, interlaced his fingers with hers and dropped his voice to a quiet, confidential tone—'I would definitely like to do this again.' He pressed a sweet kiss to the back of her hand. 'Goodnight, Kate.'

'Night,' Kate said—amazed she'd managed to say anything through what must have been the largest, dopiest grin she'd ever worn—as she leant on the door frame and watched Max stroll off along the corridor, a slight spring in his relaxed stride.

Chapter 37

Sunday morning was glorious. Kate opened her bedroom window, took a deep breath and smiled. On first glance the view appeared similar to the previous day's. Another azure sky, more mild lavender-scented air and the same uninterrupted vistas of neat lawns giving way to rolling green fields. But on closer inspection, everything seemed brighter and more vibrant, close to sparkling.

Her dress couldn't have been more perfect for such a sunny day. As she descended the stairs to the lobby, Kate smoothed the skirt of the navy-blue fabric and, her gaze wandering over the pattern of miniature rainbows, her smile widened. It was one of her favourite designs: full of hope, colour and happiness.

And she was hopeful, even if hope wasn't making her hands tremble. That was nerves. Today the case would be closed and their team had the chance to triumph. All she had to do was focus for a few more hours and temporarily shelve any intrusively bewitching, seductive thoughts about a certain kiss with a certain foxy individual. How hard could that be?

On entering the games room, Kate spotted Bella at a nearby table, already gleefully demolishing a pile of hash browns. She looked up from her plate and waved at Kate, who did her best to return an innocent smile as she approached. Kate hated keeping things from her friend, but Bella was another powerful incentive for putting any non-pure thoughts about Max out of her mind. If Bella caught on that she and Max had been canoodling, there would be little chance of getting her to concentrate on anything else. And today they needed everyone's head firmly in the game. Besides, it was only a kiss, for heaven's sake. True, it had been amazing, the sort of kiss that made you hear angels sing, see stars and—

'Morning,' Bella said as Kate arrived at the table. 'What's up?'

'Nothing! Nothing at all,' said Kate, giving herself a mental shake for losing focus so quickly. 'Everything's fine. Just great. Why do you ask?'

Bella stared at Kate, her eyes narrowing. 'Are you worried about presenting this thing later?'

'Yes!' Kate chuckled, partly in relief. That had been close. 'You got me. I can't hide anything from you.'

Bella's eyes narrowed further, until they were sharp slits of suspicion. Oh no. She'd overdone it.

Kate hardly dared move as she gave Bella her best innocent face. 'Hmn,' said Bella. 'That seat's free.' She pointed at the chair one away from hers, which would— hallelujah!—leave the stuffed deer's head behind Kate. Perhaps she would be able to enjoy her breakfast seasoned with only the lightest pinch of guilt.

'Great. Thanks. I'm just going to—' Kate motioned towards the buffet and scurried away, hoping that Bella would be so busy digesting her cooked breakfast she would have little energy spare to ponder Kate's bizarre behaviour.

The buffet tables were busy and, while she waited for her chance to serve herself some divine-smelling bacon, Kate found herself humming and tapping her fingers against her plate.

Her pleasingly jaunty rhythm was interrupted by a deep, smooth voice. 'Good morning. Another great dress today, I see.'

Max's own outfit was a plain contrast to Kate's rainbows. He was once again flawlessly smart in a crisp white shirt unbuttoned at the neck. His hair was neatly styled and Kate felt a small pang of disappointment at the disappearance of the alluringly tousled locks of the previous evening. And the practically indecent T-shirt. All of which led her back to their knee-trembling kiss in the darkened corridor. Something he said he wanted to do again.

'Kate?'

Kate blinked at Max, a burning flush racing up her neck. On no. She had been gazing at him, a dopey smile on her face, like a daft lovesick teenager. *Say something, Kate! Something smart and witty!*

She tucked a strand of hair behind her ear and said, 'Hi.'

Oh fantastic, Kate. Really smooth.

Fortunately, Max didn't seem to have noticed she had lost the power of speech. He returned her smile. 'I came to get some tea, would you like some?'

'Um, yes please.'

'Right, I'll take it over to our table. Although'—Max

stepped closer, his lips inches from her ear, and whispered—
'getting tea was an excuse to come over and talk to you.'

Oh. The incipient rumbles of hunger in Kate's tummy transformed into quivers of excitement. 'Why?'

'Well, firstly, because I like talking to you. And also because I wondered if you'd already told the others about the study and the secret—' He broke off and his gaze darted to the guests from other teams surrounding them. His caution was wise. As far as they knew, they were the only ones to have found the secret room in the study and the jewels. Giving away their sole advantage at this point would be foolish. He cleared his throat and tried again. 'Told the others about *what* we discovered last night.'

'Not yet.'

'And you haven't told Bella yet about anything else we did last night?'

Max's gaze dropped to Kate's lips, causing the heat in the skin at her neck to shoot up into her cheeks. She turned to load her plate with bacon, giving herself an excuse to hide the worst of the blush from Max and escape his patient, penetrating stare. But, when she met his gaze again, his face was possibly pinker than hers. Hold on. He wasn't embarrassed by their kiss, was he?

'I haven't …' Kate stammered, the thought that Max might regret having kissed her making her tongue leaden. 'No, I haven't spoken to her—'

'Not that I'd mind,' said Max, the words tumbling from his lips. 'Obviously, I'd happily tell everyone.'

He'd happily tell everyone. Obviously. Kate's pressed her lips together to prevent them curling into another dopey grin. It also helped her resist a sudden perverse urge to leap onto the nearest chair, throw her head back, close her eyes and bellow, 'I snogged Max Ravenscroft, it was bloody fantastic and he wants to tell everyone!'

Blissfully unaware of Kate's dramatic thoughts, Max continued. 'But, what with Paul being here, it might be best not to mention it right now?'

Oh yes. Paul. And just like that, she was back to the need to shelve things. How long had she managed to focus on the case and ignore everything else? She'd lasted about two minutes before daydreaming about Max again. She had to do better.

'I doubt it'd help the team concentrate on solving the case,' said Max. 'And I know that means a lot to you. But if you want to tell them, that's fine by me.'

'No, it's OK,' said Kate. 'You're right. I'll tell Bella later. It'll save you having to tell Ethan.' She glanced across the room to where Ethan and Bella had their heads close together, probably gossiping. 'Those two seem to tell each other everything. Anyway, she's going to be annoyed enough we didn't tell her about finding the secret r—' Kate broke off, casting a mistrustful glance at the guests either side of them. 'I mean, that we didn't tell her about the other thing we found last night. In the study.'

Bella would be livid. She had so longed to find a hidden compartment in the safe and they'd found a whole room. And a full Bella tirade wasn't something Kate wanted to face on an empty stomach.

'I don't think we need to rush to tell her though,' Kate said, sliding a triangle of toast onto her plate and ignoring the increasing grumbles from her tummy. She glanced up at Max. 'Just in case, I'll wait to finish breakfast before breaking the news.'

Chapter 38

'I can't believe you found'—Bella cast a glance over her shoulder and dropped her voice to a hiss—'a ruddy secret room and didn't come and get me!'

Kate swallowed the last of her bacon. 'Sorry, but it all happened really quickly, there wasn't time. Plus it was small and dusty. You didn't miss much.'

'Not much! Just the missing jewels—'

'Shh!' Kate shot a nervous smile at the few diners on other tables who had turned towards Bella's rising tone. Fortunately what she had said was likely to be masked by the sound of the scraping of crockery and cutlery and subdued conversation.

Paul, who was sitting in front of a large arched window, was backlit by a shaft of sunlight. Kate found herself grimacing whenever she tried to look directly at him. 'Only an hour until we present,' he said. 'We should run through our theories again.'

Bella cast a sideways glance at Kate and raised an

eyebrow as if to say, 'Who does this guy think he is?' Kate lifted her shoulders in a subtle shrug. Paul had a tendency to take charge. A quality which was valued at his work, but when he'd arrived late—and not exactly been invited—to a murder mystery weekend and made a minimal contribution to his team's investigations, a wiser man might have let someone else—and probably Bella, if he wanted to be safe—take the lead.

Under the table, a foot brushed against the toe of Kate's left shoe. Unless Bella was performing an impressive feat of contortionism, the culprit had to be Max. Not that you'd know it. Anyone else would have assumed he was absorbed in admiring the display of rifles on the wall opposite him and finishing the last morsels of a golden almond croissant.

Mmm. Kate sighed as she gazed at the pastry and the man eating it. Delicious. Her mind wandering back to their kiss, Kate trained her stare on the pristine white tablecloth and returned the pressure on Max's foot. A smile stole onto her lips and the fine hairs on her arms stood on end as her memory served up a dessert of details which—

'Kate?' said Paul. 'Why don't you begin?'

Kate blinked rapidly under the pressure of Paul's stare and the razor edge to his voice. His tone had been growing progressively sharper and his expression stony ever since he had heard about her and Max's night-time adventure. Perhaps, like Bella, he believed he should have been first in Kate's thoughts.

'OK.' Kate laid her palms on the table and spread her fingers. 'Our victim is Adrian Grieve. An apparently successful promoter, producer, businessman and investor. Father of two daughters. Found dead in his study—'

'Found *murdered* in his study,' said Bella. 'Don't undersell it. Remember what Roger Merryman said: "Only foul play here."'

'All right. Murdered most foully in his study. Stabbed through the heart with his letter opener, the safe emptied of a very valuable cache of jewels.'

Kate nodded at Max, inviting him to continue. He returned the nod and said, 'Whoever did this staged the scene so it would look as if an intruder had stolen the jewels and killed Adrian Grieve. But Kate figured out that Mr Grieve was most probably poisoned and already dead when stabbed. The relatively peaceful position of the corpse, the lack of convulsions, bleeding or vomiting—'

'Gah! Do you have to?' Bella clutched her stomach. 'I'm digesting here!'

Undeterred, Max continued, 'It suggests barbiturate poisoning.'

'Yes, yes,' said Paul, pausing in spreading strawberry jam on his toast to brandish his knife dismissively, 'but it's the suspects that are key.' He pointed the knife at Kate and the piercing nature of his gaze, combined with the sharp blade coated in a red, blood-like residue, made her squirm in her seat. 'You've ruled out Lucille Palmer because she has no motive, an alibi, and doesn't have the temperament to poison anyone or stab them in the back?'

'Correct,' said Max and Kate in unison, causing Paul's gaze to harden further as it shuttled between them.

Paul continued, 'And Archie Forbes can't be involved because he's ... how did you put it earlier?'

'A gullible innocent who couldn't keep a single one of the many secrets involved in executing a clandestine operation,' said Ethan. Kate was impressed. Ethan must have been paying more attention to the mystery aspects of the weekend than she'd thought.

'So, having ruled out two of the characters, that leaves us with the sisters and Lorenzo Corsini,' said Paul. 'The flashy Italian count—if that's who he really is. He comes across as a total grifter, a gold-digging parasite. And we're supposed to believe he's aristocracy?'

Bella snorted. 'Sounds bang on, if you ask me.'

Before Bella could climb onto the table and start bellowing 'the Internationale', Kate jumped in. 'Lorenzo is definitely involved. His cufflink was in the secret room where the jewels are stashed. And then there's the list.' She brushed a few toast crumbs from the notepad lying beside her plate. 'The mocked-up newspapers and magazine in the library feature stories on a string of jewel thefts from high society figures since late February. Which happens to be exactly when Lorenzo entered the country. Every place a crime occurred, usually a large house, hosted some kind of gathering just prior to the theft. And Lorenzo and Pamela attended all of those parties. Though the real smoking gun was in a tiny article about investigators looking into the disappearance of a diamond necklace from the Lake Como villa of the Dossi family. It went missing in September 1931, when Lorenzo met Pamela at a party at a house on Lake Como. The soirée was starry enough— featuring some Hollywood A-listers—that it got a mention in an article in one of the copies of *Star Style* left in the library. And who was at that gathering? Lorenzo Corsini and Pamela Grieve.'

'Like I said, a total grifter,' said Paul. 'So Lorenzo robbed

Adrian Grieve, but he didn't have an obvious motive to kill him, did he? Leaving us with the question: which of the sisters was in on it with him?'

Ethan tapped the tabletop and turned to Kate and Max. 'You think Pamela is our best bet?'

'Yes,' Max said. 'Nancy harboured enough resentment towards her father and has a temper that could have made an explosive cocktail, pushing her to kill Adrian in a moment of rage.'

Paul leant forwards. 'And she told me she had the sleeping pills.'

'That's true,' Max said. 'But killing her father by drugging him, that's calculated, cold-blooded. She'd need a stronger, longer-term motive to engage in the planning involved.'

'And she's nicely set up for life with the daft husband,' said Bella. 'So she wouldn't have done it for the cash.'

'And she doesn't want the house either. She hates it.' Kate glanced about her, taking in the dark wood panelling and shotgun display, and felt a twinge of sympathy for Nancy's negative view of the Old Grange.

'Pamela it is then,' said Paul. 'What's her story?'

Kate opened her mouth to respond, but Bella laid a gentle hand on her wrist. 'Let me have a go at this.' She took a deep breath. 'Pamela has no memories of her mother. She grows up with a grumpy older sister who abandons the family home while Pamela is a teenager, leaving her alone to bear the brunt of her father's domineering, controlling nature. Over time she becomes desperate to escape. And then, her prayers are answered! A dashing Italian aristocrat, a philanthropist who moonlights as a gentleman thief, sweeps her off her feet. What follows is a whirlwind romance, a passionate, intoxicating affair with the devastatingly handsome, hot, sexy Italian—'

'He's not that good-looking,' said Ethan, his nose wrinkling in disgust at his fiancée's enthusiastic description. 'He was oily. Smarmy.'

'He's also fictitious, darling,' said Bella, swaying to kiss Ethan's cheek. His grimace disappeared and, as the couple shared a smile, Kate's spirits rose. After their stormy disagreement the previous evening, Ethan and Bella appeared to have entered calmer waters.

'Where was I? Oh yes!' Bella flicked her shiny hair over her shoulder. 'Whirlwind romance. Desperate dreams of escaping her tyrannical father. But her suitor lacks funds and a timely visit from the insurers plants a seed in her head, an idea of what her father might be worth dead. Then she's prescribed sleeping pills—much needed after lying awake night after night imagining pushing her dad down the stairs—and the parts of the plan start to come together. They can be free of Adrian, swipe the jewels, claim the insurance, inherit half the estate, get the life-insurance payout and be free to embark on their charitable schemes. Sadly, she didn't realise the estate was practically bankrupt ...'

Bella trailed off, her gaze narrowing. Kate followed her stare to a table across the room, where Dave, the pale chinless joker and murder mystery weekend sceptic she had met in reception back on Friday afternoon, had dashed into the room and was rambling and gesticulating at his teammates.

'What's happening over there?' asked Paul.

'I'll check it out.' Ethan threw his napkin onto the table. 'Back in a sec.'

It was chuckles and smiles all round as Ethan was greeted warmly by their competition. But, as the conversation progressed—with increasingly dramatic hand gestures being deployed on both sides of the chat—Kate's sense of trepidation grew. What was going on?

'I'm going to the lobby,' said Ethan as he strode back to their table.

'Why?' asked Bella. 'What's happening that's got them so excited?'

'The information board,' said Ethan. 'Dorothy Williams told one of their lot'—he motioned to the other team—'that she's going to post the autopsy report any minute. And I want to get there before anyone snags it.'

'Would anyone do that?' asked Kate.

'To make sure they win fifty grand?' Bella snorted. 'People would do a lot worse than destroy a piece of paper.' She turned her gaze to Ethan. 'Remember that Kate's promised us a generous wedding present if she wins, my love. So don't walk. Run!'

Chapter 39

She'd been right.

The autopsy on Adrian Grieve confirmed that the cause of death was a lethal dose of barbiturates. The letter opener had pierced his heart, but it hadn't been beating at the time.

The tips of Kate's fingers trembled as she clutched Ethan's phone and zoomed in on the blurry picture of the report. She would have punched the air with triumph, but a worrying niggle had caught her attention.

'The bottom of the page isn't in the photo,' she said.

'I know, sorry,' said Ethan. 'I did my best, but it was a miracle I got a photo of any of it what with Roger Merryman swooping in.'

'Mr Shifty?' Bella, who had pressed her temple against Kate's to get a better view of the photo, twisted round in her seat to look up at Ethan. Kate turned too, to check they were alone. While she agreed with Bella's opinion of Roger, it probably wasn't wise to be bad-mouthing him so loudly.

Unbothered by who might be eavesdropping, Bella prompted Ethan to spill the beans. 'What's he been up to now?'

'I got to the lobby and Dorothy must have just posted the report because I saw her walking away. Then Roger comes rocketing into the room. I swear he was bright pink. And that was something to see, given his tan is orange.' Ethan shook his head. 'I don't know why, but I got this feeling about what he was going to do, so I got my phone out and took the best photo I could in a rush and at a distance. A second later, Roger ripped the paper off the board.' Ethan raised a hand, balled his fingers into a fist and jerked it downwards violently. 'He tore it into pieces as he marched off, still pink and muttering to himself. I don't think he even saw me.'

'Lucinda was definitely onto something,' said Max.

'Of course she was,' said Bella. 'Lucinda knows what she's talking about. She's got her fingers in all the pies. Literally and figuratively.'

'Whatever's going on, it's played into our hands,' said Paul. 'It looks like we're the only ones who have seen this and it backs up our theories.'

Our theories? Kate cast an incredulous glance at Paul. He'd always had a tendency to 'organise' others, but taking credit for their work wasn't something she'd expect from him.

'Ethan, mate?' Paul trained his gaze above Kate's and Bella's heads, zeroing in on where his best friend was hovering behind the women's chairs. 'Did you see any other teams in the lobby?'

As Ethan ran through his story again, Kate tapped

her fingertips against her notepad. Despite having her poisoning theory proved, something was bothering her, like an itch deep inside her brain.

'Hey,' said Max quietly. 'What's up?'

'It's probably nothing,' said Kate.

'But?'

Max's stare was insistent, but encouraging. Kate met it and said, 'Derek Jones.'

Max blinked, taking a moment to follow her train of thought. 'The missing persons case?'

'Yeah. I keep thinking, why would Archie have been briefed with so much detail on it if it was irrelevant? Why—'

'It's a red herring!' Paul boomed, his interruption landing into their private conversation like a grenade. Kate stared at him, open-mouthed. She had forgotten how bat-like his hearing could be when he wanted to use it. The sort of preternatural sense that allowed him to call out a kid whispering at the back of the assembly hall.

Kate tilted her head from side to side, considering Paul's outburst. 'Perhaps. But then I also keep coming back to the letter opener. That Nancy was asked to return it a couple of months ago and then it happened to be used to stab her father? Isn't that too much of a coincidence?'

'That's exactly what it is, Kate,' Paul said, with a sigh of exasperation. 'Another red herring to draw our suspicions towards Nancy and away from Pamela. Not everything here has to be significant. It makes sense to throw plenty of dead ends in to confuse us. We know that Roger Merryman is going to great lengths to stop any of us from winning this thing. He's obviously going to have included loads of circumstantial details which may seem significant but are designed to throw us off the scent, isn't he?' Paul pushed to standing, leaning forwards with his fists resting on the table. 'Let's not let him distract us. We have a good solution to present. I suggest we all get a coffee and then we can move on to discussing who is going to present it.'

The crystal bead trim on Bella's red halter-neck top glittered as she rose from her chair. 'Why does there need to be a discussion? Kate should do it. It's mostly her work.'

A trickle of ice ran through Kate's veins. Oh no. There was no way she'd be able to—

Paul snorted and straightened. 'That's not happening, is it? I mean, Kate's done well at putting the facts together, but public speaking isn't her thing. She struggled to get through a short speech at the school Christmas show when all she had to do was thank the parents for coming. How is she going to run through our entire theory in front of an audience?'

Kate stared at Paul and, for a moment, the chill of fear was pushed aside by a hot tremor of indignation. There was only one way he could have known about her stammering performance at the Christmas show: bloody Kirsty. She must have crept out of the office to skulk in the shadows and have a good laugh at her.

Some of the anger must have seeped into her stare. When Paul caught her eye his gaze quickly slipped down to the floor. 'I need a coffee before we sort this out.'

He marched off towards the coffee machine and Bella muttered, 'Why, thank you, Paul. I'd love a cup of tea. You're such an angel.' She rolled her eyes. 'Ethan, I'm guessing you'd like a coffee?' Ethan nodded and Bella dropped her hands onto Kate's and Max's shoulders. 'Would you guys like anything?'

Kate shook her head and Max said, 'I'll come and get mine now, save you trying to carry everything.' The sound of Bella's heels clacking across the floorboards covered his voice as he leant a little closer to Kate and said, 'Are you OK? Are you sure you wouldn't like tea?'

Max's open green gaze roved across Kate's face, but the crinkle of concern between his eyes stopped her from drifting off into a peaceful contemplation of his gorgeousness. Did she look that awful? Perhaps a drink was a good idea. 'Tea would be lovely. Thank you.'

Now he had a task to perform, the wrinkle at the bridge of Max's nose vanished. He sprang to his feet. 'I'll be back in a minute,' he said as he made to follow Bella.

Kate laid her hands in her lap and stared at her fingers. The soft cotton of her dress was smooth and comforting against her palms. *Breathe*, she told herself. *You won't have to present the case. And, even if you did, Bella and Max would help—*

'It's amazing, when you think about it.'

Kate glanced up. Ethan was lounging in the chair to the left of Max's. One side of the collar of his teal polo shirt was folded up, the other down. Kate guessed this was the result of Bella trying to convince him not to wear it turned up. She had strong views on such things.

'What's amazing?' she asked.

Ethan smiled and lifted his left foot to rest it on his right knee. 'How well you and Max have got on this weekend. I always saw you two as rivals at the Friendly Club and I didn't know how things would go. Especially as you haven't been in touch for ages, except for Christmas cards, and I'm not sure how much that counts.'

Kate blinked at Ethan in confusion. 'Christmas cards?'

'Yeah. Max asked me for your address in Reading so he could send you a card. I admire him for being so organised. I never manage to get around to it.'

Max had asked for her address? She had never received anything from him. Had he not used it? She frowned. 'When was this?'

'Shortly before we moved down to London, so that would have been the first Christmas you were in Reading, right? We were so busy with the move I didn't manage to get my parents a card, let alone think about …'

Ethan kept talking, a cup of steaming tea was placed in front of her, and Max slid back into his seat, but Kate was insensible to it all. The sound of the world outside her own mind had fallen away, drowned out by the click, click, click of her brain as it slotted together pieces of a puzzle she hadn't known existed until a moment ago.

Closing her eyes, Kate held up her conclusions to the light, checking for cracks. But there wasn't the tiniest flaw in her logic. All she needed to confirm her theory was the guilty party to confess.

Her eyes snapped open. Staring at the ghostly curl of steam rising above the delicate white cup on the table and clenching her fingers into fists, she waited for Paul to return.

Chapter 40

'They didn't have decaf.' Paul harrumphed as he slumped into his chair and opened the first of the pile of pink sugar packets he had thrown onto the table next to his cup. 'And no sweetener. I thought this place was supposed to have everything …'

Kate stared at her white knuckles as Paul rambled on. *Speak up*, her inner voice instructed. *You've listened to him rabbiting nonsense for long enough.*

She raised her head, fixed Paul with her steadiest stare and shot her words at him like bullets. 'You are a liar.'

'Sorry?' Paul's gaze dropped to the sugar packets. Ugh! Did he honestly think Kate was accusing him of telling untruths about the hotel's supply of sweetener?

Kate inhaled slowly, as if she was sucking in enough air to be able to breathe fire. 'I said: you are a liar. You are a lying, pathetic'—she narrowed her eyes as she mined her memory for the best insults she'd heard traded in the playground—'leaky bucket of worm slime.'

'Wh— I—' Paul's jaw dropped and his eyes widened, his face a picture of bafflement. 'Kate, I—'

'The book subscription, Paul.'

Slowly, Paul's mouth closed and his gaze, which had been so direct and surprised, turned shifty. He knew exactly what she was talking about. The lying git.

To her left, Max's chair creaked as he fidgeted. Kate longed to reach for him, but she had to deal with Paul first.

'Kate.' Paul held up a hand, a placating palm angled towards her. 'There must have been some kind of misunderstanding, I don't know—'

'You forgot my birthday,' said Kate. 'It was close to Christmas, you were having a stressful time in your new job, we were in a new town. It's understandable, if hurtful.' The edge of Kate's mouth trembled as she remembered the drizzle of sadness which had fallen on her when Paul had wolfed down the toast and coffee she'd made him for breakfast and left without a mention of her birthday. A sadness which had swelled into a stalking cloud of gloom as the day went on and there were no surprise phone calls or flower deliveries. She'd had to face facts: he had forgotten. The thought had hollowed her out. To allow Paul to take his dream job she had left her parents, friends and a school she adored, but she'd done it because she loved him and wanted him to be happy above all else. Was remembering to say happy birthday too much to ask in return?

And even then she had made excuses for him and had almost persuaded herself it wasn't such a big deal after all when she'd got home and found the book-sized parcel on the doorstep.

'But then you got so, so lucky, didn't you?' said Kate,

fixing Paul with a laser-like stare. 'A book had been delivered. The first in a monthly mystery book subscription. A wonderful, thoughtful, perfect gift. And the bookshop had accidentally left out the notecard with the sender's name and message on it.' She had stared at the shining gold details on the cover of the book, a beautiful hardback copy of *Murder on the Orient Express*, and her heart had threatened to burst with relief and joy. It had to be from Paul. After all, her parents and Bella had already sent gifts, so who else could it be from?

'And when you got home, your gullible girlfriend, instead of asking you about it, thanks you for the lovely present and tells you how brilliant you are.' Kate winced, remembering how she had thrown herself at him, gushing about what a fantastic surprise it was and how she had worried he'd forgotten, but of course he hadn't and she was sorry—oh my God, she'd apologised—for having doubted him. 'And I assumed you looked stunned because I was overdoing it, not because you had no idea what I was talking about!'

Paul kept glancing towards the exit, no doubt calculating how quickly he could escape. A sheen of sweat glistened on his forehead. Good.

'It was such an easy con to keep up too, wasn't it?' said Kate. 'You intercepted the arrival of the book each month, opened the parcel, removed the notecard and presented it to me. And I fell for it, thinking it was a touching gesture.'

'Kate,' Paul said. 'If you let me explain—'

'Oh, I'd love to.' Kate folded her arms over her chest. 'Come on. What have you got to say for yourself?'

Paul eyed each member of the group nervously. 'It

wasn't … You're making it sound worse than it was. It wasn't like I planned it—'

The sound of Kate's mirthless chuckle was drowned out by the gasp of disgust which came from behind her chair, where Bella was standing with her hands on her hips. 'Bloody hell, Paul!' Bella said. 'Even by your standards this is some breathtakingly epic dickishness.'

'Bella,' Ethan said, making a token effort to defend his friend from a Bella onslaught.

'No Ethan, he is not getting out of this one,' Bella said. 'He has been keeping this going for … it must be two and a half years!'

'And we spoke about it yesterday,' Kate said. 'You could have come clean then. How were you going to get out of this? I was going to find out eventually.'

'I don't know,' Paul said, mumbling his words to the tablecloth.

Ethan, perhaps in another attempt to take some heat off Paul, asked, 'But if it's not Paul, who got Kate the books?'

The chair to Kate's left creaked again. Max had covered the lower half of his face with his hand, but his neck had a telltale rosy glow. Kate smiled and the desire to hurl cutlery at Paul was replaced by a yearning to press her lips to the blush above Max's collar. *Poirot's Christmas. Lord Edgware Dies. The Adventures of Sherlock Holmes.* They'd been reading the same books at the same time for months.

'Max. Obviously!' said Bella, rolling her eyes at Ethan's question. 'Who the heck else would send Kate mystery books? And he asked you for her address right before her birthday. I should have put two and two together at the time but, like Kate, I was too busy giving Pinocchio here'—she jabbed a finger in Paul's direction—'the benefit of the doubt.'

While Bella continued to vent her indignation, Kate took a break from glaring at Paul—her eyes were starting to smart—and twisted towards Max. She touched his knee and waited for him to lift his gaze, which he had fixed on the arm of the chair.

Eventually, he shifted his hand to the side of his face and looked up at her through his dark lashes. His green gaze was calm and expectant, as gorgeously golden as ever. But it was the sight of his cheeks, which were tinged the same red as his neck, which made Kate's heart skip. Gently, she trailed her fingertips back and forth across his knee, hoping to channel the affection and gratitude she would have wanted to show him years ago—and which Paul had effectively stolen—into the gesture. 'Thank you,' she said, her voice a hoarse whisper. 'Give me a minute to sort this and then we'll talk. OK?'

Max nodded, a faint smile passing over his lips.

'... completely unbelievable!' Bella thumped her hands onto the backs of Kate's and Max's chairs, making both of them flinch. Apparently she hadn't finished with Paul yet. 'And are you going to apologise to Kate, and to be fair, to Max too?'

In the vacuum of silence which followed Bella's tirade, all attention swung towards Paul. He stuttered and wrung his hands, his gaze shuttling among them, searching for a sympathetic listener. Eventually, he settled on Kate and, in contrast to Bella's strident tone, his words were quiet and careful.

'Kate, I'll admit that I didn't handle this as I should have. I'm sorry, OK? I was going to tell you, back at the beginning. But you loved it so much and were so happy, I couldn't bring myself to tell you. And they kept turning up month after month and it got harder and harder to say anything. I'm sorry. Just ...' He lifted his gaze to the ceiling for a moment, perhaps calling for divine assistance. 'Tell me what I can do to make it up to you. I know I have a mountain to climb, but I'm good at that.' He laughed nervously at his own joke, but cut his mirth short when no one joined in. 'I'll do anything, Kate. Tell me, what can I do?'

Kate raked Paul with her gaze. This would always be a joke to him. A game in which he believed he was the only one who knew the rules. And she had considered not taking the job in Knowleswood, not moving home, because of this guy!

Kate closed her eyes and, exhaling slowly, released the simmering anger which was making her fingers twitch. As her lungs emptied, the muscles in her shoulders released and a calm hush settled over her. It was time to let it all go. Everything she had ever felt for Paul, both the good and the bad.

Taking another breath, Kate pictured herself strolling to the centre of her memory closet. With cool determination she closed the lid onto the jet-black box marked *Paul*, nailed it shut, and drop-kicked it into the gloomy depths of the room. Hopefully, lurking back there in the darkness was a friendly oblivion monster who would do her the great favour of eating it.

Kate pushed to standing. She wasn't sure she'd ever be

a world-conquering super-sleuth, but this decision was one thing she was certain she had right.

'You want to know what you can do for me, Paul?' Kate steadied herself against the table and stared him square in the eye. 'Finish your coffee and pack your bags. I want you to leave, and the sooner the better.'

Chapter 41

'Why didn't you cancel the subscription? I didn't contact you with so much as a thank you. You must have thought that was odd.'

Kate's question floated in the pleasant breeze which drifted over the gardens, scattering the light perfume of the bright flowers either side of the path. It had been a good idea to take a walk in the grounds. After Bella and Ethan had decided to help Paul collect his things—Bella whispering to Kate that she was only going to make sure he actually left—Max had suggested they step outside and Kate had been delighted to agree.

The crunch of gravel under her sneakers and the warmth reflecting off the Old Grange's honey-toned façade were comforting and helped relax the knots of tension in her shoulders. Although she was still on edge. As well as odd, Max must have thought her ungrateful and rude when she didn't acknowledge his kind present. The very idea made her chest tighten.

Max shrugged in response to her question. 'Taking out the subscription was a bit of an impulse decision. I wasn't sure it was a good idea. When I didn't hear back from you, I thought it might have been for the best that you didn't respond. I kept meaning to cancel it. But it was a job on an unending to-do list. I was so preoccupied with Mum. And then ...' He sighed. 'This will sound daft.'

Kate looped her arm around his and gave his bicep an encouraging squeeze. 'I doubt that. Go on.'

'The place that sends the books. It's a little local bookshop near my parents' house and I always get the impression from what the owner tells me that they're usually one day's takings away from having to close down for good. A couple of months after your birthday, I went in to cancel and'—he glanced at Kate before returning his gaze to the path ahead—'instead of cancelling your subscription, I ended up taking one out for me as well.'

Kate laughed and swayed into Max, giving him a playful nudge. He met her gaze and smiled. 'You must be their favourite customer,' said Kate, grinning.

'Possibly,' said Max. 'You know, I did think something weird must have happened for you not to have got in touch. Perhaps you'd sent a message and it had gone astray?' He shook his head. 'But I'm glad I didn't cancel it. Sometimes, I'd be reading one of the books and I'd wonder if you'd already finished it. I could picture you with your concentrating detective face, figuring out the whodunnit before the grand reveal.'

Max's stare had turned unfocused, fixed on a point in the distance but unseeing. His forehead was a concertina of creases and one side of his bottom lip was trapped under his front teeth.

Kate tapped his cheek with her index finger. 'Hey! Is this supposed to be my concentrating detective face?'

Max's expression relaxed into a grin. 'Of course.'

'Oh good Lord alive. No wonder I've had a headache. Please tell me the next time I'm doing it so I can stop.'

'Definitely not. It's one of my favourites.'

Kate's insides fizzed with happiness. She smiled and said, 'You have more than one favourite?'

They rounded the corner of the building and approached the columns of the main entrance porch. Max shrugged again. 'No. It's all your face after all. So just one really. Just you.'

Kate tightened her hold on Max's arm and stopped walking, forcing him to come to a halt beside her. His sweetness had set her cheeks glowing and, at a loss for a response that could measure up, she decided it was about time she delivered a message that was two and a half years late.

'Thank you,' she said, her gaze meeting his. 'For the books. Some months it was the only thing I had to look forward to.' She rose to her tiptoes and slid her arms around Max's neck. With her cheek resting against his, she murmured, 'Thank you, Max.'

Max wrapped his arms around her back, matching her squeeze. 'You're welcome, Kate.'

The spring breeze lifted Kate's hair and sent a whisper through the sycamore trees lining the Old Grange driveway. Max held her close and Kate's world narrowed to the booming of her heart, her pulse picking up as Max dipped his head and teased her neck with a cluster of slow, achingly promising kisses.

A distant sound nudged at the edge of Kate's bright bubble of happiness. It was irritatingly insistent. Was— Was that shouting? And ... breaking glass?

Max stilled, his lips hovering tantalisingly above the sensitive skin at the base of Kate's neck. Kate made a small moan of frustration. 'You hear that too?' she asked.

He raised his head to meet her gaze before turning to stare at the hotel entrance and the source of the noise. 'Maybe we don't *have* to investigate?' he said, his tone unconvinced.

Kate closed her eyes, savouring the feeling of Max's fingers stroking delicious circles along her spine. 'We don't have to,' she said, her voice hoarser than was entirely decent. 'Perhaps we could—'

'I'll kill you, Merryman!' The threat was distinct, though muffled by the front door. Kate and Max shared a glance and began to trot towards the hotel.

'Should we get involved?' asked Kate, scurrying to keep up with Max.

'I'm not letting Roger Merryman die before you win his game,' said Max, his expression determined as he opened the door and let Kate pass. 'Whoever's after his blood can wait until after we've presented.'

Chapter 42

Broken glass and lily stems littered the floor of the lobby. The oppressive scent of the flowers permeated the muggy atmosphere. On the right of the room, Roger Merryman crouched behind a sofa, the top half of his face poking out above its red velvet back. To the left, Dave—his chinless face puce with rage—was being restrained by the rest of his team while Dorothy Williams attempted to talk him down.

'Sir, please calm yourself.' Dorothy used her stern but fair principal's tone and held up her hands towards him. 'We can talk about this—'

'That rat'—Dave made another lunge for Roger, surprising his friends, who redoubled their grip on his shoulders, and Roger, who squeaked and ducked further behind the sofa—'is a con artist and a cheat!'

Dorothy, who clearly possessed all the courage as well as the integrity in the Merryman organisation, stepped closer to Dave, whose fury suggested his first experience of a murder mystery party had converted him from sceptic to believer. 'I'm sorry your solution wasn't the one we were looking for,' she said. 'But I guarantee you, I've had the solution in my possession since Friday, I opened it earlier this morning and no one is yet to present a theory which tallies with—'

'That money should be mine. I know I was right. You posted the autopsy report and he took it down before we could see it. He's actively sabotaging the players!' Dave continued to rant and struggle as his friends dragged him to the exit. With a final heave, they practically carried him over the threshold, forcing Ethan and Bella to swerve aside to avoid the mass of flailing limbs.

'Whoa,' said Ethan, picking his way between glistening patches of water and glass to join Kate and Max at the foot of the stairs. 'What's his problem?'

'He believes he should be fifty thousand pounds richer,' said Max. 'And is angry about Roger Merryman taking the autopsy report off the noticeboard. But apparently he didn't get the solution to the case right. You missed him hurling death threats and what appears to have been a vase of lilies at Roger.'

Over at the sofa, Dorothy was helping Roger to a seat. He was quivering so violently he resembled a tweed-clad orange blancmange.

'It's disappointing,' said Bella. 'But who throws glassware around and threatens physical violence because they lost a game?'

The others stared at Bella. Their silence and raised eyebrows spoke volumes.

'What?' Bella's gaze shuttled between them. 'You don't think I would ever— Come on, guys. Give me some credit!'

318

'Babe,' said Ethan, 'a few minutes ago you told Paul if he ever bothered Kate again you'd make his life a living hell.'

'Exactly!' Bella put her hands on her hips. 'You've proved my point. I didn't threaten him with death and I didn't throw anything.'

'Excuse me.' Dorothy Williams approached them, pushing her red-framed glasses up to the bridge of her nose as she neared. 'I'm sorry about the commotion.' She glanced over her shoulder to the sofa—where Roger had reclined with one arm thrown over his eyes—and sighed. 'Unfortunately as the prize fund has grown, these sorts of incidents are no longer unexpected.'

Wow, thought Kate. How many previous mystery weekends had ended in punch-ups and shouting matches?

Dorothy ran a hand down the front of her purple satin blouse, smoothing non-existent creases. 'There may be a slight delay before you can present. If you give us twenty minutes, we'll be ready for you in the library. Who will be speaking for your team?'

Kate's breath caught in her throat as all eyes turned to her. The recent drama had distracted her from the looming inevitability of the presentation. But now it appeared there was no avoiding it.

'I've already said it,' said Bella, 'and I haven't changed my mind. Kate should do it.'

Bella's show of confidence in her raised a weak smile from Kate, which quickly became a grimace as her stomach cramped.

Max touched a hand lightly to her elbow. 'I agree with Bella,' Max said. 'But if you would really rather not present, I'll do it.'

The relief was immediate: it was as though Kate had been standing in a deluge of stress and Max had opened an umbrella over her head. She exhaled, the tightness in her chest releasing. 'Thank you,' she said.

'You're sure?' Max wore a small frown of concern as he scanned her face. 'I don't want to steal your thunder. And I may need you to chip in if I get something wrong or lose my thread.'

'That's fine,' Kate said, the words rushing out as she held Max's gaze with her most imploring stare. 'I can do that. I'd like to do that. Honestly.'

Dorothy nodded. 'Excellent. I look forward to seeing you all in the library.'

'Ms Williams,' Ethan said, halting Dorothy's retreat, 'I don't want to keep you back, but'—Ethan dropped his voice to little more than a whisper—'I saw Mr Merryman take down the autopsy report from the noticeboard. The bloke who's just been dragged out of here might have got overexcited, but he wasn't wrong about that. What happened?'

Dorothy threw another glance at Roger—still playing the supine diva on the sofa—and lowered her voice to answer. 'Mr Merryman said the report I posted was incorrect. That it was from an old version of the game and would have led players down the wrong path.'

Bella narrowed her eyes, watching every tiny muscle movement in Dorothy's face. 'But you're not convinced by his explanation?'

'No. There have been a few things this weekend ...' She paused, weighing her words. 'Unusual incidents. Things which have caused me concern. But I can only assure you that I am doing everything in my power to ensure fair play.'

Oh great, thought Kate. If Dorothy was concerned, it didn't bode well for their chances of winning, did it?

Perhaps sensing a swell of despondency in her audience, Dorothy stepped closer. She gestured for them to lean in, a coach signalling her team to come in for a pep talk. 'Between us,' she said, 'I have high hopes for your team. You've taken the game far more seriously than most. You would be deserving winners. All I can do now is to wish you all the best.' She raised an eyebrow as she turned to walk away. 'Good luck!'

Chapter 43

It was impossible to tell how Max felt as he was laying out their case. His insides could well have been turning somersaults, but goodness he looked smooth. *Foxily* smooth.

The suspects sat on a row of curved-back wooden chairs facing the library fireplace. Max wandered up and down in front of them, often speaking to the floor rather than any member of the audience. Roger Merryman and Dorothy Williams stood either side of the mantlepiece like a pair of mismatched fire irons. In the middle of the mantle shelf, propped up against a gaudy golden carriage clock, was the large scarlet envelope Dorothy had produced for inspection at the Friday afternoon welcome meeting.

Max explained their case, repeating what they had discussed at breakfast, although with a fluency and logical progression which made Kate gawp. She'd watched Max reveal his solutions at several Friendly Murder Parties, but she had been so annoyed with him she had failed to notice how good he was at it. Lucille Palmer seemed to agree, although her admiration appeared to be more for Max's physique than eloquence. Her dark stare rarely left Max's torso and when he turned away from her she took the opportunity to examine his rear. And while Kate couldn't blame her, she did feel a stirring of indignation at this woman openly ogling her Max.

She's an actor, Kate. You're being ridiculous, she reminded herself. More to the point: when had she started thinking of Max as *hers*?

It took Max fewer than ten minutes to come to their last, and most damning, piece of evidence. He ran through Kate's list of parties and robberies, gradually building a case for Lorenzo to be unmasked as a gentleman thief.

'Pah!' Lorenzo waved a hand to dismiss the accusation. Wearing a navy suit and crisp white shirt, he was the picture of innocent nonchalance. 'Ridiculous. There were hundreds of people at these events you mention. I barely remember some of them. And yet you claim these little lists of yours prove I emptied Mr Grieve's safe?'

'No,' said Max, aiming his lopsided smile at Lorenzo and crossing his arms. Kate sighed wistfully as she ogled Max's biceps which bulged and flexed as he interlaced his arms.

Focus, Kate! Listen to him!

'Last night we found the jewels stashed in the secret room behind the bookcase in the study.'

Nancy Grieve's gasp was barely audible underneath her husband's exclamation of, 'What the dickens?'

Max pressed on. 'And on the floor in the same room we found this.' Max held up the silver cufflink, the mother-of-pearl inlay glistening in the sunlight. 'I believe you own its twin, Mr Corsini.'

There was a moment of stunned silence. A low sound came from Nancy Forbes, which escalated to a shriek of fury, and she launched herself at Lorenzo, screaming. 'I knew it was you! You filthy, despicable scoundrel! I'll see you hanged for this! You scum—'

Staring agog at Nancy clawing her way towards Lorenzo while spewing insults, Kate half rose from her seat to intervene. Blimey, the woman was stronger than she looked. And she was amazingly agile for someone wearing half a tonne of black wool and crepe.

But before Kate could get to her feet, Archie and Dorothy sprang forwards to hold Nancy back while Max and Pamela Grieve formed a human shield in front of Lorenzo. Lucille spun out of her chair to calmly observe the ruckus with her back pressed against the wall, twirling her long black cigarette holder between her fingers.

The whole incident was over rapidly and Kate's pulse had barely had a chance to quicken before Archie Forbes was once again holding his wife tightly against him.

Perhaps sensing it was best to wrap things up as swiftly as possible, Max raised his voice to carry over Nancy's weeping and said, 'In conclusion, having explained their motives, we believe that Pamela Grieve and Lorenzo Corsini worked together to poison Adrian Grieve. The stabbing happened post-mortem—'

Kate's lips flickered into a smile. Max really did like that word.

'—to create the impression Mr Grieve was killed by an unknown intruder who climbed through the study window, committed the murder and stole the jewels.' Max nodded at his audience, his green eyes flashing with satisfaction. 'Thank you.'

A swell of pride moved Kate to clap, her hands moving before she'd had a chance to consider whether it was appropriate. Max had been brilliant. Clear, concise and convincing. Fortunately, she was saved from embarrassment by Bella and Ethan joining her. And when Lucille also began to applaud—clipping her dainty fingers together in a series of sharp slaps—Max was forced to acknowledge the praise. He inclined his head, a bashful smile lifting one side of his mouth, and motioned for the rest of the team to take their place next to him at the front of the room.

Kate trailed Bella and Ethan, her gaze flitting between Roger's and Dorothy's faces, her hands trembling with anticipation. How had they done? Had they got it right?

The signs were promising. Dorothy was beaming. Lorenzo and Pamela were clinging to each other, her eyes brimming with tears and his mouth set into a firm line of anger, a muscle twitching beside his eye. Was that what guilt looked like? Kate bit her lip. Perhaps they'd done it?

'Well done!' Dorothy's smile shone in her dark eyes, as bright as the frames of her glasses. 'I'm delighted to say—'

'Yes, well done,' said Roger, ploughing over Dorothy's speech, 'An impressive performance. Particularly good work on finding the jewels.' His smile sharpened. 'Such a shame it's not the solution'—he pointed to the envelope on the mantlepiece—'we were looking for, though.'

The ticking of the mantle clock thudded into the silence that followed Roger's words. Glancing at the various stunned expressions around her, a heaviness settled on Kate's shoulders. All that work, for nothing. And she'd been convinced they stood a chance.

'But ...' Dorothy stuttered, her gaze shuttling between Roger, the cast and the detective team. Nancy had stopped crying, her grief appearing to have vanished as she exchanged glances with the other cast members whose knotted brows reflected her own confusion.

'But I read it this morning.' Dorothy snatched up the envelope, opened it, pulled out the paper inside and, as her gaze see-sawed down the page, her jaw dropped further.

'I'm terribly sorry,' said Roger, his smarmy grin telling Kate he was anything but. 'Again, though, well played. I am impressed and I don't say that often. But never mind. The important thing is that you enjoyed yourselves. And we would love to see you again. As I like to say, better luck next time!'

Dorothy held up her hand and took another run at a whole sentence. 'But, Roger, I don't understand—'

'For goodness' sake, Dorothy!' Roger's smile twisted into a snarl. 'Does their solution match the identity of the culprit as detailed on that piece of paper?'

'No, but—'

'Well then.' Roger's smile returned. He clapped his hands together and to Kate the echo was the sound of another box being nailed shut, the one which contained her dreams of amateur sleuthing glory. 'That brings another wonderful Merryman's Murder Mystery weekend to a close. All that remains is to thank you for—'

'Wait!' Kate took a step towards Dorothy and Roger, her mind whirling. That couldn't be it. They'd worked so hard, everyone had found their case convincing and Max had presented brilliantly. There had to be another way. Maybe something in the rules to give them another chance to—

'The rules.' Kate turned to Dorothy. 'At the welcome meeting you said that he'd'—she flicked her gaze to Roger—'agreed to change the rules so all teams get two chances to present. We've only used one. So we get another try, don't we?'

Kate's words took a moment to sink in, but when they did Dorothy straightened, pushed her glasses up her nose and squared up to Roger. 'Ms Brannon is right, Roger. After the recent rule change, they have the right to present again. I'm sure you wouldn't want to deny them that right. After all, you're always such a champion of fair play.'

Kate hardly dared to breathe as Dorothy watched Roger, fixing him with the sternest of glares. Never mess with an ex-head teacher. They'd seen it all.

Among the cast, Dorothy's announcement seemed to have triggered a union meeting. They shuffled on their seats, huddling together for a private chat, possibly to decide whether having to sit through another grand reveal fell within their contractual obligations.

Unlike the actors, Bella saw no need to keep her thoughts to herself. 'Ha! That's right, we do get a second chance!' She jabbed a finger at Roger before muttering, 'Come back from that, you orange-faced weasel.'

Perhaps hardened by the shocks of having various guests lobbing projectiles and death threats at him over time, Roger recovered quickly. 'Of course,' he said, stretching an arm along the mantle shelf. 'It simply slipped my mind. Possibly because none of our other teams availed themselves of the opportunity. After all, it can be difficult to come up with one theory, let alone two.' His cold stare scanned each member of the team and, as it passed across her, Kate shuddered. 'Do you have another solution you would like to present?'

Ah. Maybe their moment of triumph was premature. Kate glanced at Max who raised his shoulders in an infinitesimal shrug. Double ah. Apparently Max was also missing a handy backup theory. Drat.

'Pft!' Bella rolled her eyes. 'Kate will have at least half a dozen solutions. We just have to decide which one we like the most.' Bella tapped Kate's shoulder. 'Right, Kate?'

Chapter 44

Kate opened her eyes to be greeted by the cheerful cascade of rainbows decorating the skirt of her dress. Unfortunately the colourful symbols of hope did little to raise her spirits, although sinking into one of the armchairs in the corner of the library and dropping her head to her knees had helped combat her dizziness and the high-pitched whine in her ears.

Ethan, Bella and Max formed a screen around her, while on the other side of the library Roger and Dorothy were engaged in an energetic and occasionally loud conference with the cast.

Gingerly, Kate straightened and rested her head against the cushioned backrest. But lifting her head only doubled her wooziness and, even worse, she had uncurled from the brace position just before Hurricane Bella struck.

'What do you mean you've "got nothing"?' Bella hissed, glaring at Max and then down at Kate. 'This is your *thing*. How do you not have another idea?'

Kate covered her face with both hands. Burying her head in the sand wasn't a long-term solution, but it might win her a couple of minutes' peace. The droning in Kate's head had quietened to a dull buzz, but she didn't yet feel strong enough to take on Bella. Or string together a new explanation for Adrian Grieve's murder under her friend's demanding glare and even more demanding questions, which were the verbal equivalent of a taser.

The muffled thud of approaching footsteps offered a reprieve. Kate peeked out between her fingers to see Dorothy stop her stride between Ethan and Bella.

'OK,' Dorothy said, pressing her palms together. 'We have a way forward.'

She opened her mouth to continue, but was beaten to the punch by Bella. 'What is going on? You thought we'd got it right, didn't you?'

Kate uncovered her face and trained her gaze on Dorothy. *This* she wanted to hear.

Dorothy glanced over her shoulder, waited for the cast and Roger to leave the library, lowered her voice and said, 'Mr Ravenscroft's presentation did tally with the solution I read this morning and that was in the envelope over there.' She pointed to the mantelpiece. 'It was the solution the actors had been briefed to expect. But when I opened the envelope a few minutes ago, the solution inside was different.'

Ethan's brow crinkled. 'How is that possible?'

Sharing in a collective frown, they all fell into silent contemplation. It was Max who broke it. 'When Nancy went for Lorenzo.'

Max might as well have told Ethan that invisible aliens

had changed the envelope's contents. His friend stared at him, his face the image of confusion. 'Huh?'

But Kate understood instantly. 'Ugh!' She ran her hands through her hair. 'We were all distracted by Nancy trying to gouge out Lorenzo's eyes. Roger switched the envelopes.'

'He must have had another one in his jacket. Probably had it there all weekend in case.' Bella snorted. 'At least his hideous jackets proved useful.'

'I fear you're correct,' said Dorothy. 'It's the only explanation that makes sense.'

'When you think about it,' said Max, 'Roger's gone to a heck of a lot of trouble to make sure no one wins. It's awful, but also … a little brilliant?'

'I don't see how he's that smart,' said Ethan. 'How hard is it to switch an envelope?'

'Max means the effort he must have made to ensure the mystery had more than one viable solution,' said Kate. 'He may have come up with several. He could have a wad of envelopes padding out his garish jackets, ready to switch out if a team presented the one Ms Williams had in her safekeeping.'

'Bloody hell,' said Ethan. 'He really doesn't want to part with that fifty grand. Does he not have it?'

'I believe he may have spent it,' said Dorothy. 'And I suspect paying the money to a winner would mean Roger having to make some unpleasant lifestyle adjustments.'

Kate nodded. It was as Lucinda had said. Bye-bye, car. Bye-bye, couture clothing and fancy watches.

Dorothy sighed. 'I've bought you about twenty minutes to work up another presentation. The actors weren't thrilled about the unexpected overtime, but I talked them round. Roger has taken them for refreshments to apologise for the "mix-up" and brief them on what he claims has always been the one and only correct solution to the game.'

Desperate for a single silver lining, Kate asked, 'Can Max present again?'

'No. Sorry,' said Dorothy. 'The rules are clear: one of you must present alone. But, having already had his "turn", it cannot be Mr Ravenscroft.'

'Oh,' said Kate, her voice a feeble whisper. How was she going to put a theory together and communicate it to either Bella or Ethan in under twenty minutes? And why wouldn't the ringing in her ears stop? She groaned and lowered her head into her hands.

Bella rubbed Kate's upper back. 'Don't worry, Kate. We can do this.' She looked up at Dorothy. 'Ms Williams, you've seen the solution. Could you not give us even a teeny hint?'

Dorothy's mouth twisted into a moue of pain. 'I have red lines I can't cross. But I would encourage you to dwell on the things Mr Merryman went out of his way to stop the guests seeing.' She cast another glance over her shoulder. 'I should go. See if I can slow them down a little. I'll leave you to your deliberations.'

The team drifted into another pensive silence. Outside the library windows the clouds shifted in the spring breeze. A shaft of sunlight flooded their corner of the room, bringing light, warmth, but sadly little inspiration. And, in the absence of a miraculous epiphany, the group fell back on their individual strengths.

Bella organised. 'Ethan, love. What time will it be in twenty minutes?

And Ethan asked a daft question. 'Why?'

'Because that's our deadline!'

'Oh! Quarter past eleven.'

Max crouched down next to Kate and tapped her knee, a small gesture which soothed her jangling nerves. She lifted her head to meet his patient green stare. In a calm low voice, he asked, 'Is there anything I can do to help?'

'You're already helping.' Kate reached for his hand and gave it a squeeze. 'Thank you.'

'What about the autopsy report?' asked Ethan. 'Roger practically threw himself at the noticeboard to take it down. It has to be crucial.'

'But we have a picture of it,' said Bella. 'Nicely done, by the way.'

'Thank you. I'm just sorry the bottom of the page was missing. That could be important.'

'You did your best.' Bella pecked Ethan on the cheek. 'Anyway, there's that doctor as well. The one Roger was trying to kick out. Kate got to speak to him, that has to be—'

'Guys? Guys!' Max waited for Bella and Ethan to grant him their attention. 'Maybe we should give Kate some space. To think.'

'Surely four heads are better than one,' said Bella. 'I know I'm not on your or Kate's level of Christie nerdom, but I've watched enough *CSI* and *Napier* to know how to catch a killer. You ask Ethan'—she patted Ethan's chest with the back of her hand—'I always pick out the guilty party, don't I, babe?'

Ethan nodded enthusiastically. 'She does.'

'Seriously, I'm never wrong,' said Bella. 'And I reckon,

whatever that doctor said to Kate, it all hinges on that. From what Lucinda said, it sounds like Roger wanted to bundle the man into the boot of his car and drive him out—'

'Shh!' Kate held up her hand, a string of light bulbs beginning to glow inside her head. Bella wasn't wrong, was she? She'd been right about who the victim would be. Right about Max. And she had been right about the actors not being able to stay in character all weekend—or had she? 'I think I might have something.'

'Does it involve me being right?' asked Bella.

'Yes—'

'Excellent! I knew it!'

'But not about everything.'

Bella gasped in mock outrage. 'How dare you!' She grinned. 'Go on, what did I get wrong?'

'You might have to give me that twenty quid back.'

'But you caught the actor playing Lorenzo chatting on his smartphone. That's clearly him breaking character.'

'Perhaps. But you'll be pleased to know you were right about Dr Chase. There was something he said ...' She glanced about. Where were her notes?

'What do you need?' asked Max.

'My notepad. And your notebook, if you don't mind?'

Ever the efficient, conscientious scribe, Max lunged to where the items were resting on one of the bookshelves behind Kate's chair. 'Here.' He handed them to Kate. 'My pen is in there, should you need it. It's a good one, it writes well, but I can always get you another if you'd prefer—'

Kate grabbed his hand, cutting off his adorable babbling in mid-flow. 'This is terrific. Thank you.' Her smile slipped. 'There is one other thing.'

'What? Hang on.' Max pulled a chair from the front row, placing it so they were sitting face-to-face, their knees touching. 'Please give me something to do.'

'Oi! Sherlock and Watson,' said Bella, planting her hands on her hips. 'We're still here, you know. What do *we* do?'

'Um … Could you help Dorothy delay Roger and the actors? And maybe, I don't know …' Under the pressure of Bella's stare, Kate's mind could only come up with the failsafe British activity for anyone at a loose end in a crisis. 'Could you find us some tea and biscuits?'

Bella grinned and turned to Ethan. 'I think you'll agree it'd be best—'

'If you run interference on Roger and the actors. Yes, yes.' Ethan smiled and rolled his eyes as Bella punched the air. 'I'll get on with team refuelling duties.'

'I love you,' said Bella, and the couple shared a quick kiss before strolling away hand in hand, Bella issuing further instructions all the way to, over and beyond the threshold.

Peace descended on the library like a fresh blanket of snow. Kate closed her eyes and exhaled, listening to the distant creak of floorboards, swish of doors and the reception phone ringing unanswered. And gradually, the buzzing inside her head faded and she was confident that when she opened her eyes again the library would appear in full colour and sharp focus.

A little time like this and she would be able to puzzle it out. Although—she reasoned, her stomach lurching—the problem of what came next remained.

'Kate?'

'Am I doing my concentrating detective face?'

'No. But something's still bothering you, isn't it?'

'Ugh!'

'And there we are. Frustrated noise.'

Kate chuckled, then shook her head. 'I must work on my poker face. And noises too, apparently.'

Max smiled and nudged her knee with his. 'Come on, Holmes. What's up?'

'I just—ugh!' Kate thumped her palms against the arms of the chair. 'I might be able to figure this out but I can't present it. It's all'—she raised her hands above her head and shook her fingers—'a huge jumble I need to straighten out. And I don't know if there'll be time to explain it all to Bella or Ethan.'

'Hmn.' Max stared into the black depths of the hearth. It was empty, but Max must have seen something there that Kate couldn't. His brow lifted and he blinked rapidly, a glimmer entering his eyes. 'Earlier, when we were interviewing suspects, you were fine, right? You didn't find it difficult? It didn't make you unwell?'

Kate thought back to the interviews. Apart from a couple of hairy moments with Nancy—including one where she had been tempted to slap her for being horrendously rude to Max—she had found them fairly painless. And certainly panic free.

'I was fine,' said Kate. 'But it wasn't like presenting.'

Max nodded. 'I have an idea.' He reached out and took Kate's hand in his. 'I need to check the finer points of the rules with Dorothy to see if it's allowed, but if it is, I think we can sort out the presentation problem. If you'll trust me to look into it.'

A ripple of warmth coursed from Max's hand up along Kate's arm. She met his steady stare and her head cleared. Max would sort it out. She trusted he would. Back in their Friendly Murder Club days, she had believed Max lived for the individual win. That he sought personal triumph at the expense of everyone else. But she had been wrong. Then, as now, he had her best interests at heart.

She squeezed his fingers and smiled. 'Of course. That sounds promising.'

'OK. You put your genius to finding another solution to the case.' Max rose, planted his hands on the arms of Kate's chair, leant down and kissed her forehead. 'I'll find a way you can deliver it.'

Chapter 45

Leaving a rattle of polite coughing and fidgeting behind him, Max took the seat next to Kate and balanced his notebook on his knees. He glanced over his shoulder, no doubt checking that the library and its occupants were finally organised to his exact specifications.

Kate stared down at her own notes. The pages were vibrating as her left knee jiggled, a nervous movement her rational mind recognised as absurd and unhelpful but apparently had no control over.

The coughing at the back of the library ceased, replaced by some pointed throat-clearing and Dorothy's clear commanding voice, which carried over Kate's head. 'Ms Brannon, whenever you're ready.'

Kate closed her eyes, inhaled and gave herself a stern pep talk. *Breathe, Kate. Breathe and, while you're at it, stop your ruddy knee bouncing.*

A warm, firm grip settled over her knee. It stilled immediately but—as her gaze travelled up from Max's hand to meet his confident green stare—her heart skipped.

Without breaking eye contact, Max gave her leg a gentle squeeze and withdrew his hand. Kate read the gesture, and his steady gaze, as, *I'm here if you need me. You've got this.*

Lorenzo Corsini and Pamela Grieve sat directly opposite Kate and Max with their backs to the grand fireplace. The arrangement of the seating was purposefully similar to that used during their earlier interview in the music room. In a corner of her consciousness, Kate was aware of the other cast members, Roger and Dorothy, and Bella and Ethan, elsewhere in the room. They had been allocated precisely placed seats so they were behind Kate and out of her eyeline. All this was—thank goodness—within the game's rules.

Max's last, and possibly most important, requirement was that the solution to the game be taken out of the scarlet envelope and held in Dorothy Williams' hands, under the watchful eye of Bella, for the duration of Kate's presentation.

Hearing Max directing everyone to their positions in a no-nonsense, stern tone had been rather distracting. She had been trying to revise her arguments but, when he had announced that no one was to speak unless Kate addressed them first, the back of Kate's neck had prickled with heat. At one point he had slipped into French to answer a question from Lucille and Kate had considered leaving the room to prevent herself drooling or flinging herself into his arms.

Focus, Kate! Time to get this show on the road.

With difficulty, Kate swallowed and said, 'Good morning, Mr Corsini. Miss Grieve. I would like to start by returning to the jewel thefts which Mr Ravenscroft already touched on.' Kate paused while Lorenzo and

Pamela nodded in agreement. Normally the actors on a Merryman's Murder Mystery would 'reset' between each guest's solution, entering each presentation with no memory of what had come before. However, as Kate and Max were on the same team, it had been agreed that Kate would not have to repeat any of the theories Max had presented. This was to save time and had gone some way to mollify the exhausted cast.

'However,' Kate continued, 'I'd like to begin by clearing up a matter which, at first, appears to be separate from the case of Adrian Grieve's death. I believe it is vital, but it is also something of a tangent, so I ask you for your patience.'

Lorenzo rolled his eyes and yawned. Pamela's gaze was fixed on the shelves to Kate's right. Hmn. How would they react to some specific information?

'I want to talk to you about a missing persons case which has been making the news recently. A young man called Derek Jones.'

Lorenzo remained the picture of disinterested nonchalance, although he did bring his gaze down from the ceiling. Pamela, however, stiffened.

Good.

'Derek Jones, a humble lad from a working family in East London, at the tender age of seventeen became the surprise heir to the Dukedom of Berkshire. The dukedom is one of the oldest and wealthiest in the country. Overnight, Derek went from obscure nobody to being only a few years away from becoming one of the richest, most powerful men in the land. Despite intensive media interest, little news reached the public about him over the next four years. I imagine his family had him under lock and key, putting him through some intensive and possibly rather boring duke training. Unsurprisingly, perhaps, shortly after reaching majority on his twenty-first birthday, Derek decided he'd like a break from his family and went off on a trip around continental Europe. But then …' Kate lifted a fist and splayed her fingers as she whispered, 'Poof! The young duke vanished.'

Both Pamela's and Lorenzo's gazes were locked on her. Excellent. Her experience telling afternoon carpet time stories was paying off. Thank you, Julia Donaldson.

'Mr Forbes let Max and me in on a secret: it seems Derek has been kidnapped and, once his family pay the large ransom, he will be returned any day now. Isn't it interesting how the timing of Derek's case lines up with elements of this one? Derek Jones goes missing in Europe just over a year ago. Pamela Grieve meets Lorenzo Corsini in Italy about nine months ago. Adrian Grieve passes away this weekend and Derek Jones reappears next week.

'And that leads me to wonder if, rather than having been stashed in some kidnapper's cellar for the last year, Derek Jones has been hiding in plain sight. He changed his hair colour—ginger will always draw attention—to a dark brown and shaved off his equally red facial hair. He's been busy, enjoying some freedom before having to settle into his place in high society. He even found love, was lucky enough to have it returned, and got engaged. Finally, he's ready to return to the shackles of his unexpected dukedom. But he might want to keep the dark hair and clean-shaven face. They suit him.'

Kate tilted her head, fixed Lorenzo with a penetrating stare and said, 'Isn't that right, Your Grace?'

Chapter 46

Kate's accusation was a flame to a powder keg, setting off an explosion of noise behind her.

'Impossible!' shrieked Nancy Grieve.

Lucille Palmer hooted with laughter.

Bella gasped.

And, most distractingly, Archie Forbes reacted with, 'Bally unbelievable, complete shocker, what?'

Kate kept her eyes on Lorenzo and Pamela, but Max turned in his chair. The fine cotton of his shirt was pulled taut as he twisted to fire an admonishing glare at the noisemakers. Kate took a moment to appreciate Max's broad chest and strong arms, as impressed by his physique as his ability to silence the room with a single steely glance. That had to be the football coach coming out. The man would be a terrific asset in any bedroom—*class*room, classroom!

Oh good Lord. Kate ran a hand over her lips and flicked her gaze back to her suspects. She bet Poirot never had to deal with this sort of thing.

Lorenzo shifted in his seat and opened his mouth to speak, much to Kate's relief. Was she right? Would she have to push him into a confession?

Lorenzo took both of Pamela's hands in his and stared into her eyes. Pamela blinked slowly and raised her shoulders in a small shrug. This was apparently permission, because—still clasping one of Pamela's hands—Lorenzo turned back to Kate and said, 'All right. It appears the jig is up.'

It cost Kate greatly not to grin. He had spoken in the same Cockney accent she'd heard the previous morning when she had 'happened upon' Lorenzo while gargoyle spotting. At the time she had assumed the East London accent belonged to the actor playing Lorenzo, breaking character to use his phone. But she hadn't actually seen his phone because he was, in fact, engaged in a face-to-face conversation with someone—presumably Pamela given he'd addressed them as 'my love'—who was hidden from Kate by the tower wall. They must have been lying in wait for any of the murder mystery guests to pass by with the purpose of being overheard and had probably repeated the same trick several times over the weekend.

Lorenzo shrugged. 'I'm Derek Jones. I also happen to be the thirteenth Duke of Berkshire. The details of my disappearance and the reasons for it are almost exactly as you have outlined.'

'And your desire to not be the duke, for a little longer at least, and to evade your found family, explain you adopting the identity of Lorenzo Corsini and avoiding photographers?'

Derek nodded. 'I've always been a natural mimic. I

found the Italian accent easy to pick up by listening to the locals in Tuscany. As easy as it was to pick up'—he paused, lifted his nose and, when he spoke again, his wide Cockney vowels had disappeared, replaced by an series of sharp vowels and consonants that would have been at home at any Court gathering—'this terribly posh accent. Although my elocution teacher did despair of me at times.' He grinned. 'Everyone kept telling me I was lucky and I should be grateful. I was, but I was also a prisoner in grand houses that weren't my home, suffering through mind-numbingly dull lessons about the peerage, etiquette, what my life would become. An endless list of responsibilities and duties. I wanted to escape. And then I did.' He sighed and his gaze turned wistful. 'Europe was amazing. I felt so free and I wanted to enjoy it for a while longer. So'—he pointed at his hair—'it was quick work to change my hair colour, shave, and Lorenzo Corsini, minor Italian aristocrat, was born.'

Kate's gaze snagged on Max's notebook. On a fresh page, he had written her a private message in his neat script:

Brilliant. Can't believe I didn't see it before.
You're doing great, keep going.

Her cheeks warming, Kate glanced at Max and they exchanged brief smiles before she did as he suggested. 'Miss Grieve'—she paused to let Pamela drag her adoring gaze from Derek's face—'I presume your father discovered your fiancé's true identity a couple of months ago which is why he decided to give his blessing to your marriage?'

'Yes. Father always liked Derek when he knew him as

Lorenzo,' said Pamela, 'but he wasn't sure he could give me the life and … security he wanted for me.'

'What Pam is trying to say, with adorable tact,' said Derek, 'is that her father was concerned that Lorenzo Corsini was penniless. However, a rich duke was more the kind of husband he had dreamt about for his daughter. I'm not a prince'—he lifted an eyebrow, suggesting to Kate that he thought of himself as nothing less than a king—'but at least by marrying me his little princess would become a duchess.'

'And did Mr Grieve know his future son-in-law had a successful sideline in jewel theft?'

Derek opened his mouth to reply, but Pamela squeezed his hand and shook her head, urging caution. 'It's fine, darling,' said Derek to his fiancée. 'I think everyone here understands how unlikely this story will sound. That a young man, a wealthy English duke, disguised himself to live as an Italian aristocrat and then, on finding English high society to be nothing more than a cabal of lazy, parasitic, stupid, exploitative, penny-pinching, selfish, uncharitable—'

'You've made your point, dear,' said Pamela, graciously interrupting her future husband with a brief touch of his knee. Impressed, Kate gave her a grateful nod. If Derek had continued, she feared Bella would have come bounding up to the front of the room to shake his hand and plan a workers' revolution.

'Thank you, my love.' Derek patted Pamela's hand. 'Pam knows I can get carried away. I didn't grow up with money. And I want to use my newfound wealth to help others who haven't had my incredible luck.'

'By stealing?'

Derek tapped his index fingers to his lips, pondering. 'You seem to have a keen mind, Ms Brannon, and an excellent imagination. So perhaps you would be happy to explore a theoretical situation?'

'Thank you,' said Kate, impressed that Derek had remembered her name. 'And yes, that's fine. Please continue.'

Derek drew in a long breath. 'Let us imagine a young man who tries to persuade wealthy—I mean grotesquely, incomprehensibly wealthy—individuals, to donate an amount of money which would be a pittance to them to a worthy cause. Miserly, miserably, they refuse to donate. The young man, hypothetically, sees an opportunity to force a donation in the form of a piece of jewellery which won't even be missed. And he takes it.'

'And you, Miss Grieve?' Kate turned to Pamela. 'You knew—theoretically—about this philanthropic, though still criminal, pastime?'

Pamela fidgeted with her lace collar. 'I suspected from the very start at Lake Como. But it wasn't until England that I caught—*may* have caught him. I was sympathetic to his reasons and'—she slid her arm around Derek's—'it brought us closer.'

A strangled sound, somewhere between a gargle and a whistle, came from the back of the room. Without turning, Kate knew it was Nancy Grieve. It had to be hard. On the one hand her future brother-in-law was indeed a wrong'un, and the admission of his crimes would have confirmed many of her suspicions. On the other, he was also the Duke of Berkshire, a man she would spend the rest of her life feeling obliged to treat with deference.

Unmoved by her big sister's struggles, Pamela gazed into Derek's eyes, her stare a little unfocused. That one is completely love-drunk, thought Kate. Derek Jones truly was a fortunate man. He'd found a woman who loved him when she believed he was a poor charming thief. He would never have to worry that his wife had married him for his title and money. However, she was sure Adrian Grieve would have been very interested in both those things. Enough to overlook Derek's recent criminal history.

'Your Grace, in addition to knowing your true identity, was Mr Grieve aware of Lorenzo's—hypothetical, of course—Robin Hood-style activities?'

Derek's and Pamela's previously frank stares slid away from Kate's face and they shifted on their chairs, the wood creaking in complaint. Pamela returned to fiddling with her collar and Derek adjusted his jacket before answering. 'No, I don't believe he was.'

Kate scanned the couple's body language, almost certain she had just been told a lie. However, as events with Paul earlier that day had revealed, her track record in spotting huge fibs wasn't the best. A second opinion would be most welcome. Fortunately, Max's pen was already scratching against his pad. He underlined a word and lifted his hand to allow Kate to read:

A clear lie. But why lie about it?

Kate's pulse skipped. She knew the answer to Max's question. Derek and Pamela did too, and the knowledge made them so uncomfortable that they were squirming like small children who had been playing tricks with itching powder. That was an afternoon at work Kate would never forget.

'So, to be clear'—she settled her stare on Derek, who was twisting his cufflinks in circles—'Mr Grieve knew nothing about your connection to a successful series of jewel thefts? And any knowledge of your talents in the area of forced wealth redistribution had absolutely no connection to his untimely death?'

Pamela's breath quickened. Derek glanced at his fiancée, the crease between his eyebrows deepening. Unusually, even though she was looking at two people who were the living image of discomfort, Kate's knees were steady and her stomach settled. The answers to her questions were crucial and she was happy to wait for them. At her side, Max appeared to share her calm state. His pen hovered over his pad, where his latest note said:

Wait for it. One of them will crack any moment now.

As if on cue, Derek growled. 'Look,' he said, his gaze flicking between Kate to Max. 'I don't deny what you've said about my disappearance and haven't refuted your ideas about my—theoretical and not strictly legal—activities while I was Lorenzo. But, you have to believe me: I did not kill Adrian Grieve.'

'Oh, but I do believe you,' said Kate, interlacing her fingers and trying to ignore how Max's posture had stiffened in surprise. She cleared her throat and continued. 'You see, Your Grace, I'm certain you didn't kill Mr Grieve because I know who did.'

Chapter 47

'How?' Pamela's whisper rang through the silence in the library, her dark eyes wide and shining. 'How do you know?'

Goosebumps formed on Kate's arms. Pamela's questions only supported her suspicions. Wouldn't the natural response to someone saying they knew the identity of your father's killer be, 'Who is it then? Tell me!' Indeed, muffled voices and the scraping of chair feet at the back of the library suggested that was exactly what Nancy Grieve was trying to jump up and shout while her husband attempted to restrain her.

To her left, Max's pen flew across the page:

I might have to escort Nancy from the room.
But hopefully I'll get to stay because I'm really looking forward to this.

Max shot another glare over his shoulder and the commotion quietened. Facing front once again, he mouthed,

'*Sorry,*' to Kate and flashed her an encouraging smile which did little to soothe the gooseflesh on her arms. Her gaze travelled from his shining eyes downwards to linger on his lips—

Steady, Kate! Not long now.

'Sorry, Miss Grieve,' said Kate, leaning forwards and tilting her head to put Max into the safety of her blind spot. 'You asked me how I know who your father's killer is. Well, it was your family physician, Dr Chase, who put me onto the solution—'

A small noise, a cross between a sneeze and cough, disturbed the peace. Max spun in his seat but this time when he faced Kate he grinned, a rather wicked glint entering his eyes, and scrawled her a note:

Just Roger Merryman choking on the prospect of defeat. You've got this!

A smile on her lips, Kate scanned her own notes. They were short on motivational quotes, but skimming them gave her a moment to readjust her features into a serious game face.

'Miss Grieve, Dr Chase told me that a year ago he advised your father to have some tests,' said Kate. 'He doesn't know whether your father did or not, but suspects he didn't. However, I believe Mr Grieve went to one of the best doctors in the country for a barrage of specialist tests which, sadly, led to bad news. You see, Dr Chase said that when he examined your father's corpse his eyes were yellowed. He assumed this was a sign of cirrhosis caused by excessive alcohol consumption. But I think Mr Grieve's liver was failing because of another long-term illness. I'd guess cancer, which had spread to his liver from elsewhere.'

Tears welled in Pamela Grieve's eyes and rolled silently down her cheeks, but she continued to stare at Kate as if entranced.

'And I believe that Mr Grieve, having been given a limited time to live, set out to make the most of it,' said Kate. 'To have a last hurrah, a world tour which overshadowed the others. Mrs Palmer has told us about the lavish party at the Plaza in New York. It sounds fantastic.'

Pamela sniffed. 'It was. Daddy was delighted with how it went. I hadn't seen him laugh so much in months. He said he felt decades younger.'

'I suspect he had always been an energetic, dynamic person. I imagine he found it hard to accept he was ill, and it certainly wasn't something he wanted anyone else to know about in case they wanted to give him sympathy. Adrian Grieve was not a man who accepted anyone's pity. Which is why he went to lengths to avoid Dr Chase, in case the family physician spotted any signs of the disease. He didn't even tell Nancy. But he couldn't hide it from you, Miss Grieve. You spent too much time together for that.

'I can imagine that the thought of a slow decline with the incumbent indignities of being weak and dependent must have horrified him. I wonder if part of the reason for the extended world tour was that he hoped to be in the middle of an extravagant soirée on the shore of Lake Como or raising a glass of champagne at the Plaza and'—Kate clicked her fingers—'pass away. Perhaps Adrian Grieve's greatest wish was die as he lived: swiftly. To burn brightly like a shooting star and vanish in a final flash of light.'

Both Pamela and Derek nodded. The movement was tiny, almost imperceptible. But it was agreement, and Kate would take it.

351

'However, for all the parties and jollity, your father was worried. Not about himself, but about you, Miss Grieve. Your sister, she was happy in a marriage which would give her a lifetime of security. But his little princess … he wanted her to be safe. And that was going to be a problem, because he knew your inheritance wouldn't be enough to provide for you, or indeed give you anything at all. He lost a lot of money in the Crash, and settling his debts—including those he ran up on his final world tour—would wipe out the value of the estate, including this house. And that brings me back to the life-insurance policy—'

'We've heard enough!' Derek wrapped his arm around Pamela, who continued to weep quietly. 'Accusing Pam of killing her father for some paltry life insurance, it's ridiculous.' Derek's eye's flashed and nostrils flared. 'And, frankly, monstrous!'

'I'm sorry to upset anyone, Your Grace,' said Kate. 'But if you'd let me finish, you'd know I wasn't about to accuse Miss Grieve of murder.'

'Let her finish, Derek,' said Pamela in a small voice. 'I just want this all over with.'

'Very well.' Derek levelled a poisonous glare at Kate. 'May I suggest you hurry up and get to the point, woman.'

'And may I suggest,' said Max, sitting forwards and aiming a deeply lethal stare of his own at Derek, 'that you exercise a little patience, *Your Grace*.' The honorific was hissed, entirely ungraciously, from between Max's clenched teeth. 'Ms Brannon is about to reveal the culprit of a serious crime and will take all the time she needs in order to do so.'

A short staring match ensued, which Kate found rather

more thrilling than she probably should. And by the time Derek looked away—his mouth twisting as if he had been forced to swallow incredibly sour medicine—Kate's heart was thudding so hard against her ribcage she was concerned Max would hear it.

Max leant closer to Kate and murmured, 'Sorry for interrupting.'

Kate lifted her hand to her neck, which was warm where Max's breath had whispered over it. 'That's OK. Thanks.' She shifted on her seat and wiggled her toes which were in danger of going numb. Where had she been? Oh yes. Adrian Grieve's worries.

'From the moment Adrian Grieve received his terminal diagnosis,' Kate said, 'he had a lot to think about. I suggest that his two main preoccupations were how to ensure his younger daughter received something by way of inheritance and how to avoid a lingering death. He was a clever, ingenious man and I imagine he came up with more than a few solutions to these problems. But I'd bet it was as he became better acquainted with Lorenzo Corsini'— Kate nodded at Derek—'that the plan came together.'

'That's it!' Derek jumped off his seat and threw his hands in the air. 'I've been more than patient, but you insist on coming back to your wild accusations. You are aware of who I am, who my family are and I simply don't have to put up with your insolence. I've already told you I am not a murderer, but everything always comes back to me and—'

'I'm *not* saying you're a murderer,' said Kate, putting a firm hand on Max's shoulder and pushing him back onto his chair at the same time as lifting herself to her feet. 'I'm not accusing anyone here of murder, for the simple reason that the killer isn't in this room.'

Kate paused. It was an unnecessarily dramatic touch, but she couldn't help herself.

This might be the only time you get to do this, Kate. Enjoy it. Wait for the inevitable—

A chorus of gasps and shouts of disbelief went off like a string of firecrackers behind her. Kate smiled.

'What on earth do you mean?' Derek all but shouted, his cheeks an angry scarlet. 'Explain yourself!'

'My pleasure,' said Kate, adopting a chilly tone that would have made Sherlock Holmes proud. She stared into Derek's eyes and continued, 'Adrian Grieve's killer isn't in this room because the person responsible for conceiving, plotting and staging his death is none other than ... Adrian Grieve.'

Chapter 48

Rather than add to the noisy disbelief in the room, Kate's latest claim acted like a jab to a mute button, cutting off the hullaballoo in an instant and leaving stunned silence in its wake.

It was probably best to follow Derek's suggestion and get on with it.

'It was something Dr Chase said,' said Kate. She gestured for Derek to take a seat and waited for him to finish gawping at her and sit before sinking back onto her own chair. 'He apologised for making a rather macabre comment: that Adrian Grieve would have been pleased with the manner of his demise. He meant that Mr Grieve wouldn't have wanted to die from anything as run-of-the-mill as old age. But, the way I see it, of course Adrian would have been pleased with his dramatic death because it was *the one he chose*. How could someone who had always wanted to be fully in control of every aspect of their life be content to leave the details of the end of it up to chance?'

The tears had dried on Pamela Grieve's face, leaving sooty mascara smudges under her eyes. Kate gave her a sympathetic smile. 'Whichever way we approached this case, I kept seeing a story about a father and his daughters, but particularly you, Miss Grieve, his little princess. Your father would have done anything for you, and you for him. Everything hinges on that. On how much you loved each other.'

Her eyes filling with tears again, Pamela whispered, 'It was just the two of us for the longest time. I would have done anything ...'

Pamela's head drooped and her shoulders shook. Kate shuffled to the edge of her seat and—to hell with the rules and the fact the woman was an actor—reached across the gap between them to touch the back of Pamela's hand. It was cold, but when Pamela clasped Kate's fingers, Kate was surprised by the strength of the woman's grip.

'I'm guessing you started having trouble sleeping because you were so worried about your father's declining health,' said Kate, speaking softly, trying to catch Pamela's lowered gaze. 'You were prescribed barbiturates to help you sleep. And that's where your father first got the idea of a peaceful way he could take his leave whenever he wanted.

'But the insurance company wouldn't have paid out in the event of your father taking his own life. He needed another idea and, as luck would have it, you brought home Lorenzo Corsini and his string of jewel thefts. Did you tell him about that or did he guess?'

'He worked it out,' said Derek, the venom now absent from his gaze. 'He was a smart one. Saw everything. Knew

356

which parties we went to, read about the thefts. Put two and two together and made four.' He huffed a laugh. 'And at a time when no one else had even thought to put Lorenzo Corsini into the equation.'

'Not just smart and observant,' said Kate, 'but also able to capitalise on the things he saw. He realised he could turn the string of thefts to his advantage. Why not stage a robbery here? The police would see it as part of a pattern. The murder would be blamed on the intruder, allowing the life insurance to be collected. The insurance money for the jewels would also be paid to Pamela and Nancy, and Pamela could either keep the jewels—although having them reset would be wise—or sell them.

'All the details of the plan are important because Adrian Grieve was meticulous,' said Kate. 'He'd come here, to his family home where he had many happy memories. He'd thrown one last party, both because he loved parties and because it would give him a chance to settle his affairs. He invited Lucille Palmer to tell her he was releasing her from her contract and because he loved her company. He did the unusual thing of telling Nancy he was proud of her, asked her to watch over you, Miss Grieve, and gave her your mother's pearls, knowing what was about to happen to the rest of her jewellery.

'Having said his goodbyes to the people he loved, I imagine he said goodnight to the staff and, certain that he would be left undisturbed in his study, he waited for you and your fiancé to join him there.'

Kate gave Pamela's fingers a final squeeze before letting go. She lowered her voice to a gentle murmur and asked, 'He prepared his final drink himself, didn't he?'

'I couldn't have done it.' Pamela lifted her head. Her face was a picture of desolation, her dark eyes emptied by loss. 'But it didn't matter. Daddy wanted us to be entirely innocent, so when we got to the study, he had just finished the drink.' She sniffed, her lips twitching as she tried to control her tears. 'We talked. He wanted to reminisce about Mother and look at her picture. He started to feel sleepy and so we helped him to his desk. Exactly as he'd planned. And I held his hand until … until he fell asleep.'

A single tear splashed onto the skirt of Pamela's dress. The poor woman really needed a tissue—

'Here,' said Max. Blinking back tears of his own, he removed a tissue from a small packet and offered it to Pamela, who took it wordlessly.

Her tummy twisting, Kate took in Max's watering eyes as he returned the packet to his jacket pocket. She should have been more sensitive. It was inevitable that Pamela's story about her dad would stir Max's memories of his mum. An ache blooming in her chest, Kate reached for Max's hand and wrapped her fingers around his. He returned the pressure but he kept his gaze trained on the ceiling.

Enough. It was time to close the lid on this case.

'Your Grace,' said Kate, focusing on the member of their small group who wasn't in obvious emotional distress. 'I presume you opened the study window, made the footprints outside in the flower bed and dealt with other practicalities?'

'Yes.' Derek nodded. 'I cleared out the safe, put the jewels in the secret room—Adrian had showed me how to open it. And then …' He shuddered.

'The hardest part,' said Kate. 'But, I would guess, the part Mr Grieve had been the most insistent about. I imagine he gave you detailed instructions and would stand for no deviation from them. For his death to appear as a murder, he wanted you to stab him. He wanted us to think the murderer could have glimpsed the letter opener on his desk and, in a moment of opportunism, snatched it up. But the supposed murder weapon was, in fact, a careful choice. Although'—Kate raised her eyebrows as another former red herring became a revealing clue—'I imagine finding the letter opener missing and having to insist Nancy return it was a slight wrinkle in your father's plan. And I'm sure he understood why Nancy had taken it, him being so fond of it himself. After all, he had given it to your mother, Miss Grieve, as a wedding gift.' Kate closed her eyes, casting her mind back to Adrian Grieve's fond words for his late wife during their brief after-dinner chat. 'He told us, earlier that evening, that he felt your mother's presence more and more and that they'd spent many happy hours together in his study. So although to an outsider the stab wound looked like a brutal injury, it was actually a last poetic, even romantic gesture. That he wanted his fake murder to involve plunging a knife that was a love token, bearing his beloved Cora's initials, into his heart.' Kate shuttled her stare between Derek and Pamela, holding their gaze. 'Adrian Grieve left this world in exactly the way he wanted. All you two did was help him die peacefully, according to his own wishes. And, while the law might disagree with me, I don't see any crime in that.'

Chapter 49

At the back of the room, Nancy Grieve's subdued weeping ramped up into all-out wailing. It was a nerve-grating, siren-like sound, but it had the decided upside of instantly drying Max's eyes. A deep crease between his brows, he tipped his head in the direction of Nancy's histrionics and exchanged an eye roll with Kate. Some people refused to be upstaged, even if they had been forced to sit in the wings.

Fortunately, before Nancy could throw herself on the floor or start rending her garments, her howling was drowned out by thunderous applause. Kate frowned. The volume of the clapping was surely enough to shake the dust from the highest bookshelves. Even with Bella's enthusiastic whooping in the mix, how were seven people making that much of a racket?

The air around them vibrating, Kate and Max twisted in their seats to find an extra dozen people filling the space at the rear of the library. Kate recognised a couple of members of the hotel staff and some guests from other teams, who followed Bella's lead to join another round of cheering.

Max leant closer so his lips were next to Kate's ear, allowing her to hear the low rumble of his voice beneath the other noise. 'I hope you don't mind, but I agreed with Dorothy that a few more people would be a good idea. Some staff, a couple of the other guests who hadn't left yet. More witnesses in case Roger tried any more shenanigans. Or, indeed, skulduggery.'

'Good idea.' Kate grinned as Max rose and extended his hand to help her up.

'I think you may have cracked the case,' said Max, placing his hand on the small of her back as they rounded the chairs.

Kate gave a mock gasp and nudged his shoulder. 'Jumping to conclusions, Max? Honestly. Whatever next?' She smiled at him as she stole a glance at their still-clapping audience and her cheeks began to heat. 'However, on this occasion, you might be right. What happens now?'

'I don't know,' said Max, taking a step back and joining in the applause. 'But I suggest you take a bow before they riot.'

With great reluctance, knowing that her face must be an oh-so-attractive shade of beetroot, Kate gave a quick bow, followed by a pantomime curtsey, which—from the laughter—the crowd seemed to enjoy.

Dorothy Williams bustled out of the crowd, heading directly for Kate and Max. In her hand, trapped in a vice-like grip, was the scarlet solution envelope.

'Ms Brannon, Mr Ravenscroft.' Dorothy beamed at them and waited for the audience to fall silent before continuing,

'In case you were in any doubt, I'm delighted to tell you that you have won. You had it spot on, Ms Brannon. You and your team are officially Merryman's Murder Mystery winners!'

Dorothy's announcement brought on another round of cheering and applause, but Kate's attention slid past the gathering of smiling faces to the far wall, where Roger Merryman was sitting alone. He was staring into the middle distance having apparently entered a trance. He appeared to be mumbling to himself and every few seconds he would raise his hand to rub the back of his head. 'Is Mr Merryman all right?' asked Kate.

Dorothy glanced at Roger. 'He'll be fine. After a period of readjustment.' She stepped closer and dropped her voice. 'He'll soon realise having to pay the prize money is the least of his worries. The potential damage to the Merryman's brand, should details of Roger's more questionable actions get out ... Well, we'll have to wait and see, won't we?' She patted Kate on the upper arm and gave her a proud smile which no doubt had been bestowed on thousands of sports day champions and academic achievers. 'But you don't have to worry about all that,' Dorothy continued, 'because I will personally be making sure you get your winnings. Now, if you'll excuse me, I have paperwork'—she cast a dark glare in Roger's direction—'and Roger to deal with. I'll be in touch soon.'

Dorothy slipped across the room and vanished between two chattering groups of onlookers. Kate stared after her and was sliding into a daze of disbelief when a gentle touch to her wrist made her startle.

Gently, Max took her hand in his and Kate's heart

hummed as he flexed his fingers to bring their palms closer. She glanced up to meet his gaze and found the gold flecks in his eyes shining, lit up from within by his dazzling smile and reflecting the bright, shimmering joy filling Kate from head to toe.

They'd done it. They'd beaten one of Merryman's famously unbeatable puzzles. And, while the crowd's adulation seemed mostly reserved for her, she couldn't have done it without Max.

She stepped towards him and laid a hand on his chest. A lump had formed in her throat and she was relieved there was a way to show him her gratitude which required few words.

Kate lifted her eyes to meet Max's stare. 'Thank you,' she whispered before rising to her tiptoes and pressing her lips to his.

Chapter 50

It was tempting to get lost in the kiss. To dwell endlessly on how perfectly Max's strong hands held her waist, the softness of his hair under her fingertips, the lightest brush of stubble against her cheek. It was tempting, but sadly impossible. For while her pulse boomed in her ears, another sound was far louder.

'I knew it!' Bella shrieked and, at her rallying cry, the crowd came together again to erupt into a final round of celebration.

Kate giggled and rested her head against Max's shoulder, happy to let her hair curtain her face from public view. Keeping a tight hold on Kate's waist, Max—his grin returning—faced the rest of the room and raised a hand. 'Show's over, folks. Thank you.'

Carried away on a tide of excited chatter and chuckles, the visitors drifted out of the library giving Kate and Max time to exchange a smouldering glance and draw breath to speak before Bella and Ethan bowled across the room.

'You. Were. Brilliant!' said Bella, bouncing on the spot with barely contained glee. 'Honestly, we should have filmed that. They could add it to the Christmas TV schedule. Give all the Poirots and Marples a run for their money.'

Kate chuckled. 'Nice try with the flattery, but I still want my twenty quid back.'

'No problem.' Bella's lips curled into a wicked smirk. 'As long as I'm still getting that generous wedding present you promised me.'

Ethan tsked disapprovingly. 'Bella ...'

'No, that's fine. A deal's a deal.' Kate glanced at Max. 'As long as Max agrees.'

Max shrugged. 'It's your money. You figured this out. I just sat there and fought the urge to punch Duke Derek on the nose.'

Kate smiled, but a niggle of discomfort itched the base of her throat. Max was being generous, but it wasn't right. She and Max were a team and should split the winnings. Perhaps she could convince him—

'Max, sweetie, could you help Ethan carry the last of our luggage to the car, please?' Bella batted her eyelashes and shone her best wheedling smile at Max.

'Of course.'

'Come on, mate,' said Ethan, stretching an arm across Max's shoulders as they made for the exit. 'I could do with a hand. I'll never understand what she puts in the cases. She claims it's stuff for her hair, but I swear it must be bricks or something ...'

Bella waited, impatiently tapping her foot, until she and Kate were alone in the library. 'Oh my God! Bloody well done.' She threw herself at Kate, who staggered and grabbed the back of a chair to save herself from collapsing under a Bella-shaped ball of elation.

'Thank you,' said Kate. 'I still can't believe I actually won.'

'No. Not the game, silly.' Bella drew back, so Kate could better appreciate the despair with which she rolled her eyes. 'Well done on getting together with Max. He's a keeper. And think about the wedding now.' She closed her eyes and did a shuffle of impish delight. 'Paul will *die* when you show up with Max on your arm. And it serves him right. Something else to look forward to.'

'You might be jumping the gun a bit. Your wedding is eighteen months away. I don't know if—'

'Pft! That man has been daft about you for ages. I'd bet that twenty quid he'd walk through fire for you. And he's one of the groomsmen, so he'll be there anyway. It'll happen.'

Kate smiled, imagining dancing with Max at the reception, swaying cheek-to-cheek on the dance floor under a swirling shimmer of starry lights. And he would look beyond gorgeous in a three-piece suit—

'You're picturing him all suave and practically edible in the morning suit, aren't you?' Bella grinned. 'To help you, the tie is an emerald green. That should make his eyes look totally dreamy—'

Kate thumped Bella playfully on the shoulder and giggled. The tight packets of tension in her shoulders seeped away as Bella returned her nudge. 'Come on,' she said. 'Let's find Ethan and Max.'

Arm in arm, they wandered down the corridor to the

lobby. The click clack of Bella's heels mingled with the bubbly sound of their giggling. It was the most they'd laughed together all weekend and Kate was reluctant to let her friend go now she finally seemed to be more her old self. 'Do you have to rush off?' Kate asked.

Bella's sparkle faded, her smile replaced by a wince of regret. 'Sorry. Another big day at work tomorrow. I have to get home to prep for it.'

'Sorry.' Kate was apologising to communicate her sympathy for Bella's situation but also to express her regret for having inadvertently brought her friend's mood crashing down. 'Is everything OK with Ethan? I heard you two having a bit of a disagreement last night.'

'Oh, that. That was nothing.' Bella waved her hand dismissively. 'We fight but we make up. This one was a bit worse because of wedding stress and work stress. None of that helps. But it's fine.'

They reached the lobby as Max and Ethan came in from the car park. 'Perfect timing,' said Ethan. 'Your luggage-stuffed chariot awaits, m'lady.' He gave Bella a mock bow and received a kiss on the cheek in return. Taking his fiancée's hand, he turned to Kate. 'When will we be seeing you again, Kate? Hopefully before Christmas?'

'Actually, I'll have to let you know what I'm doing.' Kate clasped her hands together, her resolve hardening as she spoke. 'I'll be busy with moving and my new job.'

'The job in Knowleswood?' Ethan's brow furrowed in confusion. 'You got it?'

'Well, duh! They'd be stupid not to take her.' Bella squeezed Kate into another hug, stepped back and said, 'Well done, again. If there's anything I can do to help with the move, let me know. I'm hoping to have a break from work this summer.'

'And it's your dream to spend it hefting all my belongings up the M40?'

'Of course. It's not like I'll be doing the heavy lifting. Max will lend a hand, won't you?'

Max smiled at Kate. 'With pleasure. If you'll have me.'

'Oh, I'm sure she will,' said Bella, a smirk of pure smut quirking her lips. 'Come on, Ethan.' She seized Ethan's hand and turned to the exit. 'Let's leave these lovebirds to it.'

Chapter 51

Casual loitering was not in Kate's natural skill set.

Leaning against one of the fluted limestone columns flanking the hotel entrance, she had checked her phone ten times, smiled and nodded politely at several arriving and departing guests, and pretended to be fascinated by the gravel of the driveway.

Five minutes had been successfully killed by stowing her bag in her car, but now she had exhausted all productive ways of occupying herself while waiting to catch Max before he left.

Behind her the door swung open and a tall figure emerged. Her heart leapt, then dropped. The dark-haired man—wearing jeans, a pale pink polo shirt and a broad smile—was not the one she had been hoping to see. Although he was incredibly familiar. She narrowed her eyes, taking in the large brown eyes and thick brows. Wait a minute. Was that Lorenzo Corsini, Derek Jones, Duke whatever his name was?

'All right?' He grinned and extended a hand to Kate. 'I'm Ben. I wanted to say, you were fantastic.'

Kate shook his hand, staring at him agog. His rising intonation was unmistakeable. He wasn't Italian, Cockney or a posh English aristocrat. 'You're Australian! That's amazing!'

Ben chuckled. 'Thanks. I put a lot of work into my accents. It's nice to have someone notice. Seriously though— Oh, great, here he is!' Max had barely crossed the hotel's threshold before Ben grabbed his hand into a hearty shake. His eyebrows flying up in surprise, Max gave Kate a questioning sideways glance. 'You two'—Ben pointed at Max and Kate—'make a great team. Best I've seen and I've done a few of these. Congrats!'

'Um, thanks?' said Max.

'Pleasure.' Ben grinned and, with a cheery, 'Catch ya later,' strode off in the direction of the car park, leaving a stunned Kate and Max staring after him.

Max blinked first. 'Australian,' he muttered to himself. 'I would never have guessed that.' He turned to Kate. 'Do you have to rush off?'

'No, not at all. I've got loads of time. Nothing else planned today.' Kate winced inwardly. *Stop talking! You're making yourself sound pathetic.*

'In that case,' said Max, 'would you like to go for a last walk around the place before we leave? Admire the gargoyles and grotesques?'

'I'd love to.'

They wandered along the path arm-in-arm. Kate closed her eyes and turned her face to the gentle sunshine. Bees buzzed over the flower borders, birds sung and swooped overhead, and Max was a warm, steady presence at her side. It was another beautiful day, they had cracked the case and she had made some important decisions. There was just one remaining wrinkle in an otherwise perfect moment.

'Max?'

'Hmn?'

'The prize money. We should split it fifty-fifty.'

'Absolutely not.'

'We were a team. I couldn't have done it on my own. And I'll feel terrible about it. Please.'

They arrived at the tower. Max tipped his head back and narrowed his eyes to stare at the dragons above. 'Tell you what. If you make a donation to my local hospice, that'll do me.'

'But that still doesn't seem fair—'

'And, if you insist, you could buy some new football equipment for my kids. Final offer.' He lowered his gaze to meet hers. It was steady, resolute. She wouldn't change his mind.

'All right. But—' Kate's lips curled into a sly smile. There might be no changing Max's mind, but perhaps she could bend the bargain a little—'on one condition.'

'Yes?'

'I'll be living back in your neck of the woods soon and I was thinking …' She slid her hand down his arm, wrapped her fingers around his and pivoted to face him. 'This weekend has made me remember how much I enjoyed the regular mystery parties.'

'Even with the incredibly annoying, over-competitive oaf trying to spoil your fun?'

'Even then. Anyway, it turns out he's mostly misunderstood and has his good points.'

'Oh really?' Max raised an eyebrow and stepped towards Kate. He placed a hand on her waist and applied a gentle pressure to draw her against him.

'Hmn.' Kate laid her hands on Max's shoulders, her gaze dropping to his lips. Max began to lower his head, but Kate leant back a little. She needed to finish what she was saying before she could lose her thread in a glorious kiss haze. 'Just—and please tell me if this is a bad idea—but once I've settled in and the new school year is underway, perhaps in the new year ... we could revive the Friendly Mystery Club.'

Max's smile stretched into a grin. Encouraged, Kate continued, 'I believe you know of a local bookshop that might want to host it? I mean, it could be worth their while. They'd probably sell a few copies of *And Then There Were None* to the attendees, if nothing else.'

'I'd be very happy to ask them.'

'You are their favourite customer, after all.'

'I told a couple of people at work I was coming here this weekend and they sounded keen. I reckon they'd come.'

'It's a start. There's the old gang too.'

'Gillian and Peter certainly owe you.'

'Bella will help round them up. Her and Ethan might be persuaded to make a cameo occasionally.'

'Sounds to me like you've got everything covered.' Max smiled and made to dip his head towards hers once again. With a nip of regret and a small wince, Kate held up a finger to halt his advance.

'Sorry,' she said. 'But I don't have quite everything

covered. Maybe, as critical research for the reconstitution of the club, we could nip down to Devon one weekend before Christmas? Drop in on Greenway and see if the spirit of Agatha can inspire us.'

Max tilted his head and the shards of amber in his eyes glinted gold in the sunshine. 'That's your best idea yet. But'—a furrow appeared between his brows—'Christmas is a while away. I suggest we have some planning sessions in the meantime. And, as I have taken a serious interest in the long-term welfare of that dragon of yours, we should get dinner. I insist.'

'I would love that.'

Kate grinned. A happy, bubbly feeling was dancing around her tummy. She suspected it was the dragon purring.

Max smiled and his gaze dipped, once again, to her mouth. 'And now that's all settled, *please* can I kiss you?'

Her legs turning to jelly in anticipation—good Lord, the man had powers—Kate's eyes drifted shut. Quickly, she raced to bundle all distracting thoughts of the future into a large rainbow-coloured box, leaving the lid tantalisingly ajar and her mind free to focus on the present as Max's lips found hers.

Also by Claire Huston

If you enjoyed Kate's story, you can return to the Comptons with Lucinda, the area's best caterer and Bella's stepsister …

The Only Exception
(Love in the Comptons Book 2)

Lucinda Green knows something is missing from her life. But what? Her catering business is enjoying modest success and she loves her cosy house, even if she does have to share it with her irritating ex-fiancé.

Whatever's making her unsettled and edgy, Lucinda's certain that a lack of romance isn't the problem. How could it be when she doesn't believe in true love?

But Lucinda's beliefs are shaken by a series of electric encounters with Alex Fraser, a newly notorious actor who gradually proves himself to be infuriatingly funny and smart, as well as handsome.

Not that any of that matters. Because Lucinda doesn't believe in all that 'The One' nonsense. That's the rule.

But doesn't every rule have an exception?

And you can find out more about Lucinda's friend Becky, the Comptons' resident miracle worker …

Art and Soul
(Love in the Comptons Book 1)

Struggling single mother Becky Watson longs to revive her career as a life-fixer, working miracles to solve her clients' problems, no matter how big or small. Since the birth of her two-year-old son she has been stuck preventing wedding fiascos for the richest and rudest residents of the Comptons, a charming, leafy area of southern England known for its artistic heritage.

So when semi-reclusive local artist Charlie Handren reluctantly hires Becky to fix his six-year creative slump, she's delighted to set him up with a come-back exhibition and Rachel Stone, the woman of his dreams.

Though they get off to a rocky start, Becky and Charlie soon become close. But as the beautiful Rachel becomes Charlie's muse, Becky is forced to wonder: will giving Charlie everything he wants mean giving up her own happily ever after?

Or maybe you fancy an escape to an idyllic country village?

Elle's A to Z of Love

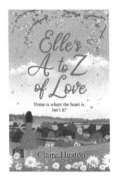

Haileybrook, a beautiful village in the peaceful Cotswolds countryside, is most people's idea of heaven on earth.

Born and raised in this small slice of paradise, Elle Bea can't wait to leave.

It should be easy, but every time she packs her bags for exotic adventures, old loves and loyalties pull her back.

Will Elle be forced to forget her dreams of far-flung places and epic romance, or can she grab one last chance to have it all?

An uplifting, romantic story about friends, family and the relationships that make a place a home.

Acknowledgements

Thank you for reading *Clues to You*. I hope you enjoyed it, even if you solved the mystery long before Kate and Max. If you can, please consider leaving a spoiler-free review on Amazon as this will help other readers to find the book.

Writing can be a lonely business, and I'm delighted that my publishing dream team continue to work with me. Thank you to my brilliant editor, Alison May; my proofreader and tireless finder of misplaced modifiers, Imogen Howson; Gail Bradley for another lovely cover and Sarah Houldcroft at Goldcrest Books for transforming my manuscript into a book.

A book is little use without readers. Thank you to Rachel Gilbey at Rachel's Random Resources for organizing my cover reveal and another brilliant blog tour. A huge thank you to the bloggers who took part and to all the other bloggers who have used their precious free time to feature and review *Clues to You*.

Thank you to the Romantic Novelists' Association and particularly the members of the Birmingham Chapter for their ongoing support.

Thanks to my husband and to Liz for listening to me going on about book stuff when I'm certain they have far better things to do. A special thank you to my mum for carefully reading the manuscript and persevering late into the night when her 'eyes were out on stalks'.

This book would not exist without the influence of Agatha Christie. While I've always been a fan of her books, writing my own murder mystery has given me a new appreciation of her genius. I have no idea how she managed to keep coming up with such ingenious plots, and at such a rate!

Choosing to create a murder mystery set in the 1930s allowed me to procrastinate by doing literary, scientific and historical research. If, like me, you enjoy Christie's mysteries and would like to know more about the poisons featured in them, I highly recommend *A is for Arsenic: The Poisons of Agatha Christie* by Kathryn Harkup. I imagine Max has read this book at least twice.

Meanwhile, a fascinating look at the fate of grand English country houses and their owners in the early twentieth century can be found in *The Long Weekend: Life in the English Country House Between the Wars* by Adrian Tinniswood.

Finally, Kate is shocked when the fictitious Lucille Palmer tells her that her name was chosen by the readers of a gossip magazine. However this is what happened to real Hollywood actress Lucille Fay Le Sueur, whose far more famous stage name—Joan Crawford—was chosen by the readers of *Movie Weekly*.

About the author

Claire Huston lives in Warwickshire, UK, with her husband and two children. She writes uplifting modern love stories about characters who are meant for each other but sometimes need a little help to realise it.

A keen amateur baker, she enjoys making cakes, biscuits and brownies almost as much as eating them. You can find recipes for all the cakes mentioned in her first novel, *Art and Soul*, at www.clairehuston.co.uk along with over 150 other recipes. This is also where she talks about and reviews books.

You can also find her on:

Instagram: @clairehuston_author
Twitter: @ClaraVal
Facebook: clairehustonauthor
Pinterest: claire_huston